ALL IN

By Nell Stark

Running with the Wind

Homecoming

The Princess Affair

All In

By Nell Stark & Trinity Tam

everafter

nevermore

nightrise

sunfall

Visit us at www.boldstrokesbooks.com

ALL IN

by
Nell Stark

2014

ALL IN

ISBN 13: 978-1-62639-066-9

This Trade Paperback Original Is Published By
Bold Strokes Books, Inc.
P.O. Box 249
Valley Falls, NY 12185

First Edition: June 2014

CREDITS
EDITOR: CINDY CRESAP
PRODUCTION DESIGN: STACIA SEAMAN
COVER DESIGN BY SHERI (GRAPHICARTIST2020@HOTMAIL.COM)

Acknowledgments

I was first introduced to poker in graduate school and played sporadically during my dissertating years. The buy-in was $5, the blinds 5 cents/10 cents. Everyone else in the room was always male. I could never remember the winning order of hands, and I always asked silly questions, but the boys were happy to take my money and I was happy to soak up the ambience. I'm grateful for all they tried to teach me, even if it never stuck.

Since I wear my heart on my sleeve and have the poker face of a puppy, I needed to do quite a lot of research for this project. Two books were especially helpful: Gus Hansen's *Every Hand Revealed* and Deke Castleman's *Whale Hunt in the Desert*. Despite my effort, my first draft required substantial revision. I am fortunate enough to have both a wife (Jane) and an editor (Cindy) who are well-versed in the game, and I am more grateful than I can express for their help.

Jane not only fine-tuned my poker sequences—she also supported and encouraged me throughout my writing process. Like a gambler, I would feel on top of the world one moment, only to hit rock bottom the next. For her love, patience, and guidance, I am eternally grateful.

As always, Cindy Cresap's editorial wisdom and advice—coupled with her wit and humor—have honed both the style and substance of this book, and I deeply appreciate her input. I also remain indebted to Radclyffe for giving me the opportunity to publish with Bold Strokes Books, and I would like to thank all of the wonderful, hardworking, and selfless people at BSB—Sandy, Connie, Lori, Lee, Jennifer, Paula, Sheri, and others—for helping to market and release quality product year after year. The members of Team BSB, including our many fellow authors, continue to inspire us, and I count you all in my extended family.

Finally, thank you to the many readers who have been so generous with their support and feedback over many years. This book is for you!

For Jane, *la miglior fabbra*

CHAPTER ONE

W e're late!" Nova let the screen door bang shut behind her and turned toward the driveway. Sunlight glinted off the hood of her Jeep, and she raised one hand to shield her eyes from the glare. It was a beautiful morning by anyone's standards—the sapphire sky was broken only by small, cottony cloud wisps borne on a warm spring breeze. Next door, Mrs. Bransen's pink terrycloth bathrobe fluttered as she watered the white carnations encircling her mailbox. She looked up, scowling fiercely across the narrow strip of grass separating the two houses. Nova smiled and waved. Nothing was going to dampen her good mood on the day she became a homeowner.

"Don't get your panties in a twist," Emily called from inside the house, prompting an even deeper frown from Mrs. B. "We have plenty of time."

In a burst of practiced motion, Nova vaulted into the driver's seat, slotted the key into the ignition, and gunned the engine. Emily climbed aboard the conventional way a few moments later. "I see we've managed to piss off the bitch again. And since when are you a morning person?"

"Don't worry about her." Nova grabbed her Oakleys from the cup holder as she accelerated down the street. Mrs. B hadn't been happy when Nova and five of her fellow graduate students had rented the house two years ago. And once she'd figured out they were all lesbians, her front yard had become a forest of anti–marriage equality signs. She probably thought they were all sleeping together.

Nova grinned. About that, at least, Mrs. B was right. "We'll never have to see her again after today."

"Thank God." Emily leaned back in her seat. "Do we have time to stop for coffee?"

"No. But I'll buy you breakfast once I'm done at the bank." Nova glanced over in enough time to catch Em's grimace. "Did you know that sixty percent of all coffee drinkers claim they *need* a cup of coffee in the morning? How's it feel to be in the majority for once?"

Em cracked one eyelid. "For someone who gave up on school, you know too much."

"Never let school interfere with your education," Nova quipped. The quote was one of her favorites.

"How'd you do last night? Rake in the big bucks?"

"Didn't log on. I was too busy packing." Nova rarely missed the chance to play at least a few hands of online poker, but in this case, the promise of moving had trumped her need for a fix.

The new house was a beauty. Set on a hill, its backyard had an oblique view of Palo Alto and the San Francisco Bay. It boasted Brazilian cherry floors, an orange tree out front, and four bedrooms. That was clutch, because Nova wanted her privacy. They all had to double up in their current house, and most of the time, it hadn't been a problem. But now she could turn the master bedroom into her own personal poker haven, to be shared by invitation only.

As she accelerated onto the highway, she pictured how they would spend the summer. While Em studied for the bar, Sandra and Monique plodded away at their doctoral research, and Liz and Felicia wrote their dissertations, she would spend her days surfing, her evenings grilling out on the redwood deck, and her nights playing online hold 'em. The sweet life.

When she pulled up to the bank, Em halfheartedly reached for the handle. "Don't." Nova rested one hand on her shoulder. "Stay here and take a little nap or something."

"Sure you don't want me to come with?"

"For the closing? Yes. To get a check cut? No. Just relax." Nova moved quickly toward the doors. Her nose wrinkled as she breathed in stale air laced with the scent of carpet cleaner. The sooner she got this over with, the sooner they could go have breakfast at her favorite café overlooking the water.

She had two choices in tellers: a twenty-something brunette with brightly painted nails, or a stout, middle-aged man. That was a no-brainer. As she stepped toward the woman, she smiled to show off her dimples. The teller was probably straight, but it never hurt to be charming. Just in case.

"Good morning…" Nova glanced down at the nameplate pinned to one lapel, just above the barest hint of tan cleavage. "Diane. I need a bank check, please."

"I can certainly help you with that." Diane barely even glanced at her before turning to her monitor. The sharp clacks of her swift typing exuded professionalism. Chagrined, Nova wondered if she was slipping. "What is your full name?"

Nova cringed. "Annie Jump Novarro. But you can call me AJ." Ever since the age of six, she had insisted on going by her initials. Inside the poker world, though, she was Supern0va, reigning Royal Flush champion. "Nova" for short. Increasingly, her online handle was becoming more real than her given name.

Diane didn't react to the invitation. "Account number and driver's license, please?"

"Here you go."

"And the amount of the check?"

"Four hundred and forty thousand dollars." Nova waited for Diane to register surprise at the large number, but her face remained expressionless. Tough crowd. How many twenty-four-year-olds were there who could meet the bank's demand for a forty percent deposit on a one point one million dollar home?

When she had walked through the door a month ago to apply for her mortgage, she'd been whisked into one of the little cubicle offices by a sallow-faced loan officer who informed her that she was a "high-risk investment" due to her profession. Nova smothered a smile as she thought back on that conversation. She had known going in that banks didn't much like lending money to young professional poker players. But as she had told the dubious loan officer, "High-risk investments are the only kind worth making." So what if she didn't look good on paper? She had almost a million dollars of poker winnings to her name. So far.

"There seems to be a problem, Ms. Novarro."

Shaken out of her reverie, Nova frowned. "A problem?"

Diane spun the computer screen to face her. "Insufficient funds."

Nova stared at the screen in disbelief. It claimed she had just over thirty-one thousand dollars to her name. A wave of fear closed over her head, and her ears began to ring. "There's been some kind of mistake," she managed to choke out, belatedly realizing just how trite those words must sound. "I had the money transferred yesterday."

"Perhaps you should check with your transferring institution."

"Yes." Nova forced the word out between lips that felt suddenly numb. "I'll do that right now. Thank you."

She retreated to the far corner of the bank, where an ATM machine flickered in invitation. When she tried to thumb through her contacts list, she realized her fingers were trembling. She had to stay calm. Take deep breaths. In goes the good air; out goes the bad air. This was all a simple misunderstanding. Maybe there had been an Internet glitch yesterday when she put in her transfer request to Universal Account Systems, the holding company for her online poker bankroll. All she had to do was to give them a call. No problem.

But instead of a ringing phone or a human voice, a series of beeps pierced her ears. "We're sorry," a mechanical voice coolly informed her. "The number you dialed is not in service."

"No." Nova fought the urge to sink to the floor as dread swept through her, tying her stomach in knots. "No, no, no. This is not happening." Desperately trying to keep the panic at bay, she opened the Internet browser on her phone and navigated to the website where, less than twenty-four hours earlier, she had arranged for her money to be transferred.

What she saw made her stumble into one of the bucket seats in the waiting area. Gone was the homepage to which she was accustomed. Instead, the seal of the United States and the seal of the FBI framed a block of text that sent her churning stomach right into her toes. The feds had shut down Universal Account Systems pending an investigation into money laundering.

Her funds were out of reach, perhaps indefinitely. There would be no house. No master bedroom poker haven. No redwood deck. Nowhere for any of them to sleep tonight. Head pounding, ears ringing, Nova staggered toward her car. She opened the door, collapsed inside, and, not wanting to meet Em's gaze, rested her forehead on the wheel. Visions of Brazilian cherry floors and flowering orange trees shattered behind her eyes.

"What happened?" Em's voice was shrill with alarm. She laid a hand on Nova's shoulder, but it didn't feel comforting. "AJ? What's going on?"

"There's no money," she croaked.

"What do you mean, there's no money?"

Still unwilling to look up, Nova fumbled for her phone and passed it over. A few seconds later, Emily cursed. "What the hell? How did this happen?"

At first, Nova didn't answer. She wanted to disappear. She wanted to punch something. She wanted to vomit. Anxiety constricted her throat, making it impossible to suck in a deep breath, ushering in the familiar claustrophobia. As the suffocating tightness pervaded her chest, she latched on to the strategies she'd honed since childhood.

1842 x 2359 = 4,345,278. The square root of 3,969 is 63. 57^4 = 10,556,001... As she forced her brain to focus on the numbers, the pressure slowly began to ease.

"Are you okay?" Em squeezed her arm. "AJ? You're scaring me."

Nova took a long, slow breath, and when her lungs didn't seize up, she dared to raise her head. Her cheeks were tingling slightly, and dark flecks danced at the corners of her vision. She'd come close to hyperventilating. So much for preserving even a modicum of cool under pressure.

"Damn it," she whispered. "Brazilian cherry floors! An orange tree out front!"

"Can you explain to me what this"—Em brandished her phone— "means? The government can't just take your money away from you, can they?"

Em's questions twisted the knife in her gut, but they also forced her to think. "They can. It's happened before."

"It has?"

Nova held out her hand for the phone. Now that her brain was working again, her priorities were falling back into order. "I'll explain the whole thing later. Right now I need to make a call. And I need you to do me a favor."

"What is it?"

"Get on the line with our landlord and try to get our house back."

❖

Moonlight filtered through the broken blinds in the living room, illuminating the nearly empty pizza box on the table. Felicia's psychotic cat had destroyed the slats last year in an attempt to catch something on or outside the window. Doubtless, the replacement cost would be taken out of their security deposit once they moved out. Whenever that was.

Nova broke a tiny piece of crust off her uneaten slice and rolled it between her fingers. Thankfully, their landlord had not yet found other renters, and he'd been happy to sign them to a new contract. At an increased price, of course. Even Em's formidable negotiating skills had failed in the face of their desperation. They weren't homeless, but they were paying almost twenty-five percent more than last year.

Nova reached for her beer, found it empty, and wearily got to her feet. "Anyone need another?" At the resounding affirmative chorus, she headed for the kitchen, carefully picking her way around towers of haphazardly stacked boxes in the process.

As she returned with an armful of bottles, the front door closed behind Monique, who had been obliged to stay on campus late to teach her Intro to Computer Science class. The original plan had been for her to meet them at the new house, and she looked none too happy at the radical change. Hands on her hips, ebony hair curling around her shoulders, she cut an imposing figure.

"AJ, I love you. But what the hell!"

"Are we really going to have to live here for another year?" Liz's voice was plaintive.

"I almost went and told off Mrs. B this morning." Sandra, seated at Liz's feet, wrapped her arms around her knees. "Glad I was too lazy."

Nova's jaw clenched at their whining. Instead of doling out the beers, she dumped them onto the carpet. "Have a little heart, will you? I know we've all had a shittastic day, but do you really have to make me feel worse? I lost almost a million fucking dollars!"

Monique sat down. Liz seemed chagrined. When Nova retreated to the couch, Em gently patted her knee. "We're just trying to understand what happened."

Nova scrubbed her palms across her face and tried to rein in her temper. She had singlehandedly torpedoed their plans. They deserved to be frustrated. They also deserved answers. She reached for a beer and poured her anger into twisting off the cap.

"Okay. Online gambling's been illegal since 2006 when Congress passed a moronic act called UIGEA that made it so banks can't fund gambling sites. So now, if you want to play, you have to transfer money through a third party—a company that will hold or transfer your bankroll."

"But isn't that still illegal?" Felicia asked.

"Well, it's kind of a gray area, because the holding company isn't a bank. They're always ostensibly selling something. Mine sells phone cards."

"Phone cards?" Liz's brow wrinkled in confusion.

"Let's say I want to deposit ten thousand into my account. I arrange to purchase ten thousand dollars' worth of phone cards, which I can either sit on or transfer to my poker account at Royal Flush. It works the same way if I want to cash out from my poker account."

"That's money laundering." Monique was shooting her a hard stare.

"Call it what you want!" Nova could feel her blood pressure rising. "The whole law is bogus. Poker isn't a game of chance like fucking roulette or craps or baccarat. Poker is a game of skill. The law shouldn't even apply!"

For a long moment, there was silence. "But it does," Sandra said finally.

"Yeah. It does." Nova's anger began to ebb, and fatigue rushed in to fill the void. "Somebody in the government must have been tipped off to what my holding company was doing, because now my money is frozen. And I have no legal recourse to get it back."

"What are you going to do?" Emily asked.

Feeling a headache coming on, Nova rubbed her temples. "I don't know. I put a call in to Royal Flush. They sponsor me. I'm hoping…" This was the hardest part. "I'm hoping they'll take care of me."

She looked around the room, taking in the dubious glances. "You guys, I'm sorry. I'm sorry I put you through this. I—" A telephone ring interrupted her. It wasn't coming from their landline, but from her laptop. The name flashing on the screen was Evan Hunt, her contact at Royal Flush. "I have to take this. Back in a bit."

In her haste to leave the room, she almost tripped over a box protruding out into the hall. Thankfully, the balance she'd honed for years on the surfboard came to her rescue. As soon as her feet were back under her, she accepted the call.

The screen resolved into a slightly pixilated image of a dark-haired man in a turquoise jacket, seated behind a desk. Colorful posters advertising several online tournaments, all sponsored by Royal Flush, hung behind him. Nova had only met Evan once, at an event in London the year before, but he hailed her like an old friend.

"Nova, baby, how you doing?"

She turned into the room she was currently sharing with Emily. Its bare walls mocked her. "Honestly, Evan? Not that great."

"Understandable, understandable."

"Do you have any idea how this happened?"

Evan's used car salesman's smile faltered. "Well, our best guess is that your transaction got the feds' attention."

Nova dropped into the worn leather chair. "What?" She felt as though she'd taken a blow to the head. "I did this?"

"Oh, they won't come after you personally. They must have been watching UAS for a while, and your transfer was probably the—"

"Nail in the coffin." Nova felt like she might be sick. How many people had been affected? How much money had been frozen? Would they ever be able to get it back? What if someone had really needed that money, not just for a house but for their kid's college tuition or medical bills or—

"Look, don't beat yourself up. If it hadn't been you, it would have been someone else."

"You think it was only a matter of time?"

"I'm sure it was."

His certainty made her feel slightly better, until she realized he was probably just saying what she wanted to hear. Swallowing hard, Nova decided to lay all her cards on the table. Bluffing had never been her strong suit. She'd never told a convincing lie in her life, and now wasn't the time to start.

"I'm going to be honest with you. Without my online bankroll, I don't have a lot of options at this point."

"Nova, Nova, Nova." He clucked his tongue and shook his head. "Would we leave you out in the lurch? You're the champ! You're our girl."

His voice sounded as slick as his hair looked. "I am?"

"Of course!" Evan leaned closer to the camera. "I spoke with

David Sterling this afternoon, and here's what we're prepared to do. The World Series of Poker starts in just over a month. We'll fly you out to Vegas and put up the ten thou buy-in for the main event."

Nova frowned. Free travel and a free spot in the most popular poker event in the world? That sounded good. Too good. Free lunches were as mythical as unicorns—especially in the gambling world.

"What's the catch?"

"Catch? There's no catch, baby—just a deal. If you win a bracelet, we'll get you set up with a brand-new contract. If you don't, we'll part ways amicably."

"Wait a minute." Nova blinked hard, trying to make sense of the words rattling around in her head. "You're saying that if I win the main event, Royal Flush will continue to sponsor me, but if I don't, you'll cut me loose?"

"You got it."

"Evan, I've never played a hand of live poker in my life. In my life! And now you want me to win *the* event at the biggest poker tournament on earth?"

He raised his hands in a gesture that was probably supposed to be placating. "Listen to me. You're one of the best online players in the world, but you're still a new kid on the block, without a lot of international cachet. The online game is dead in America—at least for the moment. So if you want to keep your career alive, either you move overseas, or you learn to win live hands."

Nova leaned back in her chair. Online and live poker played by the same rules, but otherwise, they were night and day. She had tried to watch the World Series of Poker on television a few times but always ended up switching the channel. Online poker was fast, furious, and anonymous. Live poker seemed so ponderous and messy by comparison. Besides, she was a numbers person. Not a people person. And the odds of this plan working were extremely slim.

"Deal or no deal?" Evan prompted her.

"No deal!" Nova pointed her index finger at the camera. "The *professional* live poker players are always talking about how crazy the main event is. Now that it's gotten so huge, it's practically a crapshoot. Craps is a game of luck, Evan. I don't play games of luck. I play poker. I'm not staking my entire future on a roll of the dice."

"Hey, you can leave the deal on the table if you want. No sweat. We'll find another player to stake. As you said, there are plenty of 'em out there."

His cavalier dismissal inspired a surge of adrenaline that would've been pleasant in any other context. Desperation warred with fear as her mind raced, quickly cataloguing and then discarding possibilities.

Suddenly, a solution materialized. "Counter offer!" she exclaimed, more loudly than she'd meant to. "You do what you said you'd do. But you also stake me in two other events. If I win the bracelet at any one of them, Royal Flush continues to sponsor me."

Evan scratched at his chin, appearing to mull this over. "No deal," he said finally. "Some of those games have steep buy-ins. But if you want to use your own money to enter another event, then sure. Win one bracelet, any bracelet, and you're golden." He flashed a sharp, white smile. "Literally."

Nova rubbed her sweaty palms on her jeans, glad he couldn't see the movement. How was she supposed to hide her nerves while betting millions at a live table, when she could barely hold herself together right now? But if she didn't accept his terms, the only other option was finding a job to pay the rent. That, or going back to school.

"Hell no," she muttered under her breath. And then she looked into the camera and straightened her spine. "Okay. Done."

"Excellent. You're coming to Vegas, baby!" He flashed her the thumbs-up. "I'll fax over some paperwork and then cut you a check. One of the hosts at Valhalla owes me a favor. I'll ask her to show you the ropes once you're there."

"Great." Nova tried to sound enthusiastic, but she wasn't sure she pulled it off.

"Oh, and one more thing." He waggled a finger at her in clear admonishment. "Quit talking to yourself. That's a surefire giveaway at the tables."

The screen went blank. In an effort to ease her cramped shoulders, Nova tilted her head back to stare at the ceiling. The room seemed smaller than it had this morning, even though she knew that was just her mind playing tricks. Instead of freaking out, she had to focus—to try to process what had just happened.

She was going to spend the summer in Las Vegas playing poker. Live poker. With her entire livelihood on the line.

CHAPTER TWO

He's *dead*?" James's voice bounced between the cubicle walls and the low ceiling to fill the office.

Vesper stopped typing in mid-sentence. There wasn't much capable of torpedoing her concentration—certainly not James, whose bombastic outbursts were as reliable as splitting aces in blackjack. Under ordinary circumstances, she would have ignored him. But two minutes ago, he'd been in the middle of a conversation with his secretary about Davis Beauregard's compensation package for his upcoming trip. Beauregard was Valhalla Resort and Casino's top spender, and James never let any of them forget it. His entire career had been built on the man's coattails.

Lenny poked his head around the wall of her cube. His eyes were wide. "Holy shit. Has the Killer Whale gone belly-up?"

"Sounds like it," she whispered. The office was suddenly as quiet as a graveyard.

A Texas oil tycoon, Beauregard had earned his nickname over a decade ago by placing gargantuan bets at the craps table. He habitually wagered hundreds of thousands of dollars on a single roll of the dice. Anyone who gambled even half as much was known as a "whale," but Beauregard was the fiercest of them all. And now, if James's sympathetic stuttering into the receiver was any indication, he was gone.

Vesper stared at her screen without truly seeing it. She didn't like James, but in that moment, she felt sorry for him. The life of a casino host was almost as uncertain as the luck of the gamblers they served. At least he had plenty of other fish in the sea. She thought of her own small client base and felt a twist of anxiety.

"Did Beauregard seriously bite it?" Lenny asked loudly. James must have hung up the phone. She rose from her chair and walked toward his cube, where the entire office was quickly assembling. From her vantage point, all she could see was the shiny crown of his bowed head.

"Heart attack. Last night." He raised one fist and brought it down on the desk with a dull thud. "Motherfucker!"

Vesper turned away. By now, there wasn't so much as a glimmer of naïveté left in her heart, but that didn't mean she had to like his attitude. Worse, everyone around him was commiserating. "Rough luck," she heard one man say. "I'm so sorry," said another, as though James were the one who had been closest to the dead man.

For a long moment, there was silence. Vesper had just opened her calendar to double-check that everything was in order for the Hamiltons' visit, when he spoke again.

"Maureen, send something tasteful and expensive to the son. Eugene."

"Of course. And to the widow as well?"

"Why not?" James said after a pause. "But don't go overboard. She never showed an ounce of interest in anything but jewelry shopping."

He was already pursuing the bereaved family, Vesper realized. They were the ones with the money now, and he was going on a full-court press to ensure they gambled it at Valhalla. In fact, this same conversation was probably happening in casino offices up and down the Strip. Davis Beauregard had been loyal to Valhalla for two decades, but his heir was up for grabs. Eugene was about to be hunted as fiercely as Moby Dick.

James seemed to have written off the widow, though. Priscilla. Vesper had seen her frequently over the years—a plump woman with neatly coiffed white hair who always wore large earrings, bright colors, and gem-encrusted necklaces. She concentrated on the image and tried to remember whether she had ever seen Priscilla trying her own hand at a table or slot machine, but she couldn't recall. As she stared blankly at the bouncing roulette ball that was her screen saver, an idea began to coalesce. What if she let the boys fight over Eugene and set her own sights on Priscilla?

She had a few spare minutes, and there was no sense in wasting them. After saying a quick good-bye to Lenny, Vesper hurried down to the mall level of the casino. First, she stopped at the spa and ordered a basket of their high-end skin treatment products to be shipped immediately. Then, she went to the jewelry store and chose a Cartier brooch in the shape of a starfish, made with eighteen-karat gold. When the saleswoman told her that she couldn't comp it, Vesper ignored the shrill voices in her head—one of whom sounded like her mother—insisting that she walk away. Instead, she paid the three thousand dollars with her own credit card. Her palms broke out in a sweat as she signed the receipt, but she forced her hand to remain steady. This was a gamble, and as a rule, Vesper avoided rolls of the dice. Sacrificing a chunk of her savings account was completely counterintuitive, but neither could she afford to pass up this kind of career opportunity. If she managed to nab Priscilla Beauregard, she would call it a worthy investment.

A hot rush of shame washed through her at the mercenary thought. Was she really no better than James? With a shake of her head, she signed her name to the receipt and glanced at her phone. This wasn't the time to engage in self-recrimination. The Hamiltons' plane would land in just a few minutes.

When she stepped out of Valhalla's employee entrance, the cool desert breeze made her pull her shawl more tightly across her shoulders. The temperature had peaked in the high eighties today, but with the onset of darkness, the heat had fled. She walked quickly toward the curb, where a long row of black limousines waited. Bypassing the super-stretch varieties, she approached a slightly more modest car sporting the vanity plate UR XS. After a quick rap on the window, she ducked into the back.

"Good evening, Ms. Blake." Jeremy turned to acknowledge her across the lowered privacy partition, his sparkling eyes belying the formality of the greeting. His curly black hair was neatly trimmed, and his baby face was partially masked by a goatee. A hint of aftershave lingered in the air—spicy, but not too strong. His sports coat was neatly pressed, and the collar of his shirt was stiff with starch.

"Hello, Jeremy."

"Carl and I placed a bet on whether TJ's bringing a girlfriend. Want in?"

Vesper laughed. "Do I ever want in?"

He smiled at her in the mirror. "Someday you will. Carl and I have a bet riding on that, too."

"Of course you do." Vesper knew she was in the minority of casino employees who didn't partake of the gambling culture they peddled to others. Enticing others to take risks was her job. Avoiding them herself was her life.

"Which side did you take?" she asked, wondering what TJ would say if he knew his relationship status had inspired Valhalla's employees to wager their hard-earned money.

"He won't bring anyone here," Jeremy said confidently. "He's been nursing a crush on you for years."

"Which he'll outgrow soon enough, if he hasn't already." Vesper suspected her own love life was a bigger topic of conversation than their clients'. She didn't particularly want to think about that.

"We'll see in a few minutes."

After that brief exchange, Jeremy focused on driving. That was part of what made him so good at his job—he read people well and adapted to what they wanted. They had met several years ago in a Psychology of Gambling course at UNLV, where they'd been assigned to the same peer group for final projects. Jeremy had been on crutches as he struggled to rehab a knee injury and return to the basketball team. Vesper was employed as a floorman at Valhalla and trying to find a way to move up in the ranks. They had worked well together, taking the bulk of the project from their lackadaisical group members and receiving the highest grades in the class.

The following February during Chinese New Year, Valhalla's fleet of cars had been overbooked. As a newly promoted host, Vesper suddenly found herself unable to deliver the free ride from the airport that she had promised to her middle roller. Desperate, she had reached out to Jeremy. When he proved willing, she sent him to the airport in a rented car. On the ride back to Valhalla, the client had mentioned his fondness for March Madness and his disappointment at not having been able to score tickets to the UNLV game that weekend. Jeremy had promptly called a former teammate and secured him a third-row seat.

That's when Vesper had realized that she and Jeremy were truly cut from the same mold. She'd managed to convince the Valhalla fleet supervisor to hire him, and now he was her go-to guy. In any other car, she would've felt obliged to double-check that champagne was chilling in the fridge. Here, she could relax. As much as she ever did, at least.

As she watched the glittering rows of light gradually give way to the dark desert, a large, flashing billboard caught her eye. The logo of the World Series of Poker—three black and white chips with red lettering—gleamed against a green background presumably intended to resemble felt. The annual tournament would begin in a few weeks, and if Valhalla's room reservations were any kind of indicator, it would be a record-breaking year.

How fitting, to have seen that particular advertisement on her way to pick up the Hamiltons. The WSOP felt like a kind of anniversary to her. Three years ago, she'd been mired in the drudgery of life as a floorman—creating dealer schedules, overseeing the maintenance of the casino equipment, and keeping a cautious eye on clients who seemed too lucky. She had taken care to do her job well, even as she watched the hosts with a mixture of jealousy and admiration. They hobnobbed with the high rollers—not only on the floor, but also at concerts, fights, and exclusive parties. Sometimes, they were invited out to a client's property, or to join him on vacation. But Vesper didn't care about the perks nearly as much as she cared about the power. Power and influence clung to casino hosts like their tailored suits.

She had done what she could to get ahead—to show her bosses that she had what it took to sit at the big boys' table. She went above and beyond her banal duties, becoming friendly with the middle rollers and offering them as many comps as she could scrape together from the hosts' leftovers. Her shift supervisor had alternately praised her ingenuity or cursed her aggression, but he never showed her a pink slip. She was good. He knew it, and she knew it. But she hadn't been able to slip so much as a toe through the door until the morning three years ago when James had suckered her into babysitting…

As she stooped to inspect the contents of a box on one of the lower shelves, Vesper's lower back twinged, reminding her that she'd been on her feet for most of the night. Blinking hard, she forced herself to focus. Checking inventory was the most monotonous part of her shift, and after an exceptionally busy night, she was having trouble staying focused. Fortunately, as soon as she finished this, she could retreat to her apartment on the northwest side of the city. It was small, but her balcony had an oblique view of Mount Charleston. After a long soak in a hot bath, maybe she would sit outside with a book and a glass of wine. Or better yet—retreat to her bed and sleep away the afternoon beneath her crisp, white sheets. Perfect.

"Vesper!"

Sighing at the interruption, she turned toward the door of the supply cage. The voice belonged to James, one of the Valhalla hosts. They all looked as though they'd been cut from the same mold—male, gray suit, tasteful tie, slicked-back hair. His was dirty blond streaked with gray.

"Hi, James."

"You're wrapping up, right?"

"That's right." He undoubtedly wanted something from her. She could always say no, of course, but she probably wouldn't, and he knew it. Every host at Valhalla routinely exploited her ambition.

"I need a favor. My guy Hamilton has taken it into his head to stop losing at craps and buy into the main event."

Everyone at the casino knew about Theodore Hamilton Sr. A partner at a private equity firm in New York City, he often came to Vegas on weekends to test his luck. Vesper glanced at her watch. The Texas hold 'em tournament was slated to begin at noon, just under an hour away. "Is he any good?"

"Who gives a shit!" James smoothed his hair with one hand. "I hope he loses it all on the first hand and gets back to rolling the bones. But in case he doesn't, I need you to keep an eye on his kid, Teddy."

Vesper was too exhausted to curb her disdain. "Who brings a minor to a casino without someone to look after him?"

"They were supposed to golf. The heat wave got in the way, and the nanny he hired can't be reached."

The nanny had probably gone AWOL because the kid was a spoiled brat. How could he not be? She had grown up among wealthy, entitled children, and with one exception, they had all been rotten eggs. The back of her neck prickled at the thought, and she firmly closed the mental door on those memories.

"C'mon," James said. "It won't be so bad. He'll probably just want to play video games all day."

"Then why don't you do it?"

"I'm due at the airport."

Vesper rolled her eyes. "Bull. You're jumping ship because your guy stopped firing it up at the table."

James didn't even bother trying to deny it. "Okay, look. If you do this, I'll throw in a reservation for two at Barri."

She crossed her arms beneath her breasts, considering. The promise of a meal at Valhalla's most exclusive restaurant would have been more tempting if she had any dating prospects, but James was clearly desperate, and she liked the idea of him being in her debt.

"Fine."

Relief washed across his face. "Yes. Perfect. Thank you. You're my girl!"

Vesper favored him with her best withering glance, and James quickly turned away. As they caught an elevator, she realized she was finally about to see one of the fabled Asgard suites—Valhalla's second most luxurious style of room. The only better accommodations were the Celestial Palaces, reserved for the highest of high rollers—the aptly named "whales." High rollers wagered thousands on a blackjack hand or a roll of the dice. But whales put down tens or hundreds of thousands on single bets and could win or lose millions within a matter of hours.

The Hamiltons' suite boasted sky blue walls, white trim, and lofty ceilings that made it feel even larger than it was. The foyer ended in an alcove with a window seat and a view of the Las Vegas Strip. To the left, three bedrooms branched off a corridor illuminated by vaguely Teutonic-looking wall sconces. James led her to the right, into a spacious kitchen complete with an island, its chrome appliances gleaming in the overhead lights. Vesper caught a glimpse of the dining room—its long, dark table standing out against walls the color of a rosy sunset—before they turned again.

This room was less formal than the others. A stone fireplace was set into one wood-paneled wall, a sheepskin rug lying before it. Two leather couches and a love seat were arranged to take advantage of both the fireplace and of the large television hanging on the perpendicular wall. Vesper paused in the doorway to observe its sole occupant. Theodore Hamilton Jr. lounged on the couch watching the Dodgers game and drinking a thick, vaguely chocolate-colored drink that she guessed was some kind of protein shake. Despite his choice in beverage, he was thin and lanky. Designer jeans rode low on his hips, and the sleeves of his polo shirt fit loosely around his arms. But when he turned to face them, she saw he had inherited his father's strong jaw and brilliant green eyes. They narrowed in clear displeasure as he inspected them.

"Teddy, my man!" James sauntered over to the couch and stuck out his hand. For a moment, it looked like the kid would leave him hanging. Finally, he reached out for a perfunctory shake.

"Hi."

"There's someone I want you to meet. Vesper Blake, Teddy Hamilton. Teddy, Vesper will be spending the afternoon with you."

"You mean she'll be babysitting me."

James laughed nervously. "Did I say that?" He edged toward the door. "You guys have a great time."

Teddy's gaze moved to Vesper. She watched him look her over and caught the flare of attraction in his eyes before he deliberately turned back to the television. "Make yourself at home, I guess," he said, sounding utterly bored.

Vesper remained standing, mind racing as she vacillated between two choices. Teddy was clearly bitter about being left behind while his father took in the poker action. He was also stubbornly faking his disinterest in her. She could either take a seat on the couch and passively watch him for the rest of the day, or she could step up and practice her hosting skills on *him*. He came from a wealthy gambling family. Maybe if she took the initiative to show him a good time, she would be rewarded. He might not be able to wager thousands on one spin of the wheel, but one day, that would change. And when it did, he might just remember her.

She had nothing to lose and everything to gain—a rare event in her world. Suddenly determined, she stepped into his line of sight. "All right, TJ. What would you most like to do right now?"

He frowned up at her in clear confusion. "TJ?"

"Honestly, I think 'TJ' suits you better than 'Teddy.' But if you don't like it, I apologize."

"Don't." He sat up straight and turned toward her, his expression thoughtful—as though he had never considered that he was in charge of his own name. "I do like it."

"Well then, TJ, you still haven't answered my question. What would you most like to do?"

"Watch my dad play poker."

Vesper wasn't going to dignify that with a response. She arched one eyebrow and waited him out while rapidly considering and discarding possibilities. She couldn't bring him onto the casino floor, and no live footage of the WSOP tournament was broadcast in the casino for obvious reasons. There was no way he could watch his father try to survive day one of the main event.

After a brief staring contest, he looked away. "Yeah, I know. I can't."

The seed of an idea opened in her mind. "How old are you?"

"Eighteen."

She gave him a look.

He bristled. "What? Do you want to see my ID? I turned eighteen last month!"

She held up one hand as he reached for his wallet. "I believe you. Do you play any poker?"

He snorted. "All the time at school."

Now that she had his full attention, she perched on the edge of the couch. A bit of subtle flattery seemed in order. "College?"

He shook his head. "Boarding school. I'm entering Dartmouth this coming fall."

Vesper played a hunch. "Did your dad go there, too?"

A flash of surprise crossed his face. "How'd you know?"

"Lucky guess." She pretended to be momentarily interested in the ball game to give herself time to think. The kid had a serious case of hero worship for his father, and she fleetingly wondered what that must feel like before forcing herself to focus. He couldn't go into the casino, but what if she brought the casino to him?

"Next question. What's your favorite food?"

"Buffalo wings. Why?"

"Mild? Medium? Spicy?"

"Medium. What are you—"

"And to drink?"

"IPA. The hoppier the better."

Vesper laughed. "Root beer it is."

"Root beer?" The words dripped scorn.

"You're going to have to trust me, TJ." She stood and moved toward the door. "I need to make a few phone calls. Enjoy the game for a bit."

"Sure." Clearly disappointed, he turned back to the television. He probably thought she was blowing him off.

Vesper turned into the dining room and caught sight of her own bemused smile in the large gilt mirror hanging on one wall. Teddy craved the privileges of full adulthood, and on the one hand, she couldn't blame him. But on the other…when she was his age, she had already been living on her own for a year. Adulthood came with far more headaches than perks.

And then she shook her head at her own thoughts. By the looks of things, Teddy had been born with a silver spoon in his mouth. He probably had a trust fund already valued at more money than Vesper would ever make in her life. But if she played her cards right today, when he came of age and began to gamble with that money, he would take his chances at Valhalla.

She pulled out a chair at the highly polished mahogany table. The first call she made was to the cashier. The second was to the concierge. And the third was to the closest thing to a friend she had at the casino—Isabella Martin, one of Valhalla's Hospitality Managers. For this plan to work, she needed a few more people, and Isabella managed plenty.

Once she was finished, Vesper went into the kitchen and pulled out a stack of plates and several glasses from the cabinets. The sounds must have triggered Teddy's curiosity, because he appeared in the doorway a few moments later.

"What are you doing?"

"Preparing." Vesper wanted to ramp up the suspense as much as possible.

"For?"

"You'll have to wai—" She was rescued by the door chime. "Ah. Here we are." Vesper strode toward the door, Teddy trailing behind her like a puppy. She opened it to reveal one of the cashiers holding a small lockbox.

"Vesper," he said as she took it off his hands. "Hello, Mr. Hamilton."

"Thank you, Michael."

"Don't forget about these." With a flourish, Michael produced two fresh decks of cards from the pockets of his blazer.

"Grab those for me, TJ, will you?" Vesper let the door close behind them and returned to the dining room. This time, Teddy was practically snapping at her heels.

"What are we playing?"

Vesper set the box down on the table and reached up to her neck where a long gold chain held two small keys. She looped the chain over her head, selected the larger of the two, and slotted it into the box. Pausing to glance up at Teddy, she saw that he was completely riveted. Slowly, she raised the lid to reveal several pristine rows of white, red, blue, and green chips.

An eager smile lit up his face. "Poker?"

"This is a thousand dollars' worth of chips. They're on me. A few of my coworkers will arrive in a few minutes, and then we'll play. Five-dollar, ten-dollar blinds. Fifty-dollar maximum raise."

"Excellent." Teddy slid into one of the chairs and cracked his knuckles.

"We'll play like the final table of the main event—until one person takes it all."

He frowned. "But I can't cash these out."

"No. But your dad can."

"Right." His eyes gleamed in excitement, and he leaned forward eagerly as she began to shuffle the cards.

By the time Vesper heard the door open six hours later, the dining table was littered with empty bottles of root beer and plates piled high with picked-clean chicken wings. She laid her cards on the table and watched Teddy's focused expression shift into one of anticipation. He had managed to eliminate both of Vesper's coworkers and was in the lead by about two hundred dollars.

"Well, well." Theodore Senior surveyed them from the threshold, the corners of his mouth twitching. "What have we here?"

"Dad, Vesper. Vesper, Dad." Teddy, flush with excitement over his pile of chips, spoke quickly. "We had two other players, but I knocked them out. How'd you do? And you gotta try these wings."

Theodore sat and proceeded to regale them with the story of how he had played well early on but managed to lose it all trying to bluff the previous year's WSOP champion. Teddy listened avidly, and then began to share the story of one of the more exciting hands he had played. But his father cut him off.

"How did this"—his gesture encompassed the table—"all come about? And where is James?"

Teddy shrugged. "He left."

When Theodore's face creased in a deep frown, Vesper felt a surge of satisfaction. James was in the doghouse, exactly where he belonged. "James asked me to look after TJ while he was otherwise engaged," she said smoothly.

"TJ?"

"I like it, Dad."

"I see." As Theodore inspected her, she forced herself to meet his intent gaze. "And this was your idea?"

"Yes. TJ wanted to watch you at the tournament. I thought this would be the next best thing."

"Speaking of which," Teddy said, "Can we get back to it? I have a few hundred more dollars to win."

"She doesn't seem like the type to give up easily, son." Theodore glanced between them before reaching for the cards. "I'll play the role of dealer for the rest of the night. Let's hope you don't take after your old man."

The illuminated sign at the airport entrance snapped Vesper out of the memory. Her gambit that night had paid off much sooner than she had believed possible. Theodore Senior had fired James immediately and claimed Vesper as his new host, essentially forcing Valhalla to promote her. Then, he had proceeded to recommend her to all of his "Dartmouth contacts."

That was how he explained it. But the men who called her—and they were all men—varied widely in age, so Vesper knew he couldn't have actually attended college with all of them. She hadn't asked any questions, and they hadn't volunteered any answers. After a few months, he had rewarded her discretion by explaining that he was the president of the Board of Trustees of the Sphinx, a male-only secret society at Dartmouth. She had looked up the organization online, but learned little more than what he had told her. It was all very clandestine, but one thing was clear: the brothers of the Sphinx were good at making money.

Reflecting back on that first meeting made Vesper feel oddly nostalgic. TJ had seemed so very young. In the years since, he had grown in both stature and character, though thankfully, he hadn't completely abandoned the enthusiasm she'd found so endearing. In just a few days, he would celebrate his twenty-first birthday at Valhalla with several of his closest friends. Vesper hadn't been lying when she'd said she was honored that he had chosen the resort to host his celebration, but she also had a selfish motive. Many of TJ's friends would become high rollers themselves someday—if they weren't already. The party would serve as her calling card.

As the terminal came into view, she leaned forward to inspect her appearance in the small mirror. Subtle makeup eliminated the shadows beneath her eyes, and her lip gloss enhanced the natural rosiness of her lips. Her pale green dress revealed the curve of her collarbone and the tan expanse of skin below her throat without exposing any cleavage. There weren't many female hosts in Vegas, but most of them flaunted their bodies almost to the same degree as the escorts their clients often demanded. Some even crossed that line, offering themselves up as part of the casino's comp package. The thought put a sour taste in Vesper's mouth. Even if she were attracted to men, she would never allow that to happen. She wanted her clients to see her as a professional, not as an object. So far, her plan was working well. Over the past three years, she'd only had to fend off a few overtures.

Jeremy pulled into the limousine parking area and was out his door fast enough to open hers. She shook her head at him and smiled as she stepped onto the pavement. As they walked toward baggage claim, they chatted idly about the upcoming poker tournament and how busy Valhalla was about to become. Once inside, Jeremy took up a position near the proper carousel, the placard emblazoned with *Hamilton Family* hanging limply at his side. He had brought it out of habit, she suspected. This would feel more like a family reunion than a client pickup.

She spotted Theodore Senior first, his arm linked with that of his wife, Marisa. Slim and beautiful, she was allowing her dark hair to go silver. Vesper had always felt strangely reassured that she was content not to have it artificially colored. TJ followed behind them, visibly scanning the crowd. She had seen him most recently in January, when the family had all celebrated the new year at Valhalla. Then, he had been as tall as his father, and in the intervening months he had gained another inch. His gray T-shirt clung to his toned chest and arms, and his shaggy dark hair hung low over his eyes. Vesper could appreciate his attractiveness from a purely aesthetic point of view, but all she really wanted to do was to ruffle his hair like a big sister.

"Good evening, Mr. and Mrs. Hamilton," Vesper said as they approached. "Good evening, TJ. Welcome back."

"Good evening?" TJ grinned at her as she shook his parents' hands. "Why so formal, V?" He stepped around his father and drew her into an embrace. "It's good to see you," he murmured as he released her.

Vesper stepped back gratefully. She didn't want his parents to get the wrong idea. Also, he was wearing too much cologne. As they walked toward the car, she ran through the usual questions—how their flight had been, whether they had any special requests, and if any of their plans had changed.

"Are you looking forward to the party?" she asked once they were seated in the limo.

"Hell, yes." TJ's emphatic answer earned a frown from his mother, but he wasn't paying her any attention as he uncorked the bottle of Moët.

"I'm glad. Jeremy will pick up your guests as they arrive, and they'll be staying in the suite next to yours."

"Great." He poured a glass expertly, the frothy head rising just above the top of the flute. "Care for some?"

"I'm fine, thanks."

TJ looked disappointed and passed the glass to his mother.

"Thank you, Vesper, for helping us with all of these preparations." Marisa smiled at her.

"It's my pleasure."

"And we're all set for the fight tomorrow?" asked Theodore Senior.

"Eighth row center, as usual." Vesper's phone rang and she quickly opened her purse. "Excuse me for a moment."

"Vesper! Evan."

She winced, immediately wishing she had ignored the call. Last year, Evan, who worked for the online poker company Royal Flush, had tipped her off that the wife of one of his prize poker players liked to pour his winnings into the slot machines. Vesper had comped her a shopping spree and convinced them to move from a regular room in a rival casino to a Midgard suite at Valhalla. Ever since, they had been loyal customers. And every time they visited, the wife lost thousands, if not tens of them. Now, Evan was going to ask her to return the favor. His timing couldn't be worse.

"Hi, Evan."

"So, remember that poker player I was telling you about a few weeks ago? The one who won our big tournament last year and is coming for the World Series?"

"Yes, I remember," Vesper said, maintaining her cheerful tone even as her stomach began to sink. She was already overbooked for the next two months. She didn't have time to pay attention to anyone else—especially when that person probably wasn't planning to throw large sums of money into Valhalla's lap. One baccarat player like Theodore Senior was worth a hundred poker players.

"She's flying in tomorrow to get some practice in before the tournament. I'll send you the flight information. Can you just do me a favor and make sure she settles in okay? This is her first time in Vegas."

Another babysitting gig. Just perfect. "Of course," she said, hoping her irritation hadn't seeped through. "I'll look forward to seeing the details."

"Great. I'll be in touch."

He hung up almost before the last syllable, leaving Vesper feeling suddenly overwhelmed. This job caught up to her quickly sometimes. Determined not to let her exhaustion show, she tucked her phone away and turned back to the Hamiltons with a practiced smile, apologizing for the interruption.

CHAPTER THREE

Nova walked down the stairs toward baggage claim, feeling as though she was moving in slow motion. Everyone around her seemed in a hurry—the man who jostled her elbow as he hustled down the stairs, the family chattering excitedly as they pushed their laden cart toward the exit, the woman flinging her arms around a man's neck for a passionate kiss before they turned toward the door. Clearly, they had heard the call of the Strip and were eager to heed it.

A small space opened up in front of the baggage carousel as a young couple turned away, smiling, and Nova edged her way into the gap. Hands jammed into her pockets and shoulders hunched, she watched the bags travel round and round. Moments later, her duffel appeared, sliding down and tumbling once end over end before it was stopped by the narrow ledge. The whole scene reminded her of a roulette wheel, and she felt an odd sense of vertigo, as if in empathy with her luggage. Then the moment passed, and she hoisted the bag onto her shoulder.

Evan had told her a car would be waiting at the airport, and after glancing around the room, she caught sight of her name on a placard. The man holding it was probably around her age, if she had to guess, though he was trying to look older by wearing a goatee. He extended his hand as she approached.

"Ms. Novarro?"

"That's right."

"Welcome to Las Vegas. I'm Jeremy, your driver. May I take your bag?"

"I've got it, thanks." She shifted the strap on her shoulder and patted it for emphasis.

"Right this way, then."

The sliding doors opened, admitting a blast of hot, dry air. The smell of baked asphalt and car exhaust made it suddenly difficult to swallow. Here she stood in the middle of the desert, hemmed in by arid land, stranded hundreds of miles from the sea. As her panic rose, Nova fumbled for her water bottle and drank deeply. This was ridiculous. She wasn't stranded. She had come of her own volition and could leave anytime she pleased.

"Your host, Vesper, is occupied this afternoon, but she has arranged to meet you for a drink this evening." He presented her with a cream-colored business card on which *10 p.m., Sól Bar* had been written on the back in flowing cursive. "How was your flight?"

"Fine, thanks." Nova was glad he wanted to talk. Conversation helped with her anxiety.

For the next few minutes, they chatted idly about banal topics—the weather, and and how crazy it was that what had once been a tiny oasis was now the gambling epicenter of the universe. When they reached the limo—a stretch car, Nova realized with some surprise—she finally surrendered her bag and stepped into the ample interior. The cool scent of leather and pine enveloped her, and she tipped her head back against the seat to ease the tension in her shoulders.

"Do you surf?" Jeremy asked as he slid into the driver's seat. "I couldn't help but notice the logo on your bag."

"Yes, I love it." Nova had won the duffel in an amateur competition at her local surf club several summers ago. "You?"

"Absolutely." He paused briefly as he pulled out onto the road. "I grew up in Santa Barbara and was at Rincon every chance I got."

"What brought you out here?" She couldn't imagine a die-hard surfer being content with a landlocked life.

"I got a basketball scholarship to UNLV."

"What was your position?"

"Point guard. But I blew out my knee sophomore year, and the money went away. Haven't managed to get back on a board since then, either."

"Ouch." The worst Nova had suffered was a broken arm, back in her adolescence. The thought of being stuck in a knee brace made her cringe. "I'm sorry."

"Thanks. Water under the bridge." He met her eyes briefly in the mirror. "So, you play poker professionally?"

"That's right." Nova found herself reluctant to share more details. She loved talking about poker in the online forums—rehashing past victories, analyzing lost hands, debating the best strategies. There, she was a goddess, revered by those who aspired to be like her and hated by those jealous of her success. But now, as she looked out the window toward the bristling Vegas skyline, the self-doubt that had been gnawing at her ever since that fateful day at the bank returned full force. Here, she was a stranger in a strange land.

Thankfully, Jeremy didn't follow up with another question. Nova tore her gaze away from the window and opened the mini fridge. It was stocked with three bottles of champagne, and she stared at them for several long seconds before reluctantly closing the door. The soft haze of an alcohol buzz would soothe her nerves, but today, she needed to stay sharp. She would check in, get the lay of the land, and then begin her live poker-playing career—preferably at a low-stakes table populated by tipsy tourists.

"Have you ever stayed at Valhalla before?" Jeremy asked.

"I haven't." Nova didn't want to let on that she had never stayed anywhere in Vegas. "Got any insider tips?"

"Have the salmon eggs benedict at Barri. That's the nicest restaurant. And the pool on the fiftieth-floor terrace is a little smaller than the one on the roof, but its view is almost as good and it's usually not as crowded."

"Thanks."

The word died on Nova's lips as Jeremy turned onto the Strip. Even in the harsh light of midday, it presented a spectacle. To her left, the Luxor pyramid towered over the surrounding buildings, black walls gleaming like onyx. At night, she had read, a spotlight shone from its apex so brightly that it was visible from space.

She had no more time to admire it as Jeremy guided the car into the heart of Sin City. In the days before her departure, Nova had done extensive online research about the Vegas Strip. Not wanting to seem ignorant, she had even taken a "virtual tour" of several of the major casinos. There was the New York, New York, encircled by a massive roller coaster, its Statue of Liberty welcoming the rich, the bold, the strong of constitution. Across from it, a massive lion guarded the entrance of the MGM Grand, its gaze as implacable as Fortune herself. Next came the Paris, its replica Eiffel Tower casting a long shadow across the broad street where the Bellagio's fountains danced merrily, rising and falling from an immaculate pond that summoned another surge of longing for the ocean. Then came the wide, Roman arches of Caesars Palace, sprawling in the shadow of the Mirage's tall towers. And there, at last, was Valhalla, its curved granite walls glinting dully in the sun.

It had been built, she'd learned, in the style of the ancient Norse ring forts—a perfectly circular castle with doors at each of the four compass points. Three cylindrical towers jutted up past the walls, connected in several places by gently sloping archways. Each conical roof was crowned by a large sculpture of the beast for which it was named: Dragon Tower, Raven Tower, Wolf Tower. The statues were made of some kind of white stone that glittered fiercely, fracturing the light into slivers of rainbows that played along the walls of the keep.

Jeremy pulled into the circular driveway, stopping the car so that her window was perfectly aligned with the massive gray door leading into the hotel. "Here we are," he said. "I'll grab your bag."

Nova fished up a twenty-dollar bill from her wallet as Jeremy swung the duffel onto the curb. Immediately, a bellhop appeared, but she waved him away. "I appreciate the ride." She reached out to shake Jeremy's hand. "Take care of that knee."

He nodded. "Good luck in there."

Nova turned toward the door. From the car, she had thought it too was made of stone, but now she realized the effect was the product of a masterful mural designed to appear as a bas relief sculpture. The centerpiece was a gigantic tree, its roots spreading out along the bottom of the door and its branches extending to the top. A sinuous dragon, scales painted with exquisite detail, lay curled among the roots, while an eagle perched on the branches. Nova had read about this, too: Yggdrasil, the world tree of Norse mythology.

She took one step forward and the doors slid open, splitting the tree vertically down the middle. Impressed despite herself, she stepped into the lobby. As her eyes adjusted from the glare outside, her ears were filled with the sound of rushing water and the faint musical tinkling of slot machines somewhere in the distance. She blinked, and her vision cleared to reveal a large, circular fountain, its basin illuminated by blue lights. A tall tree rose from its center, and this one was very much alive. White flowers appeared between clusters of green leaves, illuminated by a skylight overhead. A stone sculpture of a stag stood near the base of the tree, its head bent as though it were drinking from the pool. The fountain was refreshed by streams of water flowing from the creature's antlers.

Not wanting to seem like a tourist, Nova moved toward the check-in area. The employees standing behind each computer screen wore light gray jackets, their lapels stamped with the same coat of arms decorating the golden shield on the wall behind them. Its blue background had been divided into thirds, one for a black raven in flight, one for a silver wolf in mid-stride, and one for a red dragon, its wide jaws belching a plume of flame.

"Next guest, please."

She stepped up to the marble counter where a young, clean-shaven man took her ID and credit card, reciting in practiced language how pleased he was that she had chosen Valhalla for her accommodations. Again, she declined the service of a bellman, not wanting to have to dole out any more tips than necessary.

As she waited for the elevator, a nearby digital marquee tried to entice her to a baccarat tournament that had been going on since noon. That sounded about as appetizing as the "authentically prepared lutefisk" on the restaurant menu. She'd never even learned the rules of baccarat. What was the use, when Lady Luck presided over it, two-faced and fickle? She would rather burn her money. All thirty thousand dollars of it. The elevator chimed, and with a sour twist of her mouth, she stepped inside.

Her room, on the twentieth floor of Raven Tower, was barely wide enough to fit a queen-sized bed and a small nightstand. At the bed's foot was a dresser, and next to the dresser, a desk. The adjacent wall boasted one window, barely larger than an arrow slit, with a view of the neighboring tower's gray wall. If she craned her head just so, she could make out a thin slice of the parking lot. Charming.

Nova dropped her bag on the desk and went into the bathroom. It, too, was small, but the alternating rows of white and blue subway tiles were cheerful, and she felt herself smile at the sight of a rainfall showerhead set into the ceiling above the tub. That would feel heavenly later.

She braced her arms on the ceramic counter and examined her reflection. Women often praised her bright blue eyes, but today they were dull and bloodshot from a poor night's sleep. Early this morning, she had pulled her hair back into a messy bun, and several strands had escaped during the flight. She tucked them behind her ears and frowned. Her face seemed too angular—severe looking, almost—and her gray cargo pants hung precariously from her hips. Most women would have felt ecstatic at having lost a few pounds, but Nova liked the way she had looked, the person she had been. This new, changed face was on the cusp of gaunt and oddly pale despite her tan. Confidence had abandoned her. She had better learn to bluff, and soon. Displaying weakness at a poker table was like swimming in shark-infested waters with an open wound.

She clenched her jaw and escaped the mirror. There was no time like the present, right? She should go downstairs. Find her sea legs. Get rid of the jitters. Afraid to stop moving, she scooped her room key off the desk with one hand and patted her pockets with the other. A few minutes later, she was marching determinedly out of the elevator, past the fountain, and into the casino, bypassing the rows of jangling slot machines in search of the poker tables.

The baccarat tournament was harder to ignore. She heard it before she could see it—a wave of sound that ebbed and flowed as the crowd reacted to the players' fortunes. Still, she was committed to bypassing it entirely until she turned a corner and came face-to-face with the masses. They milled about between her and the double glass doors fifty feet away, over which "Poker Hall" had been stenciled in a vaguely runic-looking script. With a sigh, she began to gingerly pick her way through the mob.

But the undertow was strong. Halfway along the periphery, Nova paused when the loudest shout she'd heard yet erupted from the onlookers. Curious despite herself, she edged closer and rose onto her toes for a glimpse. Beyond the gathered bystanders was a room full of gaming tables ringed by a low railing. The tables were cut in half-moon shapes, with the dealer seated on the straight edge and six players arrayed around the curve. The surface was covered in gold and white lines and symbols, vaguely reminiscent of crop circles or cave drawings. At the corner of each table, a small backlit sign atop a pole indicated that baccarat was being played.

The entrances to the room were cordoned off with velvet ropes, and casino staff dressed in crisp white shirts and black suits were stationed evenly around the periphery. Similarly dressed tournament managers, distinguished by the tags affixed to their lapels, walked the floor, stopping occasionally to monitor the tables and answer questions from the players. One standing at a nearby table caught Nova's attention. Her skirt suit, a rich honey in color rather than black, draped elegantly against the swell of her breasts and the curve of her hips. Gentle ringlets of auburn hair curled down past her shoulders. She was wearing a nametag as well and Nova strained to get a better look.

"What the fuck?" A large man wielding a yard-long glass of frozen margarita like a scepter listed drunkenly into Nova. She recoiled from the intrusion into her personal space. "What the fuck?" he repeated, to no one in particular. The crowd parted, giving the man a wide berth. Nova took the opportunity to edge away from him and press closer to the rail. Wanting another glimpse of the beautiful woman, Nova scanned the room but was disappointed when she was nowhere to be found.

Her attention wandered back to the nearest table, where a new hand was beginning. The dealer flipped over four cards, and the audience leaned forward eagerly. When, moments later, he turned over two more, several of the players groaned. One of them pushed back from the table as the dealer collected the last of his chips. The crowd broke into polite applause as the busted player left the field.

"What just happened?" Margarita man was back. He pulled a crumpled booklet out of his pocket, nearly sloshing his drink on Nova and several nearby patrons. He waved the sodden booklet in front of him like a white flag of surrender. "Wait. I got the rules right here."

The glass tipped precariously again, but this time Nova reached over and took it from the man. She placed it carefully on the floor by the rail. "Dude. Watch it."

The man blinked once as he attempted to focus on Nova's face, then his eyes dipped to her breasts and a large smile stretched across his face. "Sure, baby. I'm Matt." He held out a pudgy hand, its fourth finger encircled by a gaudy class ring. His palm was moist with sweat.

"Whatever." Nova ignored the outstretched hand. Unconsciously, she wiped her own hand on her pants.

The dealer called for bets and the players stacked their chips in the marked circles in front of them. Two cards were dealt to either side of the table. A third card was dealt to the right. More chips exchanged hands, and another player busted out. The remaining players jotted notes onto scorecards with small golf pencils. Nova watched as a few more hands were played in this fashion. Her gaze drifted to the other tables nearby, and she quickly sized up each game before moving on to the next. This was how she had played online poker—running several tables at a time, subconsciously registering the patterns and rhythm of each game while instinctively processing the mathematical odds. The familiarity of the exercise calmed her.

After a few minutes of watching, the puzzle pieces fell into place. She must have made some derisive sound, because Matt looked from the table to her and back again. "What?"

"This has to be the dumbest game ever invented."

"Why? I don't get it."

Nova wanted to leave. She had forgotten about the crowd while she was caught up in figuring out the logic at the tables, but now the press of bodies against her was making her claustrophobic. Also, the cards were calling and she was itching for some action. Not baccarat—these fools could keep their silly game. The poker hall was just over—

But when she turned, she found herself completely hemmed in. The audience had grown while she was deciphering the rules. At this point, there were two options: create her own path or wait for a break. For a moment, she entertained the idea of plowing her way through the throng, but the thought of touching all those strange bodies made her nauseous. How had she gotten herself into this predicament? And then she remembered: the redhead in the sexy suit. Nova scanned the floor again to no avail. She sighed, suddenly wishing for a yard-long margarita of her own.

Matt poked her in the shoulder with a fat finger. "Tell me what's going on."

Nova flinched at the contact. The fat bastard sure was persistent. Maybe once she had explained the rules, he would go away. "Basically, the highest hand wins." She gestured toward the table where a new round was just about to start. "The dealer deals two hands, one for the bank and one for the player. The players get to choose before the deal whether they want to bet on the bank hand or the player hand."

"Don't the players have to bet the player hand?"

"No. Stupid, right? They can bet on either." Nova looked back toward the table where another round was starting.

The dealer dealt a two and a three to the player hand on her right and then a king and a seven to her left. After a dramatic pause, the dealer turned over a four for the player. The dealer paid out the lone bet covering the player hand and scooped up the bets for the bank. The audience burst into applause.

"But the bank had seventeen there! I thought you said the higher hand wins?" Matt rubbed his temple furiously and glared at Nova. A small crowd leaned in to hear the explanation. Apparently, Matt wasn't the only baccarat novice there.

"Well, there are no double digits in this game. If your cards add up to double digits, you drop the first digit and go with the second. A seventeen is played as a seven." Nova held up her hand, curtailing the question about to be asked by Matt and at least three other audience members who had homed in on the conversation. "I know. It's random. And ridiculous. Who wants to play a game that is really all about lucky guesses and poor math?"

The circle of people gathered around Nova and Matt nodded their heads and rumbled in agreement. A pit boss standing by the rail shushed them and whispered a warning to be respectful of the players.

"You figured this out just by watching?" Matt was looking her in the eyes now, instead of at her chest. His respect had clearly jumped up a few notches, not that she cared. "They've only played a couple hands!"

Nova shrugged. "I'm good with numbers."

This time, of the six players at the table—all of them male—three had bet on the bank hand, two on the player hand, and one on a tie. The dealer turned over the bank hand to reveal an eight and a three, and the player hand to reveal a two and a seven. One of the unlucky men shook his head in disgust, while both who had bet on the player hand smiled. The dealer turned over the third card to reveal another eight. The crowd gasped, and the players' smiles faded as quickly as they'd come.

"What the fuck was that?" Matt's exclamation earned another shush from the pit boss.

"A tie, apparently." Nova watched the dealer sweep everyone's chips off the table except for the lucky gentleman who had wagered on a tie. As he was paid out, she did some quick mental math. "I guess that pays eight to one."

Matt's eyes widened. "Did you just calculate that on the spot?"

"Mm." Nova stifled a yawn. Where was the fun in this? How could all these people care so deeply about something that was entirely the product of chance?

Another hand finished, and more players busted out and left. The dealer paused the game briefly as players were consolidated from other tables. The remaining players studied their scorecards while the relocation happened. Pockets of bystanders began to break away during the lull, lured by promise of riches in other parts of the casino. Nova waited impatiently for the crowd around her to thin. Just being here had put her on edge. Maybe she needed some time to acclimate. She could take a nap, or try out the pool. Get her head screwed on straight. Later, she could play some video poker at the bar to warm up before sitting at a table next to real people.

"What's with the notes?" Matt gestured at the players.

Nova ignored him, scanning the casino floor. The game was idiotic and boring, and his inane questions were like nails on a chalkboard in her ears.

"What's with the notes?" Matt repeated louder, this time leaning over the rail while pointing.

The pit boss cleared his throat. "Back away from the line, please." Matt swayed slightly but complied.

Finally, a path materialized before her. Nova turned to go, but Matt grabbed her forearm with a sticky hand. "Wait. What's with the—"

"What the hell?" Nova tried to jerk her arm out of his grasp, but he held on.

"I don't…" Matt blinked stupidly at Nova.

A wave of anger flooded her system with adrenaline. "Let go!"

She pulled her arm back sharply just as he released his grip. For a moment, she teetered on the backs of her heels, arms flailing as she tried to keep her balance…but then gravity prevailed. She fell backward and knocked over the tall margarita glass, splashing the pit boss and players at the nearest table. Somebody screamed, and a flurry of chaos ensued as people alternately edged away from the commotion and pushed in closer to see what was happening. In the midst of it all, Nova found herself sitting in a slushy puddle.

"Oh shit." Matt turned and pushed his way out of the throng, breaking into a staggering run as he headed for the casino exit.

Nova tried to stand up, but a strong hand held her in place. "Wait right there, miss." Nova wanted to rip the arm away but stopped herself when she saw the badge and gun. She slumped against the rail. Other security guards showed up and started diverting the crowds away while tournament managers saw to the players.

"I'll take it from here, Brady," a firm, feminine voice declared.

Nova looked up and stopped cursing her luck. The woman in the golden suit was even more beautiful from up close. A pair of low heels showed off her slim, toned legs and well-manicured toenails. The gentle swell of her hips and breasts made Nova's palms ache. The pale blue shirt below her jacket was open to the second button, and the skin at her throat was smattered with freckles. Sun-kissed.

When Nova realized she had just given the woman a blatant once-over, she blinked. Hazel eyes met her own, a chameleon swirl of brown and green and just the barest hint of gray. Nova dropped her gaze to look for the nametag she'd spotted earlier, but it was partially obscured by the suit's lapel.

"May I speak with you for a moment?" The woman's smile was practiced and pleasant, but there was an edge to her voice.

Nova felt a little dizzy, as though her skin had absorbed the margarita. When the woman extended her hand, she reached out to take it…only to realize that her fingers were as sticky as her backside. Quickly, she scrambled upright. "Sure."

The woman led her out of the press of humanity, toward an unoccupied place along the wall. After a glance around the room, she met Nova's gaze. "I understand you've been experiencing some frustration this afternoon. The spilled drink was unfortunate, but I could see it was an accident. Why don't you take a break for a while to cool off?"

"I'm freezing already. The AC is blasting in here." Nova flashed a grin other women had claimed to find charming. "But if you want to come upstairs, maybe we can warm up together. Room 2074."

A light flush bloomed along the stranger's cheeks. "You've mistaken my intent. I've received complaints about your commentary from several players. I'd like to request that you keep your disparaging opinions to yourself throughout the remainder of the tournament."

Nova recognized bullying when she heard it. Resentment flared, and she braced one hand on the wall to lean in closer. "I was explaining the game to a drunk guy. Last time I checked, this was still a free country."

"You were badmouthing the game to a crowd of people, within hearing of players who have spent their hard-earned money to enter this tournament." The woman's tone was as chilly as a Scandinavian winter. Was she really just a soulless casino executive? That would be so disappointing.

"So if I ponied up the thousand bucks, you'd be waiting at my elbow instead of taking my elbow to escort me out?"

"Even if you were playing in the tournament"—the woman paused to give her a skeptical once-over—"I'd still ask that you be respectful of the game."

Who could respect a game that was entirely dependent on luck? For a moment, Nova was tempted to go on another diatribe, but with an effort, she swallowed the words. Valhalla's management probably wouldn't think twice about throwing her out on her ear, and she was almost certain they'd insist she pay for her room. She couldn't exactly afford to flush her limited funds down the drain. Still, she wasn't about to let this woman get away with steamrolling her.

"Well, I'd like to ask that you respect prospective clients. Do the higher-ups pay you to be this condescending?"

"Excuse me?" Her eyes narrowed, and Nova could feel the waves of prickly indignation rolling off her like the approaching tide.

"What was that look for?"

"What look?"

"The 'you don't belong within five hundred feet of this room' look?"

"I didn't—" The woman shook her head sharply. "This conversation is ridiculous."

"Finally, we agree." Nova held out her non-sticky hand. "I'll promise to forget all about it if you will. We can seal the deal with a drink."

"I don't think so." The delicate muscles along the woman's

jawline flickered. "I trust you'll find another way to entertain yourself this afternoon?"

Without waiting for a reply, she spun on one heel and walked back toward the tournament. Nova watched her skirt swirl against her thighs, desire trumping her annoyance. How did such a beautiful woman become so cold, so…corporate? Nova was suddenly possessed of an insane urge to save her from herself—to whisk her away from these artificial lights and inauthentic people. Would she thaw under the desert sun? Or melt away entirely?

"Oh for fuck's sake," she muttered. This was Vegas. Beautiful women were a dime a dozen, and most were probably just as snooty as that one had been. She'd be worse than a fool to let this most recent brush-off get under her skin.

For a moment, she deliberated escaping to her room, sacking out on the bed, and turning on the television. But when she pictured herself there, she could practically feel its cramped walls closing in on her. No thanks. Resolutely, she turned to face the poker hall. Behind its frosted doors were plenty of people just waiting to lose their money. She was a professional. A champion. She belonged there.

It was time to get to work.

CHAPTER FOUR

Vesper didn't particularly care for boxing, but she could put on a good show—much like the two men facing off in the ring. Tonight, Valhalla boasted the best fight in town, and the arena was at full capacity. Beside her, TJ slid his thumb and middle finger into his mouth, and she braced herself for the sound of his shrill whistle. When the bell signaled the start of round four, she clapped and leaned forward, feigning interest. He had wagered five hundred dollars on the outcome of this bout—though officially, the bet had been made by his father—and for his sake, she hoped he won. For her sake, she hoped he lost. Such was the dilemma of a casino host.

On his far side, Theodore Senior was also thoroughly engrossed by the fight. He had removed his sports coat and rolled up his sleeves to reveal tan forearms. A ten-thousand-dollar Rolex encircled his right wrist. He had already won three times that at the baccarat tournament this afternoon, but Vesper wasn't worried. Easy come, easy go. She was always glad when her clients began their trips on a hot streak. They were likely to gamble more money than if they started off cold.

As TJ's chosen boxer put his opponent in a headlock, her phone, tucked into her jacket pocket, began to vibrate. She whisked it up to her ear before realizing it was her alarm. Time to leave. When she glanced at the ring, the boxers had been separated. Taking advantage of the brief lull, she leaned closer to TJ.

"I have to run. Is there anything I can get for you before I leave?"

He turned to her with the broad grin that probably charmed women from here all the way back to New England. "Nah, V, we're golden. Catch you later."

As she slid out of her chair, she noticed their glasses were nearly empty. On her way out, she caught one of the waiters by his elbow and pressed a fifty-dollar bill into his palm. "I need a fresh round of beer for the Hamilton party. The older gentleman is drinking the porter. The younger likes IPA."

"On it."

The waiter darted away, and Vesper continued toward the exit. The beer itself would be comped by the casino, of course, but General Grant would ensure that no one on the wait staff made the mistake of asking for TJ's ID, as they had been trained to do. His birthday was only a few days away, and he was under the watchful eye of his father. There was no reason why he shouldn't enjoy himself.

Vesper allowed herself a moment of pique that enjoyment wasn't on her own radar for the evening. She needed to sleep, not waste her time having a drink with Royal Flush's most recent online poker champion. Poker players held a certain fascination to the general public, but they weren't very valuable to casinos—unless, of course, they also gambled in other ways. Valhalla took a five percent rake from every poker pot, but even high-stakes games didn't produce anything close to the cash flow from a high roller on a losing streak at craps or baccarat or blackjack. The odds of this woman being able to help Vesper's career were low. This appointment would be a one-way street, and she didn't have time for those.

Sól Bar was at the base of Dragon Tower, and its décor set it apart from the rest of the casino. Named for the deity of the sun in Norse mythology, it was decorated in shades of orange, red, and gold. Its leather booths and stools were dyed a deep russet, and the tables and countertops were coated with beaten copper that glinted under the overhead lights.

As Vesper scanned the people sitting at the bar, she realized she had forgotten to look up this woman's photograph. "Nova" was the only name Evan had provided in his message—the player's online handle, she presumed. She searched for someone sitting by herself. Everyone was in pairs or groups, except...

Realization struck at the same time as the disruptive woman from the baccarat tournament turned her head. For the second time that day, their eyes met. Hers were the kind of blue Vesper had seen in photographs of the Caribbean. They widened, and then after a moment, a rueful grin curled the corners of her mouth before it was replaced by a smirk. Vesper focused on keeping her neutral expression in place, but it was difficult not to let the mask slip to betray her irritation. Another argument with this stubborn and self-righteous Lothario was the last thing she needed right now.

"Nova?" she asked, forcing the syllables into a pleasant tone.

She stood as Vesper approached. "Couldn't stay away, could you?"

Vesper almost turned around. Instead, she took a deep breath and kept moving until there were barely two inches between them. "Evan asked me to help you." She pitched her voice low, and clipped her words so they were sharp as ice. "But if you make one more suggestive comment, I won't stay another minute."

Nova held up her hands in a gesture that could either be protest or surrender, and Vesper found herself distracted by the play of muscles beneath her tanned skin. Ruthlessly, she quashed the unwanted surge of desire.

"Stay or go as you like. No one's making you do anything."

Vesper slid onto the stool next to her and gestured for Nova to do the same. "I keep my promises."

"Evan mentioned you owe him a favor."

"That's how this business works." Vesper signaled the bartender. She rarely indulged in a drink while working, but she wanted one now.

"What'll it be, Ms. Blake?"

"Gin and tonic please, Jim, and whatever my…friend is having."

"Ma'am?"

Nova considered for a moment, looking between the torn label of her empty beer bottle and the shelves of hard liquor behind the bar. Suddenly, her eyes gleamed.

"I'll have a Vesper. Please."

Jim started to laugh and then pretended it was a cough. Whatever was showing on her face made him hurry off to do their bidding. Nova sat calmly on her stool, looking too innocent. Obviously, she liked to push the envelope. She was a gambler. Of course she did.

"What? It's a great drink. 007 knows how to make 'em. And a distinctive name, too. Were your parents Bond fans or very religious?"

"Neither." Vesper was not about to confide in her. This was an unpleasant task to check off her to-do list, not a date.

Nova spun in the stool to look at her head on. She had cleaned up a bit from the afternoon, exchanging her stained cargo pants for a low-slung pair of jeans. Her blond hair hung down in layers that extended just past her chin in front and gradually lengthened in the back. She was attractive. Very. And an ass, Vesper reminded herself.

"I know this is awkward," Nova was saying. "But are you really going to hold what happened earlier against me? Didn't you see the drunk guy who started the whole fiasco?"

"Security spoke with him. The spilled drink wasn't the problem."

"No, apparently my lack of respect for the game was the problem." Nova fixed her with an intent stare. "Tell me the truth. You know just how much of an edge the house has. Do you *really* respect the people who walk in here and throw their money away, night after night?"

Vesper was through with niceties. "Are you even listening to yourself? You're a professional poker player. You do the same thing."

"You couldn't be more wrong."

"And you couldn't be more infuriating!" Vesper knew she was allowing herself to be baited, but she couldn't seem to help it. She raised her glass and took a sip before she completely lost her cool and threw it into Nova's face. "You wager money on hands of poker. You're a gambler. That isn't up for debate."

"Is there an element of luck in poker? Yes." Nova pushed a stray strand of hair away from her mouth, and Vesper suddenly couldn't look away from her lips. Wet from the drink that shared her name, they shimmered tantalizingly. As her stomach pitched and rolled, she sipped from her own glass. Was this some kind of hormonal quirk? Mentally, she began counting the days backward, only to lose her focus when Nova's tongue darted out to apply a fresh sheen of moisture.

"…game of skill," she was saying. "For those who can calculate the odds, at least."

Vesper took another sip, wrestling with her composure. If she so much as betrayed a hint of attraction, Nova would torment her for as long as she was staying at Valhalla. Deliberately, she injected her voice with scorn. "Knowing the odds isn't foolproof."

"Of course it isn't. But neither is a quarterback's throwing game or a pitcher's fastball. No one debates that football and baseball are games of skill, even though luck plays into the outcome."

She was good at arguing. Vesper didn't want to admit to herself that she was enjoying their verbal sparring session. "But what about the other parts of the game? Bluffing. Reading people."

For the first time since the beginning of their debate, Nova hesitated. She tried to mask it by drinking deeply from her glass, but Vesper could sense the anxiety that sharpened her movements.

"True." Nova took another sip. "In online poker, there is no body language, only patterns. So it still comes down to math—even the bluffing."

"And that's why you respect sports bettors, but not baccarat players?"

Nova braced one arm on the bar and leaned closer. "I respect sports bettors who do their research and poker players who know their numbers. I don't respect idiots who roll dice or flip a card and expect to win something for nothing."

Her speech struck a note of sympathy in Vesper. Entitlement. That's what Nova was critiquing, and her words held more than a kernel of truth. Unbidden, memories flashed across Vesper's mind like a 3-D film, inviting her to reach out and touch: the prickly armrests of the white cane chairs in the Chelton family's solarium; the vast expanse of perfectly manicured grass outside floor-to-ceiling windows; tall, sweating glasses of pink lemonade doctored with the contents of Samuel's flask.

It was a scene she had enacted a hundred times: Samuel lording it over them all at the head of the glass-topped table, flanked by his twin, Sabrina, and their younger brother, Simon. Vesper and Horatio, the butler's boy, rounded out the group. The game was always Texas hold 'em, because as Samuel often said, *All the other versions are gay.* The Monopoly money they played with was falling apart, the dollar bills more tape than paper. No amount of air-conditioning could ever adequately cool that room, and their playing cards were always slightly damp with sweat and condensation.

Vesper could feel the ghosts of those cards between her fingertips, the quiet rustling sound they made, as though she had captured a butterfly in her palms. She was the best shuffler of them all—even better than Samuel—and whenever it was her turn to deal, Sabrina would stare at her hands.

An echo of the confused desire she had felt back then set her heart to pounding, and she raised her glass again only to realize she had reached the bottom of it.

"Vesper?" Nova's voice was soft, the brush of fingertips against her shoulder even softer. No trace of her abrasiveness remained. "Are you all right?"

No. She wasn't all right. She had thought herself beyond the reach of those memories. Dead to them. A flashback that strong hadn't happened in years. But as she signaled Jim for another drink and felt Nova pull her hand away, it suddenly made sense. Here she sat, next to a woman she didn't want to find attractive, discussing the game of poker. What could be the more perfect trigger?

The fresh G&T arrived, and Vesper clutched at it, downing half the glass in two quick gulps. She turned and plastered a smile onto her face. "I'm sorry about that. I just remembered something I neglected to do up at my office. I'll need to be going."

Nova frowned, opened her mouth, and then closed it again. "Okay," she said slowly. "Well, it was nice to meet you."

"Likewise." Vesper extended her hand and tried to tell herself she didn't feel anything when their palms slid together. "Every Monday night, a group of poker pros—live poker, I mean—play a cash game in one of the Celestial Palaces. No limit hold 'em." She released Nova's fingers and took a step back. "I'll tell them to expect you next week."

Her obligation fulfilled, she turned and strode briskly away. At ten paces, the urge to glance back over her shoulder was overwhelming, but instead of giving in, she ducked her head and walked even faster.

CHAPTER FIVE

Nova tried not to betray her awe as she stepped onto the swirling marble floor of the Morningstar Palace. She had known it would be lavish and was no stranger to luxury herself, but this defied even her expectations. The domed atrium was two stories high, its walls painted in shades of gold and blue. Chandeliers hung from the ceiling, their light reflected by large, gilt mirrors. The dome itself was a darker blue than the walls and had been painted with an image of the evening sky, its stars joined by thin golden lines into foreign configurations. The Norse constellations, if she had to guess.

Matching pairs of French doors on either side of the room were closed and curtained, and Nova briefly wondered where they led. But what commanded her attention were the twin staircases curling up toward a balcony at the far end of the hall, their marble steps covered by a crimson runner. At the top, two men were having a conversation. The one leaning against the balustrade and holding a snifter half-filled with bronze liquid looked vaguely familiar. Both were dressed casually, and Nova felt a rush of relief that her black chinos and green collared shirt wouldn't be out of place. As she followed the butler across the room, the soles of her Doc Martens echoed beneath the dome, and the men glanced her way.

Ryan Davenport. That was his name. She had seen it in the credits of many an action-adventure film. One of her roommates—Liz, if she was remembering correctly—had enjoyed putting on those kinds of movies as a pretext for sex. They would start lying side by side on her bed as the opening credits rolled, but the action, both on screen and off, always escalated quickly. Dimly, she remembered Liz saying something once about Davenport enjoying poker. He must be their host tonight.

The memory made her chest ache. She missed Liz. And Emily. And Felicia. And Sandra. And even Monique, who had stayed angry the longest after the snafu with the bank. They were good friends who always had her back, and comfortable lovers without many expectations. Of course, there had been drama at times, but they'd always worked their way through it. Here, no one was looking out for her, and if she wanted to blow off steam, she'd have to do it with a stranger. That held no appeal whatsoever.

Vesper Blake, on the other hand, held plenty of appeal. Nova didn't think she had imagined the nascent chemistry between them, but she hadn't caught so much as a glimpse of her since their aborted conversation last week. She had received only one message—a handwritten note delivered by the concierge, which read simply: *Monday night, 9 p.m., Morningstar Palace. You're on the list. Best, V.* Not exactly the warmest and fuzziest of missives.

"Mr. Davenport," said the butler, jerking Nova out of her own head. Silently, she chastised herself. She couldn't afford any lapses in concentration tonight. "This is Nova."

He frowned, and Nova felt her heart sink toward her feet. Had Vesper been lying about the list? Or worse—had she tricked Nova into making a fool of herself? But then his face cleared. "Oh—you're the online poker player, right?"

"That's me." Nova hoped she sounded confident.

"Welcome." He nodded toward the double doors beyond the stairs. "We're gathering in the sitting room."

Nova ascended the stairs briskly, keeping a firm hand on the small backpack slung over one shoulder. In it were a tin of Altoids and an envelope containing ten thousand dollars in hundred-dollar bills—almost a quarter of her liquid assets. It felt heavy, but she knew that was just her imagination playing tricks.

She stuck out her hand toward Davenport when she reached the top. "Thanks for having me."

He looked her up and down and grinned faintly, radiating a GQ sort of charm that doubtless appealed to every straight woman on the planet. "Good to see you." His shake was firm and brief, but Nova found herself gobsmacked with screaming gaydar. Struggling to maintain her composure, she nodded as he introduced the other man as Kevin Gunn, lead singer of a popular band she didn't like and a "close friend" of his. Sure, he was.

"We'll see you inside," said Davenport, leaving her to face the tall double doors alone.

She took what she hoped was an unobtrusive deep breath and let her palms come to rest on the ornate gilt handles cast in the shape of sinuous dragons. The doors themselves were made of dark wood carved into ornate interlocking knot patterns that made her dizzy when she looked too closely. She tested the handles surreptitiously before giving them a strong push.

The doors swung open, silent on their hinges. Nova moved forward into a room dominated by its large, stone fireplace in which flames crackled merrily, offset by the low whir of cool air blowing through the vents. Luxury and waste were synonymous here, apparently.

An oval table with a surface of blue-veined marble occupied the center of the room, surrounded by chairs upholstered with golden leather. Six of the ten chairs were occupied, but as she moved closer, the raven-haired woman seated halfway along the far side was the only one to rise. Her three-inch stilettos put her eye to eye with Nova as she moved forward with the confidence of a tightrope walker.

"I'm Delilah, your dealer for the evening." She held Nova's hand twice as long as Davenport had.

"Nova. Pleasure to meet you."

"Likewise." Delilah cocked her head. "Shall we get you settled?"

Nova heard the unspoken request. In order to take a seat at the table, she had to hand over her money. Ten thousand dollars, just for the privilege of playing. As she let the backpack slip from her shoulder, she flashed back over the past several days. By forcing herself to sit in the poker hall for hours on end, she had managed to make almost two thousand. Now, she was about to risk five times that in a single night. If she won, she could potentially multiply her earnings tenfold or even more. If she lost...

Nova reached into the bag and closed her hand around the envelope inside. "Here you go," she said as she forced her suddenly stiff fingers to release it into Delilah's palm.

"Thank you." Delilah swept a pale arm toward the table. "Please, sit."

The prospect of sitting down between two strangers was never appealing, and it hadn't gotten easier with practice. The people in Valhalla's poker room were mostly tourists, and they tended to be both chatty and clueless. But right now, as she looked around the room and recognized three of the best live poker players in the world, she found herself oddly nostalgic for the company of amateurs.

They were all men, but that was where their similarities ended. Damon Magnusson was tall, whip-thin, and completely bald. He had won the main event at the WSOP two years in a row. The year before that, he had claimed a bronze medal for his native Norway as a biathlete in the Winter Olympics. The press had dubbed him "Ice Man." Kris Winston, aka "Kris Kringle," sat next to him, hands clasped across his prodigious belly. His poker career was as long and illustrious as his white beard.

Across from Winston, Jonah "Mac" MacArthur was hunched over his smartphone. Mac had gotten his start on the Internet, and he had parlayed that fame into a highly successful live career. Pudgy and pasty, with thinning mouse-brown hair and chunky glasses, he might not seem like much of a role model, but Nova would count herself lucky if she could emulate even a fraction of his success. Like her, he had a head for numbers, and when he wasn't playing poker, he was playing the stock market. Over the past month, she'd read every interview of his that could be found on the Net in the hopes of picking up a few tips on how to make the transition from online to live poker. Would her name be familiar to him, she wondered. There was only one way to find out.

She slid into the chair next to his, but when he didn't look up, she was obliged to make eye contact with Ice Man. His stare felt like a laser, dissecting her with cold precision. Forcing herself not to look away, she surreptitiously wiped her palm on one leg before extending it across the table.

"I'm sure you get this all the time, Damon, but great play last year at the final table."

His hands were as cool as his mannerism. "And you are?"

"Nova." His expression remained blank, and she hurried to add, "Until just recently, I've been playing online."

Finally, Mac raised his head. "You took Royal Flush's hold 'em tournament last year, right?"

"That's me." Nova didn't know whether to feel relieved or apprehensive. Mac had just laid out her credentials, proving she belonged. But with credentials, came expectations. Mentally shrugging off her insecurity, she swiveled to face him. "Good to meet you, Mac."

A blonde wearing a white blouse and a short black skirt interposed herself between them. "May I get you anything to drink?"

Nova desperately wanted to have a double of whatever Davenport had been drinking, but social lubrication would also dull her wits. She had to stay sharp tonight. "Sparkling water, please."

"Same." Mac watched the woman walk away before turning back to face her. "So, you're entering the World Series this year, I take it?"

"Unoriginal, I know." She gave him a quick smile, hoping it smacked of confidence and not nerves, and looked across the table. "It's a pleasure to meet you as well, Kris."

"Hello." He seemed disinterested but shook her hand anyway.

Delilah appeared at her elbow, then, with a rainbow of poker chips. As Nova arranged them within easy reach of her left hand, she realized that most of her fellow players had bought in for more than she had. She would begin the game short stacked, playing catch-up and vulnerable to all in moves.

Swallowing hard, she hoped her dismay didn't show. The Ice Man could sniff out weakness like a bloodhound. Fortunately, everyone's attention shifted away from her when Davenport entered the room with Gunn and another man in tow. He paused at the head of the table.

"Welcome, all. Let's have introductions before we start trying to take each other's money."

After the low rumble of laughter, Kris began, followed by Damon. Nova paid careful attention as the others took their turns: Claude, a soft-spoken filmmaker from France; Jerry, brash chef of a restaurant she'd never heard of; and Will Taylor, a retired NBA star whose name was dimly familiar. As each presented himself, she took note of their mannerisms to compare to their behavior during the game. This was the part of live poker that gave her headaches. She was used to calculating pot odds and for watching her screen for patterns in others' play. But monitoring their body language while trying to control her own wasn't part of her skill set. Over the past few days, she'd been practicing on the tourists with some success, but this group would prove much more challenging to read.

"Shall we get started?" Davenport looked to Delilah once the introductions were finished.

"The game, lady and gentlemen, is no limit hold 'em. Fifty-dollar, one-hundred-dollar blinds." She held up a small white disk. "The button will begin with our host." She slid it along the polished surface of the table, and Davenport caught it expertly just as it slipped off the edge.

Delilah's lacquered nails caught the light as she began to deal. Nova trapped her two cards beneath her fingertips, dragged them toward her, and took a peek. Five of hearts, eight of clubs. Not the worst of hands, but nothing to brag about, either. There was a slim chance she might be able to build a straight, but when Taylor promptly bet another hundred into the pot, folding was a no-brainer. Most everyone else folded as well, except Jerry and Damon, who called. She watched them closely as the flop came nine of clubs, queen of diamonds, and two of clubs. Taylor didn't hesitate before throwing in five hundred dollars, nearly doubling the pot. Jerry folded immediately but Damon re-raised to a thousand and Taylor called. When Delilah produced a turn that was the four of clubs, Taylor checked. Damon immediately checked behind him.

Nova couldn't help but lean forward in anticipation. Much had been written about Damon Magnusson's loose-aggressive style. He played a variety of starting hands and was notoriously difficult to read. Damon's re-raise after the flop could have been a sign of a strong hand. Two pair or trips. Then again, he could have been overbidding a draw hand such as a straight or flush to try and stay Taylor's betting and buy a free card while the pot odds were still cheap. The raise also could have been an exploratory bet to ascertain just how strong Taylor's hand was. Damon's check after the turn was interesting indeed. Was he still waiting for his straight to hit or was he nursing a monster hand?

The river was the ace of hearts, and the corners of Taylor's mouth twitched as he pushed four purple chips into the center. Two thousand dollars. Damon took just a moment to consider before pushing all of his chips into the pot. "All in."

Nova gasped. Taylor cursed and leaned into the table as if getting closer would grant him magical insight into Damon's hole cards. Damon had bought in for fifty thousand dollars, same as Taylor. The pot had been less than three thousand dollars before the all in. This was a serious over-bet by any standard. The Norwegian was flexing his muscle early.

With a long, drawn-out sigh, Taylor tossed his cards face up into the muck. He was folding but he wanted to show everybody that he'd hit two pair, aces over queens, when the river came. Someone clapped. Damon simply shrugged and raked in the chips without showing his own cards. His aggressive play didn't surprise her. She'd watched him on television many times, and he always played that way.

Davenport passed the button clockwise to Claude, which meant it was Nova's turn to pony up the big blind. She tossed a black, hundred-dollar chip into the center and prayed Lady Luck would grant her a decent starting hand with which to defend her money. She had learned long ago to play more aggressively when the rules of the game forced her to commit to the pot.

This time, Delilah dealt her both the jack and ten of spades. Something to work with. Careful not to betray even the slightest hint of her satisfaction, she watched the other players. Mac raised, Kris, and Davenport called; the rest folded. Damon's decision to fold inspired such a surge of relief that she gave herself a silent scolding. He might be one of the most aggressive players in the world, but he wasn't the only dangerous one. Kris and Mac had won plenty of tournaments, too. They just weren't quite as flashy.

The flop revealed the two of hearts, eight of diamonds, and queen of clubs. She had a decent chance at drawing an inside straight, and the pot was a beautiful rainbow, making it unlikely that anyone would be able to put together a flush. That queen might prove to be problematic, of course, but there was a fifteen point four percent chance of either the turn or the river being the nine that would almost certainly make the pot hers. Her pulse trip-hopped at the thought.

She had expected Mac to bet, but when he slid two black chips into the center, Nova had to work hard not to express her confusion. Two hundred dollars was just less than half the value of the money in the center—a clear underbet. The sweet spot for most professional players hovered between two-thirds and three-quarters of any given pot, and Kris surprised her by calling instead of raising. When Davenport did as well, she debated only briefly before doing the same. Re-raising on an inside draw would be aggressive, and she would be playing her table position well to do so. But the game was young and she hadn't quite gotten a bead on the other players' betting patterns yet. Holding her breath, she watched Delilah flip the turn card.

The three of hearts smiled serenely up at her. No problem. There was now a flush draw on the table but it was unlikely any of the remaining players would have stayed in the hand for a runner-runner flush draw. Mac bet three hundred dollars, another underbet. Kris folded. Davenport looked at Mac, then back down at his cards. Nova wondered if that meant he was unsure of his next move, since he obviously hadn't forgotten which two cards he was holding. Finally, he called. Nova pushed three black chips into the pot. Her chance of a nine had fallen to seven point seven percent, but as long as the pot odds remained decent, she was going to see this through. The pot now held two thousand one hundred and fifty dollars.

Delilah met each of their eyes before revealing the turn card. When Nova saw the nine of spades, she fought not to react. The straight was hers, and the threat of a flush was neutralized. She had the "nuts," the best possible hand, and now all that remained was to coax as much money as possible out of her opponents. She wasn't sitting alone in her bedroom, Swedish House Mafia blaring from her laptop's speakers. She couldn't talk trash at the computer screen or spin triumphantly in her swivel chair. Instead, she reached for her water and sipped with what she hoped appeared to be nonchalance, praying that one of them would lead out with a sizeable bet. When Mac dropped three hundred more into the middle, she clutched hard at her pant leg beneath the table, and when Davenport called, she had another drink of water. It took all her self-control not to fling all of her chips triumphantly into the pot. She had to make a careful raise to maximize her winnings. Too much and the two men would fold. Not enough and she would squander a perfect opportunity. Carefully, Nova pushed nine black chips into the center. Nine hundred dollars. The six-hundred-dollar raise represented approximately twenty percent of the pot, too tempting to pass up. Davenport called immediately. Mac squinted at her for a moment, sighed, and then reluctantly called as well.

"Let's see 'em," Davenport said.

Mac flipped over a queen and a ten of hearts to make top pair. Nova murmured a silent thanks to Lady Luck for avoiding the flush on the river. Davenport grinned widely as he revealed the eight and nine in his hand—two pair. Nova did her best to contain a smug smile, but she felt the corners of her mouth twitch as she laid down her jack and ten. The exhilaration was a thousand times sweeter than any of her small-time victories over the past few days. This was a landmark—she could feel it. Her first live hand won against professional players.

"Damn." Davenport raised his snifter in a rueful toast.

Mac only shrugged and said, "Nice stroke of luck."

That soured Nova's mood a little, but all she said was, "Right?" as she raked in her winnings. The orange fifty-dollar chip she sent spinning toward Delilah before stacking the others atop her own piles.

As she waited for the next hand to be dealt, Nova forced herself to rehash her previous decisions. One major difference between online and live poker was the speed with which the game was played. She had been accustomed to juggling multiple hands simultaneously, which didn't leave much time for postmortems. But in live poker, she could second-guess herself until the metaphorical cows came home, and right now, she was seriously questioning the wisdom of underbetting. Big wagers were aggressive, a way to gain information about your opponents while going on the defensive. So why had someone like Mac been content to bet three hundred when he should have been betting at least five times that at the end?

The pattern became apparent as the night wore on: Kris, Mac, and Ice Man were courting Davenport. Every time he stayed in a hand, they underbet, but each time he folded, they allowed themselves to play aggressively. Clearly, they wanted to maintain their friendships with him, along with all of its many perks, and Nova was content to follow their leads. She was playing well. Why bite the hand that was helping to feed her?

By midnight, she had doubled her money and was second in chips. When Davenport called for a break, she wandered out to the suite's balcony far above the Strip. Beneath the canopy of stars, its lights glittered frenetically. Curling her hands around the metal railing, she inhaled deeply of the crisp desert air and felt the tension ebb from her shoulders. In the distance, the Luxor's shining apex gleamed like a second moon. Up here, she felt none of the claustrophobia that always began to fog her brain whenever she sat for too long at the casino tables. Maybe these private games could be her niche in the live poker world, once she had built up enough of a bankroll. They were probably played all over the Bay Area, too. She would make a name for herself at the World Series, sign a new contract with Royal Flush, and play private games in between tournaments.

Within a year or two, she might even have enough saved up to buy a new house. Whether the girls would be interested in moving in was an open question, of course. It was only a matter of time before some of them left to start careers elsewhere, or paired off into exclusive couples. Sandra and Liz hadn't spent so much as a night with anyone else in months, and this wasn't the first time Nova had wondered whether they were destined for a U-Haul.

She caught herself making a face, but at least it was safe to betray emotion out here, where none of her competitors could see. As much as she loved her best friends, she couldn't imagine a permanent relationship. Not with them, not with anyone—not even with Vesper Blake, whose image continued to pop up in her mind's eye during unguarded moments. She should reach out to Vesper to thank her for including her in this game, shouldn't she? Or was that just a shallow excuse?

The sliding door opened behind her, and Nova turned to the sight of Delilah, backlit by the bright room. "Ready for more?"

"Always." She took the same seat and briefly joined in an animated discussion between Mac and Damon about the latest blockbuster action flick while the others settled in.

"Something to drink?" the waitress asked.

All night, Davenport, Jerry, and Taylor had been drinking Johnny Walker Blue. She had never tried it. Surely, two fingers of ridiculously expensive scotch wouldn't hurt. She had doubled her money, proving she could keep pace with the pros. There was nothing wrong with relaxing her guard, just a little.

"Scotch, please. Double." She rolled her shoulders as Delilah began to shuffle, wondering whether a massage would be too extravagant an expenditure.

Her drink arrived as she made a risky decision to call a thousand-dollar bet of Damon's. She had been dealt the king of diamonds and the ten of clubs, and another king had appeared on the flop. Davenport had folded early, and Damon was bringing the big guns on this hand. A pair of kings was hardly a monster holding, but it was decent, the board didn't offer much else, and she didn't want to let Damon steamroll her. Gunn folded, but thankfully, Claude followed her lead. The prospect of playing heads up against the Ice Man sent a chill right through her.

Moments later, when the board paired on the turn with a second nine, Damon pushed two thousand into the center. Two thousand dollars—more than a tenth of the chips arrayed before her. Nova's mind raced. If she waited too long to make her decision, he would pick up on her doubts. She pushed her chips into the middle and prayed she wasn't wrong. If Damon had three of a kind, there was nothing she could do. But he'd placed a sizeable wager before that nine had materialized, and his raise was proportional to the size of the pot. She had two pair, and a ten beat a nine any day.

Claude folded, leaving her to the showdown. A dry wind blew across her mind's eye, rattling the broken slats of a saloon door. In a different time and place, that wind might have been real, but tonight, all she felt was the memory of a cool night breeze brushing up against her face like a cat.

The river was the four of spades, and Nova couldn't help but frown when she saw it. Felicia, who was Chinese American, had drilled the symbology of the unlucky number four into her head. Its pronunciation in Mandarin was nearly identical in sound to the word for "death," and the association had remained strong over centuries. Some Chinese buildings didn't have a fourth floor, so strong was the superstition. And now death had appeared on the table, bearing a shovel.

When Damon bet five thousand, Nova wasn't surprised. Did he have three of a kind? Or four? A full house? Or was he bluffing? If she bowed out now, having already sacrificed thousands of dollars, would she regret it?

Yes, she told herself firmly. Folding was not an option. Damon's style of play was notoriously aggressive, and if she so much as sneezed right now, he would probably perceive it as weakness. Statistics weren't going to help in this moment. Her decision would be based on instinct, and she wanted to believe he was bluffing. He had nothing. And even if the opposite turned out to be true, at least she hadn't lay down in the dirt and allowed him to run roughshod over her.

She called and promptly flipped over her cards. People might call her a loser after this hand, but they'd never be able to call her a coward. Damon's glacial façade didn't crack as he laid down a king and a nine, his full house running roughshod over her two pair. That four on the river had been a true omen.

"Good hand," she said, watching him scoop up seven thousand dollars' worth of her chips. In a matter of minutes, he had reduced her winnings by two thirds. But that was the nature of the game. What had been lost could always be won back. Taking a quick sip of her scotch to steady her nerves, she focused on the next hand.

But that one she lost as well, when she narrowly missed an open-ended straight. Wanting to cool off, she folded her two next hands and tried to practice watching the mannerisms of her competitors. Gunn licked his lips a lot, but was that a tell or a personal habit? And Jerry was tracing the circumference of his glass with a thick finger, but was that a sign of nerves or boredom? She raised her own glass to her lips, only to find it empty. When had that happened?

The waitress was immediately at her elbow. "Would you like another?"

She did. Oh, how she did. "No, thank you," she said with a Herculean effort.

When the big blind returned to her, she clenched her jaw and vowed to defend it. But Delilah dealt her a three and an eight, unsuited, forcing her to fold when Kris led out aggressively. On the next hand, she played the small blind to the end with a pair of queens when no higher card materialized on the board, only to discover that Gunn had been dealt pocket kings. She sat out the next hand and was subsequently dealt a pair of aces, but everyone folded when she bet out three hundred to start. Murphy's law, of course—no one wanted to play the one time she was holding pocket rockets.

After losing twice more, she was down to three thousand in chips. Her only consolation was that Claude had tanked already. Of course, he had laughed it off and bought himself back into the game for another ten thousand. Nova patted her pocket, tracing the outline of her money clip. She had cashed out downstairs earlier in the evening, and it held the two thousand she'd won from the tourists. If she lost the remainder of her chips, she could always… *No.* Refusing to let her brain finish the thought, she looked down at her latest hand. With smart playing and a bit of luck, she could regain all she had lost, and more.

But as the night wore on, the stacks in front of her continued to dwindle. Whenever she held a halfway decent hand, the pots remained small, but whenever she tried to bluff, the pot value quickly escalated beyond what she could risk. The lower her chip count became, the faster her pulse rose. When Davenport finally forced her to go all in with her last five hundred, she watched the remainder of the hand unfold in slow motion, heart hammering against her ribs. And when his two pair defeated her single, her stomach dropped into her shoes.

Show them nothing. It was the only thought she could cling to. The rest were as slippery as her palms. *Show them nothing.*

"You got me," she said, the words sounding strange on top of the heartbeat echoing in her ears. "Nice one."

"Would you like to buy back in, Nova?" Delilah asked.

She shrugged in feigned nonchalance. "Why not? I'll take another two thousand, please."

As she counted out the bills, the sour taste of fear overwhelmed the residual smoky sweetness lingering in her throat from the scotch. Her new stack of chips was woefully small compared to everyone else's, and she sat out the next three hands in an effort to regain her composure. When the big blind returned to her, she tossed a black chip into the center, only to be dealt a two and a seven. As much as she hated surrendering her blind, defending it would be folly at this point.

But on the next hand, her seven and eight of hearts proved worth hanging on to when the flop revealed the six of hearts, the nine of hearts, and the jack of spades. If a five or a ten appeared on the turn or the river, she would have a straight. If either of those was a heart, she'd have a straight flush. And any heart gave her a flush, albeit a middling one. This hand had more potential than any she'd played all night, and the surge of hope made her head spin.

Claude bet out three hundred. Jerry and Kris called. Davenport folded and Damon eyed Nova's stack shrewdly as he re-raised to three thousand. Black spots appeared before Nova's vision as she realized that to stay in this hand, she would have to go all in again. Was Damon toying with her, or did he have the better cards? His features, as always, were inscrutable, but Nova suspected he was laughing at her behind his mask.

In a rush of anger, she flung her chips into the center, earning a warning from Delilah about "splashing" the pot. Mac called, but everyone else folded except the Ice Man. When the turn revealed a five of clubs, Nova clenched her jaw so hard she thought her molars might break. A straight! She had done it, and the river gave her one more chance to make it an even stronger hand.

Mentally shoving away the surge of relief, she focused on the numbers. Statistically, there was a very good chance she had the winning hand. It wasn't unbeatable, of course, but this was as good a place as any to make her Alamo. Damon bet out one thousand, pulling his bet down now that Nova was already all in. Delilah made a second stack of chips with his bet and Mac's call. The men would be playing for both piles.

There was no use in hiding her emotions now. Leaning forward eagerly, she watched as Mac called and Delilah flipped over the river card. The eight of diamonds. Nova cringed. She had been hoping for a two or a three—something that would have eliminated the possibility of a higher straight demolishing her hopes. Damon led out with five thousand, and Mac laughed as he mucked his cards. Either the pot had gotten too rich for his tastes or his draw never came.

"Worth a try," Damon said in his clipped, accented syllables. He looked at Nova and arched one brow toward the pale dome of his head. "Shall we?"

She held her breath and showed her hand. Damon cocked his head as he looked down at the cards, his mannerisms reminding her of a raptor inspecting its prey. Suddenly, Nova knew she had lost. The certainty was a hook of pain in her gut, pulling and twisting. Her breath let out in a rush as he turned over the ten of diamonds and seven of clubs. His straight was higher, and her money was gone.

"Damn." She sat back in the chair, disbelieving. Twelve thousand dollars. She had just lost twelve thousand dollars in a matter of hours. You've lost more, and in less time, her rational brain reminded her. That was true enough, but only at online tables, when her bankroll had been in the hundreds of thousands. Before she walked into this room, her bankroll had been a whopping thirty-five thousand. And she had just lost almost a third of it.

"Good hand." Damon nodded as if her interjection had been one of admiration instead of dismay. "Rough luck."

Rough luck? For one blinding moment, she wanted to hit him, the spike of rage so strong that it burned away her anxiety. Not trusting herself, she clutched the sides of her chair to keep still. It passed quickly, but she could feel a different kind of anger building like thunderheads in the back of her brain. How had she allowed this to happen? How?

Dazedly, she looked around the table. Delilah was shuffling. Mac was watching her with a speculative expression. The rest of them were very deliberately not looking in her direction, and she wondered just how much of her volatility had been apparent for all to see. Was that why she had played so poorly? Was she even worse at maintaining a poker face than she'd thought?

"Gentlemen," she began slowly, knowing she had to break the awkward silence. "I think that's a sign from the universe that it's my bedtime."

A few of them laughed. Davenport rose when she did. "You're welcome any time," he said.

Of course she was. People who laid down their money and lost it were always welcome at a poker game. "Thank you," she said, shaking his head. "Great to meet you all. Good night."

Nova turned her back on the table and let herself out into the atrium. Its gleaming floors and opulent artwork mocked her bag, empty except for the mints rattling softly in their tin. She hurried across the expanse, head throbbing in time with her heart.

How strange, she thought as she passed under the dome, that mere hours ago, she had thought herself a legitimate member of that little club. Her nascent plans seemed so hollow and silly now—the product of ignorance and naïveté. A fish in the desert—that's what she was. Flopping around uselessly, dying a slow and painful death, baking and suffocating by turns.

She didn't belong here; that much was clear. Not in this room, nor any other in this city. She didn't belong here at all.

CHAPTER SIX

Vesper stood with her palms resting on the back of Isabella's chair, squinting down at her checkered computer screen. Beyond the glass walls of her office, the lobby hummed with activity—like a beehive, she might have said, though calling gamblers industrious was a vexed proposition at best. Doubtless, Nova and the other professionals would disagree. They always had an inflated sense of their own work ethics.

Vesper's fingers tightened when she realized where her mind had wandered. Ever since their brief meeting over drinks, Nova had been sporadically ambushing Vesper's thoughts. Despite having avoided the poker room for days, Vesper found herself repeatedly engaging in mental debates featuring Nova as her opponent. It had been oddly enjoyable to spar with her at the bar—that much she was willing to admit. But that should have been the end of it. She had discharged her duty to Evan and never needed to see Nova again.

"Bad news." Isabella's voice snapped her back to the present. "All the guest rooms are full next weekend."

"No vacancies?" Vesper regarded her dubiously. "As in *no* vacancies?"

"None. Zip. Zilch. Zero."

"Not even a few rooms that James has squirreled away somewhere?"

Isabella swiveled in her chair and shot Vesper a pointed look. "Are you accusing me of lying?"

"No, of course not." Chagrined, Vesper held up her hands in a placating gesture. Their friendship notwithstanding, it would be sheer folly to get on Isabella's bad side. As a hospitality manager, Isabella was responsible for doling out the living accommodations—not to ordinary visitors, who could be served perfectly well by a computer, but to the hosts and their high rollers.

"I do have a few open Midgard suites, though. Why not just upgrade your client?"

Vesper shook her head. "This is his first time with us, and his credit line isn't anything out of the ordinary. If I give him a suite, he'll expect one forever. If I don't…"

"You can dazzle him later. I get it." Isabella scrolled back up through the listings on her screen. "But what else can you do—oh! Someone just checked out early from a guest room. Room 2074."

The number sounded familiar, but whatever association it had triggered was just beyond her grasp. "That's lucky," she said.

"What's the guy's name?"

Vesper couldn't remember the exact spelling, so she looked it up on her phone. This particular client was a friend of one of the Hamiltons' friends—far enough removed for her to be dialing it in. "The Third," she finished belatedly.

Isabella snorted. "Don't you love Thirds? They're all megalomaniacs."

Vesper glanced toward the door that connected Isabella's office to the area behind the front desk. It was closed, but she still felt uneasy. Complaining about clients was par for the course for most of Valhalla's employees, but Vesper had learned a long time ago just how costly an overheard conversation could be.

"I mean," Isabella was saying as her fingers flew over the keyboard, "it takes a special kind of inflated self-importance to give your kid the same name your father gave you. Don't you think?"

She had a point. Samuel was a Third, and not only selfish, but cruel besides. At least, he had been when he was seventeen. Fortunately, she was spared the necessity of answering when Isabella hit the Enter key and sat back in her chair. "There. Done. Thursday to Sunday, room 2074."

The memory surfaced: Nova looking down at her, smug and arrogant despite the growing margarita stain on her pants, brazenly inviting her upstairs. Why had she checked out? The WSOP was still weeks away.

And then, as though Vesper's thoughts had summoned her, Nova appeared at the far side of the World Tree Pool. As Vesper watched through the glass, she plodded slowly across the lobby, head bent as though fighting an invisible headwind. Her hair hung loose, partially covering her face, but that profile was unmistakable. A large duffel bag hung from one shoulder, bouncing against her thigh at every step as she slowly made her way toward the front door.

"Hello? Earth to Vesper?"

Avoiding Isabella's inquisitive gaze, Vesper squeezed her shoulder and turned toward the door. "Excuse me for a minute."

Before she could second-guess her own motives, she slipped out past the front desk and walked briskly along an intercept course. When they were a few feet apart, Nova finally glanced her way, only to lurch to a stop. Her eyes were shadowed and bloodshot, her cheeks pale beneath their tan.

"Vesper." The gritty quality to her voice made Vesper's stomach flutter. "Hi."

"Leaving us so soon?" It didn't feel like the right thing to say, but then again, nothing did. This had been a bad idea. Instinctual acts always were. She should have stayed with Isabella.

Nova hesitated, her gaze shifting first to the left and then to the right like an animal trapped in a cage. "I…" The muscles along her jaws contracted as she met Vesper's eyes again. "I lost a lot of money last night. Too much…too much to stay. Here."

Vesper's surprise must have been plain to see, because Nova flinched and looked down at her feet. "Go ahead and say it. 'I told you so.'"

"All I told you about was the game." Vesper felt suddenly guilty for throwing Nova into the deep end. But that was silly. She was a professional, and the deep end was where she belonged. "What happened?"

"If you really want a postmortem, can we at least sit down?" Nova nodded toward an open bench near the water.

"Of course." As she crossed one leg over the other, Vesper automatically scanned the lobby. None of her clients were visible, leaving her free to give Nova her full attention. For the moment. Dressed in a pair of gray cargo shorts and yet another tank top—did she own any other kind of shirt?—shoulders slumped in a gesture of defeat, Nova didn't look anything like a champion.

"I was playing well," she began, restlessly rubbing both palms across her knees, "or at least, I thought I was. But then I made a few bad calls and had a few unlucky breaks, and before I knew it, I was on tilt."

"So poker *is* a game of luck?" After rehashing their debate for days, Vesper couldn't resist the dig.

Nova glared at her. "No. I stand by what I said that night. It's mostly a game of skill. I just…I guess…I'm not, apparently. Skilled." The ball of her foot scuffed at the floor. "Not at sitting around for hours, trying to get in everyone else's heads while keeping them out of mine. Playing online is so different."

Against her better judgment, Vesper actually felt sympathetic. "But isn't reading body language just a different kind of pattern recognition?"

Nova looked thoughtful. "I suppose. But that won't matter if I'm giving away tells left and right. Besides, playing one game at a time is killing me."

"How else are you supposed to play?"

"Online, I played three at a time. Sometimes five."

"Five at a time?" Vesper could barely imagine it. "How did you keep track of that many hands at once?"

Nova shrugged. "It's just numbers."

"And numbers are easy for you." Vesper had met several poker players who were math geniuses, but all had been male. She couldn't help but wonder how Nova measured up to them.

"You sound skeptical." A hint of the bravado that had so aggravated her at their first meeting returned to Nova's manner as she arched one eyebrow. "Try me."

Try me. For one blinding second, Vesper imagined leaning through the space between them and pressing their lips together. What would Nova's mouth taste like? What would Nova's hair feel like, sliding through her fingers as she cupped the back of her head? Would Nova willingly surrender, or try to steal the upper hand?

The cascade of unwanted images made her lungs constrict almost painfully. Fortunately, she had much more practice maintaining a poker face than Nova apparently did. "Try you?"

"Mental math. Whatever you like." Nova squared her shoulders, clearly excited by the prospect of showing off.

"All right…how about 3789 times 8357?"

She stared at the water for several seconds with narrowed eyes before suddenly announcing, "Three one six six four six seven three."

Vesper blinked in surprise and reached into her suit pocket. "Hold on," she said as she typed the numbers into her phone. When its response was the same as Nova's, she admitted to being impressed. "I suppose you're an ace at long division, too?"

"Why don't you find out?"

Ignoring her visceral reaction to the smug little smile curving Nova's lips, Vesper quickly multiplied Nova's former room number by the last four digits of her Social Security number. "All right: 2878712 by 2074."

This time, Nova closed her eyes as though she were listening to a particularly evocative piece of music. Vesper silently counted the passing seconds, mostly in an effort to distract herself from the sensuality of Nova's expression. She had no sooner reached nine when Nova triumphantly announced: "One three eight eight."

"Right again." Vesper refrained from telling her the significance of that particular number, of course. "Division must be especially important for calculating odds."

"Yes." Nova cocked her head. "You know a fair amount about poker theory. Occupational hazard?"

"Once upon a time, I was a dealer." She watched Nova digest that information and saw the curiosity surface on her face. It was true—she was an open book. "What else can you do?" Vesper asked before Nova launched an inquisition into her past.

"Well…nth roots are fun."

"Nth roots." Vesper thought furiously, not wanting to have to ask for clarification. "That's the same principle as a square root, but with any number? Not just two?"

"That's right."

Nova seemed impressed, and Vesper tried in vain not to let that please her. The first number to pop into Vesper's head was her mother's birthday, September fourth. Shielding her phone with one hand, she multiplied ninety-four by itself five times.

"Take the fifth root of 7339040224," she challenged.

Nova scrunched up her nose as she concentrated. "Ninety-four."

Vesper felt herself smile. "That's amazing."

"Fifth roots aren't that hard, actually. There's a trick." Nova briefly rested two fingertips on her knee. "I could teach you, if you wanted."

Her touch was gone as soon as it had come, leaving Vesper's skin feeling hot and tight. The way her body was reacting was absolutely ludicrous. Nova certainly wasn't the first attractive lesbian she had ever met in her line of work, nor the first to show interest. Admit it, a small voice whispered deep inside her head. She's the first one you've truly been attracted to. Since Sabrina, at least. Which might explain why she kept flashing back to her adolescence in Nova's presence.

"You've certainly convinced me about being a numbers person," she said, deliberately sidestepping the invitation.

"Numbers are easy. People are hard." Nova looked away toward the pool, the enthusiasm visibly draining from her. Was she mentally reliving one of the games she had lost last night? "I should go."

"Where will you stay?"

"The Motel Six a few blocks over is looking pretty good," she said, standing.

Rationally, Vesper knew she should let her leave. She wasn't the first gambler who had been forced into an early checkout, and she wouldn't be the last. But when Nova reached for her duffel, she held up one hand. "Wait. I might be able to comp you a room."

"Comp me a…but why?" Nova released a self-deprecating laugh. "I'm not one of your high rollers. Not by a long shot."

That was true enough, and Vesper fumbled to articulate her reasons when even she didn't fully understand them. For one thing, there was Evan. Nova's move to a cheap motel wouldn't reflect well on her, despite her lack of blame. But if she were being honest with herself, that wasn't her only motivation. The version of Nova she had first met, full of braggadocio and disdain, had pushed all her buttons. This humbler, self-deprecating version aroused her sympathy. Not that she intended to confess as much.

"We have a few suites that aren't being used right now. You may as well stay in one." Hoping her nonchalance was convincing, she shrugged. "But if I or one of my colleagues books a client who needs the room, you'll have to leave."

"Of course." Nova blinked tiredly. "That's really generous. I owe you. Big time."

"You do." The power trip settled Vesper's nerves. Better she be owed than vice versa. "And someday, I'll collect. For now, let's get you a new key."

She led Nova past the barricade of the front desk and into Isabella's office. "Where on earth did you—oh." Isabella cut herself off and frowned when she caught sight of Nova.

"Isabella, this is Nova, a professional poker player. Nova, meet Isabella Martin, one of our hospitality managers."

As they shook hands, Isabella looked Nova up and down. When her expression turned shrewd, Vesper knew she was in for an interrogation later. Aside from Jeremy, Isabella was the only coworker to whom she had confided her sexual preference.

"I'm setting Nova up with one of those Midgard suites you mentioned," she said, once they had dispensed with the pleasantries.

To her credit, Isabella didn't bat an eye. "Great. Have you stayed with us before?"

"Yes."

"Last name?"

"Novarro."

As Isabella's fingers flew over the keyboard, Vesper became acutely aware of Nova standing just behind her—close enough to touch, although she wasn't. Novarro. So that's where her online handle came from. Vesper hadn't paid close attention to her full name when Evan had first been in touch.

"Annie Jump Novarro?"

Vesper turned her head just in time to catch Nova's flinch. "That's me," she said, a note of resignation flattening her voice.

Vesper swallowed her laugh, but some hint of surprise or amusement must have shown on her face, because Nova sighed and crossed her arms over her chest. She recognized the protective gesture and felt guilty.

"Annie Jump Cannon was one of those pioneering female scientists back around the turn of the century," Nova said glumly. "The twentieth one, that is. My parents are math and science nerds."

So her ability was hereditary, and her parents were high achievers. Vesper wondered what they thought of their daughter's career choice.

"You're all set." Isabella reached into the top drawer of her desk and quickly programmed a key. "Room 5069. That's in Dragon Tower."

"Sixty-nine?" Nova stepped forward to take the key, a mischievous grin curling her lips. "Lucky for me."

"The room doesn't come with that particular amenity," Isabella said dryly.

"I'll live." Nova winked at her. "It's a good omen. The six and nine of hearts is the only hand I'll always play."

Vesper couldn't believe what she was seeing. Efficient, businesslike Isabella, who habitually went toe-to-toe with the most macho of the male casino hosts as she managed Valhalla's prime real estate, was flirting with the female incarnation of Casanova. Which, now that she thought about it, might be another rationale for Nova's online handle.

"I'm sure that ends well for you," she was saying.

"You'd be surprised." Nova's manner had completely changed. Vesper half-expected to see her insecurity lying visible on the floor, like a discarded snakeskin.

"Oh, I doubt it," Isabella said breezily. "Vesper, will you be showing Ms. Novarro to her room, or shall I call for a bellhop?"

"I'll take care of it," she said, before realizing Isabella had been offering her an out. Not that she needed it. Isabella might be two years her senior, but Vesper had been taking care of herself for twice as long.

"Will do."

As they walked toward the bank of elevators, Vesper glanced over to see that Nova's smug expression was still firmly in place. Minutes ago, she'd been down on her luck and ready to check into a Motel Six, and now she was strutting along like a peacock? She needed to be taken down about five pegs.

"Proud of yourself, aren't you?"

Nova laughed. "Oh, that was just for fun. She's straight."

In fact, Isabella was engaged to her long-term boyfriend. But Nova didn't need to know that and feel all self-righteous about her powers of deduction. "Most everyone is until they're not."

"Is that how it was for you?"

The question sent a wave of adrenaline sluicing down her spine. How was she so certain? No one else had ever even guessed. Part of her wanted to argue. Part of her wanted to walk away as quickly as she could manage in heels. But either way, Nova would have her answer.

"I was young," was all she said. Her fingers trembled slightly as she called the elevator. Hopefully, Nova hadn't noticed.

"How young?"

The river of mental images rushed before her mind's eye like white water, catching her up in the current. The chocolate cake, baked by her mother and festooned with fifteen trick candles. The burnt smell of the popcorn machine in the hallway outside the Cheltons' home theater. The high-pitched chatter of her school friends after Samuel sauntered by in the leather jacket he wore to ride his dirt bike. The flutter in her chest when Sabrina claimed the seat next to hers. The warmth of Sabrina's fingertips reaching out in the darkness for the first time.

Their palms had been sweaty, but that hadn't mattered. Nothing had mattered except the way their fingers interlocked like puzzle pieces. Sabrina hadn't withdrawn her hand until the credits rolled. First to reach out, and first to let go—that was always how it had been with her, Vesper realized. Ever since the beginning.

The elevator doors opened. She stepped inside without answering, and a second later, Nova followed. Vesper watched the numbers light up on the panel, expecting at least a repeat of the question, if not an insistence that she answer. But she couldn't. She just couldn't. Her throat had closed up like an allergic reaction, blocking the words.

Nova's touch on the delicate skin of her wrist felt like the brush of a live wire. "Never mind," she said softly. "I'm sorry."

"It—it isn't something I discuss." The words sounded stilted to her own ears, but they were the only ones she could force out.

"I understand."

Nova spoke with the same certainty she'd had before, but this time, she had no right. No one could understand, especially when she didn't fully understand it herself.

CHAPTER SEVEN

A s the wall loomed ahead, Nova stroked harder. At the last instant, she threw herself into a neat tuck, twisting at the end so the balls of her feet touched the slick tiles. One heartbeat later, she pushed hard off with her legs, kicking as she broke the surface to slice through the water like a knife. Breathing was an afterthought—a swift, efficient turn of her head. The ache in her shoulders, the burn in her lungs—all of it was welcome. Only the taste of chlorine on her lips detracted from her pleasure. There was nothing like swimming in the open ocean, feeling the tug of the tide against her ribs and harmonizing her breaths with the rhythm of the waves.

Three laps later, she hit her goal of one hundred and forced herself to coast to a stop. If she could have carried on forever, she might have been tempted. But work was waiting, and soon even this pool would become crowded. At six a.m., she almost always had it to herself. By seven, a businessman or two might trickle in. Half an hour later, the families started showing up. She could never envy a child his or her fun in a pool, but sharing it with them when she wanted to swim laps was nearly impossible.

The sun had risen well above the horizon while she swam. Even this early, its heat was pounding down on her shoulders and transforming the brick patio into a skillet. She hurried indoors and made two quick turns to reach the door to her suite. Her suite. Shaking her head, she stepped inside. It was still difficult to believe how quickly her fortunes had reversed. One minute, she'd been dragging her bag and herself toward Valhalla's front door, and the next she found herself ensconced in the third best kind of room offered by the resort. All because of Vesper.

Who had, once again, been impossible to find since their previous meeting. Nova could recognize a theme when she saw one. She made Vesper uncomfortable.

But that couldn't be all of it, she reflected as she rinsed out her swimsuit in the first of the two marble sinks in her new bathroom—which was almost as large as her former bedroom had been. Bypassing the Jacuzzi tub, she jumped into the shower to rinse off. Vesper had been under no obligation to comp her this suite. So why had she offered the room? What did it mean?

When she had called home to chat with whoever was around, Felicia had suggested that perhaps Vesper was one of those rare, truly generous people who enjoyed helping others. Nova had heard Emily's laughter in the background. Together, they had explained to their naïve roommate that casino hosts cared about one thing: the bottom line. Nova didn't fit into that at all. For the next two weeks, her job was the exact opposite of the high roller mentality: to make as much money as possible while risking as little as she could.

Later, when Felicia had taken her newfound cynicism off to run errands at the grocery store, Em had wondered aloud whether Vesper might have comped the room as a *quid pro quo*. But what could she possibly want? In the world of live poker, Nova's fame didn't extend much further than her tournament record and her bank account. The former was nonexistent, and the latter wasn't much better off.

"Maybe you're an investment," Em had suggested. "Or maybe she wants *you*. Is she attractive?"

"Sure," Nova said, hoping her nonchalance was convincing. Instead, she had been reminded of just how bad she was at bluffing.

"Sure?" Em laughed. "You have a thing for her, don't you?"

"I don't have 'a thing.' And yes, she's attractive. But completely unavailable."

That was the honest truth, but Em hadn't believed it. Between bouts of teasing laughter and innuendos, she managed to wheedle enough details out of Nova to pronounce that Vesper was deeply closeted and had "issues." That might be true, but hearing Emily judge her so blithely had annoyed Nova so much that she hadn't called the house since. She could still remember the pained, fearful expression in Vesper's eyes when she had asked about her self-discovery. If she was in the closet, there seemed to be a good reason for it.

Forcing her thoughts away from Vesper, she left the shower and ran the single-serving coffeemaker while she threw on a green Maverick's Surf Shop T-shirt and jeans. Then, she sat at one end of her glass dining table—her own *dining* table!—and picked up where she had left off reading Damon's book about the ins and outs of high-stakes poker, in which he analyzed the hands he had played during his second WSOP victory. The book provided a deep level of insight into his mentality and strategies, one that Nova would have been uncomfortable to betray, if she had been that self-aware. But Damon welcomed the challenge. In his introduction, he invited people to read up on his techniques, claiming that if he couldn't adapt to their knowledge, he wasn't a true champion.

Nova wished she had that kind of nerve. Instead, she had dedicated an hour each morning to studying his strategies over a breakfast of coffee, fruit, and scrambled eggs. The latter were cooked each morning in the hotel and delivered by room service. No charge.

It hadn't taken her long to realize that the math Damon used was similar to her own techniques. Calculating pot odds and probabilities was second nature to her. Reading other people, on the other hand, was not. Math could reveal whether they were a loose or tight player; whether they enjoyed taking risks or played conservatively; whether they adjusted their strategy for table position. But the only way to learn their physical tells was to be in the same room with them, which was why once her study hour was up, she forced herself out of her room and into a poker hall.

Since moving into the suite, she had avoided Valhalla's poker room. Even after less than a week, she knew the regulars there already, and in order to succeed at the WSOP, she needed experience against a wide variety of players. She'd spent that first afternoon at the Hilton and the next day at the Bellagio. Yesterday, she had run into Mac at Caesars. Her table was full, so he'd sat at another, but they'd chatted for a few minutes between hands. Their conversation had been perfectly pleasant, but Nova had felt self-conscious the entire time. No doubt, he and Kris and Damon had shared a good laugh about her spectacular flameout in the cash game.

As much as she tried to tell herself she didn't have anything to prove to him—or to anyone—she couldn't help wanting to be taken seriously by the professional live players. Just knowing he was in the room had rattled her, and her play had dropped in quality for a while before she finally got her head back in the game. That was good practice too, of course—maintaining her focus despite strong emotions.

The hardest part was having to sit still for eight consecutive hours with only a short break for lunch—a routine she forced herself to follow to build endurance for the tournament. When playing at home, Nova had fidgeted and paced her way through hours spent in front of her computer. Even while relaxing, she had trouble sitting still for long, so much so that Monique had often called her "the perpetual motion machine." But live poker demanded that she keep her ass in her chair for hours on end and that she move as little as possible, lest she betray anything to her opponents. It was torture.

Swimming in the morning curbed some of her restlessness, but by the time her eight hours were up, she was always going out of her mind. A hard ride on the stationary bike in the VIP gym followed by another few laps in the pool usually settled her down again, though, and she had taken to spending her nights watching video footage of past World Series. That was fun as well as work, but she wished she had someone to sit next to on the couch—someone who would analyze and debate strategy with her. Someone like Vesper.

Nova rolled her eyes at her reflection in the floor-to-ceiling mirror and headed for the door. She had already decided to stay put at Valhalla today. Playing against some of the regulars might help shed some light on whether she had actually learned anything over the past week. She might also be able to play more aggressively against people whose styles she knew, and that was important. Even playing eight hours a day, she had only managed to recoup a third of her losses so far. The tourist tables were relatively low stakes, which suited her budget but not her demand. If she was going to have enough to buy in to a few other World Series events, she needed to pick up the pace.

The poker hall was mostly empty when she arrived, with only one table up and running. The dealer greeted her as she sat, and while the players finished their previous hand, she took stock of each of them in turn, alert to anything in their mannerisms that might clue her in to what they were holding. Only one was familiar to her—Bill, a middle-aged, balding man who tended to play quite conservatively from what she had seen.

The rest of the table, she soon learned, was comprised of novices.

A husband and wife from Maine asked the dealer every procedural question under the sun, and an elderly woman wearing a white cardigan over a hideous flower print shirt couldn't remember the ranking order of hands to save her life. As the morning wore on, Nova grew increasingly impatient with the snail-like pace of the game. And when the woman asked for the third time in an hour whether three of a kind outranked a flush, she thought she might scream.

"Is this seat taken?" a baritone voice asked from her left.

"No, not at all." She turned to size up the new player. Tall and broad-shouldered, with hair the color of the pristine sand at Año Nuevo, he was one of those muscular, all-American boys everyone found attractive. Vesper was standing behind him, her bone white sheath dress setting off the red in her hair. A sand dollar pendant hung from a silver chain to nestle in the hollow of her throat. Blindsided by the urge to trace her delicate collarbone with one finger, Nova cleared her throat and almost sat on her hands. What was she doing here? What was she doing here with *him*? Was he her boyfriend? Had she been wrong? But no, Vesper had confessed…

"Nova!" Vesper's smile seemed forced, and her eyes were wide in surprise. "I didn't recognize you from behind."

"It's good to see you," she said, hoping Vesper could hear the authenticity behind her politeness. She folded her cards, even though she'd been dealt a jack of hearts and ace of diamonds, and stood to shake the boy's hand. "I'm Nova. In case that wasn't clear."

He laughed, his grip warm and firm. "TJ. Nice to meet you."

"Nova is an online poker champion." Vesper was clearly hurrying to make up for her lack of introduction. "She's making the transition to live poker and plans to enter the World Series this month. TJ is… well, he's my oldest client." The fond smile she gave him was more sisterly than amorous, Nova was relieved to see. "And it's his twenty-first birthday."

"Hey, congrats!" Nova clapped him on the shoulder. "Bet you're beyond ready to sit in that chair."

"You have no idea."

As he sat, Nova looked to Vesper. "I can move down if you'd like to sit, too."

"Sadly, I can't stay long."

Nova frowned, wondering if she was putting them off, but her disappointment seemed genuine enough. Then again, Vesper had probably mastered the art of seeming sincere a long time ago. Casino hosts were salesmen, and salesmen needed to make you feel like the only person in the room. Especially when you weren't.

"You work too hard," TJ said as he arranged his chips—all five thousand dollars of them, Nova realized at a glance. The first time she'd ever played online poker, she had all of two hundred dollars in her account. Did this kid appreciate his silver spoon or take it for granted?

When the hand ended, TJ congratulated the winner and introduced himself to the other players. "Did I hear that young lady say it's your birthday?" asked the elderly woman.

"She did, ma'am." That wide, genuine smile was back.

"Happy birthday, son," said the man across the table, his wife echoing him.

"But don't go easy on me," TJ said above the rustle of cards. "I'm here to play some real poker."

That earned him a laugh from several players. What a charmer. Nova smiled, when what she really wanted to do was lean over and whisper to him that he wouldn't find anything of the sort at this table. By then the dealer was passing out cards, though, so she bent her head and tried to concentrate. When a peek at her hand revealed the ace and queen of clubs, she took a half-second to school her expression before looking around the rest of the table. The elderly woman looked confused. The wife seemed dismayed, and her husband was peering down intently at his cards. He did that whenever he had a decent hand, as though he was afraid to make eye contact and give it away. Ironic.

Bill looked the same as he always did, so Nova glanced at TJ. He seemed eager, but he had also just been dealt his first hand of poker in a casino. He probably would have been excited to see an unsuited three and eight. The husband bet out fifteen dollars. The wife folded. The elderly lady took forever before calling. Bill folded. Nova called, figuring the only person she had to worry about was the husband, and maybe TJ. He also called. Relatively speaking, the pot was pretty rich, and they hadn't even seen any community cards, yet.

When the dealer flopped a rainbow—two of diamonds, eight of spades, and queen of hearts—the husband gritted his teeth. Nova guessed that like her, he'd been dealt two face cards of the same suit, and had been hoping for something closer to a flush. His clenched jaw probably meant he hadn't flopped a pair, either. Unless TJ had somehow managed to pair both his cards, her position was looking good. A glance at the kid revealed him deep in thought, which might mean anything. He was an unknown quantity, and he'd walked in with double her number of chips. She had to be cautious.

The husband checked, the elderly woman inexplicably folded, and Nova slid two green twenty-five-dollar chips into the middle. TJ called. Not raising when he had position on her was an ambiguous move. Did he want to see the next card as cheaply as possible, or was he trying to lull them into a trap? If it was the latter, his technique was working beautifully, because the husband stayed in.

He appeared to regret that choice a moment later, when the turn card appeared as the three of clubs. Scowling, he checked with a sharp rap on the lacquered wooden edge. A three didn't help Nova either, but with a pair of queens and an ace for her kicker, she was feeling solid. The only question now was whether it would be better to bet aggressively. The husband looked like he was on the verge of bowing out, but he might hang around for a small raise.

Nova pushed forward one hundred in chips. That represented almost half the pot and would probably drive out the spooked husband. She wanted to keep building the pot but at this point, every card to hit the table had a chance of beating her. She needed to weed out the weaker hands. As she waited for TJ to act, the space between her shoulder blades prickled from the knowledge that Vesper was watching. Winning this pot would at least show her that she wasn't a complete hack.

TJ called, and after a long pause, so did the husband. They all stared expectantly at the table as the dealer flipped over the river card to reveal the beautiful ace of hearts. Two pair, aces over queens. Nova struggled to maintain a neutral expression. Unless she had completely misread TJ, this pot belonged to her.

But when the husband led out with a two hundred-dollar bet, a spike of doubt lanced through her chest. Had she misjudged him, too? Had he been dealt pocket rockets and just made three of a kind? Yes, he had led out strong, but pocket aces would have merited strong betting throughout the rounds given the lack of flush and straight possibilities. Was she willing to bet two hundred dollars on that supposition?

Yes, yes, she was. The pot odds were in her favor. Two hundred dollars to win over a thousand dollars, assuming TJ stayed in. Nova carefully counted out eight green chips and tossed them into the center of the table. TJ called as well, and why not? It was his birthday. He had five thousand dollars sitting in front of him. If he'd stuck around this long, he probably had at least a pair.

"Let's see them," the dealer said, mustering a little more enthusiasm than usual, perhaps for TJ's benefit.

The husband turned over an ace and king, giving him a pair. Pleased that she had read him correctly, Nova turned to TJ as she showed her hand. For a moment, his face was blank, before he grinned ruefully and shook his head.

"Thought that might happen," he said before flipping over the fourth ace and an eight of diamonds. "Damn."

"Rough one," the husband agreed.

"Next time, TJ." Vesper's voice floated over her shoulder.

As Nova scooped up her chips, she wondered whether Vesper was happy for her. She probably hoped TJ would do well in his first gambling venture, especially since he was playing poker and not craps or roulette. The rake—the cut taken by the house from every poker pot—was somewhere in the neighborhood of five percent. That wasn't nearly as much of a moneymaker as a single high roller who dropped thousands on each toss of the dice or spin of the wheel.

As the dealer passed out new cards, Nova glanced over her shoulder. She had expected to find Vesper watching TJ or perhaps checking her phone. But Vesper was looking right at her with a contemplative expression that disappeared beneath a mask of aloofness as soon as their eyes met. Nova turned back to the table, automatically checking her cards even as her mind raced. Could Vesper actually be interested in her, somehow? Was her indifference actually a mask, or was that just wishful thinking? And should she stay in this hand having been dealt a two of clubs and a nine of spades?

At least one of those questions had an easy answer. Unsuited two and nine were not worth playing. When TJ bet ten into the pot, she was one of the three players to fold. The flop revealed the ace of diamonds, and the jack and eight of spades. Dangerous. The husband bet twenty, and Nova watched TJ closely as everyone before him called. He didn't hesitate before doing the same. She wondered whether he had a strong hand, or whether he was just feeling cavalier about spending his money.

At the turn card, the elderly woman gasped quietly. The queen of spades not only made a flush possible, but also a straight flush—or so they would all believe. Nova knew better, of course, since the nine of spades had been hers. The husband bet fifty, Bill folded, and again, TJ called immediately. Showdown time.

Since neither of them had the missing nine, Nova guessed that at least one had a flush. She watched TJ closely as the dealer flipped the river card to reveal the eight of hearts. His expression never changed, but the fingers of his right hand curled inward, as though he wanted to make a fist. But was he fist pumping in triumph, or in frustration?

The husband bet out another fifty, but this time, TJ didn't just go along for the ride. He skimmed a black chip off the top of his stack and sent it spinning into the middle of the table. One hundred dollars. Surely, the man would call his re-raise, having already invested so much money in the pot.

He narrowed his eyes at TJ and flipped another fifty-dollar chip across his knuckles. "All right, son," he said finally. "Let's see whether you've got beginner's luck."

"I think he has that straight flush!" the elderly woman said, pushing her reading glasses into her white hair.

Nova couldn't keep from shaking her head. "Full house is my guess. Eights over something—maybe jacks."

TJ's head turned so quickly she thought he might have whiplash. He regarded her intently as he flipped over his cards to reveal the jack of hearts and the eight of diamonds. "How did you know?"

"Some math, some deduction, and a little bit of luck. Congratulations, by the way." She gestured to the husband. "He has a flush. The pot's yours."

"Hey, now, missy." The husband's face was turning red. "Are you counting cards?"

"Counting cards?" She laughed. "This is poker, not blackjack. The deck is reshuffled after every hand."

"So?"

Was this guy a moron, or just dense? "So it's not possible to count cards in poker."

"Then how did you know what I have in my hand?" A vein was throbbing in his neck.

"I didn't know. I guessed you made a flush on the turn, given that you increased your bet at that point. And when the eight paired on the board, I figured TJ must have a full house or else he wouldn't stay in."

"Unless I was playing stupidly," TJ added.

"Well, sure." She shot him a grin. "There's no accounting for stupidity."

"I've had enough of this," the man grumbled to his wife. He stood and collected his chips. "Let's play the slots for a while."

"Works for me," the dealer said under her breath as they walked away.

Nova laughed. "You're welcome." The casino would take much more of his money at the machines. In her next breath, she caught Vesper's scent—a breath of jasmine tinged with strawberries. Her body must have categorized it unconsciously; until now, she hadn't even realized Vesper *had* a scent. It was subtle but present, and it made her stomach flip-flop.

She turned to the sight of Vesper with one hand on TJ's chair, head bent as she spoke softly to him. After a moment, she pulled back. "So, I'll see you tonight."

"See you," he said distractedly as he organized his winnings. She wondered how he could be so dismissive in her presence. Was he gay? Or did he somehow know that *she* was?

And then her thoughts disappeared at the warm pressure of Vesper's hand squeezing her shoulder far too briefly. "Try not to bait the amateurs," she murmured, but her lips were curling just enough that Nova knew it was a joke. "Too much."

She was gone before Nova could muster a reply. Instead, she sat blinking down at her cards, wondering how the whisper of a scent and the faintest touch of a hand had set her head spinning. Automatically, she picked up her cards, but as she put them back down she had no idea what they were.

"Nova?" TJ nudged her. "You calling?"

"Hmm?" Nova suddenly realized that everyone was looking at her, and that there was already sixty dollars in the pot. "Oh. No. I fold. Sorry."

She had completely spaced out. Poor manners…and poor strategy, too. She had to be able to maintain her concentration, even in the presence of a beautiful woman. If some green kid like TJ could stay focused better than she could, she'd be in serious trouble at the tournament.

A few seconds later, he mucked his cards. As the others played out the hand, he leaned toward her. "Can you teach me to do what you do?"

What you do. There wasn't anything all that special about her methods, but maybe he'd never run into a professional poker player before. "You mean figuring out someone's hand? It's an inexact science, you know."

"Sure, but it's still a science. I want to learn how to think that way about poker."

"Okay." Nova had written a few columns about strategy for Royal Flush's player blog, but she had never sat down one-on-one and coached another person. Hopefully, she'd be a decent teacher. The last thing she wanted was TJ getting frustrated and taking his complaints to Vesper. "Happy to help."

"Great." He leaned a little closer. "And you should come to my birthday party tonight."

Who invited someone to their birthday party five minutes after meeting them? "I'd love to, but—"

His kilowatt smile cut her off. "Vesper will be there. She organized it."

For the second time in as many minutes, words failed her. Was TJ playing matchmaker? If so, why? And didn't those kinds of schemes always end up in disaster?

"I'll put you on the guest list. Room 6035. Come by any time after ten."

"Um…thanks."

By then, the dealer was shuffling again, and TJ immediately bent over his new cards. Nova could only follow his example. The irony would have made her smile, if she hadn't been working so hard on her poker face.

CHAPTER EIGHT

Vesper was watching the caterer arrange sushi roll after sushi roll on the dining table when her phone rang. The number was unfamiliar, but she answered it quickly. Her cell was unlisted, and the only people who called it were coworkers, clients, or prospective clients. This must be one of the latter.

"This is Vesper Blake."

"Hello, Ms. Blake. This is Priscilla Beauregard."

Every nerve in Vesper's body went on high alert, and she quickly ducked into the closest unoccupied room, which just so happened to be the office. Its glass desk sat before a window with a view of the Strip, and its mini-fridge was stocked with the complimentary bottle of Johnny Walker Gold she had ordered herself. Right now, she wanted a shot to settle her stomach.

"Mrs. Beauregard. Please allow me to express my condolences."

She sniffed, whether because of tears or in dismissal, Vesper couldn't tell. "I received your gifts."

"It's the very least I could do on behalf of Valhalla. Your husband was respected and admired by our staff."

"His *money* was respected and admired." Her voice cut the air like a dorsal fin.

Vesper gripped her phone more tightly. One thing was clear: the Killer Whale's widow didn't like bullshit. And if Vesper didn't adapt to that quickly, she'd probably be hearing a dial tone sooner rather than later.

"That, too."

Mrs. Beauregard's laughter sounded like the bark of a seal, but higher pitched. Vesper wanted to join in but bit down on her lower lip and forced down her hysteria. It was time to step up and play ball.

"Did you enjoy the gift, I hope? I know you received many."

"Why do you think we're having this conversation? You did your homework, and I can tell."

Vesper wanted to be pleased with herself, but she didn't dare. "What else can I get for you, ma'am?"

An exasperated sigh was her response. "Nothing, if you ever call me ma'am again."

"I understand, Priscilla. And please, call me Vesper."

"Good. Now. For starters, you can get me one of those fancy Celestial Palaces next weekend, and a premium level spa treatment for three more. I'll be bringing my best friends."

"Excellent." Vesper scrabbled in her purse for the small notebook and pen she always kept ready to hand. "And how much of a credit line would you like?"

"How much did my husband have?"

"Usually three million over the course of a weekend."

"With you. Or rather, that sycophant, James. Davis gambled at a few other places that gave him just as much."

Vesper knew he'd gone to other casinos from time to time, but had they really extended him that kind of credit? They might have, she supposed, especially if they were trying to woo him away from staying at Valhalla.

"Double his number, Vesper, and I'll never even put so much as a pinky toe through any other door."

Vesper could practically feel the blood draining from her face. A six-million-dollar credit line when Priscilla had never so much as placed a bet? Her bosses were not going to like that. At all. "Are you sure you plan to gamble that much, ma—Priscilla?"

"It's not about how much I gamble, Vesper. Surely you must know that." Her voice could have withered a rose in full bloom. "It's about who has the biggest dick."

The sudden vulgarity made her press down so hard with the pen that she punched a hole in the page. "And that's what you want," she said slowly.

"That's what you're going to get for me."

Vesper only narrowly stopped herself from saying she would try. That wasn't what Priscilla wanted to hear. "May I call you at this number with confirmation of the details?"

Priscilla gave her a fax number instead and then hung up before she had finished saying good-bye. Vesper collapsed into one of the leather chairs in front of the desk and quickly jotted down a few more notes. When she was finished, she stretched her legs out in front of her and rested her head on the back of the chair. The Killer Whale's wife was coming to Vegas with friends and she'd chosen Vesper to be her host.

James was going to go ballistic.

The thought made her smile until she realized she had reservations to book and a massive credit line to secure. After checking in with the caterer, Vesper spent the next twenty minutes on the phone. She was arguing with the casino manager about the credit line when one of the staff cracked the door and mouthed, *They're here.*

"Steve, I have to go. The Hamiltons need me. Just remember: this is the Killer Whale's widow, and right now, the only place she wants to spend her money is here." Vesper didn't know that for a fact, of course, but she had a feeling that Priscilla hadn't been lying about her intentions. "Pour yourself a drink, do some mental math, and find it in your heart to authorize six million."

Before he could answer, she hung up. As she smoothed the front of her dress, she caught her reflection in the darkening windows. Her hands were still trembling, and no wonder—she had never spoken to Steve that way before. But she had also never hosted for someone with as much money or clout as Priscilla Beauregard. If she was going to rise to the next level of her career, she was going to have to leave her comfort zone from time to time—to move beyond assertiveness to downright aggression.

When Vesper took a deep breath and clenched her hands into fists, they stopped trembling. It was time to focus. This was the homestretch of TJ's party. The guests—his parents, their closest family friends, and a dozen peers from college—had enjoyed dinner at Barri followed by Cirque du Soleil. Now they had returned to the suite for sushi, sake, cocktails, and a black sesame crème brûlée cake. She had to admit it—TJ was turning into a man of discerning tastes. Before his request, she hadn't even realized it was possible to *make* a crème brûlée cake.

As she left the office and turned toward the foyer, she met Theodore Senior and Marisa in the corridor. He was loosening his tie with one hand, while the other remained around Marisa's waist. Vesper's smile was genuine. Watching them together almost made her want to believe in true romance.

"Ah, Vesper," Theodore said. "There you are. The show was great."

"I'm glad you enjoyed it."

"The kids liked it too," Marisa chimed in. "They'll be up soon. One of them convinced Teddy to play a few dollars at a slot machine in the lobby."

"If he hits a jackpot, his head won't fit through the door." TJ's first day of casino gambling had been a success for him. He had made several hundred dollars at the poker table before getting lucky at craps to the tune of just over a thousand. His father, on the other hand, had lost almost ten thousand playing blackjack. An ideal trade-off where Vesper was concerned.

"Is there anything else I can get for you tonight?" she asked.

Theodore glanced at his wife before answering. "Not at all. But I did want to let you know that I've invited my colleague, Bizmark, to join the festivities when he arrives later on."

Vesper reached for her phone. "Bizmark Deloreo, correct? His flight is slated to arrive in just under an hour. I'll let Jeremy know that he should encourage him to come up."

"Perfect, thanks. And please tell Jeremy that he's welcome as well."

"It's been a lovely day for Teddy," Marisa added, smiling. "Thank you for taking such excellent care of us."

Vesper tamped down the part of herself that warmed to the praise. She was more comfortable thinking about what to do next, and that involved finding the birthday boy. After wishing them good night, she kept moving. By the time the door opened, she was waiting expectantly in the foyer.

"V!" His face lit up when he saw her, and she found herself immediately enveloped in a rum-scented hug. As he pulled back, she caught sight of his wide smile and slightly glazed eyes. By the look of it, Theodore Hamilton Jr. was happily tipsy. "You shoulda been at the show!"

"I'm glad it was fun. Get anything off the slots?"

"Nah. Maybe tomorrow." His friends filtered past, but he made no move to join them. "Oh, meant to tell you at dinner. I invited that poker player. Nova. She said she'd give me pointers." He bent his head so that his mouth was close to her ear. "And she's cute."

Vesper froze. Was she going to have to break the news that for the second time in his life, he'd developed a crush on a lesbian? The first time had been hard enough. She didn't want to have to do it again, especially not on his birthday. Steeling herself, she looked up…only to find him trying to waggle his eyebrows. It wasn't really working, but she got the point. He wasn't the one attracted to Nova. He thought *she* was, and he was trying to set them up.

All she could do was laugh. "Are you kidding me?"

"C'mon, Vesper," he wheedled. "Don't you ever get lonely?"

The question felt like a blow to the chest, and for one agonizing moment, she couldn't take a breath. He was more drunk than she'd thought. Sober, he would never have said something so callous.

He frowned then, perhaps realizing his error, but before he could say anything, one of his female friends swept in to take his arm. Amelia had brown hair and brown eyes, and her face was too angular to be beautiful, but no one was better at making TJ laugh. On more than one occasion, Vesper had caught her watching him longingly. "Come on, Ham," she said, using the nickname preferred by his college friends. "Ethan's going to eat all the spicy tuna rolls if you don't hurry."

He looped his arm through hers. "We can't have that! You coming, V?"

"I'll be right behind you." She followed them slowly, his words echoing in her ears. *Don't you ever get lonely?* Of course she did. Drowning herself in work wasn't a good solution, but it was certainly better than the alternatives. Falling in love wasn't safe, and safety was still her first priority.

She stood near the door and watched as TJ piled sushi on his plate and accepted a glass of sake from Amelia. After stepping outside briefly to call Jeremy, she touched base with the caterer and then with the butler. Feeling restless, she walked through the public areas of the suite and paused to double-check on the sitting room. It had been arranged to accommodate a poker game, which TJ would undoubtedly crave at some point.

Poker made her think of Nova, but when she caught herself smoothing the lapels of her suit jacket, she stalked back toward the party. Yes, she found Nova attractive. No, she did not want a relationship. It was that simple.

On returning to the dining room, she quietly joined in when Ethan led the group in a raucous, atonal rendition of the "Happy Birthday" song, and she clapped along with the others when TJ cut his cake. With every passing second, her anticipation grew, despite her best attempts to distract herself with idle chatter. What was Nova playing at? Was she trying to be fashionably late?

When Jeremy finally texted from the airport that he was bringing a rather intoxicated Mr. Deloreo back to the hotel, she decided to meet them in the lobby, if only to give herself a break from the waiting.

"You're being ridiculous," she whispered at her reflection in the gleaming metal walls of the elevator.

She sat on one of the benches and stared at the World Tree Pool, watching ripples move across its surface as new water fell rhythmically from the antlers of the stone stag. She realized this was the same bench where she and Nova had sat and talked only days ago. Had she chosen it tonight by coincidence or subconsciously? And why was everything suddenly reminding her of Nova?

Don't you ever get lonely?

With a shake of her head, Vesper forced her thoughts out of their rut and instead began to mentally review the dossier she had compiled on her latest client. Bizmark "Biz" Deloreo was the newest member of the Sphinx's board of alumni trustees. He was also thirty-six years old, a political king-maker in New York City with an unrivalled war chest of money and connections, and unmarried. His preferences ran to Davidoff cigars, single malt scotch, rib eye cooked black and blue, and the Yankees. Could he be more stereotypical? Her mouth twitched at the thought. She was about to find out.

Whether he was playing a caricature of himself or not, her job was to entice him to gamble as much money as possible over the course of the coming week. With some digging, she had discovered that he had made past trips to Vegas, but until now, he had always stayed at the Luxor. Theodore Senior had opened the door for her by arranging the board meeting at the Valhalla, but it was up to her to reel Mr. Deloreo in.

The first step was to make him feel special. She'd successfully outmaneuvered several other hosts at last week's meeting and had managed to get him an upgrade from an Asgard suite to a Celestial Palace. A bottle of Macallan 18 and a box of Davidoff Grand Cru was waiting on his dining table. She had baited the trap. Now all she had to do was keep him happy while the house milked him for all he was worth.

Squaring her shoulders, Vesper angled her body toward the door. The mental exercise had left her feeling more focused and balanced than she'd felt all night. When Mr. Deloreo first saw her, he would find her attentive, not distracted.

When, seconds later, the doors slid open, she recognized Jeremy and rose from the bench. He was moving slowly, rolling a large suitcase behind him, and keeping time with the unsteady gait of the man walking beside him.

"Vesper!" Jeremy's hail sounded oddly relieved. He shot her an intense look that seemed like some sort of warning. "This is Mr. Deloreo."

"Well, hello, hotness." The stocky man who stepped forward had short, dark hair, liberally coated with product to stick up like porcupine quills. His face and neck were mottled, and his breath, as he approached, stank of whiskey. "You're the lucky lady looking for me. I'm Biz."

Before she could move or protest, he leaned in and kissed her full on the mouth, one arm snaking around her waist in a clumsy attempt to grope her butt. Shocked, she took a quick step backward, barely restraining herself from shoving him in the process. Jeremy dropped the suitcase and jumped forward to steady her. A quick glance at his face revealed his anger.

Her palm tingled with the desire to slap Biz's flushed face, but she didn't dare. Still reeling, she forced herself to assess the situation. He was visibly drunk, but he was still a member of the board and an associate of Theodore Senior's. She had to be as respectful as she could manage. But if he tried to grope her again, all bets were off.

"Mr. Deloreo?" Vesper stuck out one hand—more to keep him away than out of a desire to touch him again—and smoothed the front of her dress with the other. "I'm your host, Vesper Blake. I've been coordinating with your secretary."

"Who will be fired for neglecting to tell me how fucking hot you are."

"We only spoke on the phone." Vesper felt a wash of sympathy for the poor woman who handled Biz's daily affairs. "Shall we get you checked in?"

He leered at her. "And then you'll be my date at that party for Hamilton's kid."

"I'll be happy to show you to Mr. Hamilton's suite," Vesper said, hoping the refusal in her subtext would reach his liquor-addled brain.

"After you, sir." Jeremy's voice was smooth, but as he reached past Vesper, he whispered, "I'm coming up with you."

She nodded in acknowledgment, hoping he could sense her appreciation. Thankfully, the available clerk at the front desk was a middle-aged man named Dale, and Biz behaved himself through the check-in process.

"Would you like to stop by your suite first, Mr. Deloreo?" Vesper asked once he had surrendered his bag to the bellhop.

"Only if you'll come in with me."

She stared up at him, wishing she were taller and waiting for him to realize that she was deliberately ignoring his come-ons. After a long pause, his mouth twisted into a grin. "Fine, sweetheart, let's party first. Give you a chance to warm up to me."

As they walked—and Biz stumbled—toward the elevator, Vesper tried to engage him in small talk by asking if this was his first trip to Las Vegas. Unfortunately, he proceeded to regale them with stories in lurid detail from his best friend's bachelor party earlier in the year. Fortunately, the VIP elevator was an express, and the ride was short.

"Here we are," she said, cutting him off in the middle of a story about two strippers. Jeremy matched her pace as she walked briskly down the hall, forcing Biz to hustle behind them.

"Slow down," he complained. "Where's the fire?"

As they approached the door, the party became audible. Laughter and shouts mingled with the heavy beat of the electronic music TJ enjoyed, but the noise seemed well contained. When she rang the buzzer, Biz moved in close behind her. *Trapped.* The old panic welled up from her gut at the sensation of his breath puffing against her ear, and every muscle in her body turned to steel. If he touched her now, she wouldn't be able to hold back a scream.

"What's the kid's name again?"

"TJ." She forced out the letters between clenched teeth, fighting instincts that clamored for her to bring all her weight down on the instep of his closest foot.

When the door opened, she bolted inside, a racehorse out of the starting gate. "Ms. Blake?" the butler asked in alarm.

"Sorry, Tom," she managed to say, hoping he attributed her breathlessness to the sudden movement. "I misstepped." Pulling herself together, she glanced back toward the door. Jeremy was looking between her and Biz and frowning. "Is Mr. Hamilton still in the dining room?"

"I believe he's now in the sitting room."

"Thank you. This way, gentlemen." As she led them deeper into the suite, the music and voices grew louder, and her pulse began to slow. Surely, Biz would be on his best behavior in the Hamiltons' presence. She was safe, now.

She turned the corner, gaining line of sight into the sitting room. Theodore Senior was opening a new bottle of sake. Amelia, Ethan, and several more of TJ's male friends were seated at the table...and at its head, Nova was shuffling a deck of cards.

Nova. Just when Vesper had managed to forget all about her, there she was. Her dark purple shirt was open down to the second button, revealing a tan expanse of skin, and Vesper's heart lurched into another gallop. As though she could hear it, Nova looked up. The cards fluttered between her fingers as their eyes met. For once, her smile was open and relaxed, without any hint of predatory interest.

"Hey, look who's back," she said to TJ.

"V!" Even that syllable sounded more intoxicated than it had an hour ago. Maybe she should start watering down his sake. Then again, if his father was pouring, who was she to interfere? "Nova's the designated dealer. She's gonna show us all her tricks!"

"Great. But will you remember them tomorrow?"

"Oooh, burn," said Ethan over Amelia's laughter.

"'Course I will!" TJ protested. "And, hey, Jeremy! What's up, man?"

Belatedly, Vesper remembered why she was there—to introduce

Biz. Once Jeremy had finished conveying his birthday wishes, she gestured toward him. "And this is Mr. Deloreo, who works with your father."

"Indeed he does." Theodore Senior came around the table with his hand extended. "Glad you could make it. How are you, Biz?"

"Very well, sir, very well," Biz said heartily. "Thank you for inviting me to celebrate your son's birthday. Congrats, TJ."

Vesper couldn't believe it. Biz was apparently one of those drunks who could—up to a point, anyway—turn on a fair impression of sobriety whenever he wished. As long as he also pretended not to be a letch, the rest of the night would go smoothly. Smothering a sigh of relief, she moved away from him toward the sidebar. One glass of sake would help steady her nerves.

"I've got it," said Jeremy, ever the gentleman. He took the opportunity to lean in close. "You okay?" he asked under his breath.

"Yes. Thanks. That was…unpleasant."

"That's one word for it." He shot the unsuspecting Biz a dirty look. "I'm going to grab some food. Want anything?"

"I'm fine." Vesper nodded toward the game. "I want to watch some of this."

She had to pass behind Nova to take a seat and found herself momentarily captivated by the different shades of blond in her hair. Some were so dark as to be almost brown, while others were nearly white. Most dominant were the strands that glittered like spun gold under the lights, and Vesper suddenly wanted to know what they would feel like, sliding through her fingers. When she realized where her mind had drifted, she hurried toward the first open chair and took a long drink.

"Vesper," said Nova, drawing out the middle consonants in a sultry hiss. "Glad you've joined us. Shall I deal you in next hand?"

"No, thanks. I'm just here to watch."

"C'mon, V!" TJ slurred. "Play a few rounds at least."

Nova arched an eyebrow. "It *is* his birthday."

"Yeah! It is! Please?"

She glanced across the room to where Biz was conversing with Theodore Senior. When they began to move toward the doorway, she relaxed a little more. The party was going well. Her clients were taken care of. Surely, she could allow herself to join in the game for a little while.

"All right. Just a few hands."

A few hands came and went, and turned into more. The chips were already paid for, which made them free money, but old habits died hard, and Vesper had always favored a conservative style of play. She won occasionally, lost sporadically, and folded often. It was fun to play in a no-stakes environment, but even more enjoyable was the banter around the table. TJ and his friends kept up a running commentary of trash talk that made her feel oddly jealous. In her adolescence, she had dreamed of getting a scholarship to UT-Austin—or, if necessary, taking classes at one of the Houston community colleges and transferring in as a junior. Before that dream, and all others, had shattered, the university experience had seemed so romantic. A part of her still pined for it, apparently. It was impossible not to ask, "What if?" Would she have found a strong circle of friends, as TJ had? What career path would she have followed? Would she look back on those years of her life with nostalgia instead of hiding from the memories?

"Hmm. This one's tricky."

Nova's voice was a welcome interruption, jolting her back to the present. When Vesper looked down the table, she couldn't help but stare. Nova was twisting her hair into a bun as she squinted down at the five community cards. At the end of each round, she had taken to trying to predict each remaining player's hand before they showed their cards. About two-thirds of the time, she was right. The kids loved it, and even Vesper had to admit that her ability was impressive.

"Come on, let's hear it," said Ethan.

But Nova wouldn't be rushed. She brought her right hand to her mouth and closed her teeth around one of the thin black hair bands encircling her wrist before sliding it off and threading it through her hair. The practiced motion was strangely alluring, and Vesper reached for her sake glass only to find it almost empty. She wanted another, but grabbed the carafe of water instead.

"Okay. Ethan, you have a high-middle pair. Maybe nines, maybe jacks. TJ…" She looked between the table and the birthday boy. "I'd guess you were dealt pocket rockets or pocket kings. The problem is, I'm pretty sure Amelia has a straight."

"I hit it on the river," Amelia said proudly, revealing her two pocket cards.

"With an inside draw? You got *lucky.*" Ethan sounded disgusted as he turned over the jack of spades and the three of diamonds. "Can't believe you hung in there with all of Ham's re-raises."

"I was bluf-fing!" TJ hiccupped on the last syllable and turned over the ace of hearts and the two of clubs.

"That's why I kept calling," Amelia said dryly.

"Damn." Ethan shook his head. "Should've known."

"He fooled me, too." Nova gathered up the cards. "Another hand?"

"Of c-hic-course," said TJ.

Ethan blocked his arm as he reached for the sake bottle. "Water from now on, bro."

Clearly intending to argue, TJ took a deep breath only to hiccup even more loudly. Amelia touched his shoulder. "He's right, Ham. You don't want to boot, do you?"

TJ looked between them before conceding with a noisy sigh. "Fine." To Vesper's relief, he took the brimming glass she offered and gulped it down noisily.

Nova was just beginning to distribute the cards when Biz's voice filled the room. "Dealer! I want in on this round."

Vesper's stomach twisted. She looked up as he moved deeper into the room, silently praying that he would choose a seat on the far side of the table. But then his eyes met hers and that sloppy, suggestive smile returned to his face as he headed directly for her. Behind him, Theodore Senior stood in the doorway.

"My wife and I are turning in," he announced. "Enjoy the rest of the night. Thanks for being here. Happy birthday, son."

"'Night, Dad."

Don't go, Vesper wanted to call after him like a frightened little girl. But she was a casino host, not a child, and he was not her father. She had never had a male protector, and she didn't need one now.

"Is your evening going well, Mr. Deloreo?" she asked as he took the chair next to hers. Perhaps, if she continued to treat him with professionalism, he would get the hint and back off.

"It's much better now, hon."

"My name is Vesper," she reminded him, making her voice as cool as she knew how.

"And what a sexy name it is."

Ignoring him, she glanced toward the head of the table as she picked up her cards. Nova was frowning at Biz, and for a moment, it looked as though she might say something. Vesper caught her eye and shook her head once before focusing on her cards. Biz was a dog. He would quit his bad behavior if no one paid attention.

At first, it seemed her instincts were correct. Over the course of the next few hands, Biz alternated between drinking and regaling the kids with stories from his Dartmouth days. A few of TJ's friends seemed especially interested to hear what the Greek system had been like in his time. But just as Vesper began to relax, Biz yawned, stretched, and rested one arm along the back of her chair. Nova immediately bristled. Amelia looked uncomfortable. TJ just seemed confused. Vesper turned her head and stared at him until he looked up.

"Something you need, hon?"

"Yes. The back of my seat."

"Oh!" He moved his arm away, but not before giving her shoulder a squeeze. "Sorry about that. Hand has a mind of its own."

She sat back but couldn't manage to relax. Tension gripped her neck and shoulder muscles as she remained alert to Biz's every movement. A few minutes later, her vigilance was justified when he put a hand on her knee below the table and began to slide it up along her inner thigh. Clamping her teeth around a startled cry, she trapped his hand with her own and pulled it away. The anger that had been simmering since his first unwanted advances in the lobby boiled over. Enough. That was *beyond* enough. She refused to sit here and be groped by her own client. Only her sense of professional decorum stopped her from publicly reprimanding him.

"Excuse me, all," she said, pushing back her chair. "I should check in with the caterer."

As she left the room, she heard the scrape of another chair across the floor. "I need to piss like a racehorse," Biz announced. "Be right back."

A sense of dread made Vesper's chest tighten. Was he really going to use the facilities, or was that an excuse for him to pursue her?

Walking briskly, she turned into the empty corridor and hurried toward the dining room and kitchen. She was probably just being paranoid, but the sooner she was back in a room full of people, the better.

"Vesper, wait!"

Damn it. Her instincts screamed at her to break into a run, but she mastered the impulse and spun to face him. At least if they had it out here, she could give him a piece of her mind without humiliating him in front of the Hamiltons or their guests.

"Mr. Deloreo," she said, leveling a finger at his chest as much for emphasis as to ward him off, "your conduct tonight has been completely inappropriate. I am your host, not your call girl. We have a professional relationship, nothing more. If you cannot respect that, I will find you another host."

He held up both hands and offered her a wide, white smile that he probably thought was charming. "Look, babe, I didn't mean to offend you. I apologize."

Vesper almost called him on his use of "babe," but decided to focus on the apology instead. "Thank you."

Biz took a slow step forward. "You gotta lighten up, though. You're wound so tight." He shook his head. "I can show you a good time. Get you to relax. You'll thank me later. Promise."

"I am *not* interested." Adrenaline brought Vesper to the balls of her feet. Her raised arm trembled. "Now, if you'll excuse me, I—"

With surprising quickness, he moved closer and closed his hand around hers. She had nowhere to go but backward, and her teeth jarred together as her back hit the wall. Still smiling, he loomed over her, his heavy, liquor-stained breaths puffing against her face. In that moment, a wave of pure terror paralyzed her. She couldn't speak. She couldn't think. Her brain was trapped between the past and the present, and she had nowhere to go.

And then the wave passed. Beyond it was the memory of her training. As his thighs pressed against hers, she let her body go limp beneath his touch. His smile widened.

"There, that's better," he crooned, leaning in for a kiss. "I know you want—"

Silently, and with every ounce of force she could muster, Vesper smashed her left knee into the space between his legs. The sound that burst from his chest was half a scream, half a shout. It was the most beautiful thing she'd ever heard. As he slumped forward, she slipped beneath one arm and raced for the door. Out. She had to get out, before he could—

"Whoa!"

She collided with something—*someone*, she realized from their exclamation—and was thrown off balance. Strong arms came around her waist and she pulled at them, clawing with her nails, refusing to be trapped again. Every breath felt like fire in her lungs.

"Vesper!"

The voice was feminine. Familiar. She stilled, blinking hard against the moisture in her eyes. Other voices, most of them male, were shouting questions. Someone was moaning. From somewhere nearby, a different female voice announced in trembling tones that she had called security.

"It's me. It's Nova." The words were soft against her ear. "You're okay. I've got you. You're okay."

Vesper blinked again, and her vision cleared enough to make out the blurry outline of Nova's face. The commotion went on around them, but here, in the circle of her embrace, she felt untouched.

"Nova." She shuddered as the haze of panic subsided. Memories rushed to fill the gap: Biz's unwanted advance, his hand gripping hers, his body trapping her against the wall. Suddenly, even Nova's hold on her was more than she could bear.

"Please," she said hoarsely, gripping Nova's wrist where it lay against her stomach. "I need to—"

She let go immediately. "I'm sorry. Did I hurt you?" Nova looked over her shoulder. "Did *he* hurt you?"

Swiping at her eyes, she fumbled for the words. "He…"

"What did you do to her? What the fuck did you do?" The voice was TJ's, deeper and angrier than she'd ever heard it. When she focused, she saw him standing over Biz, hair disheveled and fists raised. His friends had filtered into the corridor.

"N-nothing!" Biz's voice was high and thin.

"You're lying!"

Slowly, wincing and groaning, Biz pushed himself to a kneeling position. As he braced one arm against the wall in an attempt to stand, Theodore Senior emerged at the end of the hall, shirtless except for silk pajama pants. The muttering and murmuring trailed off.

"*What* is going on here?" he asked in a tone that made it clear he expected to be obeyed.

"Biz hurt Vesper!" TJ's gaze never wavered.

"I didn't." Biz dragged himself upright, one hand still covering his genitals, and looked between TJ and his father. "We were just talking, and then that…that *bitch* attacked me!"

TJ pulled his right arm back and punched Biz squarely in the face. It happened so quickly Vesper thought she had imagined it, until she blinked again and saw Biz back on the ground holding his left cheek. As she watched, blood trickled from his nose and dripped onto the carpet.

The sound of a commotion drew her attention away. Theodore Senior was restraining TJ with both hands on his shoulders, telling him repeatedly to settle down and back away. No one was attending to Biz.

"Motherfucker!" Biz shouted. "You fucking bastard!"

"Enough!" Theodore's voice cracked through the air. He looked around at the people milling about in the hallway. "We need hand towels, a bowl of water, and ice. Now."

As several of TJ's friends scurried off, Theodore turned to look directly at Vesper. "Biz had his say. Now I'd like to hear your side."

Vesper nodded, feeling dazed. Why would he believe her over the testimony of one of his Sphinx brothers? Was this it—the end of her relationship with the Hamiltons? Had she just jeopardized every business partnership she had cultivated for the past several years?

The first time she tried to speak, no sound emerged. She swallowed hard, cleared her throat, and tried again. "Biz has been making sexual innuendos all night." Her voice was hoarse, and it trembled a few times at the beginning, but hearing her own words out loud somehow made her feel stronger.

"When I left the poker game, he followed me out here and offered to…to 'show me a good time.'" Out of the corner of her eye, Vesper saw Nova's fingers curl into her palms. The visceral response surprised her enough to make her pause. Did she need to worry about Nova becoming violent, too?

"Vesper?" Theodore asked.

"I'm sorry." She tried to swallow again, but her mouth was dry. Where had she been? "I told him I wasn't interested. He came closer, grabbed my hand, and tried to kiss me. My back was to the wall." She shivered. "That's when I…reacted."

Biz staggered back to his feet, a towel filled with ice held to his cheek. His other hand, stained rust-red with his own blood, was gesticulating at her. "Attacked! You fucking attacked me!"

Theodore rounded on him. "I said, *enough.*" The cold anger in his voice gave Vesper a glimmer of hope. Was there a chance that he would take her side?

The two-tone chime of the doorbell drew her attention to the door. Casino security. She wondered which of the night shift officers was standing outside. Over the past few years, she had worked with them all, but only as a liaison—never as someone involved in an altercation. Vesper felt her cheeks grow hot. Would this change the way her coworkers looked at her? More importantly, would she even have a job tomorrow?

Theodore answered the door and admitted Shaun, an ex-Marine who kept his head as bald as an egg. He rarely cracked a smile, but he was fair and efficient. "Vesper, TJ, Bizmark, and I will speak with the security officer," Theodore announced. "The rest of you: good night. This party is over."

Feeling as though she was going to her own trial, Vesper turned to follow them. A few feet away, Amelia was cradling TJ's right hand in both of hers as she held ice against his knuckles. "Keep the ice on for ten more minutes," Vesper heard her say just before she rose onto her toes and kissed him on the cheek.

At the sound of her own name, spoken softly and urgently, Vesper realized Nova had come up next to her. Nova stretched out one hand as if to touch her shoulder but then apparently thought the better of it. Vesper was about to say something inane about how she wished Nova hadn't had to witness the conflict, when she spoke.

"I want to wait for you, and then I want to see that you get home okay."

Automatically, Vesper shook her head. "That's really not necessary."

"I know. You'd be fine on your own. But I just..." For a moment, she looked away, grimacing. "Think of it as a selfish request. Another favor I owe you. Please."

She looked so earnest, so serious, and Vesper realized she wanted to say yes. When this discussion was over, no matter what had been decided, one thing was clear: she wouldn't want to be alone.

"Mr. Hamilton," she called, tearing herself away from the stormy, blue-gray depths of Nova's eyes. "Would you mind if Nova waits in the sitting room for me?"

"That's fine." Theodore's tone was as perfunctory as the hand gesture he used to beckon her forward. "This way."

Vesper swallowed hard against a fresh surge of dread. She didn't look back as she followed him down the hall, but she could feel the weight of Nova's gaze—like a massage between her shoulder blades—until the office door closed behind her, severing the connection.

CHAPTER NINE

Nova balanced the tray on one hand, her other clutching the necks of several empty sake bottles. As she walked carefully down the hall, her eyes were drawn to the small splotch of red that marred the bone-white carpet—the only tangible sign of the evening's violence. Unbidden, her mind replayed Vesper's narrative. When the glasses on the tray began to clink together, Nova realized her hand was trembling.

Vesper's voice had trembled too, as she told them how Biz had cornered her. She had been remarkably self-possessed in the wake of that insanity, but hearing the quaver behind her words had made Nova see red. If TJ hadn't already knocked the bastard down, she might have been tempted to try.

She turned into the kitchen and set down the tray with a sigh of relief, briefly shaking out her arm before loading everything into the dishwasher. Alone in the sitting room, surrounded by empty glassware, she had quickly gone stir-crazy. The housekeeping staff would have cleaned everything up in the morning, but staying in motion helped to keep her anxiety at bay. Even so, as she rinsed out the sink and wetted down some paper towels, she couldn't help but wonder what was happening in that office. Was Vesper in trouble? Would Biz press charges against her and TJ?

The sound of a door opening made her drop the sodden towels next to the sink. When she emerged into the hallway, Vesper was having a tête-à-tête with Mr. Hamilton. She hung back, wanting to give them privacy. Surely, the Hamiltons didn't blame Vesper for the fracas, did they? Out of the corner of her eye, she saw him briefly rest one hand on her shoulder before disappearing back into his office. Vesper bowed her head and took a long, deep breath. She seemed overwhelmed, and in that instant, Nova wanted nothing more than to hold her.

Instead, she cleared her throat. "Hi."

Startled, Vesper looked up. Almost immediately, the professional mask slid into place, erasing the lines of fatigue around her mouth and the furrow between her brows. It was an impressive defense mechanism. "Nova. I didn't see you."

"Sorry. Didn't mean to sneak up." The moment was quickly becoming awkward. She wanted to ask how the conversation had gone, but not here. Instead, she glanced at her watch. "It's past one. You must be exhausted."

"I'm a little tired."

Nova wanted to grab her by the shoulders and lean in close and tell her to stop dissembling, but this wasn't the time or the place. "How do you usually get home?"

"The city bus."

"It's stopped running by now."

"I'll call a taxi." Vesper mustered a forced smile as she moved toward the door. "It was nice of you to offer to see me home, but I really am fine."

Nova waited until they were outside the suite before calling her bluff. "Bullshit."

"Excuse me?"

She knew Vesper meant to sound affronted, but her retort mostly came off as defensive. Nova looked to both her left and right before replying, and when she found the corridor deserted, she leaned in close.

"You were sexually and verbally assaulted tonight by one of your clients. You are not *fine*." As she spoke, Nova watched closely for any sign of a chink in Vesper's armor. It came as a quickly suppressed quivering of her lips. Nova wanted so badly to slide her arms around Vesper's waist in comfort, but she also didn't want to touch her in any way without an invitation. Especially tonight. To keep herself honest, she shoved her hands into the pockets of her pants.

"Vesper." She softened her voice. "You've had a long, difficult day. Stay in my suite tonight."

Nova knew Vesper was considering the offer when she didn't reply right away. She drew herself up to her full height, eyes narrowed. "I'm not sleeping with you."

Nova felt like she'd been punched in the stomach, and a haze of red tinged her vision. "Are you kidding me? Do you think I'm some kind of predator, like Biz?"

Visibly chagrined, Vesper held up her hands. "I'm sor—"

"I know I've been flirtatious. But for fuck's sake, Vesper, what kind of monster would I have to be to want to coerce you into sex after the night you've had?" Head throbbing, she took a step back. "We don't know each other well. I get that. But it kills me to think I've given you that kind of impression."

"You haven't," Vesper said quickly. "It's me. My...issues. And what happened tonight."

Heart pounding, her chest rising and falling with quick, shallow breaths, Nova struggled to master her emotions. She had to calm down. Whatever Vesper thought of her wasn't important. Not right now.

"I overreacted. I'm sorry. I just want to help, okay? My suite has a sleeper sofa." She tried to smile. "Which, of course, you know. I'll sleep there. You can take the bed."

Vesper's eyes flickered as she searched her face—for what, Nova couldn't guess. "Okay," she finally said, the word barely above a whisper.

The elevator ride down was quick and silent. Nova wedged herself into the corner, wanting to keep plenty of space between them. Vesper remained near the doors, looking straight ahead. Her dress—a deep, navy blue that fell to just above her knees—was complemented by matching heels that showed off the contours of her shapely calves. When Nova caught herself staring, she closed her eyes until the elevator came to a halt.

Once they were inside the suite, she moved quickly toward the bedroom. "Let me just grab something to sleep in, and then it'll be all yours."

"I can take the sofa," Vesper said, trailing behind her. "Really."

"No way." Nova fished around in her duffel until she found a T-shirt and a pair of boxers. On second thought, she grabbed a tank top and pair of mesh shorts and set them on top of the dresser. "Okay.

These are clean, if you want them. The door locks, by the way. And the bathroom's around the corner. Which you probably also knew." Realizing she was babbling, she beat a hasty retreat toward the door. "Good night."

If Vesper replied, Nova didn't hear it. She went first to the fridge for a bottle of beer, and then to the couch. Exhaustion was making her eyes burn, but she could still feel her heart fluttering quickly against her ribs. Too keyed up to sleep, she reached for the remote. It didn't take long to find a terrifically awful B-movie about sharks, but even that couldn't hold her attention.

Above the sounds of the film, she heard the bathroom door close and the water begin to run. What was Vesper thinking? How was she feeling? Nova tried to imagine herself in Vesper's place, but it wasn't easy. Was she angry? Frightened? Worried? Their mentalities were so different. She would be terrible at Vesper's job—at anticipating the whims of the wealthy and catering to their every desire.

The water shut off. Nova held her breath but remained facing forward, part of her hoping Vesper wanted company instead of sleep. A moment later, the sound of the bedroom door being closed dashed that hope. That was all for the best, of course. Instead of moping about it, she should follow Vesper's example and sleep. She stood, intending to transform the couch into a bed, but decided in favor of just crashing on it as-is. The closet yielded a pillow and blanket, and she settled in to let the film bore her into sleep. But as the minutes ticked past on the TV clock, her thoughts continued to race.

And then the door reopened.

"Nova?" Vesper's voice was quiet. Had Nova been asleep, she wouldn't have heard a thing.

"Hey." She sat up so quickly her head spun. "Couldn't sleep?"

"No." Vesper stopped near the armchair, but didn't sit. She had looked amazing in that dress, but she looked even better now. The tank top was a little too big for her, but from the way it draped over her breasts, Nova could tell she had forgone a bra. The shorts were a snugger fit, though she had rolled them once at the waist. Her hair hung down past her shoulders in auburn waves that were slightly disheveled where her head had rested against the pillow. This slightly rumpled, very human version of Vesper was even more attractive than the assertive, professional woman who had first caught Nova's attention.

"My brain won't turn off. Would you mind if I raid your mini-bar? I'll have the staff comp it all tomorrow."

"No need for that." Nova heard the hoarseness in her own voice. "Take whatever you like. Actually, wait—I'll help."

The bar revealed several small bottles of middle-shelf vodka, whiskey, and rum. Together, they carried them to the coffee table. Nova returned to the fridge for a half-full bottle of orange juice and a few cans of Diet Coke. She watched as Vesper emptied one of the rum bottles into a shallow glass and then filled it with orange juice. The efficient movements of her arms made her breasts sway slightly beneath the shirt. Nova's mouth felt as dry as the desert outside her window, and she reached for the whiskey.

Vesper sat back in the armchair, crossed one leg over the other, and stared down at her knees as Nova racked her brains for a safe conversation topic.

"Did you go to Stanford?" Vesper asked, her attention focused on the white "S" sewn onto the fabric of the shorts.

"Yes." Nova wondered if that changed her opinion at all. Had she just become more respectable in Vesper's eyes?

"What did you study?"

"As an undergrad, mathematics. As a grad student, game theory."

Vesper raised her eyes and smiled, just a little. "Of course. So I should be calling you Dr. Novarro?"

Nova's stomach did a loop-the-loop. "Ah. No. I dropped out a few months before I was set to defend my dissertation."

She waited for the judgmental frown, but Vesper's expression never changed. "Why?"

"Poker." Nova took a sip from her glass to fortify herself. This wasn't at all the direction she had expected their conversation to go. "By then, I was playing online a lot and making good money. I hadn't done much work and would've bombed my defense."

"I see." Still, Vesper's face betrayed nothing.

"You're very difficult to read." Nova hadn't exactly meant to blurt that out, but there was no going back now. "Your poker face is everything mine should be and isn't."

Vesper drank deeply from her cup. "I've had a lot of practice."

The note of sorrow that inflected her words roused every protective instinct in Nova's body. "Do you want to talk about it?"

Vesper rested her glass in the palm of her hand and rotated it slowly, staring into the swirling liquid. "I suppose I do, or I wouldn't be sitting here right now."

Nova was confused. She'd figured that Vesper was still upset—or at least unsettled—by what had happened at TJ's party. What did her poker face have to do with that? "I don't want you to feel uncomfortable," was all she said.

"Me, neither." Vesper met her gaze again, lips twisted in a self-deprecating smile. "But what happened tonight...it's brought something back, for me. Something I've tried hard to forget. Avoiding the uncomfortable doesn't seem to be working."

Nova was squeezing her own glass so tightly she feared it might break. Carefully, she set it down on the table. "The way Biz treated you tonight...that's happened before?"

She nodded. "Once. When I was sixteen. It was a lot like tonight, actually. Nothing *really* bad happened, but—"

"Vesper." Nova couldn't stand to hear her talk like that. "Biz harassed you. Repeatedly. That's awful. No one should have to stand for being treated that way."

"I know." She was staring down at her lap again. "I just...I've never been hurt. Physically. For which I'm thankful. So many other women have gone through so much worse."

"We're talking about you right now." Nova did her best to gentle her voice, despite the fury boiling in her blood.

"It's a long story."

"I'd like to hear it, if you want to tell it."

Vesper nodded again and visibly squared her shoulders. "My mother works as the housekeeper for a very wealthy family in Texas. I grew up of an age with their middle child, Sabrina. We started to become...very close...when I was fifteen."

Very close. Nova didn't need that spelled out for her. She wondered what Vesper had been like at fifteen. Had her face been rounder, her smile bright and ready? Had her movements been clumsy as she adjusted to a recent growth spurt? Had her eyes been bright and credulous, instead of guarded? Maybe not, if she had been forced to keep Sabrina a secret. Lying was the most basic survival skill of the closet.

"Her older brother found out the next year." Vesper's eyes had become unfocused as she remembered. "First, he threatened me. Then, he…he came on to me." She tossed her head back and drained the contents of her glass. "I suppose it was really the same thing."

"The same thing?" Nova didn't want to make Vesper relive all the details, but she also needed to understand.

Vesper's gaze snapped back into focus and locked onto hers. "We tried to be so careful, but he overheard us talking about Valentine's Day. Sabrina said she wished she could hold my hand in public, and then she kissed me. I'll never forget how happy I was in that moment."

"What happened then?"

"Samuel—that was his name—ambushed me in the room I shared with my younger sister. My mother was taking her to a birthday party, so neither of them were home. It's funny, the details you remember, isn't it?"

Her voice had become breathless, as though she were close to tears. They were probably necessary, but if Nova had been in Vesper's shoes, the last thing she would want was to lose control of herself. Silently, she held up another bottle of rum. When Vesper nodded, Nova bent her head to mix the drink, giving her a chance to regain her equilibrium.

"Thanks." Vesper's fingertips brushed hers as she took the glass. Nova didn't want to imagine what they would feel like on her face, on her breasts, on her hips. Not now.

"Anyway, he told me that he'd seen us kissing. That he would tell his parents, and my mother would lose her job. By the time he was finished threatening me, he had backed me into a corner." Vesper's tongue darted out to moisten her lips. "He said he would make me a deal. He touched my hair. My face. He said if I slept with him, he wouldn't tell."

"Oh, God. Vesper." Nova could feel the strain in her wrist tendons as her fingernails dug into her palms. She wanted to hit something, like she'd wanted to hit Biz, earlier.

"I knew he was lying." Vesper's laugh was mirthless. "He wanted me, but he would never have kept our secret. So I told him no." She shivered. "Fortunately, all he did was force me to kiss him, and…and touched me, a little. Just m-my breasts. Then he laughed and left."

When she took another sip from her drink, Nova forced her hands to unclench and followed suit. This was a nightmare—a nightmare that Biz had forced her to relive. Vesper could lose her *own* job, this time.

"I didn't know if I could save my mother's job, but I had to try. So I packed a bag and took the bus downtown to where Samuel's father worked. When I told his secretary there was an emergency that had to do with Sabrina, he saw me right away. He was sitting behind a black marble desk, and behind him, there were floor-to-ceiling windows with a view all the way to Lake Houston. It was beautiful."

The flickering light of the television screen sent shadows dancing across her face like an echo of a caress. Dread swirled in Nova's stomach as she leaned forward to catch every word.

"I told him I had fallen in love with his daughter. That we'd been seeing each other. And then I told him a lie: that it had been my idea, my initiation. I said I would leave, right then, and never come back. He would never see me again, and neither would Sabrina...as long as my mother was able to keep her position. He was so angry, and I think he wanted to believe me. He yelled at me for a while, then told me to get out."

"Where did you go?"

"Albuquerque. By bus. My cousin is...gay...too. And he was going to the university then. He lived in an apartment with three other men. I lived there for a while. Got a fake ID. Worked."

She tossed back the rest of her drink. For a long moment, the only sound was the thud of Nova's heartbeat in her ears. Her entire body was on high alert, and her chest ached dully in empathy with Vesper's remembered pain. There were so many questions she wanted to ask, but Vesper had already shared so much. She was emotionally raw, and more vulnerable than Nova had ever seen her.

"You're incredible," she finally said.

"No." When Vesper shook her head firmly, her hair swished against the stark outline of her collarbone. "I did what I had to do."

Nova was tempted to argue with her—to point out all the ways in which she had sacrificed her own well-being for that of others: her mother, her sister, her girlfriend. But Vesper had just laid bare a traumatic past, in the wake of an awful day. A debate was the last thing she needed.

"That's not how it seems to me," Nova contented herself with saying. She hoped Vesper could hear her sincerity.

"I should never have taken the risk that I did." Vesper's voice grew stronger and sharper as she chastised herself. "By being selfish, I put my family in danger. I should've known what would happen if Sabrina and I got involved."

"Vesper, c'mon." Nova almost reached out to touch her hand, but pulled back at the last second to rest on the arm of the chair. "You're being too hard on yourself. You were a kid."

"I was sixteen, and the daughter of a housekeeper. I knew enough about how the world works."

Nova didn't know how to respond. Clearly, this line of self-recrimination was well-trodden ground for Vesper. Nova wasn't going to be able to change her mind overnight, or perhaps ever. The thought was saddening.

Her hand was still awkwardly resting on the chair, so she moved it to Vesper's glass. "Another?"

"No. Thanks." When Vesper leaned forward to glance at the clock, the light from the screen threw her face into sharp relief, accentuating the dark circles that were materializing beneath her eyes. They didn't matter. She was still impossibly beautiful. "I should sleep. We both should."

Together, Nova's rebellious brain finished, unhelpfully. "That's probably true," she said lamely. But when Vesper began to gather up the bottles, she stood, shaking her head. "You go ahead and crash. I'll put this stuff back."

"Are you sure?"

"Positive."

Nova bent to the task but was brought up short by the heat of Vesper's palm soaking into her shoulder. She froze in the act of clutching half a dozen of the small bottles to her chest.

"You're a good listener," Vesper said softly. "Thank you."

As quickly as it had come, the touch was gone.

"Sweet dreams." Nova could only hope she didn't sound as bereft as she felt.

Again, the bedroom door closed. She cleaned up quickly and returned to the couch. Turning off the television plunged her into a darkness broken only by the red numbers on the digital clock below the screen. The suite was quiet. In the bedroom, she imagined Vesper was tucked under the blankets. Did she sleep on her back or on her stomach? Did she prefer to wear pajamas, or sleep in the nude?

Frustrated with her wayward thoughts, Nova rolled onto her side and closed her eyes. Desiring Vesper right now, in the wake of her confession, made Nova feel no better than the men who had abused her. Lying perfectly still, she focused on taking deep, even breaths. When that didn't lull her into sleep, she began mentally working her way through the Fibonacci sequence. But while her mathematical mind smoothly summed the progressively larger numbers, her imagination refused to quiet. Instead, images of a younger Vesper began to resolve before her mind's eye: a frightened but determined Vesper confronting Sabrina's father, Vesper waiting at a street corner for the bus that would take her into exile, Vesper sleeping fitfully on a ratty couch that smelled of beer and cigarettes.

Once she had been a runaway, living out of a single bag. Now she was a casino host, wearing expensive suits and hobnobbing with millionaires. How had she done it? Nova wanted to know every step, every misstep, and everything in between. But just because Vesper had chosen to confide in her once, didn't mean she had a right to know more. If anything, she now had a better appreciation for why Vesper was so tight-lipped.

Nova flipped to her other side, looked at the clock, and flopped back onto her pillow. Almost three. Ridiculous. Tomorrow would be a world of pain. With a heavy sigh, she forced herself to concentrate on Fibonacci and his golden ratio. The mathematics of his sequence was predictable. Dependable. Unlike life. Unlike poker.

Unlike love.

CHAPTER TEN

Vesper woke with a start. Everything felt wrong. This wasn't her bed. This wasn't her room. The taste of rum lingered in the back of her throat, and her head was throbbing dully. A surge of panic propelled her into sitting position and she blinked rapidly, trying to make sense of the world. The bed was empty and she had clothes on. Those were good signs, though they would have been better if the clothes belonged to her.

Then, she caught sight of the "S" embroidered onto her shorts. In a rush, the memories returned: Biz's unwanted advances, TJ's strong right hook, drops of blood on the snowy white carpet. Nova giving up her own bed. The panic that had suffocated her every time she tried to close her eyes. Rum and orange juice and secrets revealed.

She turned her head to glance at the clock. 5:27. Her alarm would sound in three minutes. Part of her wanted nothing more than to turn it off, fall back onto the mattress and let herself sleep as long as she was able. But that was a pipe dream. The casino manager, Steve, would hear about the altercation with Biz when he arrived this morning, if he hadn't already. She had to be ready to defend herself as best she could.

Anxiety drove her out of the bed, where she quickly threw on last night's dress. After a brief stop in the bathroom, she grabbed her purse and headed toward the door, only to be brought up by the sound of light snoring. The gray, predawn light filtered through the blinds, illuminating Nova as she lay supine on the couch. One of her arms was dangling off the edge, and Vesper took an involuntary step forward before reining herself in. Nova didn't need her help. But she did deserve her thanks, and Vesper took a moment to carefully backtrack to the desk. She wrote out a quick note and left it in between the two bathroom sinks, where Nova was sure to find it.

At this time of day, the casino was nearly empty and lightly staffed. Even so, Vesper went out of her way to leave by the employees' entrance, in the hopes that no one would see her wearing yesterday's clothing and assume she was doing a walk of shame. That sort of gossip would travel at light speed, especially where she was concerned. Then again, some version of last night's events was probably already making the rounds.

The more she thought it over, the clearer the landscape of her choices became. Ultimately, her options boiled down to two: she could proactively pay Steve a visit, or wait for him to call her into his office. If she decided to approach him first, she might come off as too assertive, or even aggressive. But if she waited, did that make her a coward?

As the day dawned, so did an epiphany. She could have it both ways, so long as Jeremy was willing to help. A golden-crimson sunrise made the bus stop's steel bench gleam as she quickly typed out a text. *Something happened after you left last night. Please call me when you see this.* Isabella was always making fun of her for writing her text messages out in complete sentences, using proper punctuation, but it was a habit that made Vesper feel more professional, and she refused to give it up.

She shared the bus home with only one other passenger, a drunk businessman who had passed out on the rear bench. As she leaned her head against the window and closed her eyes, she wondered how much he had lost. More than he could afford to, by the look of it. Only time would tell if she had done the same. If the chips didn't fall her way, she might be unemployed within a few hours.

But even if her job was safe, her actions last night had repercussions. She had confessed more to Nova than she should have. No one knew that much of her story. No one. Isabella knew a part, as did Jeremy. TJ knew her sexual preference, but not much else. Even Geoffrey, the cousin who had taken her in, remained ignorant of Samuel's threat and her confrontation with his father.

Knowledge was power, and in her weakness, she had offered up that power to someone she barely knew. Trust was a fantasy. All she could hope for now was that Nova would never have a reason to use anything she'd said against her. At least, Vesper reflected as the bus pulled over at her stop, she had been smart enough to hold back her real name—though she wasn't naïve enough to imagine it couldn't be found with some digging.

Two hours later, after a long, hot shower, two cups of coffee, and a phone conversation with Jeremy, Vesper returned to Valhalla. This time, she walked through the front doors in her most expensive suit—a gray Donna Karan with an off-the-shoulder jacket. She had pinned her hair back into a bun and applied subtle layers of makeup to hide the darkness beneath her eyes. As she skirted the World Tree Pool, her phone vibrated. She pulled it out of her pocket and felt her pulse jump. Text from Jeremy.

just left steves office. i told him wut that fucker said & did. how r u doing?

When Vesper had called him earlier, he was buffing his car in the Valhalla lot in advance of his first airport pickup. She had filled him in on everything that had happened after he'd left TJ's party—everything except her spending the night in Nova's suite, of course. And then she had asked him to report Biz's verbal harassment to Steve. To his credit, he had done so right away.

Thank you, she texted back. Now all she could do was wait.

On her way to her office, she passed several fellow employees, all of whom she greeted by name without breaking stride. Was she imagining their curious glances, or had they already heard rumors? In an attempt to shake off her paranoia, Vesper glanced down at her phone again and launched her "To-Do List" app. Putting her life on hold while she waited for Steve to call her in would be ridiculous, not to mention ill-advised. Priscilla Beauregard would arrive in just over a week, expecting to be treated like royalty. Making the preliminary preparations for her visit would be the perfect distraction.

Vesper had booked spa appointments for Priscilla and her friends, assigned Jeremy to pick them up at the airport, and arranged for a private viewing of Valhalla's latest jewelry selections when her cell phone began to buzz. *Steve Syrano*, the display proclaimed, and Vesper's palms immediately grew moist.

No. Keep it together. You have nothing to hide. Not when it comes to yesterday, at least.

"Good morning, Steve," she said, proud her voice remained steady.

"Vesper, I need you in my office right away."

"Of course." She disconnected the call and rose from her chair. As she walked past her coworkers' cubicles, she couldn't help but wonder whether this would be the last time she saw her cubicle. If she had to start over at a different casino, how would that work? Had she built up enough cachet to be hired as a host, or would she have to take a step back and return to the floor of the pit? The thought made her stomach roll queasily. She had worked so hard to move up the ladder; the last thing she wanted was to be forced down a rung.

Not wanting to run into any familiar faces, she took the stairs instead of the elevator. The mild exertion helped to burn off some of her adrenaline, and she felt her head begin to clear. If Steve fired her and she had to start over somewhere else, she would be fine. She had done it before; she could do it again. No matter what, she would always be fine.

She turned into his office suite without breaking stride and paused before his secretary's desk. "Good morning, Hannah."

Hannah didn't look up from her screen. Her elaborately manicured nails clacked loudly against the keyboard. "You can go back."

"Thank you." Vesper curbed the impulse to roll her eyes. Hannah was only the most recent in a long string of Steve's nubile secretaries. He seemed to have three criteria: youth, waifishness, and haughtiness. By that standard, Hannah was the most successful yet.

Steve shared the suite with Valhalla's CEO and CFO, neither of whom she had ever met. Until she landed a whale, she probably never would. Priscilla Beauregard might be her golden ticket, but unless she survived this meeting with her job intact, she wouldn't have the chance to find out. The prospect of having to give up her best chance at breaking into the big leagues, all because of Biz's misogynistic harassment, sent a hot wave of anger beneath her skin. She hung on to the feeling as she knocked at Steve's door. Anger was infinitely more useful than fear.

"Vesper." To her surprise, Steve rose and came around his desk to shake her hand. "Let's sit at the conference table."

Hoping she hadn't betrayed her confusion, Vesper took the seat he pulled out for her. Their previous meetings had all been conducted across the expanse of polished mahogany separating him from whatever riffraff might chance to come through the door. Why was she suddenly being given a seat at the table, especially given what had happened yesterday?

Once they were seated, he clasped his hands. "So. I hear we had a little problem last night."

She didn't know why he was beating around the bush, but she wasn't about to join him. "If by 'problem' you mean 'a of case sexual harassment,' then yes."

He cleared his throat. "Well, about that. I'd like to avoid any unpleasantness."

"As the target of Biz's remarks, I can tell you they were both unpleasant and unavoidable."

Her defensiveness must have come through loud and clear, because he raised one hand in a placating gesture. "No one's debating that. His driver last night said as much."

Vesper offered up a silent thank-you to Jeremy and vowed to get him an especially nice Christmas present. But as the awkward silence dragged on, her anger flared again. Was he really going to make her do all of the heavy lifting in this conversation? What was he afraid of— that she would sue Biz and drag Valhalla through the mire somehow? A lawsuit might have been tempting, but hiring a lawyer was expensive, and her savings account was the product of many years of scraping.

"I'm not sure what you want me to say, Steve. He verbally harassed me for hours, touched my thigh, backed me into a corner, and tried to kiss me. None of that is acceptable."

Her candidness made him visibly tense. "Look. Vesper. Theodore Hamilton and I spoke earlier this morning, and he made it clear how highly he thinks of you." He paused then, probably wanting her to ask for details or toot her own horn. Instead, she stared at him silently, waiting. After a long pause, his Adam's apple bobbed in a hard swallow. "He's disappointed that one of his colleagues acted so callously while under the influence."

Vesper heard what he wasn't saying: that Biz had been drunk and should therefore be forgiven for not having been himself. Well, bullshit. Drunk people rarely acted in ways that were truly out of character. If anything, they became more honest, more essential. The essential Biz was an asshole—of that she had no doubt. If Steve wanted to convince himself otherwise, that was his problem.

"What do you intend to do about it?" A part of Vesper couldn't believe the words that were leaving her mouth, but the rest of her finally felt vindicated. She was speaking up for herself, taking her needs into her own hands. The sensation felt oddly like flying, and the rush made her bold. "I'll happily transfer Biz's account to whomever you choose, of course."

"That's not what he wants."

"Why should I care about what he wants?" Vesper fired back.

"He's your client."

Vesper sat back in her chair and stared at him. There it was—the bottom line. "You've never been sexually harassed, have you, Steve?" When he began to bluster, she cut him off. "Fine. I'll accept his apology and make all of this go away. Water under the bridge. On one condition: get me that six million in credit for Priscilla Beauregard."

"Vesper…"

"She's not going to use it all. And even if she does, she's good for it. Give me the line, and before you know it, you'll have her and her three best friends in here rolling up a storm at craps. Her friends will tell their friends. We both know how this works."

Steve laced his fingers together and rested them on the table, revealing platinum cufflinks in the shape of the Wall Street bull. They had probably cost a small fortune. "If you're wrong about this, you're out."

The flash of triumph felt all the sweeter after the uproar of the past twelve hours, and Vesper let it show on her face. "I'm not wrong." She pushed back her chair. "Are we finished?"

"We are." He stood and offered his hand. "Take care."

As she left the office, Vesper wondered whether he had meant the words as a generic farewell or a warning. Then she realized it didn't matter. So what if she was stuck with Biz? She could handle him now. She had proved as much last night. With a green light for Priscilla's account, she finally had the harpoon she needed to go whale hunting.

This was her once-in-a-lifetime chance. If she succeeded, she would enter the ranks of the elite casino hosts. If she failed, she would have to start over somewhere else. But she wasn't going to fail. Her weakness last night had been a temporary insanity born of stress—nothing more. Nothing in her past or present would interfere with her goals. She would make sure of it.

Nothing.

❖

Nova folded her hand and rubbed at her eyes. Maybe this had been a mistake. She had been woken three hours earlier by housekeeping's knock on the door, chagrined to discover that the bedroom was empty and it was past nine o'clock. A quick shower and a cup of coffee hadn't done much to clear her head, which felt as though it had been stuffed with cotton balls. Between the late-night drinking and lack of sleep, she was a mess—not to mention her worry over Vesper's whereabouts and emotional state.

Twice, she had almost called before deciding she would seem too pushy. Or clingy. Or both. Vesper was working. At least, Nova hoped she was. Since taking a seat in the poker hall, she had been on the lookout, even going so far as to deliberately choose a chair with a view of the door. Had Vesper's boss called her on the carpet? Was Biz trying to press charges? Or had it all blown over, and she was simply having a busy day?

All Nova knew for sure was that she was distracted and playing like crap. She hadn't taken a single day off since she'd arrived at Valhalla. Maybe what she needed was to go upstairs, take a dip in the pool, and try to nap for a while. Anything would be more productive than losing money to tourists.

A warm, heavy hand fell on her shoulder—the same shoulder Vesper had touched last night. "Hey, Nova."

She looked up and felt the surprise register on her face. "TJ. Hey." His other hand hung at his side, a bandage over the knuckles. "You all right?"

"Yeah, of course. It's nothing." He rolled his eyes. "Amelia made me promise I'd leave the damn thing on for the day."

"I'm glad you're okay." Nova patted the seat next to hers. "Want to play a few?"

He shook his head. "Actually, I'm sorry to interrupt, but…can we talk?"

This time, she tried to keep a lid on her surprise. "Sure." She signaled the dealer that she was out for a few hands and rose from her seat. "Can I buy you a drink? Or coffee?"

"I'm buying. And definitely the latter." He grimaced. "Not quite ready for the hair of the dog, yet."

"Sorry. I know it's painful."

An awkward silence stretched between them as they entered the lobby. Her best guess was that he wanted to talk about Vesper. Nova wondered just how much he knew of her story. She would have to figure that out carefully, without revealing any of the details Vesper had entrusted to her confidence.

He led her to a table near the corner of the small café area. After giving the server their orders, he rested his elbows on the rickety surface and leaned forward. "Have you heard from Vesper today?"

Nova shook her head. "You?"

"No." He frowned and began to pick at the edge of his bandage. "Did she get home okay? I remember hearing you say…at least, I thought…"

"She ended up staying in my suite becau—"

"You spent the night together?" TJ hissed.

"No!" Nova lowered her voice when a nearby couple glanced at them in curiosity. "No. She slept in the bed. I slept on the couch. Nothing happened. Nothing's going on."

"But you want there to be." It wasn't a question.

Nova didn't know whether to laugh or get angry. Did TJ think he was Vesper's matchmaker, her bodyguard, or an unlikely combination of both? "Is this what you wanted to talk to me about? Because I'm not having this conversation with you."

"Why not?" He flashed a self-deprecating smile. "I was in love with her too, once."

That was interesting enough that Nova didn't bother to correct him about her own feelings. "Oh?"

"Yeah. Made a fool of myself the second time I was in Vegas."

"How old were you?"

"Nineteen." He laughed dryly. "Every day, I would present her with some stupid gift. A dozen roses. A pair of earrings from the store." He jerked his thumb in the direction of Valhalla's shopping gallery. "Unoriginal stuff like that."

"Hey. A dozen roses are classic." Nova patted his hand, not knowing what else to say.

He shrugged. "Finally, she had mercy and told me the truth."

"The truth?"

Alarm made his eyes widen. "You mean you don't know?"

Nova had to make a snap decision that he was talking about Vesper's sexual orientation and nothing else. "That she prefers women? Yes."

Relief made his shoulders slump. "Thank God. For a second there, I thought I'd broken my promise."

Their coffees arrived then, and Nova waited until the server left before replying. "I'm sure she knows you wouldn't betray her trust. I get the impression she hasn't told many people." When he looked at her quizzically, she added, "I figured it out myself, and she didn't seem happy at all."

"You figured it out?" He whistled lowly. "That's impressive. I had no idea. You must be really good at reading people."

Nova laughed. "I'm awful at it. Good at math. Bad at human beings."

"You're seriously trying to tell me that gaydar, or whatever, isn't about reading people?"

"I guess it is." Nova sipped at her coffee, considering. "But it's very specific. Attraction is gravity, right? Bodies being pulled into orbit, or slingshotted away. You're a good-looking guy, TJ, but there's no gravity between us."

"There is between you and Vesper."

Nova wanted to believe he was right. She also didn't want to admit it. "Why are you so invested in her?"

He spread his hands in the air, palms up. "Not sure I can totally explain it. Maybe it's because she was the first person to really treat me like an adult when that was all I wanted. Or because she's the first woman I fell for. Or because underneath all that competence and elegance, she just seems so...so sad sometimes."

Nova nodded slowly. She had one answer, at least: unless TJ was bluffing, he had no idea about Vesper's past. Nova wished she could tell him how impressive it was that he had picked up on her deeply buried melancholy without knowing the cause. He was the one who was good at reading people.

"You know her better than I do," she said, even as she wondered whether that was true. Regardless, the conversation had strayed into dangerous territory. It was time for a change of topic, and turnabout was fair play. "And since you know she's off the market, what do you think of Amelia?"

TJ huffed and looked down at the tabletop, fingers straying back to the bandage on his right hand. "She's been one of my best friends since freshman year."

"And?"

"And that's it." His tone was defensive, his jaw suddenly tight.

Nova studied him for a long moment. She didn't need any interpersonal skills to tell that her question had shaken him. "Feels like gravity to me, my friend," she said gently.

"Well, don't you two look as thick as thieves."

The soprano voice, melodious with amusement, pulled Nova's head around so quickly her vision blurred. When it cleared, Vesper was standing before them, polished and resplendent in a gray suit. The jacket was an off-the-shoulder cut that revealed the delicate contours of her collarbone in sharp relief against her pale skin. Nova felt her mouth open, but no sound emerged. Fortunately, TJ spoke for both of them.

"V!" he exclaimed in clear delight. Then, mindful of their public location, he lowered his voice. "How are you doing? Do you want to sit? Here, take my seat."

When Vesper rested one hand on his arm as he tried to stand, Nova felt a stab of jealousy that she was touching him instead of her. Clearly, she was going insane.

"Relax. I just came from a conversation with the casino manager. Everything's fine." Vesper must have noticed his bandage, then, because her smile suddenly vanished. "How's your hand?"

"Oh, it's nothing. Really." He held it up between them and clenched a fist. When the bandage got in the way, he moved to rip it off.

"Don't even think about it." Nova pointed a finger at him and tried to look severe. "*Certain people* will be very unhappy with you."

As a flush began to creep up from his neck, he pushed back his chair. "You really should sit. I need to go anyway. I just…" He paused, looming above her. "Are you okay? Like, really okay? In terms of your job and…everything?"

When Vesper's smile remerged, Nova felt her stomach flip. "Never better. I promise. And thank you for standing up for me last night." She arched one perfectly manicured brow. "Though if your father didn't read you the riot act about throwing punches—"

TJ's expression soured. "Believe me, he did. I know it was idiotic. And you didn't need me anyway. You handled that asshole just fine by yourself."

"Still, I appreciate the sentiment. Just not the violence." She checked her watch. "And yes, you should go if you're going to make it to the go-cart place in time for your reservation."

"Damn, forgot about that!" He kissed Vesper swiftly on the cheek. "Thanks. See you later." Nova watched him hustle away, mostly because she knew that as soon as she gave Vesper her undivided attention, she would have trouble breathing. "He turns into a puppy around you," she said, meeting Vesper's gaze only once the words were out of her mouth.

"He's a good kid." She perched lightly on the chair. "Man. He's a man, now."

Her body language was clear even to Nova; she wasn't planning to stay long. Wanting to keep her talking, she said the first thing that came to mind. "Sounds like you've watched that transformation happen, over the years."

That got her attention. "What has TJ been telling you?"

"That he was madly in love with you when he was younger."

Her lips curved slightly. "It was just an infatuation. He'll learn the difference someday." In another heartbeat, her expression grew serious. "And what have you been telling him?"

"Nothing." Nova wanted to reach for her hand but knew she couldn't. "You can trust me, Vesper."

Vesper searched her eyes. "Thank you," she said finally, though she sounded more apprehensive than relieved. "And thank you for being there yesterday."

"You meant what you said to TJ? No negative repercussions?"

"The opposite, actually."

"Oh?" Nova was intrigued by the energy that suddenly crackled around her. Had something good come of this mess? "Do you get to be the one to kick Biz out of the casino, I hope?"

"No. But he's going to formally apologize." She looked around the room furtively and then leaned in closer. "And in return for dropping the issue, I got what I needed to entice a new client here."

Nova didn't know how to respond to that. Vesper was letting Biz get away with a slap on the wrist in order to make some kind of trade? He had *harassed* her. An apology was the very tip of the iceberg. He should have spent the night in prison, or at least be barred from Valhalla. With Vesper still his host, he would have far too much access to her. What was to stop him from harassing her again, and possibly even hurting her?

Still, in the face of Vesper's obvious excitement, what right did Nova have to second-guess her? "Someone important?" she asked, hoping her dismay wasn't obvious.

But Vesper's eyes narrowed. "You don't think I made the right decision."

"Did I say that?"

"You didn't have to." She pressed her lips tightly together in clear displeasure. "What should I have done, according to you? Press charges? Tie up my money and risk my job?"

Nova felt as though she had whiplash. Numbly, she drank from her coffee, hoping the caffeine would jolt her brain into some sort of epiphany. What on earth had just happened? Moments ago, she and Vesper had been talking like confidantes, and now she was *persona non grata* for something she hadn't even said?

Like confidantes. The thought gave her pause. Despite last night, Vesper didn't trust her at all. That's what this was about. She didn't trust Nova to keep her secrets, and she didn't trust her to reserve judgment. At the slightest provocation, she had reacted defensively. After the night she'd had—after the *life* she'd had—Nova couldn't really blame her.

"I never meant—"

"I didn't say what I did last night so you could judge me." Vesper stood abruptly. "You don't get to do that. No one does."

"I'm worried about you! Judging you is the la—"

"I don't need you to worry about me." Vesper steamrolled right over her. "And one more thing. If you don't figure out how to control your face, you won't last a single round at the main event. You can trust *me* on that."

"AJ! There you are!"

Nova's whiplash became shell shock. Numbly, she looked up just in time to register Emily's broad smile before she swooped in to plant a kiss—as familiar as it was unwelcome—squarely on her lips. Precious seconds passed before Nova had the wherewithal to pull away.

"Em? What are you doing here?"

"We've been worried about you. You never write, you never call…" She cocked her head. "That, and I wanted to see this amazing suite of yours."

Vesper chose that moment to clear her throat, and Nova's stomach did a slow roll in response. What a spectacle she was making of herself. Fumbling for some measure of poise, she gestured between the two women.

"I'm so sorry. Vesper, this is Emily, one of my roommates back home. Em, this is Vesper—one of the hosts here. The one who is comping me the suite you mentioned."

Emily gave Vesper a once-over and extended her hand. "AJ's mentioned you a few times. Nice to meet you."

"Likewise." The chill in Vesper's tone could have frozen the desert.

"Did I interrupt something important?" Em asked. "I can wait in the lobby if you'd like."

"No. We're finished." Vesper barely glanced at Nova. "Enjoy your stay at Valhalla."

She turned and walked away without looking back, leaving Nova slack-jawed and reeling. Emily slid into the empty seat and reached for her hands. Nova watched as Em's thumbs made soft circles below her knuckles, but she couldn't feel it. She couldn't seem to feel anything.

"How's everyone back home?" she asked in an effort to seem normal.

"Liz and Sandra got a kitten. I think they're getting serious." When Em smiled, Nova forced herself to mirror the expression.

"Sounds like."

"I've missed you." When Em cupped her face and slid her thumb across Nova's mouth, arousal scorched through her like a solar flare, sharp and unbidden. Relief followed close behind. She wasn't numb, after all. "How about showing me that king-sized bed of yours, hmm?"

Nova turned her cheek into Emily's palm in an effort to recapture the easy chemistry they had always shared. She had been lonely and stressed since her plane had left San Francisco, and Em was the perfect antidote. So why did the idea of going to bed with her feel like cheating? Vesper didn't even want a one-night stand, not to mention a relationship. There was nothing—*nothing*—wrong with blowing off some steam with one of her roommates.

Nova stood and extended her hand, shoulders squared in determination. The heat of Emily's palm soaked into hers, stoking the flames. "Follow me."

CHAPTER ELEVEN

The anger was a hot coal in Vesper's chest, fanned by every breath. It burned away her gratitude, her sentimentality, her self-consciousness. What the hell was Nova playing at? That…that *woman* came out of the woodwork and she turned into putty? She hadn't mentioned a girlfriend, and she certainly hadn't been acting like she was in a relationship. Had she been lying by omission this entire time, or was *Emily* an actual roommate with benefits? Either way, Nova was clearly even more of a player than Vesper had originally realized. Shaking her head, she silently congratulated herself on being smart enough to avoid acting on her attraction. She had dodged a bullet, there.

As she waited for an elevator, her indignation picked up steam. Romantic status aside, how dare Nova judge her decisions? Had *she* passed judgment when Nova confessed to having dropped out of graduate school? No. It was a crazy thing to do, especially when Nova had been so very close to getting her doctorate, but Vesper had schooled her features and listened patiently. Whereas Nova had looked at her like she was an alien as she explained how she had bargained with Steve.

Tit for tat—that was how this system worked. At every level, hosting was all about *quid pro quo*. Did she want to see Biz again? Of course not. But would it be worthwhile to continue on as his host in exchange for being able to strike a deal with Priscilla Beauregard? That was a no-brainer.

Vesper glanced down at her watch. The Sphinx board meeting had adjourned for lunch half an hour ago. She had booked them a private alcove at Barri in case they wanted to continue discussing business over their meal, and it would be wise to check in with them to ensure everything was satisfactory. The only downside, of course, was Biz.

If her presence forced him to apologize in front of the senior board members, would he resent her for it?

As she waited for the elevator, she caught sight of her reflection in the gleaming metal doors. An unexpected wave of guilt washed over her. Why was she worrying about Biz's mental state? He was the aggressor and she the victim. If anything, he should be the anxious one. Then again, he had the money, and her entire *raison d'être* was to convince him to spend it at Valhalla—a fact of which he was no doubt aware. Despite the incident last night, the power was still firmly in his hands.

The doors opened and she stepped inside, mentally clinging to the smoldering ashes of her anger. When she walked through the doors of the restaurant, she needed to present a façade as impenetrable as diamond. These were corporate men, trained to sniff out weakness and capitalize on it. There could be no chinks in her armor, or she would lose their respect. And if she lost their respect, eventually, she would lose their patronage. Gamblers would never stop pushing her limits, always seeking out the fanciest suite, the newest show, the priciest meal. Her job was to give where she chose and take wherever she could.

As she approached the restaurant's frosted glass doors, Vesper nodded to the maître d' but didn't slacken her pace. She paused only when she reached the dark blue curtain separating the smallest of the restaurant's VIP areas from the main dining room, and then only long enough to sweep the fabric aside. The five men seated around the oval table were all dressed in black or charcoal suits. She recognized three: Theodore Senior, who wiped his mouth and stood as she entered the room; Biz, who got up a moment later; and Edward Mirallo, whom she had hosted twice in the past year and refused to play any game other than blackjack. The other two had either flown in for the day or were staying at other establishments.

"Good afternoon, gentlemen," she said, plastering a gracious smile onto her face. "Is the meal to your liking, I hope?"

"It's very fine, Vesper, as always." Hamilton's tone was warm and courteous, but whether he was simply being polite or had truly put last night's incident behind him, she couldn't say.

"These snails are unparalleled," Mirallo said, patting his belly. "I don't suppose you can convince the chef to share his recipe, can you?"

"Now why would she do a thing like that," asked one of the other men, "when she wants to entice you back as often as possible?"

Vesper laughed obligingly. "I'll certainly ask our executive chef, but she tends to be quite protective of her masterpieces." She emphasized the pronoun in the hopes that Mirallo might think twice about making gendered assumptions. "Is there anything I can do for you at the moment?" She met each man's eyes in turn—even Biz's. He was staring right through her in a way that made her skin crawl, but she refused to let that show. "Very well then, I'll leave you to your meal. Please let me know if you think of anything."

She turned, but not before seeing Hamilton nudge Biz discreetly with his elbow. As she let the curtain fall behind her, she caught the sound of him excusing himself. Sweat immediately lined her palms, and she silently cursed her own nervous system. She was in a restaurant full of people. There was nothing to fear.

"Vesper!"

She turned immediately, wanting to seem attentive. "Hello, Biz." Hearing her own voice, strong and steady, added to her resolve. "Something I can do for you?"

"I need to apologize for my behavior last night." The words lacked any inflection. Either Hamilton had spoon-fed him the line, or he had rehearsed it. Or both.

Vesper forced herself to smile brightly. "We've all done something we regret after having a few more than we should."

The set of Biz's shoulders eased. "Oh? What have *you* done?" That oily smile broke out on his face and he stepped closer. "Your secrets are safe with me. I promise."

Despite being in the center of a room full of people, Vesper felt cornered all over again. She should have coolly accepted his apology and then left. Instead, she had left the door open for his chauvinist comments.

"Oh, that was only a platitude." Hoping she had somewhat redeemed herself, Vesper turned and walked away. "Enjoy your afternoon," she said over her shoulder.

Vesper's heart didn't stop pounding until she was outside the restaurant and could be sure he hadn't followed. As she walked back to her cubicle, the adrenaline began to ebb, laying bare her exhaustion. She wanted nothing more than to go home and burrow under her covers, but between arranging Priscilla's credit line with the financial department and serving as the point person for the Sphinx board members staying at Valhalla, she wouldn't see her pillow until late in the evening.

"Vesper!" Isabella's voice scattered the bullet points in her mental to-do list. "I've been looking for you all day! What did you do—lose your phone?"

Vesper found herself wrapped in a bone-crushing embrace before she could reply. Chagrined at having ignored Isabella's increasingly frantic text messages, she hid her face against Isabella's shoulder as she formulated a reply.

"I'm sorry," she finally said as she pulled back. "Today has been hectic. I had to meet with Steve."

"You did? About..." She glanced around the hallway. "About what happened?"

Vesper decided to feign ignorance, mostly because she wanted to know what the rumor mill had come up with. "Wait, what did you hear?"

Isabella grabbed her hand and pulled her into a nearby alcove for vending and ice machines. The electric hum drowned out the sounds from the corridor. "I heard you got *attacked*," Isabella whispered, searching her eyes. "By one of your clients!"

Vesper rapidly tried to weigh how much she should confess. "I wasn't attacked, per se," she said slowly.

"Per se? What the hell does that mean?" With each successive syllable, her voice rose in pitch.

"Shh. Careful." Vesper kept one eye on the passersby as she spoke. "He'd had too much to drink. He said some inappropriate things and then tried to kiss me. That's all."

"Oh, really?" Sarcasm flooded her voice. "Because I heard he also had his hands all over you and ended up pinning you to the wall!"

Vesper blinked. The rumor mill was apparently quite accurate. Too accurate. She wanted everyone else to forget those details almost as much as she wanted them purged from her own memory. "He did have a bit of a case of wandering hands."

"And the wall?"

Her attempt to tone this down was backfiring horribly. "He crowded me a little. I overreacted and—"

"Kneed him in the balls." Isabella rested her hands on her hips, glaring. "Which was brave, and not in any way an overreaction to sexual assault. Sexual assault, Vesper! Why are you downplaying this?"

"That's a strong term. It really wasn't that big of a deal."

"It's the *right* term and a huge deal! If this had happened to me, would you be telling me to stick my head in the sand the way you're doing? Because if so, you're not the person I thought you were."

Vesper felt her hands go cold. Was Isabella saying their friendship was on the line? Over this? She was reacting ten times as fiercely as Nova had. What gave her the right? Why was this any of her business?

"If it had happened to you," she said fiercely, "I sure as hell wouldn't be yelling at you. Why are you judging me? It's over and done with. I just want to move on."

Isabella opened her mouth, apparently thought better of herself, and closed it again. For several moments, she worried at her lower lip with her teeth. "I'm sorry," she finally said. "I'm just worried about you."

The echo of Nova's sentiment gave Vesper pause. Doubt seeped into the corners of her mind. At every step, she had acted to protect herself—first from Biz, and then in terms of her career. She had to trust her own decisions. They had gotten her this far.

"I appreciate that. I really do. But I've handled it. Water under the bridge, okay?"

"Is he still staying here?"

The hard edge to Isabella's tone made Vesper realize she couldn't admit to continuing on as Biz's host. "Yes. It will be fine. He was drunk yesterday and not acting like himself." The white lie came too easily. Biz had been almost as much of a creep ten minutes ago as he had been last night.

"I don't like it. Promise me you'll be on your guard? Ask security to keep a special eye on him?"

That was a decent idea, and one that would make her feel better without endangering her job. "I'll do that. And I promise." She grasped Isabella's shoulders and pulled her in for another hug. "Thanks for watching out for me. I'd better get back to the office."

She nodded. "Drinks later?"

"Let's do tomorrow. I'm completely exhausted."

"Sure. Get some rest." Isabella turned, paused, and then looked back over her shoulder. "And keep your phone handy, okay? I'm going to check in with you. A lot. Deal with it."

She hurried out into the corridor and disappeared in the direction of the elevators. Vesper stared unseeing at the flashing buttons of the vending machine, trying to refocus herself. She had too much on her plate to be able to afford any more distractions.

But as she resumed the journey to her office, her thoughts refused to obey. She had turned on Nova because of a facial expression, but she'd let Isabella say her piece. Did she owe Nova an apology, now? Or was it all for the best that she had strained the unlikely bond developing between them? Nova might be good at playing the confidante, but that didn't mean she could be trusted. Her attraction was clear, but that obviously didn't mean anything.

No sooner had the thought crossed her mind than the memory resurfaced of Emily swooping in so confidently to plant a kiss on Nova's lips. In her weakest moments, Vesper had fantasized about doing exactly that. Now, she felt betrayed, though she had no right to the emotion.

But as she sat behind her desk and powered up her computer, Vesper glimpsed a hint of silver lining. She hadn't let down her guard enough to give in to her desire, and that was a positive thing. This entire episode with Nova was a hard lesson that only reinforced what she already knew: don't let anyone get too close. She had let Nova in too far. The only person she could trust was herself, no matter how much she might sometimes wish it otherwise.

The only solution was to keep her distance. No apologies, no contact. Cold turkey.

❖

Nova raked in the pot, cutting out a blue chip for the dealer in the process. "That's it for me," she said. "Have a good one, folks."

"Same here," said Mac, seated to her left. He had joined the table an hour after her and had been playing conservatively all afternoon.

As she racked up her chips, Nova mentally added up her winnings. Just over a thousand dollars—one of her better afternoons—but still not enough. If she kept winning at this rate, she would be able to enter five or six events, not counting the hold 'em tournament. Five or six didn't give her good enough odds of winning a bracelet. She needed more money, and she needed it fast, but the only way to get it, short of robbing a bank, was to return to the cash game and risk everything all over again. If the game had been online, she would have been confident enough to join it, but the thought of walking back into Davenport's Celestial Palace made her quail inside. The fear was unfamiliar and disconcerting. Nerves were a part of the game—they helped keep her sharp. But fear was crippling, and if she didn't find a way to master it, it would follow her into the World Series.

Mac joined her en route to the cashier. "Missed you at this week's big game," he said, as though he'd heard her thoughts.

She rolled her eyes. "I'll bet. No easy money this time?"

"Oh, there was." His grin was wolfish.

"Why play with the peons, then? And tightly, too."

"Practice for the main event. The first few rounds are full of rich tourists." He gestured for her to cash out ahead of him. "If I only play with professionals, I forget how to handle the crazy amateurs."

"Makes sense." Nova stepped aside and waited for him to finish. She enjoyed running into him on the Strip—usually at Caesars, which seemed to be his preferred poker hall. He was always friendly, unlike some of the others. Damon barely acknowledged her presence whenever they encountered each other. "Must be so frustrating to get knocked out early."

"It happens to at least one of the best, every year. My goal is to make sure that's not me."

"If we were drinking, I'd drink to that."

He smiled. "Why not? It's free."

Nova hesitated. Was there any good reason not to indulge? Back at Valhalla, all that waited for her was mediocre buffet food and a night of studying past poker games. Emily had left on Sunday night to make it home in time for her clerkship duties, and since then, Nova had felt equal parts relieved and unsettled. Being with Em had always been so easy, but every moment of their impromptu weekend together had been a struggle. Nova had done her best to act naturally, and she must have succeeded to a point, because Emily hadn't seemed to notice that anything was wrong. But something was. Nothing felt…right. Even the sex had been an effort, to the point that Nova found herself faking it on their last night together. She'd never had to do that before, and the experience had been disconcerting.

Also disconcerting was the absence of Vesper, who had been actively avoiding her for almost a week. Whenever they did see each other—mostly when TJ had invited Nova to join him in some activity—she would barely say two words before finding somewhere else to be. That Vesper was still angry seemed obvious. What she was angry about, on the other hand, was unclear. There were too many options for Nova to narrow it down.

"Sure," she told Mac.

They made their way over to the closest bar and sat in the far corner. At Nova's elbow, a video poker machine twinkled invitingly. In occasional moments of weakness, when the thought of sitting down at a table and rubbing elbows with strangers made her throat tighten in a rush of claustrophobia, she gave herself a break and played against the machine. It was comforting, but not at all useful.

When the bartender stopped by, Mac ordered a rum and Coke. "Just the Coke for me, please," Nova said. "Diet."

Mac shot her a questioning glance. "You enjoyed that fancy scotch way too much to be a teetotaler."

She tapped the side of her head. "Still need to stay sharp today."

"Heading back to the tables later?"

Nova decided to confess. Mac seemed like a decent guy, and he might even have some pointers. "No. At night, I study. Mostly, I watch former tournaments."

"You're working hard." Their drinks came, and he sipped at his before continuing. "If you don't mind my asking, what's your goal in all of this? Besides making money, of course."

Nova weighed her choices. She didn't want to tell him about the specifics of the sponsorship deal, so she needed a more generic answer. "You used to play online, so you know how it is. There's just no way to do it anymore in this country. So if I want to keep playing, I have to figure out how to succeed at the live game."

"True. And it's not easy."

"What was the hardest part for you?"

"I've always been a fairly conservative player, but when I started playing live, I totally tightened up." He grinned ruefully. "People like Damon scared the shit out of me. I had no idea how to deal with that kind of raw aggression, and I'd just sit there, frozen, letting the antes and blinds bleed me to death."

"He is terrifying, isn't he?" Nova thought back to her experience at the cash game. Damon was the kind of player who took control of a table easily, dictating its pace and the other players' bet sizes by being heavy-handed with his own chips. "How'd you get over it?"

Mac laughed. "I read his book, for one thing. And then I'd sit at tables like that"—he jerked a finger toward the one they'd just left—"and try to play as aggressively as possible."

"Did it feel horribly wrong?"

"At first, yeah. It was like pulling teeth. But I made myself do it until I stopped getting queasy every time I went all in."

"That's really admirable." Nova stared at him thoughtfully. "Do you feel like doing that changed your style of play at all? I mean, you're still a relatively tight player, as they go."

"I am. And that's the other thing I realized—that I'd never make it anywhere if I tried to play against my true nature. But now, when I *should* take a risk, I can actually do it."

Nova nodded, wondering if she dared to speak so candidly about her own flaws. For a while, they drank in silence. Above the bar, a wavy mirror held the reflection of the room behind them, distorting its lines and shapes like the inside of a funhouse. Mac seemed intrigued, but Nova looked away, her pulse rising as she deliberated. He might be able to offer her valuable advice. At the same time, revealing her Achilles' heel to an opponent was a terrible idea. Unless he already knew what it was.

"So your weakness is playing too tightly. What's mine?"

He raised his eyebrows. "Sure you wanna hear it?"

"I'd better, or I'll never be anywhere near the money in this tournament."

"Well, you've clearly got a good head for numbers, and you're smart about table position."

"But?"

"Look, everyone has tells. Everyone. But yours are on par with the flashing neon lights out there." He nodded toward the exit to the

Strip. "Why else do you think we started taking all your money after the break, that night you played in the cash game?"

His words only confirmed what she had suspected, but they still weren't easy to hear. "You just needed a little time to figure me out." Nova sighed and bowed her head…and realized her left leg was bouncing. "Shit, I'm broadcasting right now!"

"Mm. You don't much like to sit still, do you?"

"No," she said bitterly. "And playing one game at a time is so *slow*. You get that, right? I tried to explain online play to Vesp—to someone, recently, and she thought I was insane for playing five games simultaneously."

"Five?" He seemed impressed. "I usually played two. Never went above three."

"I was at my best playing five. Sometimes I even did more." She sucked down the dregs of her Coke. "It's the adrenaline junkie in me, I guess."

"What do you do, jump out of planes in your spare time?"

"I surf." Vesper felt her expression turn wistful. There was no sense in hiding it. "Out on the water…it's the only time I feel relaxed. At peace. I miss it like hell."

"But surfing is as much about patience as it is about adrenaline, isn't it? Waiting for the right wave and then timing it properly?" Mac cocked his head. "Actually, that sounds a lot like poker, when it's being played well."

Nova blinked at him, teetering on the edge of a breakthrough. "That makes a lot of sense," she said. "I never thought of it that way before."

He shrugged and went back to his drink. Nova returned her gaze to the mirror, eyes tracing its crests and troughs. She flashed back to the ocean—to lying on her board, rising and falling in time to the swells, waiting for the perfect moment to begin paddling. Her chest felt hollow with need. What if Mac was on to something? She could be quiescent when she was waiting for the perfect wave. Why not, then, when she was waiting for the perfect hand?

The dealer directly behind them was shuffling his deck in preparation for the next round, his fingers made abnormally long and spindly by the mirror. She imagined sitting at that table, body planted in a chair but her mind free to float in the zone. Tranquil, surrendering to the flow, yet hyper-aware of her muscles, skin, breath. In such a state, she had control of every cell in her body.

In such a state, she might even be able to school her features enough to bluff.

CHAPTER TWELVE

Girls, a toast!" As Priscilla Beauregard raised her piña colada high, the gigantic oval diamond on her left hand refracted the shimmering lights of the nearby slot machines. Her three friends clinked their glasses with hers and then proceeded to sip delicately at their frozen drinks.

Vesper mentally reviewed their names: Mary, Susannah, Hazel. Mary was the short, stout one; Susannah the tall, willowy one who dyed her hair platinum blond; and Hazel was the shy, plump one who apologized and thanked people more than she should.

Of them all, Vesper liked Priscilla the best—and not just because she was the one with the money. Unlike Mary, Priscilla kept herself in decent shape, with only a slight bulge around her middle. Unlike Susannah, she hadn't attempted to color the salt-and-pepper hair that curled around her ears. And unlike Hazel, she spoke her mind frequently and often. In short, Priscilla Beauregard was the enemy of pretension. Vesper found that appealing, perhaps because she couldn't abandon it herself.

"Shall we continue on?" She gestured toward the room of slots adjoining Sól Bar that was next on their list of tour stops. Priscilla and company had arrived in the early afternoon, and after Vesper had explained all the features of their Celestial Palace, they had wanted a tour of the casino.

As she led them along the path through the heart of the slots, she explained what would happen when—never "if," of course—one of them hit a jackpot. They emerged from the twinkling, musical maze into the long rectangular hall that held the table games from blackjack to baccarat to Pai Gow. Where the path became a T, she paused to tell them about the daily lessons and tournaments, before guiding them down the right fork and into the room that housed the craps pit and cashier's cage. It was always noisy here, as high rollers tossed their dice and onlookers hooted and hollered in encouragement or sympathy.

"Oh, that looks so difficult," Hazel fretted, watching those huddled around the nearest table place their bets as a male shooter massaged the dice in his hand.

"The betting rules are a bit complicated," Vesper said, "but we offer daily craps lessons as well, if you're interested."

After a brief overview of the cashier procedure, they retraced their steps. This was the moment Vesper had been dreading. For the past week, she had assiduously avoided the Valhalla poker room, but she was obliged to at least mention it to her newest clients. Nova didn't play there every day, she knew, but the risk of running into her was still much higher than elsewhere. Vesper had seen her only twice since that last, heated conversation—once in the lobby and once at Sól having a drink with TJ—but on both occasions she had managed to extricate herself quickly.

Each time, she had been struck first by a bolt of pure, physical desire, followed by waves of anger, jealousy, and guilt. The feelings pursued her into sleep, where she found herself repeatedly plagued by an erotic and deeply disturbing dream. In it, she was lying naked in the pitch-dark beneath the lean, powerful body of a woman who was making love to her. Vesper always melted beneath her mystery lover, hands clenching and toes curling as the woman expertly stroked her toward climax. A heartbeat before her orgasm, a spotlight suddenly revealed the woman's face: Nova's, but where her beautiful eyes had been, bone-white dice showing snake eyes gleamed in the empty sockets. Vesper opened her mouth to scream, but instead she would wake—gasping, wet, and aching.

Never had a nightmare felt so good. She might be ashamed of the deep, visceral urges of her body, but there was no mistaking what it wanted. There was also no mistaking the risk in that desire. Vesper didn't need to be a psychologist to know that the dice were highly symbolic. Her reptilian brain might crave Nova, but the more highly evolved parts sensed danger.

With a start, she realized that she had led the ladies all the way to the threshold of the poker room, when her original plan had been to point it out from a distance. She cleared her throat and gestured toward the double doors.

"And here is our poker hall. Lessons there, as everywhere, are daily and free. We can take a closer look if you're interested." In the ensuing pause, she silently prayed that no one would speak up.

"Interested? I'll say we're interested!" Priscilla raised her half-empty glass for emphasis. "Aren't we, girls? Poker is so sexy. We watched *Casino Royale* on the private jet to get in the mood."

"I'd like that Daniel Craig to teach me poker." Susannah sounded wistful. "He has the most amazing eyes."

"I've played once or twice," Mary said, "but it's been years."

"I played strip poker in college a few times," Susannah said with a giggle. "But I don't remember the rules."

"Oh, I think I'll just watch," Hazel said nervously.

"Oh, no you won't!" Priscilla was adamant. "We'll get lessons."

Vesper, who had been trying to prepare herself, realized she was out of time. "Here it is," she said, every nerve tensing as she pushed open the doors. Immediately, she scanned the room for Nova's honey-colored hair and lean, bronze arms. Nothing. When the surge of disappointment trumped her relief, she knew she was in trouble. "Lessons are offered throughout the day, seven days a week," she added in an effort to stay focused.

Priscilla raised one eyebrow. "Private lessons."

Vesper's first thought was that she should have anticipated that demand. Her second was *Nova*. Her third was that now she had an excuse to go and see her. Her fourth was that Priscilla would probably prefer a male instructor. Her fifth was that she didn't care. Her sixth was that if she did break her silence with Nova, she would have to guard against any kind of emotional attachment.

"Of course," she found herself saying, as much to quiet her racing mind as to answer Priscilla's question. "I can arrange for a poker champion to visit your suite."

"A champion?" Susannah sounded excited. "What's his name?"

There it was—the gender bias. "This is a woman, actually. Her name is Nova. She won the largest online tournament in the world last

year, and will be entering the World Series of Poker in just over a week."
As she listened to herself brag about Nova's accomplishments, Vesper
felt as though she had entered some kind of warped parallel universe.

"She'll do," Priscilla said. "What time tomorrow?"

Vesper almost laughed. Priscilla was the definition of impatience,
and why not? She had the money to make things happen whenever
she wanted them to. Even so, Vesper wouldn't go so far as to make an
appointment on Nova's behalf.

"Let me check in with her tonight, and I'll let you know right
away."

"Excellent." Priscilla was staring at the nearest occupied table,
eyes gleaming in fascination.

Vesper agreed, with the exception of the voice of reason in the
back of her head warning her this was a terrible idea. For once, she
wanted to follow the example of the gamblers arrayed all around her
and drown out that voice.

For once, she wanted to take a chance.

❖

Nova sat on the edge of the couch, practicing her square breathing
even as she watched a younger, slightly less muscular Damon bully the
other players at his table. The sound of crashing waves filled the room,
broadcast from the suite's sound system connected to her iPod. After
returning from her chat with Mac last night, she had downloaded dozens
of hours' worth of ocean sounds. Hopefully, the rhythmic sigh of the
water breaking along invisible beaches and cliffs would help her remain
relaxed and calm as she studied past games. Tomorrow, she might even
try taking her iPod and headphones to a table. She had never made a
habit of listening to music while playing online—sometimes she did,
sometimes she didn't—but plenty of the top professional players wore
headphones. Some also wore sunglasses. Maybe she should try that,
too, not only because they would hide her eyes, but also because they
were a staple of her beach attire.

For that matter, maybe she should wear board shorts and a bikini
top to the tournament. Or a wetsuit. The mental image made her laugh.
Only then did she realize she had been zoning out for the past several

minutes. Grimacing, she leaned forward for the remote. "Focus," she muttered. "You have to focus."

The doorbell chimed. The unfamiliar sound startled her, and she dropped the remote. Its back panel fell off and batteries went skittering across the coffee table. "Damn it!"

She jumped up and hurried to the door, mentally cataloguing the possibilities. She hadn't placed an order for room service or housekeeping, and she hadn't told TJ her room number. A sudden thought made her blood pressure spike. Had a legitimate client just arrived, who actually deserved the suite? Was this a member of the casino staff, telling her she had to leave?

When she put her eye to the peephole, her heart tried to leap right out of her chest. Vesper was standing outside, dressed in a dark blue suit that made her hair seem as red as the sun setting over the Pacific. As Nova watched, immobilized by her own desire, Vesper frowned and began to turn away. As if released from a spell, Nova fumbled for the door handle and yanked it open.

"Um. Hi."

Vesper's eyes met hers, and Nova watched her pupils expand, swallowing up the green of her irises. Attraction. It was there, but only in the flickering of tiny muscles Vesper couldn't control. Otherwise, she seemed cool and professional as she turned back toward the door with a practiced smile.

"Hello, Nova. May I come in?"

"Sure. Of course." Nova backed up, trying to pull her act together as she held open the door. Vesper's arm brushed hers as she passed, and Nova's skin tingled as if from an electric charge. As she let the door close, Vesper took a few steps toward the sitting area, paused, and cocked her head.

"What exactly did I interrupt?" she asked, a note of laughter in her voice. The cry of a seagull punctuated her question, and Nova hurried to turn off the sound system.

"I was studying," she said. "And meditating. Well. Trying to."

"By doing physical violence to your remote control?"

"Oh, that." Nova turned to see her gathering up the batteries. "I dropped it when the chime went off. Still not used to a hotel room with a doorbell."

"Here you go." Vesper extended the reassembled remote.

"Thanks."

"Is your roommate still visiting?"

"Emily?" Nova felt her face go hot. Hopefully the blush wasn't visible beneath her tan. "Oh, she only stayed until the end of last weekend."

"I see. Well, I hope she had a good time."

Throughout the past week, Nova had often found herself hoping that Vesper's silence was indicative of jealousy. Jealousy was good. It meant she cared. But there hadn't been anything but mild curiosity and cool professionalism in her question and response. Had Nova misjudged her interest entirely?

As she mentally grasped for a response, Vesper's gaze fixed on the television. "When was this—two years ago?"

"Three." Nova sank into one of the armchairs, cradling the remote as gently as if it were one of the baby chicks she'd held way back in kindergarten. Her head was spinning, and not just from Vesper's nearness. This conversation felt completely surreal. Vesper was acting like nothing was the matter—like she hadn't spent the last week avoiding her. Like she hadn't sat in this room clutching a rum and orange juice for purchase while haltingly telling her life story.

Suddenly angry, Nova hit the pause button, forcing Vesper to look at her. Vesper might like playing mind games, but she wasn't interested. "I'm not sure why you're here. Is there something you need?"

"Yes." Vesper sat on the couch and smoothed her skirt along her legs. She had beautiful legs, slender and toned, but they were too pale. She was trapped, Nova realized—trapped inside that skirt, inside this building, inside this city. All day, every day. Had she forgotten the tickle of grass against her feet, or kiss of the tide on her toes? How long had it been since she'd had a vacation? Forever?

As the question crossed her mind, her anger melted away. Vesper had spent the past ten years fighting to survive, to make a place for herself in the world. Las Vegas might be a gilded cage, but she had bent its bars to her will. A daydream materialized before her mind's eye: buying two first class plane tickets to San Francisco; driving Vesper to the beach at Año Nuevo; walking along the sand as the surf frothed and bubbled around their ankles; teaching her the basics of surfing. But as quickly as it had come, the vision disappeared. She would have to win a bracelet to make that a reality.

"I need to apologize to you."

Nova struggled to refocus. "Apologize?"

Vesper nodded. "Last week, when I got angry…that was about me. I took out my own anxieties on you. I know you were concerned, and I appreciate it. I'm sorry I blew up." She leaned forward. "You didn't deserve that, especially after listening so patiently to me the night before."

Still chagrined at her own anger, Nova wanted to reassure her. "It was a stressful time. I understand." She paused, uncertain how much to say, before soldiering on. "Biz hasn't tried anything since then, has he?"

"Thankfully, he's been gone for most of the week on business. Though he'll return in a few days and stay through the World Series."

"Great," she said dryly. "Do you know his events? I can shadow him and try to knock him out, if you'd like."

Vesper laughed, and it almost sounded genuine. "That won't be necessary, but I appreciate your chivalry. And no, I don't know what he's planning." She cocked her head. "What about you?"

"My plans?" Nova shrugged and looked away. "I figure I'll enter several of the events with small buy-ins during the first few days, see how I do, and take it from there. Even if I don't win a bracelet right away, I might be able to add to my bankroll. And then there's the main event, of course. Royal Flush is picking up the tab on that one."

The plan didn't sound very convincing, now that she was describing it out loud. It was a scattershot approach, throwing seeds into the wind and hoping one of them took root. The games with low buy-ins would be packed with amateurs for that very reason, and she could hear Mac's warning in her head. The later games weeded out most of the low-hanging fruit with their steep buy-ins, but then, of course, she would have to risk more of her bankroll on a single event.

"Fair enough." Vesper was looking at her curiously. "But you still haven't explained how the ocean sounds fit in."

Nova felt her cheeks get warm. "It's kind of a long story."

Vesper arched an eyebrow. "Is there somewhere you need to be?"

"No. Of course not." Nova struggled for the right words until she realized what she was doing. The truth was the truth. If Vesper thought she was an idiot, then she could leave. Right? Right. "So, my mentality is…problematic for live poker. I'm not patient enough. And as you said last week, my face is an open book."

Vesper started to speak, but Nova raised one hand to forestall her. "I've been practicing—trying to bide my time and show no emotion—but it doesn't come naturally to me. One of the players at that cash game, Mac…I've seen him around town a few times, since then. He's kind of taken me under his wing. I guess. At any rate, we were chatting a few days ago, and I told him about how surfing is my hobby, and how it makes me feel."

Vesper leaned forward. "How does it make you feel?"

Nova forced herself to meet Vesper's eyes. They were green and deep and still, like the leaves of a redwood grove. The impulse to protect her own secrets was almost as strong as the urge to bare her soul.

"When I'm in the ocean, I feel calm. At peace. Patient, even, while I'm waiting for the perfect wave to gather." She shrugged, self-conscious. "He suggested that I try a similar approach with poker, mentally. That I might have more success that way."

Vesper stared off into the distance as she mulled that over. Nova found herself captivated by the graceful column of her neck and the shadows beneath her jawline. She wanted to kiss her everywhere—to coax heat and color into every inch of her pale skin. What would Vesper do if she got up right now, straddled her where she sat, and indulged that desire? Push her away? Pull her closer? Turn her head in indifference?

"And?" Nova blinked to find Vesper refocused on her. "Has it made a difference?"

"I'm not sure yet. I mean, I do find the waves soothing. I just don't know if what I'm doing will end up helping me improve."

"What about visualizing? Do you ever do that?"

Nova grinned. "Sure. Every time I'm dealt a new hand, I picture pocket rockets."

Vesper extended one leg and nudged Nova's calf muscle with her toes. The movement was surprisingly familiar—almost intimate—and Nova sucked in a quick breath. If Vesper heard, she gave no indication.

"Not your cards. You can't control those. I meant visualizing yourself staying calm and showing no emotion. Maybe you could do it in front of a mirror?"

Nova swallowed a snarky comment about voyeurism. "That's a thought."

Silence fell between them, then—an awkward pause that amplified the tension in the room. Nova stared down at the faint scars on her knees, feeling as though she were a teenager again. Under normal circumstances, she would have done what she usually did in the presence of a beautiful woman who piqued her interest: flirt. Not that she was all that good at it anymore, if she were being honest with herself.

After her junior year lab partner had precipitated her coming-out epiphany, the rest of college had been marked by a parade of women. Most of the female members of the Gay/Straight Alliance had considered her fresh meat, and she'd been happy to oblige. None of them lasted more than a month or two, right up through graduation. She'd had a fling with a barista during the intervening summer before graduate school but had returned to campus unattached. Then, she'd discovered the Women in Science Program, and most of her current roommates. Who needed to flirt when there was always someone to scratch the itch at home?

But being out of practice wasn't her only problem. When she thought back to how she had objectified Vesper at their first meeting, Nova wanted to slap herself. She felt no better than Samuel or Biz, even though rationally, she knew she had never crossed the line. Still. Did Vesper want to be wanted? Sometimes, Nova thought so, but until she could be sure, she wasn't going to risk aggravating the wound Biz had reopened.

Paralyzed. That's what she was. Trapped by her own guilt. A wave of claustrophobia rose to choke her, and she quickly looked up, hoping to find relief in the spaciousness of the suite. Instinctually, she focused on Vesper, who was staring at her with a thoughtful expression. The panic did a cartwheel and turned into self-consciousness.

"Is something wrong?" She tried to make light of the moment. "Did I put my shirt on backward? Ever since they stopped putting tags on clothes, I've had real trouble."

Vesper's answering smile was distracted. "Nothing's wrong. You're fine. I just have a favor to ask."

A favor. The phrase jarred her like seawater up her nose. Vesper said she had come to apologize, when really she had an ulterior motive. Nova could hear the echo of her words from their first real conversation at the bar. *That's how this business works*, Vesper had said.

Business. Was that all she was to Vesper, even now? A transaction? A tiny cog in the wheel of her plan to rise to the status of superhost? More hurt by the prospect than she could have predicted, Nova remembered the crash of the ocean and tried to school her features.

"Oh? What is it?"

She must have done a decent job, because Vesper didn't seem to notice anything amiss. "This newest client of mine, Mrs. Beauregard, asked for private poker lessons for herself and her three best friends. The first person I thought of was you."

For a split second, Nova felt honored. Then, she realized Vesper was probably just feeding her a line in the hopes that she would say yes. Not that she really had a choice. How could she turn down the woman who had been comping her a suite for weeks?

"Sure. No problem."

"Great. How's tomorrow?"

"Anytime is fine. Professional player, remember? No set schedule."

A hint of her bitterness must have shone through, because Vesper's eyes narrowed slightly. Nova concentrated on smiling and asking for details: timing, location, whether she would need to bring any equipment.

"I'll provide everything. I think they'll want to play in their suite, but I'll double-check on that and the time." She stood. "Can I text you in a little while?"

"Sure." Nova tried not to say anything else, but somehow, "Anytime," slipped out right afterward.

"Thanks again."

Instead of skirting the outside of the coffee table, Vesper took the inside track. Their knees brushed as she passed by. Nova might have been pissed off and disappointed, but the fireworks flared nonetheless. She followed Vesper to the door and held it as she left. Her hair smelled faintly of lavender. Nova wanted to feel it brushing against her collarbone as they moved in synchrony. Naked.

Damn it.

"Good night."

Vesper sounded so self-possessed. For one terrifying moment, Nova wanted to grab her by the shoulder, clutch a fistful of that hair with her other hand, and kiss her breathless. The polished veneer would slip away as Vesper melted into her embrace, a soft whimper rising from the back of her throat. She knew it would.

In another instant, the impulse had passed. It frightened Nova so much that she mumbled something vaguely approximating a good-bye and closed the door. Suddenly shaky, she sank to the floor, pulled up her knees, and rested her head in her palms. Her heartbeat was erratic and her head was pounding and she really, really didn't want to be this worked up about a woman.

Not a woman. Vesper. Who saw her as a pawn in the game of chess she was playing with her superiors.

Sitting on the floor became too pathetic—and too uncomfortable—after a few minutes, so she pushed herself up and moved toward the bedroom. On the way, she pressed the Play button on her iPod. At the first whisper of waves against the shore, she felt her pulse begin to slow. Women would come and go, but the ocean would endure forever.

It should have been a comforting thought, but tonight, she just felt lonely.

CHAPTER THIRTEEN

Vesper surreptitiously checked her phone while listening to James whine. The weekly hosts' meeting always devolved into a pissing contest, and with the World Series beginning the day after tomorrow, everyone was in a frenzy. Clients were popping up like gophers, wanting a last-minute piece of the action, and Valhalla was bursting at the seams.

"This guy is a textile mogul from Bangkok!" When sniggers greeted his announcement, James threw up his hands. "Laugh all you like, but he deserves a suite."

Crickets. Vesper tuned out the ensuing chatter. All of her clients were cared for. The Hamiltons would return tomorrow night, as would Biz. The only one of her people at risk was Nova, but if she stayed quiet, maybe James would badger someone else out of a room.

She refreshed her email and glanced at the time. Nova's third lesson with Priscilla had begun an hour ago, and she wanted to be there. Anywhere but here, but especially there. Vesper had sat in on the first lesson, where Nova had proven to be as patient a teacher as she was impatient the rest of the time. When it became clear that Hazel was never going to remember the ranking order of hands, she had helped her make a cheat sheet. When Susannah had triumphantly laid down a pair of kings without realizing she also had a flush, Nova hadn't poked fun. And when Priscilla had asked about bluffing strategies, Nova had paused before turning to meet Vesper's gaze full on for the first time that day. For once, her eyes had been unreadable—ironic, given what she had said next.

"To tell you the truth, I'm not very good. Vesper has a much better poker face. She could probably give us all some tips."

The hint of challenge in her words, combined with her unusually avoidant behavior over the past few days, had piqued Vesper's curiosity. Work kept her from attending the second lesson Priscilla had scheduled, but if she could make it out of here within the next hour, she might be able to catch the tail end of this one. She wanted to be attentive to her most important client, of course, but that wasn't the only reason for her sense of urgency. Being around Nova was…nice.

No. That was absolutely the wrong word, because being around Nova made her feel like a comet hurtling toward the sun. When had she started to crave that feeling? And why? It wasn't comfortable. It certainly wasn't safe. And it wasn't as though she knew how to manage it. Every time they were in the same room, the chemistry fizzled out into awkwardness. Just a few weeks ago, Nova had been so eager to make a move. Why was she holding back now? The attraction hadn't disappeared—of that much, Vesper was certain.

She stabbed at a new email with her thumb more firmly than she had intended. The bigger question was why she was sitting back and letting Nova set the pace. If she wanted a fling, why not go get it? Because she never had? What about all the other times in her life when she'd taken a chance? Riding the elevator up to Samuel Chelton Jr.'s office. Feeling the blast of heat on her face as she'd climbed the steps of the Greyhound bus. Presenting her fake ID at the Sandia Casino when she'd applied to be a dealer. She had always possessed the courage to go after what she needed to survive. The thought of needing another person in that way was terrifying, but that wasn't what was happening with Nova. Vesper didn't need her, but she did *want* her. Why not be proactive and assertive now, then? Why not go after what she wanted, even if it was a luxury?

Over the years, there had been other women she had found attractive, but none had ever moved her to action. Nova stirred some essential part of her that had been locked in hibernation since she was sixteen, but just because her body was waking up, that didn't mean she had to become emotionally involved. Besides, in a few weeks, Nova would be back on her beloved West Coast—with or without a bracelet. This could be the summer fling she'd grown up too quickly to have.

"Vesper!" James's grating voice interrupted her reverie. "What about this chick you have in one of the Midgards?" He glanced down at a piece of paper in his hand. "Novarro."

Vesper's shoulders tensed. "What about her?"

"I pulled her records." He waved the paper in her face. "She's a poker player who barely even plays here! Why the hell are you comping her a suite?"

"She's the reigning champion of Royal Flush's annual tournament." Vesper spoke to give herself time to think. How hard should she fight for Nova? If she gave in, James might feel slightly in her debt—unless, of course, he made her look bad in front of her peers. Then he would feel macho and vindicated.

"And I'm the reigning champion of beer pong at my college fraternity," he retorted. "Who gives a fuck?"

Vesper stared at him for several seconds, pretending to think, when in fact she had already made up her mind. She combed the fingers of her right hand through her hair, shaking out the silky ends against her shoulders. When he licked his lips, she knew he was distracted.

"You know, James, that's fine. You can have the suite." She glanced at her watch. "When does your client arrive?"

"Uh." He seemed surprised that she hadn't mounted a stronger opposition. "His flight lands at eight."

"She'll be out by five." She scraped back her chair. "I'll track her down now."

"Thanks." James still seemed confused. She smiled briefly at him before walking through the door, and then quickened her pace as soon as she reached the hallway. She had a legitimate reason to leave the meeting early, and she had denied James a clear victory. True, she had bad news to deliver to Nova, but she also had a solution in mind.

Hopefully, Nova would see it the same way.

❖

Priscilla Beauregard seemed bored as she sat sipping her Tanqueray and tonic, but by now, Nova knew it was a front. Her eyes, framed by red rhinestone bifocals, missed nothing. At the moment, Nova suspected that she was trying to figure out just how strong a hand

Hazel must have, since she was on the verge of seeing the river for the first time all afternoon. Instead of her usual move of folding after the flop, Hazel had called Priscilla's ten-dollar bet to see the turn. Then, she had confounded everyone by re-raising Mary's fifteen-dollar bet to twenty. The board was a motley rainbow: king of hearts, ace of spades, six of hearts, eight of clubs.

Hazel was one of the most conservative players Nova had ever seen, which led her to the easy conclusion that she had been dealt at least one ace, if not two. Susannah had folded, and silently, Nova encouraged Mary and Priscilla to do the same. Had Hazel been a stranger, Nova might have suspected her of lulling them in with her timid play, only to make a bid for control of the table. But unless she had completely misread her, Hazel was working with a very strong hand.

At long last, Priscilla slid a green chip into the middle of the table. "I know I shouldn't do this," she told Nova, her broad Texas vowels flowing like molasses, "but I have to know what in hell she's got!"

"I can always show you," Hazel said. Her speech was quick and quiet and clipped, the way Nova imagined a frightened rabbit would sound if it ever spoke.

"You're not supposed to do that, remember?" said Mary. "Nova said we should never give our opponents free information."

Nova smothered a smile. It was gratifying to see her lessons being absorbed. "It's true. Some players will show you their cards if everyone else folds, but I don't recommend it." She burned the top card in the deck and paused for dramatic effect before finally revealing the river card. The king of diamonds.

Hazel looked down at her cards, and then at her cheat sheet. A moment later, she gasped. Priscilla rolled her eyes. "Could you be any more obvious?"

"I'm sorry." When Hazel actually clutched the pearl necklace at her throat, Nova couldn't suppress the laugh that bubbled out of her throat. Instead, she tried to turn it into a convincing cough.

"Pardon me. Your bet, Hazel."

After some deliberation, Hazel pushed an orange chip into the pot. It was the largest bet anyone had made this afternoon.

"Fifty dollars?" Priscilla looked like she'd swallowed a lemon. "You'll bleed me dry!"

Only after Susannah rolled her eyes and Mary laughed heartily did Hazel smile. Not for the first time, Nova wondered how she had become part of Priscilla's inner circle. Brash and outspoken, Priscilla had said more than once that she admired women with "spine." How did Hazel fit in?

Grumbling, she tossed her own orange chip onto the pile and flipped over her cards. "Two pair, aces and eights. Now spill the beans."

Hazel revealed the king of clubs and the ace of spades. "Full house," she stammered. "I think."

"You think?" Priscilla snorted. "I should've folded early."

"Congratulations, Hazel." Nova gave her an encouraging smile as she pushed the chips in her direction.

The doorbell chimed. Susannah started to stand, but Priscilla gestured for her to stop. "Let the butler get it. That's his job."

Nova reached for the muck pile and began to reshuffle. "When a conservative player starts to make big bets, it's often true that they have a good hand. But it's also possible that they've been trying to lull you into a false sense of security about their playing style. They might not have anything and could be trying to scare you off." She turned to Priscilla. "When you're holding an ace and there's one on the table, it's hard to let go of your hand. I probably would've called, too."

"You're not just saying that to make me feel better, are you?" she said grumpily.

Nova pressed the heel of her palm to her sternum with a resounding thump. "You wound me. I only speak the tru"—she almost choked on that last syllable as Vesper came into view around the corner—"th."

Today, Vesper had forgone a power suit in favor of a black and ivory scalloped print dress that flared slightly just above her knees. The attire lent her a lighthearted air that was only magnified by her smile. She seemed in a good mood, but that could also be an act. In professional mode, Vesper was nearly impossible to read.

"How's the lesson going?" she asked after exchanging pleasantries with the women.

"Nova's a wonderful teacher," Hazel said earnestly.

"I have half a mind to enter this World Series she keeps talking about," said Priscilla.

"Why not?" Nova said. "There are a lot of events, some of which aren't very expensive in the grand scheme of things. The five-thousand-dollar hold 'em game is the day after tomorrow. That's half the buy-in amount of the main event."

"Will you be entering that one?" asked Mary.

"Absolutely." Nova tried to sound confident.

In the ensuing silence, Priscilla stood. "Girls, I think I'm going to take a little nap before our evening festivities." She turned to Vesper. "Nova continues to refuse any compensation for these lessons. Will you work on her for me?"

A completely inappropriate reply leapt into mind, and Nova clenched her jaw against it. Her brain insisted on painting a vivid image of exactly how Vesper could work on her—preferably in bed, naked. Her heart thumped almost painfully and her mouth went dry as she reached for the memory of the ocean in an effort to keep her arousal hidden.

"I'll certainly do my best." Vesper sounded vaguely amused. Nova didn't dare look at her. Was it possible she'd had a similar thought?

"In the meantime," Vesper continued, "is there anything you need from me? Are you still happy with your dinner reservation for six thirty?"

"That's fine. Go relax. Find us at the blackjack table later."

Nova followed Vesper down the hallway and couldn't help but admire how the fabric of her dress hugged the slight flare of her hips. Blinking hard, she tried to focus. For the past week, she had woken up periodically throughout the night from vague, anxious dreams. The tournament was psyching her out even before it had begun. She knew she should go down to the poker hall and practice, but the thought of putting in more time for measly money made her want to slink back to her suite and curl into a ball beneath the covers. Where were her killer instincts? When had she begun to fear the rush instead of crave it? Had she lost her urge to walk the knife edge between genius and insanity? When she thought back to all her nights spent in front of the computer, alternating coffee with Red Bull as she lorded over multiple online tables simultaneously, she felt as though she were remembering someone else's life. What did that mean?

All she really wanted was to share a quiet drink with Vesper and forget all about poker for a little while. She wanted to feel the way she'd felt when Vesper was confiding in her—like a real human being, instead of a desperate grinder or a stone-faced statistician. But Vesper was probably too busy, and a simple date wouldn't help to advance her career. Nova was more resigned now than bitter at having played the role of Vesper's bargaining chip, but the thought still stung.

When they emerged into the corridor, Vesper turned to face her. "I have some bad news. Management needs your suite. Right away. I'm sorry."

Nova took an involuntary step backward and her stomach began to churn queasily. She was suddenly homeless. The tournament would begin in two days. Damn it, she should have expected this to happen. During her first few days in the suite, she hadn't even unpacked, certain that at any moment she would be asked to leave. Over time, she had grown complacent, and that was no one's fault but her own. Not only would she have to start depleting her bankroll by paying for a room— she would first have to find a vacant one. Even the Motel Sixes might be booked at this point.

"Oh. Okay." Struggling not to show her dismay, she tried to muster up a smile. Vesper had been kind enough to comp her the suite. The last thing she wanted to do was to appear ungrateful. "I can't thank you enough for letting me have it for the past few weeks."

"What will you do now?"

"Hunt for a cheap hotel. Guess I'd better get to it." She raised her hand in an awkward farewell and started to turn.

"I have a different idea."

Nova raised her gaze to Vesper's and was surprised to see a blush rising to her cheeks. "Oh?"

"I have a sleeper sofa in my living room. You can stay there, if you'd like. It even has a view of the mountains."

Nova couldn't believe what she was hearing. She felt a little dizzy, and her head was ringing. Vesper was inviting her into her home? To stay? Her instinct was to accept, but... "I don't want to intrude," she heard herself say.

"I'm rarely there. You won't be intruding."

She tried to picture it: lying awake on a thin sofa mattress, staring up at an unfamiliar ceiling. Would she get any rest at all, knowing that Vesper was asleep just around the corner? Probably not. Did she mind? Definitely not. The real question was why Vesper had made the offer in the first place. What was in it for her? Nova felt like a novice playing at chess, unable to see enough moves ahead. But even if Vesper did have some ulterior motive, did that really matter? She was offering Nova something she needed—a place to sleep—and something she wanted: a chance for them to spend time together. Why look the proverbial gift horse in the mouth?

"You're very generous. Thank you." She focused back on Vesper and smiled. "On one condition, though—that you let me chip in for some groceries at the very least."

"This will sound pathetic, but I eat almost all of my meals here."

"You wouldn't if you'd ever had my frittata."

Vesper arched one eyebrow. "Just promise me you'll wash the dust out of the skillet, first."

"Not much of a cook?"

"I think it's an occupational hazard when you're around free food all day." Vesper began to move toward the elevator. "I have a few hours of downtime before I need to be back later tonight. I can take you over to the apartment now, if you want."

"I just need a few minutes to pack up."

"Text me when you're ready, and we'll meet in the lobby."

Half an hour later, as Nova walked past the World Tree Pool toward the front desk, she still felt like pinching herself. Had she really gone from living in a hotel suite, to being homeless, to being Vesper's roommate, all in the course of a single conversation?

"Checking out, please," she told the platinum blonde behind the counter. Not so long ago, she would have flirted with her, but the prospect held no appeal now. Maybe the thought should have given her pause, but it didn't. She just wanted to finish up quickly so that she could go home with Vesper.

Even the thought sounded titillating in her own head, but there was so much more to it than the distant possibility that they might end up in bed together. She wanted to see how Vesper arranged her living space, how she decorated her walls, what kind of items she kept close by. She wanted to know whether Vesper snored and how she rolled her toothpaste.

The intimacy of that particular detail brought her up short. *You're her guest, not her lover.*

"You're all set, Ms. Novarro," said the blonde, interrupting her self-recrimination. "Please come again soon."

Nova thanked her cursorily and retreated to the nearest bench. The lobby was the busiest she'd ever seen it, and it wasn't hard to figure out why. Large "World Series of Poker" banners had been strung between the massive pillars and over the front desk. Valhalla was one of the three casinos hosting the tournament, and this would be its first year hosting the final table of the main event.

"Ready to go?"

Nova turned at the sound of Vesper's voice. It was a little disconcerting to be looking up at her, and she quickly stood. "Ready when you are."

"We can take a shortcut to the bus stop," Vesper said as she led Nova toward a side door flanked by two potted plants and labeled *Restricted*. It opened onto a stifling corridor barely wide enough for the two of them to walk abreast. "Are you hungry?"

"Sure," Nova said, caught off guard by the non sequitur.

"Sure." Vesper gave her an exasperated look. "Does that mean, 'Yes, I'm starving,' or 'No, but I want to be agreeable'?"

Nova felt herself grin. She loved how easy it was to fall into banter with Vesper. "Can't it be, 'Yes, I'm starving *and* I want to be agreeable'?"

"In that case, we'll stop by the best Thai takeout spot in the city, which happens to be right around the corner from my apartment."

Nova's stomach chose that exact moment to gurgle loudly. Only when Vesper laughed did Nova realize she had never heard that sound before. "Dinner's on me," she said. "I'll have whatever you recommend."

"The drunken noodles are to die for."

The hallway culminated in another door, which stuck slightly as Vesper pushed it open. Sunlight streamed in, bringing with it a dry blast of heat. Nova stepped outside, took a breath, and coughed as the air seared her lungs.

"Damn. How do you get used to this?"

"I'm from Texas. I didn't have to. Come on. The bus stop will have shade."

"I can handle the heat," Nova insisted, not wanting to sound like a wimp.

"This is the desert, surfer girl. When there's shade, you stand in it."

"Surfer girl, huh?" As her eyes adjusted to the brightness, Nova realized they had emerged onto a narrow side street. She switched her duffel to her other hand and let Vesper guide her toward the far end of the street. "Want to hear something pathetic? This is the first time I've been off the Strip since I got here."

Vesper smiled. "You're not alone in that, believe me. Oh, good timing."

A bus marked "Spring Valley" was lumbering down the street, and Nova picked up her pace alongside Vesper's. They were the last people on board, but there was more than enough space for them to sit. Vesper waited for her to choose a spot and then took the seat immediately next to hers. What did that mean?

"Is it a long ride?" Nova asked, trying to sound normal even though their thighs were brushing.

"About ten minutes. Were you serious about having me order for you?"

"Sure." Nova immediately caught herself. "Which means, 'Yes, order me whatever you think is best.'"

"Mild, medium, or hot?"

Nova just grinned. As Vesper rolled her eyes and took out her phone, Nova silently thanked her Spanish heritage for a high tolerance to spice. No matter how crazy Vesper decided to get with her order, she would be able to handle it.

After tapping briefly on the screen, Vesper returned her phone to her purse. To distract herself from wanting to reach for Vesper's hand, Nova looked out the window. As the bus moved down Flamingo away from the Strip, the landscape changed quickly. The gleaming high-rises of the casinos gave way to strip malls and shopping centers. Every time they crossed a new side street, Nova would see an advertisement for a different housing community. The bus's windshield revealed the lofty Spring Mountains, their peaks marching toward the southwest.

The people around them seemed mostly local, with the exception of a few tourists who had chosen to wander off the beaten path. Many of the locals wore uniforms from one or another casino. Vesper was the most elegantly dressed on board. Other casino hosts didn't take the bus home, Nova realized. They probably leased fancy cars.

Suddenly, Vesper's fingers were stroking the back of her hand. Nova nearly jumped out of her skin, but the touch was as brief as it was unexpected. Normally, she would have interpreted any physical contact from another woman as a sign of interest, or maybe even an invitation, but with Vesper, she wanted to be especially careful.

"What are you thinking?" Vesper asked.

Nova wasn't going to confess that she had been thinking about how different Vesper's priorities must be from those of her colleagues. "I was wondering when you first came to Vegas," she said instead, wanting to put together the pieces she knew of Vesper's life.

The bus wasn't very full, and they weren't sitting in close proximity to anyone else, but Vesper still looked around warily before replying. "I was nineteen."

Nova rested one palm lightly on Vesper's knee, watching her face to make sure her touch was welcome. "We don't have to talk about it if you don't want to."

"No, it's fine. But maybe we can wait until we're alone?"

"Of course."

"Besides, here we are." Vesper pressed the button that signaled the driver to stop. "I always use that grocery store as my landmark."

"Oh. Good. Right." Nova felt silly for not paying more attention to the route. This was how she would have to commute to the casino from now on, after all. Because she was Vesper's new roommate. The thought still blew her mind.

Nova followed her down the steps and back out into the oven. As Vesper led her down a side street, she pointed out the pharmacy, the Laundromat, and a burger place that should be avoided at all cost because of a chronic history of food poisoning. The next door down, however, was the storefront for Bright Sun Thai. Its air was redolent of beef and peanut oil and garlic, and Nova's mouth immediately began to water. The restaurant area boasted only four tables, all of which were occupied. Behind them, the counter had been painted with a cheerful orange sun, caught in the act of rising from a turquoise ocean.

The young woman at the cash register greeted Vesper by name, but when she would have pulled out her wallet, Nova stopped her with a light touch on her arm. "My treat, remember?"

They carried the warm paper bags around the corner, where Vesper paused at a rectangular adobe building next to the local gas station and car wash. "This is it." She suddenly seemed a little shy. "I'm on the top floor. Hope you don't mind stairs."

"I've been riding too many elevators. Stairs will be good for me."

The front door had been painted aqua blue several years ago, and it could have used a fresh coat. Its hinges stuck a little as Vesper turned the key and pushed, but the hallway into which Nova followed her was brightly lit and smelled like Lysol. She followed Vesper up the wooden staircase, which needed a new coat of varnish but otherwise seemed sound. Four flights later, she trailed Vesper onto the landing and turned with her toward the door marked 3B. This door swung open smoothly onto a corridor painted the color of terracotta. Automatically, she toed off her sandals on the rug.

"Oh, you don't have to do that," Vesper said when she noticed, though Nova could have sworn she seemed pleased.

"Old habit."

The corridor forked to reveal the kitchen on the right and a small living room on the left. The tile on the kitchen floor was a pale shade of green and chipped in a few places, but the room was bright and clean. Nova followed Vesper in and set the bag down on the counter.

"So, this is the kitchen." Vesper pointed through the doorway. "That's the den, where the sofa is. And the bathroom branches off from there, too."

And your bedroom, Nova wanted to add. "Mind if I take a look?" she asked instead.

"Go right ahead."

The den was rectangular in shape, with the couch taking up most of the back wall. Nova set her duffel down next to the glass-topped coffee table and looked out the large window to her left. Below, the roof of the car wash shimmered in the heat, but directly ahead, a string of green and gray mountains loomed above the valley floor. The knot of anxiety in her chest loosened at the sight.

"Have you ever gone hiking in those mountains?" she called out as she glanced briefly into the bathroom and bedroom. The former was tiled in the same pale green as the kitchen. The latter boasted a simple queen-sized bed with a white coverlet. It was all too easy to imagine herself beneath the covers, moving languorously above Vesper as their legs twined together.

"I organized a hike for the Hamiltons once, up to Charleston Peak. It was beautiful."

Nova returned to the kitchen to see that Vesper had laid out napkins and utensils on a small wooden table in the corner, its surface inlaid with blue and white tiles. "I might have to put that on my to-do list before I leave," she said as she unpacked the takeout bags. "I'm definitely a water person, but in the absence of an ocean, mountains are the next best thing."

"TJ and his father are mountain people, as you can probably tell." Vesper's voice was slightly muffled as she rummaged in the refrigerator.

"And you?"

"I don't know. I've never seen the ocean."

The words smacked her down more effectively than a breaking wave. She couldn't imagine never having wiggled her toes in the sand; never having licked sea salt off her own lips; never having felt so small and yet so powerfully *aware* while staring at the place where the sea kissed the horizon. The ocean was a part of her, and she felt its absence like a phantom limb. But Vesper couldn't miss what she didn't know.

Vesper crossed the room holding a ceramic pitcher painted to resemble a lemon. "Lemonade," she said as she plunked it down on the table. "But I have wine and beer if you'd like something stronger."

Nova bent to fiddle with the hem of her shorts, not wanting Vesper to see her face until she was sure she had mastered her emotions. Even a hint of the pity she felt would ruin everything. "Lemonade's perfect. Thanks."

For a while, their discussion centered on the food. Vesper hadn't been wrong. Bright Sun's drunken noodles were loaded with flavor. As they ate, she shared a few stories about some of the most exotic dining requests she'd received from clients, including a man who had been intent on tasting *fugu*, the dangerously toxic Japanese puffer fish. During one of the lulls in their conversation, Nova realized she had been given exactly what she'd wished for: a relaxed date with Vesper that had nothing to do with poker.

"I might want this every night," she said, wondering whether Vesper would realize she wasn't just talking about the food.

"I confess, there have been weeks when I've eaten from there multiple times." Vesper either hadn't noticed the subtext, or wanted to ignore it.

"How did you find it?"

"The day I moved in, there was a line out the door, so I knew that was a good sign." She pushed back her plate and regarded Nova thoughtfully. "Speaking of which: I didn't mean to put you off, earlier. I don't talk about my past very much."

"I'm sorry I brought it up." Nova wasn't surprised, but she couldn't help wishing Vesper felt comfortable enough to entrust her with some of the details. "We don't have to talk about it."

"No, it's fine. I just…" Her gaze dropped to the tabletop. "More than anything, I think I'm self-conscious. I came here with practically nothing—one suitcase full of clothes, a few thousand dollars, and the number of the landlord here." She gestured to the apartment. "He's the brother of one of the dealers I worked with in Albuquerque."

"What made you leave?" Nova didn't want to press Vesper for more details than she was willing to share, but she wanted to know more than simply what had happened. She wanted to know *why*.

"I didn't have any reason to stay once I'd built up a small nest egg and my cousin graduated. I could have worked my way up the ladder there, but it was a small-time scene compared to Vegas. When I arrived, Valhalla had just opened, and they hired me to deal the card games on the graveyard shift."

"Ouch. That must have been painful. What made you choose casino work?"

"I started off waitressing in one. Pretty soon, I realized the dealers made better tips, so as soon as I could, I went to dealer school."

Nova thought back to her own life as a seventeen-year-old. By that time, she had exhausted all of the math courses at her high school and was taking more at the local community college. She was the captain of the chess team. Every spare moment, she spent surfing. She earned a little money on the side tutoring her peers, but other than that, she hadn't worked a job during the academic year. Every night, she returned to her parents' modest split-level in Claremont, where they shared the evening meal together. When she had told them she wanted to attend Stanford instead of getting a free ride at Berkeley, they hadn't batted an eye.

She had taken her privilege for granted. Guilt formed a lump in her throat, making it difficult to swallow. "You're amazing," she managed to say.

Vesper stood and began to stack their empty plates. "I did what I had to."

It was the second time Nova had expressed her admiration, and the second time Vesper had completely downplayed her accomplishments. Nova couldn't stand it. She followed Vesper to the garbage can, and when she turned around, Nova gently but firmly grasped her shoulders.

"Vesper. You left your home to protect your family. You built a life for yourself out of nothing. You've climbed the ladder from dealer to host." Nova stared down into her eyes, bright with remembered pain. "You're the most remarkable person I've ever met. I wish you could see yourself the way I do."

When Vesper started to shake her head, Nova lost hold of her self-restraint. Her words weren't working, but there were other ways to communicate. She raised her hands to cup Vesper's face and finally gave in to the pull of gravity. Vesper's mouth was soft and warm and yielding, and Nova felt more than heard the whimper of pleasure that rose from her own throat. She wasn't ashamed. Her fingertips were trembling against Vesper's jaw, but she wasn't ashamed of that, either. When had a kiss ever meant so much?

A wild, starving part of her wanted to plunge inside and claim Vesper in some deep, visceral way, and she shuddered with the effort of reining herself in. Vesper had suffered at the hands of the men who had tried to take advantage of her. The last thing Nova wanted was to be like them. Tenderly as a ripple on the water, she mapped the contours of Vesper's mouth with her own before reluctantly pulling away.

Eyes wide and cheeks flushed, Vesper looked even more alluring than she had a few moments before. As Nova watched, her tongue darted out to moisten her lips, tasting the echo of her kiss. Such a tiny movement, yet Nova found it unspeakably erotic. It was all she could do not to slide her hands down to grip Vesper's waist and pull her closer. Instead, she let her arms drop to her sides.

"I'm not sorry I did that," she said hoarsely. "I've been wanting to for weeks. But all it will take is one word from you, and I'll walk out of here. You'll never have to see me again."

Vesper didn't speak. She took one step forward, slid her arms around Nova's neck, and pulled their bodies flush. Nova had just enough time to gasp at the sensation before Vesper rose to her toes and kissed her.

This kiss was nothing like the other. Vesper slipped her tongue inside, setting off fireworks in Nova's brain. When she sucked hard, Vesper's hips rocked forward. Nova wrapped her arms around Vesper's lithe waist, clutching her tightly as her fears receded. Vesper had initiated this. She wanted it. And dear God, her mouth was so sweet.

As their tongues tangled together, Nova stroked up Vesper's spine while pulling her even closer with her other hand. When Vesper's fingernails bit into the nape of her neck, Nova was filled with the desperate urge to get closer. She leaned back against the counter and shifted her thigh between Vesper's legs, groaning when Vesper flexed her hips again in response. *Her.* Vesper wanted *her.*

"You feel so good," she whispered, flicking her tongue out to taste Vesper's earlobe before trailing a line of kisses down her neck. Vesper tilted her head back even as she continued the rhythmic, circular movements of her hips. When Nova nipped at the skin above her collarbone, Vesper cried out softly. Inflamed by the sound, Nova crushed their mouths together, feeling her control slip away as their tongues battled for dominance. Vesper's unabashed sensuality was melting away the dregs of her reason. Soon, she wouldn't be able to stop. If Vesper had been any other woman, she wouldn't have hesitated to suggest they move to the bedroom.

Instead, she pulled back. "Vesper. I—I'm losing my grip, here. I think I need to cool off."

"I'm sorry to hear that." Her voice was breathless, and her eyes glinted with a sensual ferocity.

Nova rubbed her thumbs lightly over the twin swells of Vesper's hipbones. "Does that mean you don't want me to go?"

"I don't want you to go." Vesper glanced behind her shoulder and sighed. "But I have to. The ladies will be expecting me to cheer them on at blackjack tonight." With a reluctance that didn't seem feigned, she stepped away. "I'll probably be back late."

"Okay." Nova wasn't sure what else to say. *I'll miss you* was the first thing that came to mind, but that would sound pathetic, if not downright clingy. "Any chores I can do while you're gone?" she said instead, wanting to at least make herself useful.

"No." Vesper fixed her with a stern look. "And no cramming,

either. You should relax. Sleep. The next few weeks will be manic. You'll do better with a clear head."

"A little assertive, aren't you?" Nova teased her.

Vesper walked across the kitchen, opened a drawer, and extracted a key dangling from a metal ring. She returned to press it into Nova's palm, then lightly traced the edge of her wrist with a single fingertip. "You have no idea."

Desire sliced through Nova like an invisible sword. She had no doubt that Vesper would be as demanding in bed as she was outside of it. "Just to warn you, I'm no pushover either."

"I never thought you would be." Like a cloud moving across the face of the sun, Vesper's expression grew thoughtful. She raised her free hand as if to cup Nova's cheek, but then evidently thought the better of it, toying instead with the top button of her shirt. "We're on the same page about…this. Right?"

Nova buried a surge of uneasiness. "Why don't you tell me what you're thinking, and I'll let you know."

Vesper's eyes searched her for a long moment. "I like you," she said, almost brusquely. "But I don't have time for anything serious, and in a few weeks, you'll be gone."

"That's true." Relief almost eclipsed her disappointment, which was itself unexpected. Why should she mind that Vesper's expectations were the same as hers had always been with the women she'd fooled around with? Vesper was right. In a few weeks, the tournament would be over, and then she could return to Palo Alto with a golden bracelet and enough prize money to buy the house she had promised her friends.

Only the chances of winning a bracelet seemed less and less the more she played. And the prospect of returning to her former living situation made her feel more claustrophobic than comfortable. She missed her roommates, but as the days passed, she communicated with them less and less. And even in her neediest moments, she had never craved any of them the way she had come to crave Vesper.

Refusing to think through the implications of that realization, she brushed her lips fleetingly across Vesper's, hoping to whet her appetite. "I'm up for whatever you want," she said, praying that her voice sounded more casual than she felt. "You're in charge, okay?" And then, she bent her head so that her mouth was a mere fraction of an inch from Vesper's ear. "At least, until we're in bed."

When Vesper exhaled sharply, triumph sang through Nova's veins. A moment later, though, Vesper had mastered herself enough to take a step backward, eyebrow arched in a perfect bow. "You'd like to think that, wouldn't you?" she said defiantly.

Nova had heard and felt enough of Vesper's responsiveness to be confident in her instincts. Besides, Vesper spent all day, every day making power plays and brokering deals, perfectly in control of the chaos that was her chosen occupation. Wouldn't she want someone else to take charge during intimate moments? "Go work," was all she said aloud. "I'll be here."

"I'm glad." Once the words were out of her mouth, Vesper seemed oddly flustered. Nova retreated to the sleeper sofa and pretended to be absorbed in figuring out the remote as Vesper moved purposefully around the apartment. By the time she was at the front door, Nova had figured out how to turn on the television and navigate the channels.

"Sure you can't stay here and watch cheesy TV?" she asked with a feigned nonchalance.

"Yes. No." Vesper worried at her lower lip with her teeth. "Yes, I want to. Okay? No, I can't. I'll see you later. Call if you…need anything."

She was out the door in a heartbeat, leaving Nova alone on the couch. The show played on, unheeded, as she tried to process everything that had happened over the past few hours. Last night, she had slept in a king-sized bed at Valhalla. Tonight, she would crash on Vesper's sleeper sofa. There was no place she'd rather be.

The thought should have frightened her, but it didn't.

CHAPTER FOURTEEN

Vesper stood between Hazel and Susannah, watching Priscilla roll the dice. On this, their last night at Valhalla, Priscilla had finally decided to try her hand at craps, and so far, the results were spectacular. She had started off placing ten-thousand-dollar bets, but as her confidence level rose, so had her wagers. As Vesper watched, she pushed one hundred thousand dollars in chips on the pass line.

Across the table, Theodore Senior was focused on the action, but TJ raised his head and caught her eye. From the expression on his face, she could tell he had never seen someone risk that much money on a single roll of the dice. Word had spread about the high roller in the craps pit, and onlookers were trickling in for a look. While Priscilla blew on her fingers for luck, Vesper signaled to one of the waitresses that she should get extra help. Watching a game like this made people thirsty. Quenching that thirst made them looser at the tables.

The spectators murmured as the other players began to offer encouragement. By this time, almost all of them were betting with Priscilla. Her current hot streak had lasted fifteen minutes. As her fingers curled around the dice, a hush fell over the crowd.

"Here we go," she said, her voice clear and strong. The dice skittered across the table, hit the back wall, and rebounded to reveal a five and a six.

"Yo-leven," the dealer proclaimed, his voice all but lost beneath the triumphant shouting. TJ pounded his father on the back, and Mary, who was playing to Priscilla's right, jumped up and down in her excitement.

"You did it, you did it!" she cried, throwing her arms around Priscilla.

"Settle down, now," Priscilla said, patting her hair to make sure the enthusiastic embrace hadn't mussed her updo. But she was smiling broadly, and her eyes were bright with excitement.

Three bartenders returned with trays full of complimentary drinks, trailed by a second pit boss and a security officer. Vesper nodded to them, unsurprised. This table was the hottest action in the entire casino right now.

When Priscilla pushed an even larger stack of chips onto the line, the murmurs began anew. Soon, Vesper was hearing "one-twenty-five K's" repeated throughout the throng. She didn't know whether to hope for Priscilla's hot streak to continue or to snap. The more she won, the more she would inspire everyone around her to play in the hopes of having similar luck. On the other hand, she was up well over a million dollars by now, and Vesper's bosses wouldn't like that much.

As Priscilla prepared to shoot the dice, Vesper felt her phone buzz. Jeremy. She excused herself to Mary and Susannah and retreated toward the door. "What's up?"

"Ms. Blake," Jeremy said in the tone he always used while speaking with her in front of clients. "Mr. Deloreo and I are minutes away. He'd like you to meet him in the lobby." From the strain in Jeremy's voice, she could tell he didn't like the message he was delivering.

"I'm in the craps pit, and that's where I'll stay. He can find me there if he wants. Mind delivering that more diplomatically?"

"With pleasure," Jeremy said, now sounding amused.

She ended the call and returned to the table to find that Priscilla had set the point at eight. TJ promptly made a come bet, while Theodore Senior placed a field bet. Priscilla rubbed the dice between her hands and her lips moved silently. At times like these, with an entire room hanging on the outcome of one flick of the wrist, even Vesper felt caught up in the action. As she looked at the faces around her, she saw her own anticipation mirrored and magnified. The only difference between her and them was that she never lost sight of the sword above their heads.

Vesper closed her eyes as the dice bounced across the felt. The room held its breath, then roared. She smiled as Susannah clutched her shoulder, and opened her eyes to see that Priscilla had rolled a five and a three. As she watched, Priscilla spun triumphantly in a circle. Her elation was contagious.

"Hey, sexy." Biz's voice, accompanied by a heavy, moist hand on her shoulder, popped her good mood like a bubble. "Miss me?"

"Good evening, Mr. Deloreo." Vesper put a foot of space in between them as she spoke. Unsurprisingly, he reeked of alcohol. Did he have anxiety about flying, or was he just a drunk? "How was your trip?"

"Who cares? I'm here now." His hand stroked down her arm. "Let's celebrate."

"I can arrange for you to join the players, if you'd like." Out of the corner of her eye, she saw TJ look up with a scowl, but she couldn't worry about him.

"I'd much rather play with you."

The last thread of Vesper's patience snapped. She linked her arm through his and pulled him toward the far corner of the room. Touching him at all made her nauseous, but she didn't want to cause a scene. The wool of his Armani suit was soft beneath her palm, and beneath the cloying smell of whiskey she could detect the muskiness of a recent cigar. He might wear his wealth on his sleeve, but she had faced down powerful men before. And this time, she had no intention of running.

"I refuse to tolerate this behavior from you," she said, turning her back to the crowd so he was the only one who could see her face. "We have a professional relationship. That is *all*. If you make another suggestive comment or try to touch me again, I'll report you to security."

"No. You won't." His mocking grin was insufferably arrogant. "If you do, I'll take my business elsewhere, and I'll spread the word that others should do the same." He leaned in closer, stale breaths puffing against her face. "Teddy Bear Hamilton isn't the only one with friends. By the time I'm done, no one will touch you with a ten-foot pole." He laughed. "What a shame, too. You could use a good, hard ramming."

Vesper felt her vision tunnel, until all she could see was his smug, oily face. Distantly, she was aware of her head throbbing in time with her heartbeat, but it almost felt as though the sensations were happening to someone else. Even as her pulse raced, an empty space seemed to open in her chest. Her mind had become oddly disconnected from her body. Was she in some kind of shock?

Biz took her silence for defeat. Leering down at her, he very deliberately cupped her cheek with one hand and rubbed a thumb across her lips. She could barely feel the touch. Had her face gone numb?

"I think I'll join that game now, sweetheart."

Some kind of instinctual autopilot took hold of her, then, guiding her back to the table at his side in just enough time to see Priscilla finally crap out. As Biz swaggered up to the dealer, Hazel grasped the same arm that had been linked with his.

"She just lost two hundred thousand dollars!"

"But she just *made* almost two million," Susannah said, laughing. "What a crazy night!"

Vesper's mouth smiled. Her lips formed congratulatory words. Her eyes watched the pit boss help Priscilla to gather up her winnings. Her hand signaled the bartender, and some part of her brain remembered that Priscilla was particularly fond of the piña colada. Vesper's arms opened to embrace Priscilla when she was finally able to make her way to them, and her ears heard the excited chatter of their friends. But her mind was spinning in free fall, racing ineffectually like a hamster wheel. A chill constricted her lungs, curling its icy fingers around her rib cage.

She was trapped. Again.

"Vesper?" Priscilla was standing in front of her, cheeks still flushed with exhilaration. The inch-long string of diamonds hanging from her ears glittered in the overhead lights. "You look like you've seen a ghost."

In a way, it was true. Vesper blinked and shook her head slightly. "I'm sorry. I was just lost in thought." She plastered a fresh smile on her face. "What a way for you to end this visit. I hope you're thinking about coming back?"

"What I'm thinking about is not leaving."

The words shocked Vesper out of her daze. Like rusty gears on a bicycle, her brain whirred and spun before finally settling into high gear. Priscilla's suite was set to be claimed in two days by a banker from Hong Kong—a blackjack whale who enjoyed playing poker on the side. He was a big spender and a loyal customer, and she doubted Steve would allow him to be bumped.

"But Priscilla—" Hazel began.

"I know you three need to get back home. You'll take the jet without me." She looked to Vesper. "Right?"

"Of course. I'll make the arrangements immediately." Vesper had never felt so thankful for a reason to sit in front of her computer. She wanted to be as far from Biz as possible. "Is there anything else I can do for you tonight?"

"Get some rest," Priscilla said. "You look exhausted."

Vesper refused to acknowledge her fatigue in front of her biggest client. It was a sign of weakness, and the last thing she wanted was to give Priscilla that impression. "Congratulations again." She turned and hurried toward the door, praying that some high roller had canceled their reservation within the last few hours.

TJ intercepted her a few feet from the exit. He loomed above her, frowning. "What did Biz say to you, V? Are you okay?"

"I'm fine, TJ. It's all fine."

He frowned. "Are you sure? Are you feeling okay? Did he—"

"Yes. Just a little tired." She hoped the admission would get him to give her some space. "How about you? Having fun tonight?"

"Winning's always fun. Bet I'll get smoked tomorrow, though. That five-K no limit hold 'em event must be popular, right?"

"Not for most of the professionals." Vesper patted him on the shoulder. "Don't be self-defeating. Go in confident and smart."

"Is Nova entering that one?"

Nova. Vesper flashed to the hungry softness of their kisses, the possessive stroke of Nova's hand along her spine, the needy noises she had made as the moment intensified. Desire flared, hot and bright, driving back the cold like a torch in the darkness. The relief was so intense she almost gasped.

TJ's hand on her shoulder snapped her out of the memory. "I'm sorry. You're tired. I'll let you go."

"I think she's planning to be there, yes. And I'm sorry. I'm preoccupied."

He looked at her as though he wanted to say something more—something serious—before apparently thinking better of it. "Sweet dreams."

He stepped aside, and she hurried past him without a backward glance. Her mind was a blizzard of anxiety. Even as she tried to focus and consider the various permutations that ended with Priscilla Beauregard getting to keep her Celestial Palace, her thoughts spiraled out of control. Only when she pictured Nova's face did her panic begin to recede. Vesper wanted to go home and find comfort in the circle of her arms. She wanted to lie down beside Nova in the dark and discover how their bodies fit. She wanted—

"Vesper!"

Jeremy's voice brought her up just short of the opening elevator doors. She watched them close to reveal his reflection behind her. His brow was wrinkled and his movements inflected with a jerkiness that seemed like desperation. Had something happened?

"I'm glad I caught you," he said. "Can we talk? Privately?"

There was no such thing as true privacy in a casino. "Let's go outside."

He didn't say anything until they were well away from the front door, walking slowly down the Strip as though guided by the beam of the Luxor pyramid. "Biz asked me for drugs."

Vesper wasn't sure how many more adrenaline rushes she could handle tonight. This time, the surge of energy left her feeling a little dizzy and slightly nauseous. "What, exactly, did he say?"

Jeremy's lip curled derisively. "It was something like, 'Hey, boss. Do you know where I can score with Molly?'"

She almost laughed. "Molly" was a code name invented by the up-and-coming generation for MDMA, the pure form of Ecstasy. Biz was clearly trying to relive his college glory days by getting in with the cool kids.

"I had a hard time not laughing, too," Jeremy said. "At first, anyway. But then he kept pestering me."

"What did you tell him?" Vesper considered the implications. Biz asking around for drugs had the potential to be dangerous for both Jeremy and the casino. Las Vegas might be Sin City, but the casinos were notoriously strict about shutting down illegal drug use on their premises. If Biz did find Molly, and Vesper caught him at it, she might be able to use that as a pretext to kick him out of Valhalla.

"That I didn't know anything."

"Good." When she reached for his arm to turn him back toward the casino, the satiny material of his suit jacket under her palm reminded her of touching Biz. Bile rose into her throat and she snatched her hand away.

"V? What's wrong?"

"Nothing." Vesper struggled to keep her voice light. "Thanks for letting me know."

"What are you going to do?"

"I'm not sure." She breathed in deeply, willing the cool air to clear her head. She couldn't process any of this right now. Thinking about Biz was making her crazy, and the only proven distraction was asleep in her sofa bed.

"I'll figure something out. But right now, I need to go home."

❖

Nova watched the cable box's red numbers mark the minutes. The mattress and pillow were comfortable enough, and the fan above her head kept the air reasonably cool, but she couldn't sleep. Every time she was about to doze off, a fresh memory of that kiss with Vesper would set her heart to galloping. She had tried every one of her usual mental math exercises. She had tried rereading the section on early tournament rounds in Damon's book. She had tried playing some fake poker on her phone. She had tried watching the reruns of last year's final table that were being broadcast on ESPN.

Nothing worked. She was exhausted but couldn't sleep. Vesper was haunting her. Worse, it was almost two o'clock in the morning, and Vesper had yet to return. For the thousandth time, Nova debated sending her a text before deciding against it. Vesper wasn't in any danger. She was fine. A casino host would have to work late hours, of course. She must be so tired.

With a frustrated sigh, Nova flipped onto her stomach and buried her face in her pillow. A heartbeat later, the quiet snick of a key in the lock paralyzed every cell in her body. Finally. When she could breathe again, she turned onto her side and listened to the sounds of Vesper moving around the kitchen. As her footsteps drew closer to the living room, Nova sat up and took a deep breath. "Hey," she called softly, reaching over to turn on the nearby lamp.

Its golden circle of light illuminated Vesper, frozen in mid-stride, one bare foot over the threshold and one hand poised above the bun holding up her hair. Her face was paler than it had been a few hours ago, and a thin band of shadows lurked beneath her eyes. She looked exhausted. She was also the most desirable woman Nova had ever seen.

"I was hoping you'd gone to sleep hours ago," Vesper said, taking two more steps into the room.

"I tried. It didn't work. How did you get home?"

"Jeremy drove me." Another step. Vesper's gaze was fixed on hers in a way that made Nova's skin pebble.

"Are you okay?"

"Why can't you sleep? Tournament on your mind?" The patterned dress swirled around her knees as she moved even closer.

Nova was mesmerized. "That, and other things."

"Other things?" Vesper sat on the coverlet. The lamp cast a nimbus around her, throwing her features into darkness but making her hair glow like hot coals.

"You're avoiding my question," Nova managed to say. "And I can't see your face."

"Maybe I don't want you to." Vesper angled her body toward Nova and rested one hand on her stomach. "All night, I've been wondering what your skin feels like here."

She tugged down the sheet, exposing the hem of Nova's T-shirt. Helpless beneath this unexpected onslaught, Nova watched as Vesper's hand slipped beneath the shirt and skimmed the skin above the waistband of her boxers. The caress felt like the brush of rose petals. And then it was gone.

"Vesper." Nova's throat was so dry she could only whisper. "I want you so much. But I need to know what happened. You're not acting like yourself."

"How do you know?" Vesper flicked the sheet aside and began to trace the contours of the muscles just above her left knee. Nova felt her quads spasm beneath that maddeningly gentle butterfly touch. "Maybe this is me, and the person you thought you knew was all an act."

It took all of Nova's willpower to trap Vesper's hand against her leg. "Please."

With her face still backlit, Nova couldn't make out Vesper's expression, but she knew Vesper could see her perfectly. She looked up, unblinking, at the dark pools where Vesper's eyes were, trying to telegraph the sincerity of both her concern and her desire.

"Biz was an ass again tonight. Because of who he is, and who I am, he thinks he can touch me whenever he wants."

Nova's pulse spiked and a film of red hazed over her vision. "Vesper—"

"I'm not finished yet." She laughed softly, but the sound carried no humor. "Here's the definition of irony: I don't want him to touch me, but he won't stop. I do want you to touch me, and you won't start."

Nova's heart was galloping in her chest like the wild animal she feared she'd become if she gave her desire free rein. "You're not going to regret this? And you really will tell me to stop if that's what you want?"

Vesper leaned in, releasing the light to illuminate her face. Her eyes were wide and dark, her cheeks flushed, her lips parted. "No," she whispered. "And yes."

When Vesper pressed their mouths together, Nova groaned and clutched at her waist. She managed to pull Vesper on top of her without their lips ever parting, and Vesper settled between her thighs as though she belonged there. A distant part of Nova's brain couldn't believe this was happening, but her body knew exactly what to do. She shifted one hand up to slide her fingers through Vesper's hair and deepened the kiss.

It went on for what felt like hours, until the soft, needy sounds emerging from Vesper's mouth made Nova desperate to feel her skin. With clumsy fingers, she sought out the zipper on the dress and fumbled with it. When Vesper suddenly pulled her head back, Nova went still as a stone, fearful she'd been moving too fast. But Vesper only smiled and rose to her knees before putting both hands behind her back. The movement thrust her breasts forward, and Nova's mouth began to water.

"Hey," she mumbled at the sound of the zipper's descent. "I wanted to do that."

"Next time." Vesper peeled the dress from her shoulders, slowly revealing the flushed skin of her chest, crisscrossed by a simple back bra. Nova's heart felt like a bird trapped in a cage. Dimly, her rational brain registered that Vesper had just implied this wouldn't be the only time they would be together. But as quickly as the thought occurred, it went up in flames. Vesper was shimmying out of the remaining fabric, and the sway of her hips made Nova tremble in need.

With the fabric bunched to the waistline of her matching black underwear, Vesper paused and frowned. "Are you okay?"

"No." Nova struggled to prop herself onto her elbows. She didn't know how to express what she was feeling—how to put words to the hunger tying her belly into Gordian knots.

"No?" Vesper's voice was laced with uncertainty, and Nova instantly hated herself.

"I'm afraid I'll…" She focused in on Vesper's eyes—clear and green, like polished sea-glass. "I'll be too much. Want too much. From you."

In answer, Vesper yanked off what was left of her dress. She leaned forward and slid Nova's shirt up, up over her abs, over her breasts, over her head. The friction of the fabric raised a moan from Nova's throat. Within moments, her nipples were puckering in the cool air. As she watched, Vesper leaned forward to press her mouth to the skin above her navel.

"Oh, God."

Slowly, Vesper began to trail her kisses up the centerline of Nova's torso. "How does this feel?" she asked before shifting her head to lick delicately at the hollow spaces between Nova's ribs.

Nova tried to speak but lacked the breath. "So good," she managed to choke out. Lying quiescent while Vesper worshipped her skin was almost as excruciating as it was amazing. As Vesper's lips moved higher, Nova's fists clenched and reopened fitfully. Her need to feel the heat of Vesper's mouth on her breasts warred with her desire to have Vesper beneath her, arching into her caresses.

As Vesper moved higher, she brought her hands into play, cupping Nova's rib cage and stroking the crests and troughs with her thumbs. When Nova shivered and gasped, Vesper raised her head. Her smile was full of sensual promise.

"Ticklish?"

"A little."

Vesper raised an eyebrow and pressed harder with her thumbs. "Just take it."

Nova's vision blurred and she felt herself get wet. Free of her inhibitions, Vesper was a whirlwind, and Nova was more than happy to be carried away. By the time Vesper's tongue darted out to taste the sensitive underside of her right breast, Nova was panting.

Vesper raised her head and licked her lips. "Your skin is so hot. *You* are so hot."

"Please, don't stop now. You're killing me."

"Oh?" Vesper nipped lightly where she had just kissed. "Need something?"

Nova heard herself whimper at Vesper's teasing. That was the last straw. She had to get a grip and stop acting like a submissive puppy. Clearly, Vesper knew what she wanted, and she didn't seem uncertain in the slightest. Taking as deep a breath as she could manage, Nova met Vesper's eyes.

"I need you to suck me."

Vesper's pupils swelled, nearly drowning out the green. Smoothly, she ducked her head and closed her mouth around the hard ball of Nova's nipple. The moist heat and soft pressure conspired to wring a low moan from Nova's throat. The swirl of Vesper's tongue made sparks of pleasure dance between Nova's breasts and the juncture of her thighs, and when Vesper used her teeth, Nova's hips jerked off the mattress.

Vesper backed off and settled on her heels. Her hair was a river of red flowing down over her shoulders. "So responsive," she said, toying with the elastic of Nova's boxers. "What else do you need?"

The haze of arousal receded just enough for Nova to glimpse her chance at turning the tables. "I need to see you naked." But when Vesper began to reach behind her back, Nova sat up. "Let me."

Vesper's hands fell to her sides. Nova could see the pulse fluttering in her neck. Was it a sign of excitement, or nerves? Maybe she was more comfortable being in charge, especially after the way Biz had treated her. But then Nova flashed back to their first kiss, and the way Vesper had yielded beneath her touch, and her confidence returned.

Mimicking Vesper's kneeling position, Nova reached out and ran one finger beneath her bra strap. At the same, agonizingly slow pace Vesper had used, she slipped the strap down the milky white skin of her shoulder. When she pressed a kiss to the soft place between her arm and torso, Vesper shivered.

Only after repeating her actions on Vesper's other shoulder did Nova lean forward enough to work at the clasp of her bra. She gave an internal sigh of relief when the hook detached, leaving her able to slide the swatch of fabric down Vesper's arms. Vesper's breasts were slightly larger than her own, but her nipples were small and pink instead of the deep red Nova was used to seeing in the mirror.

"You're so beautiful," she whispered, praying that Vesper would hear the authenticity behind her words. Cupping one hand behind her neck, Nova moved forward just enough for the tips of their breasts to meet. The erotic slide of firmness against softness made her breath catch. "And you feel amazing."

She bent her head to suck at the tendon between Vesper's neck and shoulder. Vesper tasted like summer rain, and Nova scraped her teeth against the taut skin, dying for more. She threaded one hand through Vesper's hair and clutched at her hip with the other.

"Kiss me," Vesper demanded.

"I am." Nova licked down into the hollow below her collarbone.

"My mouth. Kiss my mouth."

Instead, Nova pulled her head away and pushed firmly, toppling Vesper onto the mattress. In the next instant, she was covering Vesper's body with her own. She stared deep into Vesper's eyes, searching for any sign of anxiety, and found none. When Vesper arched her back to brush their pelvises together, Nova shifted to slide one thigh firmly between her legs.

"What makes you think you can order me around?" Reaching between their bodies, she pinched Vesper's nipple gently, and then, when she moaned, more firmly. "Hmm?"

"Please," Vesper gasped.

"That's better." Hearing her beg set Nova's nerves aflame. She bent her head and crushed their mouths together, channeling every ounce of misplaced possessiveness into her kiss. This might only be a fling, but for tonight, Vesper was *hers*.

As their tongues tangled together, Nova stroked one hand along Vesper's side, loving the goose bumps that rose beneath her palm. When her fingertips encountered fabric, she dipped beneath the waistline of Vesper's underwear to draw lazy circles against the soft skin of her lower abdomen. Vesper moaned into her mouth, hips rocking steadily, and clutched hard at Nova's shoulder blades. She dug in her nails, and the sweet sting of pain made Nova shudder. In all the times she had fantasized about Vesper during the past several weeks, she had never dared to imagine anything like this. The real Vesper was sensuality incarnate, light years removed from the cool professional façade she displayed to the world.

Wanting to imprint herself on Vesper's body and mind, Nova kissed her as thoroughly as she knew how. Sweat beaded up between them as their bellies slid together, and Vesper's movements grew more frantic. Nova knew what she wanted, but for the first time in her life, she didn't want the same. Not right away, at least. She wanted to tease—to fan the flames of Vesper's need for her touch until it eclipsed every other emotion.

One of Vesper's hands moved to her hair and tugged, breaking the seal of their lips. Her eyes were dark and wild, her lips swollen. "Touch me," she gasped.

Nova shook her head as much as Vesper's grip would allow. "Not yet."

"Damn it!" With a groan half-frustrated, half-needy, Vesper let go and fell back onto the pillow. Nova didn't have to be good at reading people to tell that she was only putting up a token resistance.

"You're not really upset." Nova ducked her head and flicked Vesper's left nipple with her tongue. "This is what you want. Me, making you feel whatever I want you to, whenever I want you to."

Vesper didn't reply. Her head was thrown back and her eyes were closed and her lips were parted. The shadow of a pulse was visible between her ribs. She was exquisite, and Nova's restraint faltered. It would be so easy to slip her fingers between Vesper's legs—to twitch aside that thin band of fabric and feel her heat and wetness. But no. No. If there was a next time, she might abandon patience. In case there wasn't, she wanted this to be perfect.

Nova kissed slow spirals around both of Vesper's breasts before traveling down the center of her body. She darted her tongue into Vesper's navel and tugged at the skin below with her teeth. Vesper's eyes were closed, but her head shifted restlessly on the pillow. Caught up in the throes of sensation, she was so lovely.

Nova's craving finally spilled its bounds. In one smooth motion, she rid Vesper of her underwear and moved both hands to her inner thighs, spreading her open. Vesper's sex glistened in the lamplight, inviting her touch. Nova answered the call, bracing one hand on the bed and stroking through the patch of hair framing her folds.

"Gorgeous," she whispered, dipping lower, seeking and finding the hard focal point of her desire.

"Oh—"

When every muscle in Vesper's legs tensed, Nova knew she couldn't linger. "Close already, hmm?" She bent to kiss Vesper's left breast. "Not yet, ba—" At the last moment, Nova choked back the term of endearment. "Be patient," she said instead.

Mentally shaking off the lapse, she focused on tracing Vesper's opening with one gentle finger. The hot, slick skin beckoned her inside, but she resisted, keeping her touch feather-light. She drew aimless patterns, brushing against Vesper's clit and then moving away, tongue batting at her nipple all the while. Vesper's thighs trembled and her hands scrabbled at the sheets. Her unrestrained passion was so beautiful.

"Look at me," Nova murmured. When she did, Nova pressed more firmly. Vesper cried out and closed her eyes again, head moving fitfully against the pillow. Nova gentled her touch and followed the curves of Vesper's inner lips. "I mean it. Watch me touch you."

Her body shivered, and Nova felt a new rush of wetness against her fingertips. It was all she could do not to slip inside, but she needed to see into Vesper's soul as she did. With one finger poised to enter, she stroked softly with her thumb.

"Vesper. Please." The plea finally accomplished what her coaxing hadn't. Vesper's eyes fluttered open, glassy with desire. Nova waited until they focused on her. "Tell me what you want."

"Take me. Just take me."

The soft, broken whisper made her heart thump painfully. "Yes," she said, bending down to kiss Vesper's mouth as she finally slipped inside her body. When smooth muscles clenched around her fingertip, Nova grew still. Breathing heavily, she rested her forehead against Vesper's shoulder. "God, you feel good."

"More," Vesper gasped. She gripped Nova's wrist in an effort to pull her deeper. When Nova obliged with a gentle push, another spasm gripped her finger, and she felt an answering rush of wetness from her own body.

"You're so tight," she murmured. "I don't want to hurt you."

"You won't. You won't." Vesper's nails dug into the skin below her palm. "Please."

Nova saw the need on her face and abandoned her plan to take things slow. In a single, fluid movement, she moved down the bed to wedge her shoulders between Vesper's thighs. The sight of her, wet and swollen and wanting, made Nova feel a little dizzy. When she breathed in, the musky scent of Vesper's arousal went straight to her head. She had to taste her. Now.

At the first delicate touch of her tongue, Vesper cried out. Thrilling to the sound, Nova used her spare hand to spread Vesper open before licking her again. Vesper's thighs trembled, and her fingers found their way into Nova's hair to tug her closer.

Nova's heart hammered wildly. Following Vesper's cue, she hollowed her lips and sucked even as she pushed deeper inside. Vesper's body opened to her like a flower opens to the sun, and Nova lost herself in the wet heat of her welcome. She slid inside as deeply as she could, then crooked her finger and fluttered her tongue.

Vesper's scream cut off as sharply as it had begun. Her body stilled for an instant before the climax shook her like a ship in a tempest. Glorying in the rhythmic contractions of her release, Nova shifted her hand to Vesper's abdomen, holding her in place as the invisible storm raged. She kept up the soft circles of her tongue as Vesper pulsed beneath her, every breath a shuddering gasp.

Lost in Vesper's pleasure, Nova didn't stop even when her muscles grew slack. Instead, she coaxed a series of tiny aftershocks from Vesper's body with light kisses. Only when Vesper feebly tugged at her hair did Nova finally raise her head. Flushed and breathless, blinking dazedly, Vesper looked uncharacteristically vulnerable.

An unexpected surge of protectiveness propelled Nova to cover Vesper's body with her own, framing her head with both hands. "I don't have the words to tell you how beautiful you are."

Vesper reached up to touch her face with a trembling hand, but said nothing. When she ran one thumb across Nova's mouth, Nova kissed the soft pad, then took it between her teeth and bit down gently. Vesper shivered but remained silent. What did her reticence mean? Was she still catching her breath?

Nova was about to ask if anything was wrong, when Vesper's free hand ghosted down along her flank to pause at her hip. The light, questing touch set her every nerve aflame, and her vision blurred. When Vesper turned her wrist and slid beneath Nova's boxers, she jerked and raised her hips reflexively.

"Oh my God." Nova's abdominal muscles clenched painfully. "What are you—"

Vesper pulled her head down, locking their lips and plunging her tongue into Nova's mouth. Nova groaned, battling for control of the kiss, but Vesper held her in place. When her fingers slipped down to brush against the aching focal point between Nova's legs, a surge of heat arced up Nova's spine to explode in her brain. Her sharp cry was caught by Vesper's lips.

Nova quaked helplessly as Vesper explored the contours of her most sensitive skin, stroking and circling. When two fingers dipped into her opening, only to retreat, she jerked her head free to suck in a deep, shuddering breath. "Oh, please—"

And then, in one smooth glide, Vesper filled her. Nova's breath caught in her chest as her eyes slammed shut and her arms buckled. Vesper's hand cradled the back of her neck, her soft strokes playing counterpoint to her short thrusts deep within Nova's body. When her fingers curled up to rub against a particularly sensitive spot, Nova felt herself go molten. The heel of Vesper's palm rocked against her, sending wave after wave of pleasure to pool in her belly. Ecstasy bore down on her like a shooting star, bright and hot and unavoidable. With her last ounce of strength, Nova raised her head to look into Vesper's shining green eyes. They were a beacon, pulling her over the edge.

"Come."

Vesper whispered the command, and Nova had no choice but to obey. With a groan, she clamped down around Vesper's fingers, retaining just enough self-awareness to collapse onto her elbows as her arms finally gave way. Even with her hand crushed between them, Vesper continued to stroke firmly inside her, and Nova cried out in surprise as her body convulsed again.

Consciousness receded, lapping at the edges of her mind like the tide. Her limbs felt heavy and unresponsive, as though the climax had overloaded her synapses. Had she ever been so affected by a lover's touch?

Lover. Was that the right word for this? With her cheek pillowed on Vesper's chest, Nova was dimly aware of the racing heartbeat beneath her ear. If only she could decipher its Morse code, what would it tell her? Vesper claimed to want only a temporary relationship. A fling. But was that her heart speaking? Or the walls she had built around it?

As the heat of their passion dwindled to hot coals, Nova finally faced the truth. The effortlessness of her intimacy with Vesper only reinforced what she already knew. For the first time in her life, she wanted more than a casual relationship. She wanted to try for something real.

The epiphany roused her from her lethargy, and with an effort, she lifted her head. As her gaze met Vesper's, she tightened inside. Only then did she realize that Vesper had yet to withdraw. Fleetingly, Nova wished she never would. Vesper's eyes were flecked with gray and swirling with some indecipherable emotion. She leaned forward to kiss Nova's temple.

"I'm going to come out, now. Okay?"

Nova wanted to beg her to stay. Instead, she nodded and tried to relax as Vesper slowly withdrew her fingers. Was this the first and last time? Would they share a bed again, or would Vesper think better of it? The empty space inside her ached at the thought. She rolled onto her side and buried her face in Vesper's shoulder, lest her face give her away.

"You're amazing," she said, the words muffled by Vesper's warm skin.

For a long moment, Vesper lay quiet and unmoving before she reached down to pull Nova's arm over her waist. "You, too."

Nova splayed her fingers along Vesper's rib cage, holding her close. The gesture was possessive, but fatigue made her bold. "Don't you want to sleep in your own bed?"

Vesper shifted enough to turn off the lamp, then settled back into Nova's embrace. "Not tonight," was all she said. "Not tonight."

As she drifted off, enveloped by the scent and feel of Vesper, Nova hoped she wouldn't feel differently in the morning.

CHAPTER FIFTEEN

Vesper woke to the aroma of bacon and eggs. She sat up in bed, blinking in the sunlight filtering through her blinds, mouth watering. Turning her head, she glanced at the clock…only to realize it wasn't there. This was the living room, and she was in the sofa bed.

Because she and Nova had slept together.

The memories returned in a rush, reigniting her desire. The power she'd felt as she caressed Nova into incoherence; the tender ferocity of Nova's hands claiming her body; the current of passion that had flowed between them, equal parts give and take. Vesper shivered, pulling the blanket more tightly around her as she recalled the possessiveness of Nova's intimate touches. She hadn't been with many women, but none of them had ever invested so much care into her pleasure.

In the kitchen, pots clanked together over the murmur of the faucet. None of Vesper's previous flings had ever made her breakfast, either—not that she had given anyone else the opportunity. Nova was the first woman who had ever spent the night in her apartment. Vesper felt a flicker of unease at the realization, but it disappeared at the sound of Nova whistling cheerfully. Feeling her lips curve, Vesper closed her eyes and let herself enjoy the warm cocoon of the sheets for another few minutes.

The first event of the World Series didn't begin until the late afternoon, so they had time to take things slowly this morning. Vesper felt a touch of chagrin that she had kept Nova up late on the night before the tournament. Then again, she hadn't been complaining. Far from it. If Vesper concentrated hard enough, she could hear the echoes of Nova's moans and pleas. The memory made her warm, and she threw off the blankets, uncurling her body in a long stretch. The twinge in her abdominal muscles was a welcome ache. Had anyone ever teased her so expertly? Nova called herself impatient by nature, but she certainly hadn't been last night.

Ultimately, the promise of seeing Nova cooking in her kitchen drove Vesper out of the bed. For a moment, she considered walking through the doorway naked, but something in her quailed at the thought despite all they had shared only hours ago. Instead, she darted into her bedroom and dressed in a UNLV T-shirt and a pair of yoga pants, pulled her hair into a loose ponytail, and finally opened the door.

Nova was standing at the sink, washing dishes. She didn't seem to have heard anything over the running water, so Vesper went into the bathroom to brush her teeth. When she emerged, Nova was bending over, inspecting something in the oven. She was wearing the same Stanford shorts Vesper had slept in only a few weeks ago, and Vesper paused at the threshold of the kitchen to admire how they showed off her lean, muscular curves.

"Hi," she said softly. "That smells amazing."

Nova turned around, holding Vesper's cast-iron skillet in her gloved right hand. It was practically bubbling over with a golden-brown egg mixture, and she quickly set it on the stovetop.

"Good morning." Nova's gaze never left hers as she peeled off the cooking glove. "How'd you sleep?"

"Well. You?" Vesper's rational brain was telling her to play it cool, but the rest of her wanted to touch Nova again. She compromised by reaching out to hook her index finger beneath the waistband of Nova's shorts, maintaining contact but also distance. "How long have you been up?"

"A while. My internal alarm clock is set to early."

"You must be exhausted. Do I need to apologize?"

"Don't even think about it." Nova leaned through the space between them to kiss her too briefly. "Go sit. I'll bring you breakfast. Coffee?"

"Please." Her lips tingled, their warmth spreading beneath her skin. She took a step toward the table before changing her mind and her trajectory. She turned back to Nova and cupped her hips before sliding her palms across flickering abdominal muscles covered only by a thin layer of cotton.

"Oh." Nova's entire body shivered. "You can't know how good that feels."

"To me, too." Vesper rested her cheek between Nova's shoulder blades and let her fingertips trail down until they encountered skin. Hot silk over steel—that's what she felt like, and Vesper suddenly needed to feel that skin beneath hers. Last night, Nova had taken control. Now it was her turn.

She dipped beneath Nova's shorts and swiped her fingers back and forth like a pendulum, trying to show Nova with actions what she found so difficult to say in words. Nova was so good at describing her feelings. For her sake, she would try.

"Vesper," Nova groaned. "The eggs."

She stood on her toes and flicked her tongue against Nova's ear lobe. "I'm not hungry for them just yet."

Vesper tugged Nova backward toward the table, then spun her around and pointed to the closest chair. Nova sat down immediately, eyes glazed over with want. "So obedient," Vesper murmured as she sank to her knees.

"Oh, God."

Heady with the power trip, Vesper laughed. "But I'm the one on my knees." She took hold of Nova's waistband and pulled, gratified to find no other barrier in her path. Resting her palms on Nova's inner thighs, she slowly pushed them apart. Nova's sex gleamed, beckoning her closer. She didn't fight the impulse, leaning in to place one gentle kiss on the swollen knot of nerves before pulling away to gauge the reaction. When Nova made an inarticulate sound somewhere between a groan and a whimper, Vesper did it again.

This time, she stayed put, using her tongue to explore the delicate crests and troughs of Nova's most sensitive skin. She fluttered her tongue against Nova's opening and was rewarded by a rush of moisture and a tortured moan.

"Mmm." Vesper raised her head to a sight even more exciting than Nova's sexy sounds. Nova's hands were clenched on the chair, knuckles white and wrist tendons straining. Her jaw was clenched and her nostrils flared with each rapid breath. She looked like a woman on the edge of losing control. Already.

Last night, Vesper had been afraid of saying too much, so instead she had said nothing. Now, with Nova open and needy beneath her hands, she felt no fear at all. "You like that, don't you?"

Without waiting for an answer, Vesper ducked her head. This time, she used one thumb to rub soft circles around Nova's clit while resuming the flickering of her tongue. When Nova's hips bucked, Vesper shifted her arm to hold her down. The salty sweetness of her was like nothing Vesper had ever tasted. For a moment, she wondered whether Nova's taste mirrored that of the ocean, before Nova's hand clutched her hair and pulled her even closer.

"Please," she panted, "oh, please…"

I know what you need, Vesper might have said. But she didn't want to talk anymore. Instead, she slid her tongue inside Nova's body. When she could go no further, she withdrew and returned, fucking her slowly and deliberately as her thumb circled and stroked.

Nova's hoarse shout pierced the air as she shattered, pulsing against Vesper's fingers, internal muscles convulsing wildly. To feel her release while they were so intimately connected was nothing short of amazing. Vesper dug her fingertips into Nova's thigh and curled her tongue, wanting to prolong her climax in any way possible. It must have been the right thing to do, because Nova cried out again and tightened her grip. The slight pain in Vesper's scalp was entirely worthwhile, and she didn't let up her caresses until the iron bands of Nova's thighs softened beneath her arm.

Only then did she pull back, peppering soft kisses along Nova's skin in the process. When she looked up, Nova was staring back at her, a naked vulnerability in her eyes that made Vesper's heart stutter. Then, as though Nova had become aware of how much emotion she was betraying, a shutter fell over her expression. For one insane moment, Vesper wanted to call her out—to make her confess what she was feeling. But how was that fair, when she wasn't willing to do the same?

Instead, she decided to give Nova some space in which to regroup. Retreating across the kitchen, Vesper tentatively touched the side of the skillet. "Still warm," she reported. "See? The eggs are fine."

When she turned around, Nova had pulled up her shorts. "Good thing." She joined Vesper at the stove, resting one hand on her hip and leaning in to kiss her lightly on the cheek. "They're not to be missed."

Vesper wondered what she was trying to communicate. Gratitude? Affection? Something else? "So you said." She leaned into Nova briefly, hoping to telegraph that her little touches were welcome. "Pretty full of yourself, aren't you?"

Nova grinned, hoisted the skillet, and turned toward the table. Vesper licked her lips, tasting Nova as she followed in her wake. For a while, they behaved like a normal couple over breakfast—chatting about mundane topics as though by some unspoken agreement to avoid anything relating to gambling. Slowly, Vesper relaxed into the conversation, feeling sheltered by the banality of it.

Finally, she glanced at the clock and pushed her chair back. "That was amazing. Thank you."

"I'm glad you liked it." Nova sipped at what was left of her coffee. "When do you need to go?"

"Within the hour. Priscilla's friends are leaving in the early afternoon, and I should see them off." So much had happened last night that Priscilla's victory at the craps table felt like a distant memory.

"She isn't going with them?" Nova stood and began to clear the plates. When Vesper tried to mimic her, Nova shook her head. "Let me."

"But you cooked."

"I did. But *you* never stop moving." Nova transferred the plates to one hand and briefly cupped Vesper's cheek. "Just sit. Please."

"All right." Vesper settled back in her chair. "And no, Priscilla's not leaving. I think you inspired her. She wants to play in the tournament."

"Oh?" Nova laughed. "I hope I don't come face-to-face with her tonight. She's formidable."

"She's probably feeling that way this morning, after winning two million at craps last night."

"Two *million*?" Nova whistled. "Insane. Next to that, most of the tournament games will be small potatoes."

"I just hope she enjoys herself and stays long enough to lose back everything she won."

Nova laughed and began to stack the dishes in the sink. For the next few minutes, Vesper couldn't stop watching as Nova moved competently and efficiently around the kitchen. She looked as though she had cooked a hundred meals in it, instead of just one. Her arms rippled as she washed the plates, and when she raised the skillet to return it to the cabinet above the stove, the hem of her tank top rose, exposing a tan strip of skin. Vesper's mouth went dry at the memory of Nova's firm body moving over hers, and her fingers trembled as she took a sip of lukewarm coffee.

"So," Nova said into the silence, drying her hands on the dishtowel. "You never told me what happened with Biz last night."

Vesper looked down at the floor, not trusting her instinctual defenses when it came to Biz and all the baggage he dredged up. Then she remembered that Nova already knew most of her story, and she let out her breath on a long sigh. When she looked up, Nova was leaning against the counter, staring at her intently.

"Tell me," she said softly. "It's okay."

Vesper thought about dissembling. She was good at it. Nova might not be able to tell. But what was the point? If she was really going to try to run Biz out of Valhalla, she needed a plan. Maybe one would become clear to her if she used Nova as a sounding board.

"He was drunk when he got in," she said as matter-of-factly as she could. "And touchy-feely. The two seem to go together with him."

Nova suddenly had a stranglehold on the dishtowel. "Did he put his hands on you?"

Something in her tone made Vesper want to sidestep the question. "He threatened me, and—"

"He *what*?" Nova was at her side before she could blink, looming over her, face mottled in anger.

Vesper squared her shoulders and pointed to the empty chair. This wasn't the reaction she needed, and she was going to nip it right in the bud. "Sit down, and I'll tell you. But only if you don't interrupt and you don't get crazy."

"Cra—" Nova must have seen the truth in her face, because she held up both hands and sank into the seat. "Okay. I'm sorry. He... threatened you. Goddammit."

"Yes. He did. He told me that if I didn't continue on as his host, he would leave Valhalla for a different casino."

"Good! Great, even!" Nova must have realized that she was on the verge of becoming melodramatic, because she paused. "I interrupted. Sorry."

"He also said he would take a lot of people with him. For years, the Hamiltons have brought me business, but Biz claims he can convince most of his colleagues to abandon Valhalla."

"Do you think he's telling the truth?"

The multimillion-dollar question. Vesper shrugged, wanting to seem cavalier, even if she wasn't. "I don't know. I do know that I won't take the risk."

"So you're just going to let him—" Nova clamped her lips together, but her eyes beseeched Vesper not to make deals with people like Biz.

"I'm not going to let him do anything." She took the napkin from her lap and began to smooth out its wrinkles. "Jeremy told me that Biz has been asking about drugs. If I can catch him in the act, I might be able to justify having him kicked out of Valhalla."

"Catch him in the act?" Nova's voice had lost its shrillness, but her hands were clasped so tightly together that her knuckles had turned white. "How are you going to do that?"

"I don't know yet." Vesper reached across the table and gently pried Nova's palms apart. "I'll need to keep a close eye on him, which won't exactly be pleasant. But at least as his host, I'll have the access I need."

"*Access* is exactly what I'm worried about." Nova looked down at the tabletop, clearly wrestling with how much to say. "What if he assaults you again?"

"I'm going to be careful and smart. I won't ever be alone with him." Vesper dipped each thumb into the center of Nova's hands and began to rub gentle circles against her skin. "You need to trust that I can handle this. It comes with the territory, sometimes."

"This kind of thing has happened before?"

"Not quite to this degree, but yes—I've had a few persistent clients in the past."

Vesper noted with satisfaction that her impromptu massage seemed to be working. Nova's shoulders had dropped two inches, and her eyes were taking on a dreamy haze. In that moment, Vesper wanted nothing more than to drag her back into bed and spend the rest of the day there. But she had to go. Priscilla would be waiting.

Leaning across the table, she kissed Nova lightly. "I can take care of myself. And speaking of which: it's time for me to go to work."

"I know you can." Nova sounded almost mournful as Vesper

moved away. "Believe me, I know. But you can't blame me for wanting to help."

I want that, too, Vesper might have said. The words rolled across her tongue, but she swallowed them back. "You're sweet," she said instead, glancing briefly over her shoulder before closing the bedroom door.

❖

Nova riffled the few chips remaining to her, hoping their weight in her palm and their quiet plinking would stave off the panic threatening at the edge of her mind. She was losing. Badly. The second day of the eight-handed no limit hold 'em event was almost over, but she didn't have enough chips to make it through the end of this round. By now, the blinds and antes were steep enough that she would bust out in five hands.

It took a supreme force of will not to look at her cards. She knew what they were—the ace of spades and eight of diamonds—and checking them again would send a message of uncertainty to her opponents. She should have gone all in before the flop since she wasn't likely to get a better hand with her dwindling stack. But her distraction led her to just call the ante. Oh well, she'd get to see a cheap flop, at least. Struggling to seem as disinterested as it was possible to be with a short stack, she stared off into the distance in an effort to find some serenity and wished her iPod hadn't failed a few hours ago. The sound of the ocean in her ears hadn't instantly transformed her into Doyle Brunson, but it had been comforting.

She had no one to blame but herself. Last night, she'd been so eager to get Vesper naked that she had forgotten to charge any of her electronic devices. Not that she really cared. On their way home from the first day of the tournament, she'd been careful not to put any pressure on Vesper, and once they arrived at the apartment, she had diligently begun to turn down the sofa bed. Only after Vesper had asked what the hell she was doing and then proceeded to drag her into the bedroom had Nova given her own desire free rein. They hadn't slept until the first gray fingers of predawn were fumbling at the base of the mountains, and they had woken only a few hours later, legs still entwined.

Nova smiled at the memory before she remembered the necessity of maintaining a poker face. But even if she lost the entirety of her five-thousand-dollar buy-in over the next few minutes, she wouldn't regret last night. Once again, Vesper hadn't said much, but the responsiveness of her body more than made up for her reticence.

Fighting the urge to look around the room for her, Nova continued to slide the chips through her fingers. The flop shattered her musings. Ace of clubs, nine of hearts, jack of clubs. She blinked down at it as her brain shifted gears, automatically cataloguing her probability of success. Flopping a pair of aces was good, but that nine could be a problem, and two clubs on the board were worrisome. But the reality was that her time—and chips—had run out. It was time to move all-in. Would she get any takers or would her bold move scare everyone out?

She got her answer when the young, athletic guy across the table from her in the backward baseball cap and tight Raiders T-shirt threw twice as much money into the pot as was stacked before her. Without hesitation, she moved the remainder of her chips into the center. This was it. Sink or swim.

The remaining players mucked their cards, making way for a showdown. Nova was relieved not to have to try to pretend anymore. With a shrug, she flipped over her cards. Her opponent grinned and revealed the ace of diamonds and nine of clubs. He had two pair; she had one. The only way for her to win was if both the turn and the river came up eights. With a ruthless efficiency, her brain calculated the odds of success: point-three percent. Winning might be out of the question, but she could still hope for a tie. The odds were still slim—two point nine three percent that the turn and river would be a pair higher than nine—but at least it was something to cling to.

Nova's vision telescoped as she focused on the dealer's hands, moving swiftly as he burned a card and turned over the next: the ten of diamonds, more precious in this moment than the gem it was named for. Winning had just become impossible, but her chance of a tie had just nearly doubled, to six point eight two percent. With some luck, they would split the pot and she would be granted a stay of execution.

Again, the dealer burned a card. Nova held her breath, her only thought a silent plea. But Lady Luck proved deaf when the king of spades appeared, staring up at her implacably from his bed of felt.

Fitting, that he should arrive to bury her. She exhaled slowly, then stood and extended her hand to the player who was gathering up the dregs of her chip stack.

"Nice one. Thanks, all. See you 'round."

Just like that, it was over. She had nothing to show for her two full days of play except cramped hamstrings and a five-thousand-dollar hole in her bank account. Not that she had expected to win this particular event, but it was discouraging that she hadn't even made it to the halfway point. If she wasn't going to get a bracelet, she at least needed to progress far enough to make her money back.

As she made her way past the throng of onlookers and reporters, her concern for Vesper rushed back to the fore of her mind. Her phone's battery was down to the slimmest fraction of red, and once she found a place to stand at the edge of the room, she typed as quickly as her fumbling thumbs would allow. *Busted out. How r u doing? What can I do to help?*

Knowing that if Vesper was with a client, she wouldn't reply, Nova sent a text to TJ, too. He might have a better sense of where she was. *Busted out. U?* Clutching her phone in one hand, she began to make her way slowly around the periphery of the room, scanning its occupants for a glimpse of the light blue suit she had watched Vesper put on this morning.

Same, a while ago, TJ replied. *Watching Mac @ media table.*

As far as she knew, Mac was the highest-profile professional who had decided to enter this event. It made sense that his table would be featured by the media. Without any word from Vesper, she might as well join TJ. Mac had been kind to her, and now that she was out of the running, she would be happy to cheer him on. Maybe she'd even learn something from watching him in tournament play.

The closer she got, the thicker the crowd became. Fortunately, she spotted TJ quickly and made her way over to the corner where he had staked out a place along the rail. He grinned when he saw her and pulled her into a one-armed hug.

"Hi," she said. "Sorry you got knocked out. Is your dad still in the mix?"

TJ laughed and shook his head. "He didn't make it past the second round today." Craning his neck, he looked around. "He was watching with me for a while but decided to go to bed."

Nova gestured toward the game unfolding under the portable lights. Their heat made the air shimmer like a mirage. "How's Mac doing?"

"Sitting on the biggest stack at the table and the third largest overall. Looking pretty good."

They watched in silence for a while. At first, it seemed that Mac was playing more aggressively than usual, but Nova quickly picked up on a pattern. He was eagerly challenging the short-stacked players while actively avoiding showdowns with the only other player whose chip stack was remotely comparable to his. It was proving effective, especially since his primary opponent seemed to be operating under a similar philosophy. Between the two of them, they were efficiently dismantling the remainder of the opposition. The tournament organizers, who had to ensure that the field was whittled down to one third of its initial size by the day's end, probably appreciated their strategy, too.

"Hey, look, there's Vesper."

Nova instantly lost all interest in the table. Every cell on high alert, she followed the line of TJ's arm to where Vesper stood behind the last row of onlookers. Nova relaxed a little when she realized Vesper was talking with Priscilla. Vesper's hair gleamed invitingly beneath the fluorescent lights, and Nova flashed hot at the memory of sliding her fingers through the cool, silky strands last night during an interlude of languorous kissing.

"Let's go say hi," TJ said.

Vesper saw them first. She must have caught a glimpse in her peripheral vision, because she never broke eye contact with Priscilla, but her body language changed. She shifted toward them and raised her chin slightly, a silent acknowledgment of their presence that made Nova feel possessive. Priscilla and TJ might be Vesper's clients, but she was Vesper's lover. She wanted to stake her claim in front of them—to slide her arms around Vesper's waist and kiss her neck and make her blush. Instead, she shoved her hands in the pockets of her board shorts and hung back half a foot behind TJ.

"Young Theodore," Priscilla proclaimed in her drawl. "How lovely to see you again. And you as well, of course, Nova."

Somehow, Nova managed not to laugh at the "young Theodore" comment. "How did everything go today, Priscilla?"

"How did I play, you mean?" Priscilla looked at her shrewdly. "Like crap. Though it was still exhilarating."

Nova swallowed down the urge to say something banal. Priscilla wouldn't respect that. "Can I help?"

Priscilla cocked her head. "If you're standing here right now, you didn't come out smelling like roses either, did you?"

Inwardly cringing, Nova forced herself to laugh. She wasn't about to expose the depth of her insecurity to Vesper—not right now, at least. "Truer words were never spoken. Tomorrow is another day."

"That it is." Priscilla's eyes narrowed. "Are you entering the Omaha/stud eight event?"

"Might as well. See you there?"

"I do believe you will." The shrill ring of Vesper's phone curtailed their banter. "Take it." Priscilla waved her bejeweled hand. "I'll see you tomorrow."

"Good night," Vesper said. "And excuse me." She stepped away as she answered the call.

"Good night, Priscilla," Nova echoed, never taking her eyes off Vesper. When her shoulders hunched suddenly, Nova wondered whether the voice on the line was Biz's.

A round of applause from the crowd distracted TJ, but Nova didn't care what had happened in the game. She couldn't hear Vesper's conversation, but she could try to read her lips. Had she just said "thank you"? Was that a good sign? Not for the first time since the morning, Nova wished she had a real claim on Vesper, so she could insist on helping with her mission to oust Biz from the casino. The worst part about this entire scenario was that Vesper still seemed to consider sexual abuse an occupational hazard. Nova's hands clenched automatically. As much as she admired and respected Vesper's fierce independence, Nova couldn't stop feeling that she was mishandling this entire situation in deference to the career she had worked so hard to build. But when keeping that career meant repeatedly sacrificing her safety, was it really worth it?

Vesper hung up and immediately met Nova's gaze. She seemed tense, but not fearful. Acutely aware of TJ beside her, Nova spoke carefully. "Did your evening just get busier?"

"Yes. I need to go to my office for a while."

"At this hour? Is everything okay?"

Nova felt a flash of annoyance at TJ's immediate reaction to jump to the rescue—not that she could blame him, of course. When Vesper rested a hand on his arm, her skin tingled in sympathy.

"You know as well as I do that Vegas never sleeps." She smiled, but it seemed rather forced. "Relax. Enjoy yourself." She glanced too briefly at Nova. "Both of you." She turned and hurried away, leaving them to watch her melt into the throng.

TJ sighed. "She works too hard."

"She does." Nova looked down at her watch to stop her face from betraying any hint of her unease. "It's almost midnight. I'd better catch the last bus."

"Bus?"

Nova's stomach flip-flopped. TJ still thought she was staying at Valhalla. Could she get out of this without confessing where she was actually spending her nights? "I had to give up my room to some high roller," she said, flashing what she hoped was a convincing grin.

"Damn. Must have been tough to find a place at this time of year."

"Mm." She stared toward the featured table and hoped he would let the subject drop.

"Nova." His hand on her shoulder forced her to meet his concerned gaze. "What are you not saying? Are you sleeping in a car or something? Becau—"

"What? No!" She sighed in frustration, silently damning her own expressiveness. "I'm staying with Vesper."

"You're—oh." In an instant, his frown of concern was replaced by a wide grin. "When did *that* happen?"

"Not long ago." At least she could try to be vague about the timing.

"No wonder you busted today. You must be totally distracted."

"Thanks. Thanks a lot."

He looked chagrined. "I didn't mean it that—"

She shook her head and patted him on the shoulder. "Relax. You're probably right. Just…don't make a big deal to Vesper, okay?"

He scowled at her. "Do I look like an asshole to you?"

"It had to be said. You would have, in my place."

"Probably true. And I'll say something else, too." He pointed a finger in her face, all trace of his puppyish enthusiasm gone. "Don't hurt her."

For a heartbeat, Nova was tempted to tell him that Vesper wasn't the one in danger—that she was the one for whom this was only a fling. But TJ already knew too much, and this was none of his business.

"I won't," was all she said. *But she might hurt me.*

CHAPTER SIXTEEN

Vesper ducked into the stairwell and hurried up to the second floor, heart pounding in time with the rapid click of her heels. She clutched her phone in her left hand in case Jeremy called back with new information. Their conversation had been terse, his voice low and hurried.

Biz had me take him out to this place near Green Valley Ranch. He picked up two girls there. I think they might've been getting high in the car. They wanted to stop at a liquor store, so that's where we are now. I think he's planning to bring them back to Valhalla.

His news had made Vesper feel at once triumphant and anxious, and her agitation had only increased when she considered Jeremy's situation. But he could take care of himself—she had to remember that. This wasn't the first time someone had used a limo as a drug den. It was, however, the first time Vesper had been involved. She knew how other hosts handled these moments—some cajoled, some threatened, some turned a blind eye. All of them walked the line between catering to their customers' whims and keeping the interests of the casino safe.

She paused on the landing, ran her fingers through her hair, and inhaled deeply to steady her breaths. By the time she entered the security center, she was once more in command of herself. Two levels of monitors ringed the semicircular office—fifty screens connected to almost two thousand cameras. When she first visited this room, Vesper had been surprised to learn how lightly it was staffed. Just a few security officers watched the monitors at any one time. Most of the video was only scrutinized after the fact, if a pit boss had noticed something suspicious. Tonight, the room was occupied by only one man, who looked over his shoulder at her approach.

"Hey, Vesper."

"Flying solo, Carl?" she said as she perched on the empty chair next to his.

He shrugged. "Shaun went down earlier to help out with your whale, and Dan just ran out to get us some food." She caught his quick once-over before he focused on her face. "So, what's up?"

"I have a situation developing, and I might need your help. One of my clients just picked up two women in his limo. Jeremy's driving, and he's pretty sure the women brought drugs with them. They'll be back here soon, he thinks."

Carl shook his head as he turned to the nearest computer. "What's this guy's name? I need to pull up his file."

"Bizmarck Deloreo." Saying it made her want to brush her teeth.

Carl looked over his shoulder at her, frowning. "Isn't that the asshole who—"

"Yes." Vesper's heart was suddenly racing again. Of course Carl would know about the incident from a few weeks ago, but the last thing she wanted to do was to rehash it with him now. She smoothed her dress to disguise the tremor in her hands and forced herself to roll her eyes. "He's a real charmer."

"Sounds like." Carl pressed a few buttons, and Biz's photograph popped onto the screen alongside a page of text. "Muckity-muck politician, eh?"

"He made his money in the Dot Com bubble right out of college. Switched to the big corporate scene for a while before eventually becoming a *public servant*." She didn't even try to curb her sarcasm.

Carl snorted. "Well, I'll be sure to keep an eye on him. Thanks for the heads up."

Vesper was tempted to turn around and leave. Nova might still be downstairs. Jeremy wouldn't mind taking them home. The scene unfolded before her inner eye—Nova's hand brushing across her hips as they hurried up the stairs; Nova's lips moving insistently across the nape of her neck as she fumbled with the keys. And once her apartment door had closed behind them…anticipation seared through her, burning away her anxiety. Vesper imagined backing Nova up against the wall, pressing their bodies together, holding her head in place while she licked and sucked at the delicate skin of her throat. Her imagination could easily conjure the desire that would be written plainly on Nova's face and soft, needy sounds she would make. More. There was no use in denying it. When it came to Nova, she wanted more.

But just as she was about to stand, Biz's photo caught the corner of her eye, and suddenly her memory was flashing back, back to Nova's expression this morning when they had been discussing him. Nova had all but begged her not to allow Biz to take any kind of advantage. If he did break the rules, and Vesper let Carl handle it, there wouldn't be any real consequences. Biz might be blackballed from the casino if he proved recalcitrant, but that was probably as far as Valhalla would go. And as Biz had made plain to her last night, there were many more fish in the sea.

"Actually, do you mind if I watch with you?" she asked Carl. "I'd like to see what he's up to."

"Fine by me."

Ignoring the flames still crawling under her skin, Vesper crossed one leg over the other and focused on the cluster of monitors dedicated to the front entrance. To stop herself from thinking about Nova, she asked Carl about his wife and kids. He was just launching into a recap of his youngest son's most recent Little League game when a black car pulled up. Moments later, it disgorged a leggy blonde, a petite brunette, and Biz.

"There he is." Vesper leaned forward, eyes straining to catch every detail as he exchanged some kind of joke with his companions and then pulled them in close. Together, they began to make their way inside. Was he staggering because he was drunk or high, or were his movements jerky because he had a woman on each arm?

"We'll pick him up there." Carl pointed to an adjoining group of screens displaying the lobby.

"Thanks." Vesper swiveled in the chair, tracking him as he entered the hotel. He stopped to have a conversation with the concierge, but his mouth was moving too quickly for her to successfully read his lips. As he skirted the World Tree Pool, he paused to take a selfie with the two ladies before continuing toward the elevators.

"Number three," Carl announced when the doors opened. He pointed to another monitor. "There."

Other people were waiting for the elevators, but no one else joined

Biz and the women in number three. Vesper wondered what he had said to keep them waiting. As soon as the doors closed, the brunette pressed her body to his, grinding her hips against his leg as her hand drifted down his chest. When she began to trace the noticeable bulge in his pants, Vesper quickly turned her gaze on the other woman.

Carl shifted in his chair. "You sure you want to keep watching? I have to see shit like this all the time, but you can walk away."

Vesper hardly heard him. The blond woman had opened her purse and pulled out what looked like a tin of mints. She flicked open the top and held up a small, white disc between her French-tipped thumb and index finger. Her lips moved, and this time Vesper could read them clearly. *Ready for more, tiger?*

In that moment, she would have wagered every cent in her savings account that the woman held not a mint, but a tab of Ecstasy. She watched as Biz, already panting from the hand job he was getting, opened his mouth more widely. When the woman delicately placed the tab on his tongue, he closed his mouth and sucked on her fingers.

"Looks like he found Molly," Vesper said, not realizing until she heard her own words that she had spoken the thought. Her mind felt curiously detached, as though it were floating above her body. The smoking gun had just fallen into her lap. But what should she do with it?

Carl's heavy sigh set the ends of his mustache quivering. "I'll go break up the party and read him the usual riot act. Want to come along?"

The image on screen slid out of focus as Vesper contemplated the crossroads before her. Going about business as usual was safe. It was what Valhalla would want. Because of who Biz was—and more importantly, how much he was willing to gamble—the casino would give him a Get Out of Jail Free card. Wasn't that the cornerstone of her entire career: that powerful people got exceptions to the rules? No one would blame her for slapping Biz on the wrist in the name of preserving the status quo and not ruffling feathers.

No. That wasn't true. Nova might say that she understood Vesper's priorities, but her eyes never lied, and they would tell a different story. For one insane moment, Vesper wanted to stamp her foot and scream about the injustice of it all—Samuel's hands on her breasts; Biz backing her up against the wall; and in between, all the leers and remarks and inappropriate touches she had endured from so many men over so many years. At sixteen, she hadn't had a choice. Now, she did. How many more times could she choose stability over self-respect before she lost some essential part of her soul? Vesper wasn't even sure she believed in the soul, but maybe it was the difference between her and a host like James. She still had some principles left. He didn't. This job would take everything if you let it, and for years, she had allowed it to erode her values.

No longer. Vesper straightened her spine and reached for her phone. "Don't bother, Carl. I'm going to call the police."

"What?" He looked at her as though she had suddenly sprouted a second head. "V, I know you don't like the guy, but bringing the cops into this is a terrible idea."

"He's breaking the law. And if I were a betting woman, I'd lay down money that those women are prostitutes."

"But you're not a betting woman." Carl was looking at her intently. "And this isn't a gamble—this is suicide. If you call the PD, Steve will shit a brick!"

Vesper focused on scrolling through her contacts list, forcing herself into action. "Valhalla will come out smelling like roses. We'll be lauded for taking a hard line on drugs."

"By the authorities and the goody-two-shoes, maybe," said Carl. "But calling the cops on a client is a real good way to discourage future business."

He wasn't wrong, and Steve would agree. Steve, who had the power to undo her years of hard work in an instant. Vesper's heart trip-hopped in her chest. Her thumb hovered above the green button. She watched it tremble and suddenly hated her own weakness. Nova had called her strong, but Vesper knew the truth. All her life, she had taken the steps necessary to be self-sufficient. Now, it was time to do more than simply survive.

She looked up at Carl and read the trepidation in his face. "I'll make sure Steve knows you weren't involved. But I need to do this."

Surrendering to gravity, she made the call.

❖

Vesper stood near the concierge's podium as a member of the Las Vegas police department led a handcuffed Biz around the World Tree Pool. A K9 cop followed them, her four-legged partner straining at its leash. Vesper fleetingly wished Biz had given the dog a reason to bite him. Behind them, a man in khakis and a DEA jacket gestured at the two other police officers who were playing escort to the women Biz had hired for the evening. The irony would have made her laugh, if it weren't for her growing apprehension over Steve's reaction to this spectacle.

When the lobby door slid open, a flashbulb went off, briefly turning the night to morning. After hanging up with the police dispatcher, Vesper had gone for broke and decided to call News 3. Apparently, the word had spread—several other affiliates had sent reporters, all of whom were trying to get a rise out of Biz as he was prodded toward the waiting cop car.

"What kind of drugs did you buy, Mr. Deloreo?"

"How much is your bail, Mr. Deloreo?"

"Does the governor know about your arrest?"

Finally, Biz cracked. "Shut up!" he bellowed. "Shut the fuck up, all of you!" As the echo of his voice bounced between the tall buildings flanking the street, the officer yanked open the door with one hand and guided Biz's head inside with the other.

Vesper's phone buzzed. Her heartbeat accelerated into double-time, and she almost let the call go to voice mail. But after what she had already done tonight, this was no time to lose her courage. "Hello, Steve."

"My office. Now." He disconnected the call without waiting for her response.

Resolutely, Vesper turned toward the stairs, but she paused on the outskirts of the lobby. Would this be the last time she saw it through the eyes of a casino host? Under the light of the massive chandeliers, every surface glittered and gleamed, unchanging—the same at two in the morning as it was at two in the afternoon. Time lost all meaning here. Sunrise or sunset, the slot machines sang their Siren songs. Here, yesterday's bad luck was forgotten, and tomorrow was always bright and hopeful. No wonder it was so easy to lose yourself in Vegas.

She had tried to do exactly that, but even here, the past had returned to haunt her. Someday, she would feel proud of confronting it head-on instead of hiding her head in the sand. First, she had to survive this confrontation with her dignity intact. Turning her back on the lights, she ducked into the stairwell.

This time, Steve didn't lead her to the conference table. He rose as she entered, passed her without any sign of acknowledgment, and shut the door—which she had deliberately left open—firmly behind her. He turned and pointed to the low chair in front of his desk. As she sat, heart hammering wildly beneath the smooth fabric of her dress, only one thought penetrated the fog of her anxiety. *Show no weakness. Show no weakness. Show no weakness.*

Photographs of Steve posing with various celebrities adorned his office wall. On his desk, a lacquered business card holder, carved in the shape of a playing card dispenser, caught the light of a lamp made out of horseshoes. The half-smoked cigar in the crystal ashtray was an Opus X BBMF—"Big Bad Motherfucker"—one of the most expensive in the world. When he finally sat, he adjusted his Brioni sleeves and smoothed his Hermès tie. Despite the late hour, he betrayed no sign of fatigue in his movements or appearance. Even the smallest detail of this place telegraphed wealth, power, and prestige. The space between them—only a matter of feet—felt like a chasm.

"What the fuck do you think you're doing?"

Taken aback by his conversational tone, Vesper was momentarily speechless. Even as she tried to pull herself together, a detached part of her brain couldn't help but admire his rhetorical trick. She was completely off-kilter now.

"The right thing," she finally managed.

He laughed. "The right thing. Having Bizmarck Deloreo marched out of here in handcuffs with those two cunt whores was the 'right thing.'" He smacked the desk with his open palm. Vesper started in surprise at the sharp sound. So much for showing no weakness. Clamping her mouth shut, she vowed not to speak unless prompted. He would hold whatever she said against her.

"You've always seemed like a bright girl, Vesper," he said, leaning forward and clasping his hands together. The oddly paternal note inflecting his voice gave her goose bumps, but she managed not to shiver. "Dedicated. Ambitious. Driven."

Forcing herself to meet his eyes, Vesper concentrated on regaining her inner balance as she waited for his judgment. Exhaustion hovered on the horizon of her mind, but for now, adrenaline kept it at bay.

"I thought you were ready for the big leagues," he continued. "Clearly, I was wrong. Security will escort you back to your office and you will collect your things immediately."

Even though she had been expecting them, the words were a guillotine slicing through her carefully woven safety net. Ever since she had been old enough to understand what it meant to hold down a job, her mother had reinforced the importance of employment. *Work hard and you can make your own choices*, she always said. Vesper had taken the mantra to heart, marketing herself as a babysitter at twelve and taking a waitressing job at fifteen. After leaving home, she had worked overtime and weekends to scrape by. And now she was unemployed.

A rush of anger burned away her self-pity. Was she really going to let Steve railroad her out of the casino without a word of protest? If she had decided to be strong, didn't she need to follow through? Cocking her head, she tried to emulate the casual tone that had so distracted her only moments ago.

"I don't think that's a good idea right now, Steve."

"Excuse me?" When he stood, Vesper followed suit, not wanting to give him the chance to loom over her.

"We're in the middle of the World Series. Valhalla's resources are already stretched thin. Not only am I handling the Hamiltons—Priscilla Beauregard just told me tonight that she wants to extend her visit with us. Fortunately, we now have a spare Celestial Palace." She crossed her arms beneath her breasts, mostly to hide the trembling in her hands. "I'll stay until the end of the tournament, and then I'll go without a fight."

His jaw clenching rhythmically, Steve stared at her as though she were something foul he needed to scrape off the bottom of his shoe. She met his gaze steadily, vowing to make him look away first.

"Fine." The grudging syllable was practically a growl. "Now get out of here and do your fucking job while you still have it."

She was almost to the door when he spoke again.

"And if you breathe another word to the police or the press, I will personally see to it you never work in this town again. Are we clear?"

His patronizing attitude was like nails on a chalkboard, but Vesper forced herself to swallow the retort that leapt to her lips. Instead, she glanced back over her shoulder, nodded perfunctorily, and let herself out of the office.

Relief outweighed any sense of triumph she might have felt, but as her adrenaline began to ebb, fatigue rushed in to fill the void. She left Valhalla by the employees' entrance, beckoned to one of the taxis at the curb, slid inside, and closed her stinging eyes. All she wanted was to climb into bed, burrow into Nova's embrace, and sleep for a full twenty-four hours. The thought should have been frightening, but she was too tired to be afraid.

The ride was mercifully short at this hour of the night. She found an extra burst of energy as she climbed the stairs but focused on moving quietly once she reached the landing. Nova needed all the sleep she could get, especially after a disappointing day in the tournament. They hadn't been able to talk at all, but Vesper was sure her early loss in the first event had been unsettling. She eased open the front door and hurried inside, pausing to remove her heels and let her eyes adjust.

When they did, she frowned. Through the kitchen, she could see the outline of the sleeper sofa. Why had Nova gone to the trouble of making it up? Why hadn't she just slept in the bed? There was only one good answer to that question, and Vesper didn't like it. Obviously, Nova didn't feel welcome there without an invitation. The realization made her heart ache. Much of the cocky, self-assuredness of Nova's public persona was a front, but Vesper wondered whether Nova was also being especially careful not to reopen old wounds. Still, shouldn't they be past that by now, especially after having spent much of the last two nights making love?

The thought froze her where she stood on the threshold between the kitchen and the living room. Making love? This was a fling. What they shared had nothing to do with love, and everything to do with chemistry. It was sex—fun, no-strings, feel-good sex. She enjoyed Nova's company and had even come to respect her as a poker player. But there was no room in Vesper's life for falling in love. She had spent her adult life avoiding risk, not welcoming it into her bed.

Only then did Vesper realize she was staring. Nova had thrown off some of the blankets in her sleep, exposing one muscular thigh and part of her flank. Her skin glowed silver in the moonlight that filtered through the window, and Vesper found herself mesmerized by the gentle rise and fall of her rib cage. She wanted to step forward and fit her fingers into the grooves of Nova's bones—to hold her breaths in the palm of her hand.

Asleep, unwitting, Nova looked so innocent. But she was a player at heart. That much had been obvious at their first meeting, and several times thereafter. Nova didn't want commitment, either. They were on the same page. In a few weeks, she would leave, and life would return to normal. In the meantime, she could enjoy this, couldn't she? Nova certainly didn't seem to be protesting.

Barefoot, Vesper moved quietly across the intervening space and bent to stroke the hair back from Nova's forehead. "Hey, you," she said when Nova's eyelids fluttered. "Come to bed."

"Aren't I?"

The sound of her sleepy voice, gritty from lack of use, made Vesper wet. Even so, it wasn't sex that she craved in that moment. She stepped back and held out her hand. "No. Come with me."

As Nova dragged herself into a sitting position and laced her fingers with Vesper's, her eyes cleared of their haze. "What happened with Biz? Are you okay?"

Vesper drank in the planes and curves of her nude body. She had a sudden, insane wish to be a visual artist—to capture and preserve Nova's beauty. Swallowing against the dryness in her throat, she hurried to speak. "He showed up with prostitutes and drugs. I called the police on him." With a gentle tug, she led Nova into the bedroom and briskly pulled down the sheets. "He was arrested." She made a split-second decision not to say anything about Steve's ultimatum. It would only sour the mood and distract Nova from the World Series. Nova would be far from Vegas before any of the fallout from tonight descended to torpedo her career. There was no use in making her worry.

"Thank God." Nova helped Vesper out of her suit jacket and draped it over one corner of the dresser. She turned back and gently shooed Vesper's hands away from her shirtfront. "Let me."

Vesper let her arms hang loosely at her sides as Nova undid the buttons. The quick, sure movements of Nova's fingers made her feel both desired and cared for. She couldn't remember the last time she had allowed someone to undress her. It was such an intimate act—the slow reveal, the peeling away of external defenses.

Nova slipped the shirt down her arms and laid it on top of the jacket. "You're so beautiful," she murmured, pressing a gentle kiss to the side of Vesper's neck as she leaned in to undo her bra. Once it was gone, she stroked the sides of Vesper's breasts before sinking to one knee before her.

Pillowing one cheek against her abdomen, Nova reached behind her to unzip the skirt. Vesper closed her eyes and sifted her fingers through Nova's hair, relaxing into the intimate embrace. She felt the fabric puddle around her feet, but for a long moment, Nova didn't move. Finally, Vesper felt a soft kiss against her abdomen. When she looked down, Nova was staring back, a wistful expression softening her features. Vesper wanted to ask what she was thinking, but the question caught in her throat when Nova slowly eased her black bikinis down the length of her legs. Then, after another lingering kiss, she stood.

"Let's get you to bed." She climbed in first, turned onto her side, and held out one hand.

Vesper slid under the covers and nestled her body into the curve of Nova's torso, accepting her unspoken invitation to be the big spoon. Nova settled her arm across Vesper's waist, hand splayed over her stomach, and pulled her even closer.

"Comfortable?"

"Yes. Thank you." As the words left her mouth, Vesper internally cringed at how formal they sounded.

"Sure?" Nova loosened her grip. "You just got kind of tense."

Vesper clamped her hand over Nova's before she could withdraw. "Stay," she said. "Please."

Nova's lips brushed the nape of her neck. "Okay."

Relaxation was slow in coming. When Vesper closed her eyes, she saw Biz's crooked grin and heard a mental echo of his sleazy come-ons. *I'll never have to see him again*, she reminded herself. It was a familiar thought, taking her back to her adolescence—to sleepless nights on her cousin's threadbare couch and long, dull shifts in the local casino's restaurant. In those first lonely months, she'd had too much time to think and to question her own decisions. She'd abandoned her family for their own good but couldn't even tell them. For a long time, her only comfort had been that she would never have to see Samuel again.

But everything was different now. This time, she hadn't run from her abuser—she had gone on the offensive. This time, she had fought the battle instead of fleeing from it. So what if she would be out of a job within the week? The years she had spent in the crucible of Valhalla had given her the tools she needed to make it elsewhere. Where once she had only a suitcase to her name, now she wielded comps and credit lines. And she wasn't crashing on a couch offered out of begrudging charity—she was sleeping in her own bed, in her own apartment.

With Nova.

That was different, too. Isabella was something of a confidante, and Jeremy was as much a friend as a subordinate could be. But this—the closeness, the connectedness—was something she had been subconsciously craving. It felt so good to be held, and Vesper pressed her palm against Nova's knuckles, hoping to convey the emotion without speaking. In response, Nova slid one leg between hers, increasing the points of contact of their skin.

A warm wave of contentment washed over Vesper, loosening her limbs and soothing her lingering anxiety. Melting into Nova's embrace, she finally slept.

❖

"All in." Nova felt a jarring sense of déjà vu as she pushed her dwindling stack of chips toward the center of the table. This was the fourth time in the past week that she had found herself with her back to the wall, forced to risk everything for a shot at survival. Her other gambles had ended in failure. At least this time, she was certain to walk away with some money.

The turbo no limit hold 'em event had treated her well. She thrived on its quick pace, and after days of playing tight, careful poker, it was liberating to be more aggressive in her approach. Now, she was one of ten players left standing. If she could just win this hand, she would have a decent shot at surviving long enough to see her first final table at a live event. Only eight other players would stand between her and the coveted bracelet, then.

But she couldn't get ahead of herself. Glancing around the table, she watched as three of her four opponents folded immediately. The man two seats to her right was equally quick to call, though, and she struggled not to betray her disappointment. The move made sense—he had the second shortest stack at the table next to hers. If she'd been in his position, she probably would have done the same with halfway decent cards.

Her own king and ten of diamonds was more than decent, given the flop: the nine of clubs, seven of diamonds, and king of hearts. She had high pair and a decent kicker. She wouldn't find better ground than this to make her stand, especially given the whirlwind rate at which the blinds and antes were increasing. With a flick of her wrist, she turned over her cards in near synchrony with her opponent.

Queen of clubs, eight of spades. A weaker hand than her own, and her chance of winning was just under ninety-five percent. Still, he had a few outs that might save him. She wasn't out of the woods yet, and her palms began to sweat as she waited for the turn.

When the dealer revealed the jack of diamonds, Nova's head spun. Now, in addition to having top pair, she had a shot at making a flush on the river. Even so, her chance of winning had fallen slightly to ninety-three percent, thanks to the possibility of her opponent drawing to an inside straight. He needed a ten, and fortunately, she was holding one of the four in the deck. She could only hope that the other three had been dealt to the remaining players at the table.

Nova held her breath as the dealer burned a card. She had never been taught to pray, but at moments like these, it came instinctually. *Please.* The thought was a net, cast indiscriminately. If there was some higher power out there—God or Luck or Fate—she needed its benevolent intervention more than ever before.

When the ten of clubs materialized on the felt, its cloverleaves mocking her bad fortune, Nova felt as though she'd been punched in the sternum. *No.* The word ricocheted around her brain like a stray bullet. Ears ringing, she dimly heard the spectators groan. They had been on her side, she realized. Cold comfort.

A smattering of applause broke out as her opponent stood and fist-pumped, acknowledging his victory. After a moment, Nova caught his eye and extended her hand. He shook it perfunctorily and returned to his celebration, swooping up a thin, platinum blonde in his arms. Reporters crowded near the players, eager to interview those who had survived to the final table.

Nova rose stiffly, shaking out her legs as she waited for the tournament staff to sign her paperwork. At least she had made some money. Fifteen thousand dollars—enough to recoup her entry costs over the past few days with a bit of a surplus. It could have been worse. Still, as she walked away, the weight of disappointment rested heavily on her shoulders. Fatigue crept into the crevices of her brain, a gray mist leeching the world of color. All she wanted was to slide beneath Vesper's sheets and sleep for a week surrounded by the comfort of her scent.

It was too intimate a thought, and Nova shook her head in a futile effort to dislodge it. With each passing hour, the lease on their relationship grew closer to expiring. The start of the main event was only days away, and once it was over, she would have no reason to stay. If she miraculously won a bracelet between now and then, her career would take off in a whirlwind of accolades and appearances. But the odds of finding success were dwindling. And if she didn't, then what?

The easiest course of action would be to slink back to Palo Alto with her tail between her legs, proof positive that her parents and advisors had been right all along. But she didn't want to be an object lesson, and she definitely wasn't going to return to school. That ship had sailed. Even the prospect of going home to the house she shared with her friends wasn't appealing. She had barely spoken to them in weeks. The thought of returning to her life as it had been made her stomach flip-flop like a dying fish. She didn't want to play musical relationships anymore.

She wanted Vesper, but Vesper only wanted a casual relationship. More than once, Nova had considered admitting to her growing feelings, but Vesper had been clear in her expectations. The only thing Nova would accomplish by being honest was to prematurely end their time together. Maybe it was pathetic, but she would take what she could get.

Last she'd heard, Vesper was in the craps pit with Priscilla, who was taking the day off from poker. On the way, she passed Sól Bar and almost changed course. A drink or three sounded perfect right about now. Forcing herself to resist temptation, she kept walking. She didn't need a drink; she needed to go home and sleep in order to be sharp for the six-player Omaha event tomorrow at noon.

She caught sight of Vesper first, as always. Today, she wore a sapphire blue dress and matching heels that reminded Nova of the deep sea on a clear day. Her jewelry was understated: gold teardrop earrings and a thin, golden watch around her left wrist. The overall effect was to highlight the beauty of her skin rather than its ornaments, and Nova's breath caught as she succumbed.

When Priscilla glanced her way, Nova knew she'd been caught staring. As she approached, she prepared herself for their inevitable pity. "Hot dice today, I hope?"

At the sound of her voice, Vesper turned with a smile. It only lasted a moment, but its warmth soaked deep into Nova's hollow chest. As Vesper searched her eyes, the answer to her question must have been apparent, because the expression faded. She started to raise one hand, then stopped.

"Lukewarm." Priscilla was regarding her critically. "How did you do?"

"Busted out right before reaching the final table." Nova shrugged. "I had over a ninety percent chance of winning, but the other guy made it on the river."

"I'm sorry." Vesper's voice was soft and soothing. Nova wanted to pull it around her like a blanket, close her eyes, and drift off.

"Lousy luck," Priscilla said. "Let's get a drink. You could use one, and I need a break."

"Thanks, but I really shouldn't. I need to be sharp for tomorrow."

Vesper looked at her as though she had two heads. "That's ridiculous. You've been running yourself ragged. You're a zombie right now, and all you'd do tomorrow is lose another buy-in."

Taken aback at the assertiveness of her tone, Nova struggled for a reply. Maybe she should have felt defensive, but mostly, she appreciated Vesper's concern.

"She has a point." Priscilla gestured the length of Nova's body. "Just look at yourself. The bags under your eyes could fit my luggage."

Nova felt as though she'd been backed into a corner. Though since it was Vesper doing the backing, she didn't mind so much. "Okay. You're right. I'll take a day off." Just saying the words filled her with relief. She really did need a break.

"Let's have that drink, then."

They ended up at Barri, where Priscilla commandeered a private table and ordered the most expensive items off the menu, including a five-hundred-dollar bottle of champagne. When Nova dared to ask what they were celebrating, Priscilla arched one imperious eyebrow and said, "Life. Youth. Passion."

"Cheers." Nova didn't look at Vesper as they clinked glasses. Had Priscilla figured out that they were…what, exactly? A couple? That wasn't the right word. Fucking? Nova's fingers tightened on the stem of her champagne flute. That wasn't right, either. It sounded too crass. Friends with benefits? But no, they hadn't begun as friends. Their chemistry had been undeniable since their very first meeting.

After a while, their conversation turned back to poker. "Did the speed of the turbo event make it feel closer to playing online?" Vesper asked.

"Yes. I think that's partly why I made it as far as I did." Nova reached for a piece of sushi topped by a tiny cluster of caviar, wondering when she would next eat so well. "Too bad there isn't another speed event on the schedule." Not wanting to monopolize the conversation, she looked to Priscilla. "What else do you plan on entering?"

"Oh, I think I'll hang around until the main event, as long as Vesper can find a place for me to rest my weary head."

Nova shared a brief, private smile with Vesper. Thanks to the way she'd handled Biz, Priscilla's extended stay had been a non-issue. "I hope I don't find you at my table in the early rounds," she said. "You know too much about my style."

Priscilla gave her a pointed look. "You once told me that the greatest poker players are the ones who can publish books about their strategy and still beat the pants off you."

Nova laughed. Priscilla was sharp. "Are you sure that's how I put it? In any case, touché."

"You should enter the Poker Player's Championship." Vesper leaned into Nova's space as she spoke, her gaze intent. "I can't believe I didn't think of this before. It's perfect."

Perfect. Nova took a sip of champagne to buy herself some time before she replied. That wasn't the adjective she would have used. There was a reason why she had never considered that particular event, and the reason was *money*.

"I've heard people talking about that," said Priscilla. "What is it?"

"It's the biggest mixed game event, played over five days," Nova said. "There are eight games total, starting with limit two-seven triple draw lowball and ending with pot limit Omaha."

"It's the most prestigious event at the tournament," Vesper chimed in. "The one all the professionals consider the best measure of true skill."

Priscilla's forehead crinkled. "Why is that?"

"Having to switch games each round can be very difficult," Vesper said. "It takes a lot of skill to be able to continually adjust to new rules and strategies. And then there's the buy-in."

"How much is it?"

"Fifty thousand dollars," Nova chimed in, hoping they'd drop the subject. Technically, she could afford that much, but only if she depleted her bank account. Given her performance so far, there was no way she could justify that kind of risk.

"Thousands of people try their luck at the main event," Vesper said, "but the field for the Championship is usually less than two hundred." She looked to Nova. "You'll have better odds than in any other game. And won't switching so often make you feel like you're playing online?"

Nova sat back in her chair and raised the flute to her lips. She had never thought about it that way, but Vesper's logic was sound. Without the money, though, her reasoning was also moot. Steeling herself for embarrassment, she finally confessed.

"You're probably right. But I just don't have the bankroll to do it."

Vesper's expression shifted through sympathy to guilt, and ended in a scowl of fierce concentration. For once, Nova knew exactly what Vesper was thinking. She was trying to find some way to subsidize her entry into the Championship, but there was no way that Nova would allow her to spend her painstakingly hard-earned money just so she had one more snowball's chance in hell to win a bracelet.

"I can hel—" Vesper was beginning to say, even as Nova started shaking her head.

Priscilla's voice put an end to their argument before it had begun. "I'll stake you," she said, gaze fixed on Nova. "That's what it's called, isn't it?" She took their silence for assent. "Half for half. I throw in twenty-five thousand now, and you give me half of whatever you win. How much goes to the champion?"

"Two million," Vesper said. She had since regained control of her features, and whatever she felt about this idea was buried deep below the surface.

Nova felt paralyzed. Should she say yes? Staking was a perfectly natural practice in the poker world, especially for the more expensive games, but it would also add stress to a situation that already felt like a pressure cooker. "That would be a thirty-nine hundred percent gain on your investment," she said instead as her brain automatically retreated to the simple comfort of mathematics.

"What stock option can offer you that?" Priscilla raised her champagne flute again. Streaming bubbles glinted in the light as they rose toward the surface, and freedom. "Do you accept?"

In the end, there was only one possible answer. Despite her own protestations to Vesper all those weeks ago, Nova knew the truth. Poker might be more a game of skill than a game of chance, but she was, at heart, a gambler. Priscilla was offering her a fighting chance to do what she'd come here to do—to prove to everyone that she belonged in this world. Tilting her own glass forward, she clinked their rims together.

CHAPTER SEVENTEEN

Vesper stood with one hand clutching the rail, her gaze fixed on Nova where she sat sandwiched between two men. The twenty feet separating them felt like a gaping chasm. Having lost almost half her chips a few hands ago, Nova was teetering on the brink of the abyss. Vesper didn't want to watch her flame out just before another final table, but she was the one who had pushed Nova into this, and the least she could do was to cheer her on.

"Breathe, V." TJ patted her briefly between her shoulder blades before returning his elbows to the railing. "It's not over yet."

"Let's hope not," Vesper said. She glanced at her watch. It was close to midnight. Nova had been playing for nearly ten hours straight, with only a few short breaks. She had to be exhausted. But if she could just outlast a few other players, she would make it to the final table. And then…well, if she entered it short-stacked, she might find herself exiting all too quickly. But if she could make something of these final few hands and advance from a position of power—that would be an altogether different story.

A pair of Oakleys shuttered Nova's eyes, but her hands were far too expressive for her own good. When she was feeling confident, she plucked smoothly at her chip stack, allowing the small discs to clink together softly as they slid through her fingers. When she had poor cards, though, her movements were erratic. It was a small tell, but Vesper was sure she wasn't the only one who had picked up on it. She reached for her phone and called Nova's number, silently praying that she would pick up. Nova was allowed to answer it as long as she stepped away from the table, and when she signaled the dealer, Vesper's relief was palpable.

"Are you okay?" Nova was scanning the crowd in search of her.

"I am, but you're not. Quit messing with your chips. You're broadcasting the strength of your cards."

Nova cursed. "I was trying to be so careful!"

"Just keep your hands still. You can do this." She caught Nova's eye and smiled. The weary grin she got in return made her want to drag Nova back to her bed—for sleep, not for sex.

"Thanks. I...thanks." Nova disconnected the call and returned to the table. She put her hands in her lap, and from the tension in her arms, Vesper guessed she was gripping her shorts to keep herself anchored.

"Come on. Be smart now."

She hadn't realized she'd spoken aloud until Amelia leaned in from her other side with a sympathetic look on her face. "Fingers crossed."

Vesper suppressed the urge to roll her eyes. Fingers crossed? Did Amelia really believe that luck held sway, here? More than any other event in the WSOP, this one was about skill. Nova would either prevail or she wouldn't, and luck would only be able to help her so much. Right now, she was playing too tightly—a logical response to the hit she'd taken, but also wholly predictable. Her opponents were taking advantage. Whenever she seemed to want to stay in a hand, one or another of the players would make a large bet, and she would fold. She was backpedaling right into the jaws of defeat.

As she put her phone back into her purse, Vesper's fingers brushed a smooth, curved surface. Regretting her forgetfulness, she pulled it out. She had seen the mini conch shell in the casino's gift shop this afternoon in one of those plastic bins filled with knickknacks designed to entice children. Years of living inches from the poverty line had trained her never to make impulse purchases, but she had bought the shell.

"That's pretty," said Amelia. "But far from home."

"I bought it on a whim today. For Nova." Vesper felt her face grow warm as she answered the unspoken question. "I thought she might be able to use it as a card cap, but then my day got busy and I didn't have a chance to give it to her."

"Card cap?"

"A little token to put on top of your cards," TJ said. "It signals to the dealer that you're still in the hand."

"I see." Amelia smiled at her. "Well, I'm sure she'll appreciate it."

If I can give it to her before she busts, Vesper thought. She mirrored the smile and carefully deposited the shell into her jacket pocket before turning back to the game. Even if it was a train wreck, she had to watch. If she continued to study Nova's playing style, maybe she could come up with a few more tips to give her.

In the hour that followed, antes and blinds slipped away like sand eroding from a beach. Nova's lot didn't improve; she continued to play much too conservatively. From time to time, Vesper glanced over at the other remaining table, hoping that someone there would bust so that this grueling day could end. She wanted to be supportive but wasn't sure how much more of this she could take.

When TJ and Amelia finally wandered off, it was a relief. She might feel comfortable with them, but she was still their host, which involved a certain measure of decorum. Right now, she was much too stressed and exhausted to be "on." Her headache ratcheted up another notch as the player two seats to Nova's left moved a large pile of chips into the center. He had probably bet the limit, which had grown progressively higher over the past four days. Damn it, Nova was going to have to fold again.

Except this time, she didn't. Vesper heard herself gasp as Nova pushed all of her chips into the center of the table. What on earth was she doing? Yes, the blinds and antes were wearing her down, but if this bet failed, she'd be done. A chill shivered through her, and she wrapped her arms around her chest, silently praying that Nova wasn't trying to bluff.

One other player had called, as did the original bettor, but everyone after Nova got out of the way. Vesper stood on her toes, though it did nothing to improve her view. Biting her lower lip, she watched helplessly as the dealer instructed the players to show their cards. This was 2-7 triple draw, she reminded herself. The lowest hand would win.

For a long, agonizing moment, no one moved. Finally, Nova sat back in her seat, shoulders slumped. Vesper's heart lurched into her throat until Nova pushed her sunglasses to the top of her head and smiled in obvious relief. When the dealer confirmed the cause of her happiness by sweeping the chips in her direction, Vesper almost lost her balance.

"Yes!" she whispered fiercely, managing to restrain herself from a more demonstrable display. No longer sitting on the shortest stack of chips, all Nova had to do now was to wait for someone else to bust. She had made it to her first final table.

"She had the nuts," someone said from a few feet away. If it was true, Nova had finally gotten a stroke of good luck at exactly the right time. In 2-7 triple draw, the nuts was a hand of 2, 3, 4, 5, and 7. Usually the worst of the worst, it was in this case the best of the best.

Fifteen minutes later, it was all over, as the man who had led with the limit bet earlier went all in and lost. The tournament staff swarmed both tables, cataloguing chip counts and issuing instructions for the final table. They were going to have a long night of preparation. The Championship might not be nearly as high profile as the main event, but it was still a big deal, especially to the professional gambling world. They would probably need to spend more time with Nova than with most of the other contestants, since she was a virtual unknown in the live game.

As if the thought had summoned her, Nova jogged up to the rail. In board shorts and a gray hoodie, perched sunglasses holding her hair in place, she looked like she'd spent the day on the beach, not glued to a chair.

"Hi." She rested one hand a few inches from where Nova's was still holding on to the rail.

"Congratulations." Vesper's cheeks stretched at the breadth of her smile. She wanted to lean over the barrier between them and kiss her. Everyone would see, but it was suddenly hard to remember why that mattered. "You did it!"

Nova shrugged. "Lived to die another day."

Vesper shot her a look. "Lived to win tomorrow, you mean." She reached back into her purse and held out the shell. "Speaking of which: this will bring you luck."

Nova's fingers stroked over hers as she took the talisman. "It's beautiful," she said, inspecting it.

"It matches your theme." Vesper swept her hand through the air, indicating her beach attire. "I thought you could use it as a card cap."

"That's a great idea!" Nova leaned in but apparently remembered herself a moment later and turned what had been clearly intended as a kiss into an awkward hug. "Um, thanks." She pulled back quickly. "You should go home. The vultures need me for a while."

It was just past one in the morning, and Vesper was tired, but she didn't want to return to her apartment alone. She would have to start doing that soon enough. The thought made her twinge deep inside.

"No, I'll wait. There's always work to do."

"Okay. I'll call you, then." She seemed to want to say something else but then decided against it, raising the conch instead in an awkward salute. "Thanks again."

Vesper watched as Nova was swallowed up by the throng of media. Even if she didn't win the event tomorrow, making the final table gave her a legitimacy that she might be able to parlay into other, less stringent sponsorship deals. Her career was finally taking off. Both their careers were. She had the right to feel triumphant, twice over.

So why did she feel lonely instead?

❖

In its initial configuration, the final table of the Championship had eerily resembled the cash game that had sent Nova into the tailspin that in turn had ended in her becoming Vesper's charity case. Mac, Kris, and Damon had all advanced, and during the first few rounds earlier that afternoon, the men had exchanged a slew of banter as they systematically dismantled the stacks of their three weakest opponents. Nova had played as tightly as she dared, ignoring Damon's trash talking and letting the other players knock each other out.

At the end of the previous round, Mac had gone heads-up with Kris and triumphed, so now there were only three players remaining. She still couldn't believe she was one. Unfortunately, she was also the one with the shortest stack, which meant they were ganging up on her. That was nothing personal, of course—it made perfect strategic sense. It also meant that she couldn't afford to play conservatively anymore. As soon as she was dealt even a reasonably strong hand, she would have to make a move.

From here on out, there would be no more switching from game to game. The tournament organizers had ruled that no limit hold 'em was the best way to decide the victor once the table had been reduced to three players. As the dealer shuffled, Nova counted out the 400K big blind and pushed her chips into the center. Four hundred thousand dollars. She tried to remind herself that they weren't *her* dollars. She was playing with everyone's money and would get a percentage when the tournament was over. Still, she had never been forced to lay down that large a blind before, and it was disconcerting.

No, it was worse. When she pulled her hand back, her chest suddenly constricted in a wash of anxiety. She looked out at the crowd, but it was too densely packed for her to pick out Vesper's face, if she was even there. As she tried to take deep, even breaths, the walls seemed to shudder and close in around her. Naturally, her claustrophobia would choose to rear its ugly head at the most inopportune moment.

Over the years, Nova had found that getting up and walking around often helped the panic to recede. But they had just returned from a break, and leaving the table again would signal her weakness to her opponents. She would have to work through this while sitting still, and quickly. The round was about to begin.

Leaning back in her chair, she closed her eyes and pictured the beach. Beneath the table, she wiggled her toes, imagining the warm sand sliding against her skin and the hot sun beating down on her shoulders. A card brushed her hand, rousing her from the reverie. Her heart was still pounding wildly as she glanced down at what she'd been dealt. Queen of diamonds, seven of spades. Not good enough, especially when Damon led out with a 500K raise. Whether he had the cards to back it up was unclear, but she couldn't pull off a bluff when her skin was crawling and her pulse was a drum roll. Mucking her hand, she tried not to think about how much money she'd just surrendered. Not that. Anything but that. She had to calm down.

Her next two cards were the three of clubs and the seven of hearts. Drawing to an inside straight was a vexed proposition at best, and suicide right now. She folded, as did Damon a moment later. Her small blind and his big blind joined Mac's growing pile of chips. Her next hand with a four and nine unsuited wasn't much better. She mucked her cards. Mac laughed at something Damon said. Mercifully, the words were drowned out by the murmur of the crowd, but no white noise could distract her from the fact that her chip count had just fallen below two million.

Nova closed her eyes again, but the beach fantasy just wasn't cutting it anymore. The truth was, as much as she wanted to return to Año Nuevo when all of this was over, she didn't want to do it alone. She didn't want to do it with her roommates, either. It was Vesper who belonged beside her, hair loose and skin glowing under the sun, a surfboard propped awkwardly under her arm. Nova wanted to teach her how to read the undertow and time her paddle and ride a breaking wave. Later, they would sit together at a table in the shade of a palm tree and drink fruity frozen concoctions, flirting and teasing as the sun made its bed in the ocean.

A fresh blast of the air conditioner reminded Nova that she was just shy of three hundred miles from the Pacific. Shivering, she opened her eyes and pushed her 400K big blind into the pot. Two cards slid to a halt on her patch of felt, and she reached for them, too desperate even to pray.

Pocket rockets stared back at her: ace of diamonds and of hearts. Twin scarlet letters. Suddenly, her heart was racing for an altogether different reason. Struggling not to betray her elation, Nova latched onto the rhythm of her own breaths. In and out. In and out. Slow and even, like her pulse should be. Her eyes might be protected by the shades, but the rest of her face had to remain impassive. If she didn't play this hand perfectly, she would squander her chance for a comeback.

It was Damon's turn to start the betting. If he led out aggressively, she could call. If he didn't, her choice would be much more complicated. She'd been playing so tightly that if she bet too much, she would betray her strong hand and both he and Mac would fold. But she also wanted this pot to be as large as possible so that she could recoup some of her losses.

Damon was looking at her now, eyes narrowed. Hopefully, she seemed vulnerable. Standoffish at best, Damon had barely acknowledged her presence since her abysmal performance in that cash game. All he felt for her, she felt certain, was disdain. Hopefully, she could use that against him.

When he raised 400K, she almost smiled before remembering that they hadn't even seen the flop. Damon's pre-flop re-raises were the stuff of legends, and now she was on the other side of one. The fact that she was holding two aces made it more palatable than it otherwise might have been.

Then Mac called the bet, and an icy finger of dread trailed down her spine. After a moment of utterly authentic hesitation, she slid 400K into the middle, fingers trembling from the adrenaline. Quickly, she returned her hands to her knees. Gaze riveted on the empty swatch of felt before the dealer, she waited for the cards to appear. Nine of spades, nine of diamonds, three of clubs. Nova blinked down at them, unable to swallow. If either Damon or Mac had a nine, his chance of winning had just skyrocketed to eighty-nine percent.

Mac looked from her to the pot and back again. Then, with a shrug, he pushed 900K worth of chips into the middle. It was exactly the number that would force her to go all in if she chose to remain in the hand, and he knew it. Either he had that nine, or he was trying to bluff her into busting.

Finally, her throat loosened enough to swallow. If she backed off, she would have to surrender her 900K in the next two rounds as the blinds bled her down. Lady Luck only knew what cards she would be dealt. That was no way to go out. No, she needed to put up a fight now, with aces in her pockets. The turn or the river might be kind.

She scanned the crowd again but still couldn't pick out Vesper. She saw TJ, though, clapping with his hands above his head as though she were playing soccer and not poker. The room was awash with sound, but his voice rose above the roar. "Get it, Nova!"

She pushed her shades to the top of her head, then stroked her thumb across the cool surface of the conch. For a moment, she imagined she could feel the cards beneath it, stirring like sea beasts in the depths, ready to wake. This wasn't over. She had two outs, and the aces wanted to win.

"All in." As she spoke the words, a foreign sense of calm settled over her. Was she in shock? Had her adrenal glands run dry? What was happening to her?

When Damon mucked his cards, she knew he'd been bluffing. Mac met her unshielded eyes, smiled slightly, and said, "Ladies first."

She palmed the conch and flipped her cards. The crowd's collective gasp would have been comical under any other set of circumstances. Mac's eyebrows rose, but he said nothing as he flipped over the nine of clubs and the jack of hearts. There was a smattering of applause, but also some groaning. A distant part of Nova's brain wondered whether her supporters were cheering for *her* or for her gender?

The dealer burned a card and turned over the queen of clubs. Nova knew she was supposed to feel disappointed or sad or upset, but she felt nothing. Her mind had somehow broken through the cloud cover of emotion. She only wondered how long it would last.

The dealer's hands were well manicured, for a man. Idly, she wondered whether that was a casino requirement. They moved efficiently, but time seemed to slow as he grasped the edge of the card that would decide her fate. With a flick of his wrist, he revealed it to the world.

Time stopped. Nova stared blankly down at the table. The ace of spades stared back at her, regal, impassive, victorious.

Victorious.

The room exploded into shouts and cheers, an avalanche of sound that pulled her under and turned her upside down, releasing her from the grip of her paralysis. Exultation flooded through her as the dealer pushed the pot into her orbit, leaving behind 200K as her small blind. The reminder sobered her. As much as she wanted to join in the audience's celebration, she had won a single battle, not the war. Mac had left himself with only 500K, but he wasn't finished yet. And beside her there was Damon, who had more chips than the both of them combined.

The dealer dealt. Mac, who mercifully had the button, folded his hand immediately. Damon was the big blind and Nova decided to give him a taste of his own medicine. She raised 800K and waited. A low chorus of *ooohhhhs* around her suggested that the crowd was enjoying her sassiness. After a solid minute of deliberation, he mucked his cards.

Nova hid her smile by taking a sip from her seltzer water. For the first time since this round had begun, she felt a measure of confidence. Still, when her next two cards were the ten of clubs and the five of diamonds—affectionately known as the "five and dime"—she folded. It wasn't good enough to run with, especially since Damon would be looking to recoup his losses. And sure enough, he pushed Mac all in right away.

Nova watched their showdown closely, trying to pay particular attention to Damon's facial expressions and body language, but it was like trying to guess the mind of a statue. He really was the Ice Man, and within a matter of seconds, his straight had frozen out Mac's two pair. The crowd rewarded Mac's performance with warm applause, and he rose to acknowledge it.

She stood when he did, and once he had shaken Damon's hand, Mac turned to give her a quick embrace. "Take him down a few pegs," he whispered.

As she returned to her seat, the fact that she was playing a heads-up game with Damon Magnusson with a WSOP bracelet—and a sponsorship deal—on the line finally began to sink in. A renewed surge of anxiety knotted up her stomach, and she quickly turned her head away from Damon so he wouldn't catch any hint of fear in her expression.

"Players, are you ready?" Their new dealer was a woman. Tall and blond and thin, she was the paragon of the American ideal of female beauty, but Nova didn't even feel a twinge of desire. Vesper was the one she wanted. Only Vesper.

"Yes," Damon said curtly. He laced his hands together, rested them on the table, and stared at her impassively.

"Ready." The buzz of the crowd would be her ocean, the heat of the lamps her sun. She wanted to be right here, right now, fully present—channeling her emotion, not insulating herself from it. This was the moment she'd been waiting for, the chance to carve out a space for herself in this world. To prove she belonged—not just to the Damons of the world, but to her family and friends. And to herself.

The cards thrummed between the dealer's hands, a drum roll announcing the final showdown. As the first two hit the table, Nova's vision telescoped. She was up against the most aggressive player in the world. Fight or fold, those were her options. There could be no middle ground.

The rhythm of the game caught her up, and for a while, she let it carry her. The blinds had gone up to 250K and 500K. Her first three hands were junk, and she folded them all, giving up a million in blinds to Damon within two minutes. He never cracked a smile, but she could feel the smugness radiating from him like bad cologne. Praying to be dealt some kind of weapon, Nova reached out to pull her fourth hand toward the hole camera.

Ace of diamonds, king of clubs. Big Slick. Her prayer had been granted, and this time, she wouldn't mess around by limping in. Damon, on the small blind, was first to act and he called. After a moment of consideration, Nova raised to one million, hoping he would be intrigued instead of frightened off. He called instantly. Did that mean he had a strong hand? Or would he have called no matter what?

The flop revealed the five of clubs, seven of spades, and king of spades. Mindful of Vesper's warning about her tells, Nova kept one hand on her chips and the other on the conch shell. She led out with a continuation bet of one million, once again hoping to keep Damon interested if he'd only been bluffing. But instead of calling, he tossed two million into the pot. A re-raise. Of course.

Unless he'd been dealt pocket rockets, she had top pair and top kicker. But there were two spades in the flop, so he might be chasing a flush, and that five and seven might also point to a straight. Too many options. Suddenly, her plan seemed naïve. Over half of her money was already in the pot. Calling Damon's bet would leave her with 600K. Then again, whatever he might have at some later point, she had something *now*, and that was worth defending. Nova carefully counted out a million in chips and threw them into the pot.

The turn was the four of hearts—not exactly comforting, if Damon was going after the straight. Nova checked and surprisingly, Damon checked behind her. Maybe he was still waiting for his draw? Not a spade, she prayed silently as the dealer shuffled. Please, not a spade.

When the jack of clubs appeared on the river, Nova's confidence returned. She pushed her remaining 600K into the middle of the table, hoping Damon had struck out and would fold. "All in."

When he didn't respond immediately, she managed to meet his steely gaze without flinching. What did he see when he looked at her? A worthy opponent, or a bug in need of squashing?

Finally, he called. Nova swallowed hard, gently moved the conch aside, and turned over her cards. Damon's lips twisted in disgust—the first emotional reaction she'd seen from him all day. There was only one reason for him to look that way, and her heart fluttered wildly as she dropped her gaze to his cards. The king and queen of hearts. She had won, all right. Just barely.

Hands trembling, she stacked up her chips: 7.2 million from a single pot. She had won that much before in a handful of online games, but it was a completely different experience to be able to rub the chips between her fingertips and tangibly feel her success. She realized that for the first time since the tournament began, she had a significant lead over Damon.

For the next several hands, Damon would claw and scratch that lead away, going all-in three hands in a row. The cards went cold for Nova, and as much as she wanted to face up to his aggression, she just didn't have the hands for it. Half an hour after Big Slick had staked her a seemingly insurmountable lead, Nova found herself only 600K ahead with the momentum decidedly in Damon's court. And he knew it, too. With every win, he turned to the audience and pumped his hands in the air.

As the dealer broke out a new pack of cards, Nova looked out into the crowd. A glimpse of Vesper would make her feel much better. Where was she? Had she decided not to come? Was something wrong?

"Nova!" TJ's voice rang out again. This time, when she turned to wave to him, he was pointing across the room. "She's over there!"

She followed the line of his arm with her eyes and sure enough, there was Vesper in the midst of the television crew, talking intently with a man who was probably one of the producers. Had she gotten roped into working? Nova watched as she raised her hands to gesticulate, every movement precise. Those hands had been all over her body, inside her body, tormenting and inflaming and soothing her. No one had ever touched her the way Vesper had—tenderly and possessively, all at once.

As though she'd heard the thought, Vesper looked up. Their eyes met and held, but the distance between them was too great for her to read Vesper's expression. Even so, in that instant the tournament faded away, poker faded away. There was only Vesper. Nova fought the urge to get up from the table and run to her. And then the tournament director announced that the blinds were being raised to 300K and 600K, severing their connection.

Two cards slid to a halt in front of her. She exhaled slowly and picked them up. Staring back at her were the king and ten of hearts. Finally, a decent hand. When Damon led out with a 600K raise, she didn't even think twice. She called.

The flop came seven of spades, two of hearts, eight of clubs. Disappointment hit Nova like a punch in the gut. She had missed the flop entirely. She was also playing out of position, which meant that the prudent thing to do would be to check to Damon and then fold on his bet. How she would have loved for the royals to be her magical six and nine of hearts instead. Then she would have an outside straight draw, at least. Nova looked up at Damon, who stared at her stonily from across the table. She had been trying all day to get a read on him, but it was useless. The man was impenetrable. And she was as easy to read as a teleprompter, in comparison. Nova tapped the felt, checking to him.

As expected, Damon lifted 1.2 million in chips and flicked them into the pot. The colored discs landed and rolled haphazardly around the table, causing the dealer to stop play in order to gather them up. At a cash table, Damon would have been chastised for splashing the chips. But under the bright lights of the final table, he was the king and the king could do as he pleased.

Nova felt a wave of anger roll over her. She hadn't played for over twelve hours and wagered $50K of her money and Priscilla's just to limp to the finish line behind the likes of Damon Magnusson. Chances were, the junk flop had hurt him as much as it had hurt her. Unless he was sitting on a pocket pair, he was probably still waiting for his hand to materialize as well. She was going to go down shooting this time. Nova counted out 1.2 million chips and pushed the stack into the center of the table.

The turn card was the five of diamonds, and suddenly, a plan began to form in the back of her mind. The five on the turn would have given her a straight had she been playing the six nine of hearts. Just because she wasn't dealt them didn't mean she couldn't play them, right? For the entirety of the final table, she had been fighting to school her reactions, control her tells. All of her energy had gone into creating a mask of bulletproof indifference and yet her best opponents seemed to be able to see right through her façade. She was a tight, aggressive player and Damon knew it. The last several hands had shown that without good cards, he was going to dismantle her stack in short order. Because she hadn't shown that she was willing to gamble on a losing hand.

Nova looked into the crowd where she had last seen TJ. Vesper was now standing beside him. Vesper, who had read her as a typical Casanova from the moment they met. Vesper, whose suspicions had been confirmed when Emily had come to visit.

Vesper had typecast her, and Nova had played her role to perfection, bluffing all the while. Perhaps she had been carefree and loose before, but things were different now. She wanted more of Vesper. Not just more of what they already had—so much more. Everything. And yet she had allowed Vesper to categorize their relationship as casual, no strings attached, when in reality, she was already all in.

Here under the blazing media lights, the truth had nowhere to hide. She had fallen in love. Holding Vesper's gaze, Nova pushed all of her chips into the pot. "All in."

The crowd reacted with a roar of surprise and Nova could feel the cameras swinging about to get close ups on her face and Damon's. Even Damon seemed unsettled by the turn of events, though his posture had barely shifted. He was studying the cards on the table intently, undoubtedly running all of the numbers through his supercomputer brain. But Nova was counting on more than mathematics to pull off this bluff. She was hoping that Damon had studied her online tournament wins and knew her penchant for playing six nine of hearts.

That he didn't call right away confirmed her suspicions that he was still waiting for his hand. But his hole cards could still beat hers and she would be out of the tournament. After two minutes of deliberation, Damon finally mucked his cards with disgust. The room erupted around her as Nova gathered and stacked her winnings. Damon would be pissed in a few months when he saw the televised game.

Two hands later, he was all in.

"I call." Nova's voice, at least, was strong. It carried into the crowd, which roared back its approval. Nova soaked in their support as she carefully moved her chips into the pot. Alongside Damon's, they formed a miniature metropolis, towers rising proudly to scrape the stale air.

"Players," announced the dealer, "on the count of three, show us your cards. One. Two…Three!"

The hall fell silent. Nova flipped over her hand, letting her cards spill onto the felt. Time seemed to slow as she turned her head, and for an instant, her eyes blurred. They refocused on the ten of clubs and ten of spades. Damon had three of a kind, but that wasn't good enough to beat her straight. She had done it. She had won a bracelet.

As the crowd began chanting her name, Nova scrambled to her feet and extended her hand across the table. Damon shook it without saying a word, then turned away. Numbly, Nova walked toward the rail.

Vesper. She had to find Vesper. Cameras clustered around her face as reporters shouted questions, but she ignored them all.

"Nova!" TJ's bellow swung her attention to the left. He had managed to carve out a place for Vesper along the edge and was shielding her body with his own. She hurried toward them, almost tripping over one of the camera wires in the process. TJ reached out to thump her on the back as soon as she was within arm's length. "You did it! You fucking did it!"

And then Vesper was there, right in front of her, smiling broadly. Nova wanted to vault over the rail and kiss her, but even as the thought passed through her mind, she realized her folly. The cameras were everywhere, and Vesper was still in the closet. Even an embrace might be misconstrued. Belatedly, Nova realized she should never have sought her out. The numbness spread, filling her chest.

"Congratulations!" Vesper tried to shout over the crowd.

"Thanks." Nova nodded awkwardly and stuck her hands into her pockets.

"Nova, baby!" Evan's voice boomed out behind her. "Fantastic job out there!" He rested his hands on her shoulders, spun her around, and kissed her on both cheeks.

She hadn't seen him in months—not since her last Royal Flush appearance in London. Naturally, he would come out of the woodwork as soon as she had proven her value to the company.

"Hi, Evan."

"Ready to claim your reward?"

Her reward: a two million dollar check and the golden bracelet that was her golden ticket. Everything she had wanted. Everything she had worked so hard for.

"Sure," she said. "Of course." And plastering a smile onto her face, she let him lead her from the room.

CHAPTER EIGHTEEN

It was past eleven before Vesper's phone vibrated with a message from Nova. *Finally done. Still here?*

Yes. Meet you in the lobby.

As she made her way downstairs, she smothered a yawn. Thankfully, there was a day of rest between the conclusion of the Poker Player's Championship and the main event. Unless some kind of emergency occurred, she planned to spend it keeping Nova in bed.

Her steps quickened at the thought. She hadn't seen Nova since the champion's dinner that had followed the press conference and photo shoot. The meal, hosted by several of the higher-ups from both the tournament staff and Valhalla, had transpired in a private room at Barri. Nova had invited her, along with TJ's family, Amelia, Priscilla, Jeremy, and Evan—"the people I've grown closest to in the past few weeks," as she described them.

While her performance in the Championship had been the main topic of conversation, Nova had made sure to praise Vesper liberally in Steve's presence. Even on a day that undeniably belonged to her, she was thinking of Vesper's future. Vesper didn't expect Steve to reconsider and wasn't sure she would sign back on with him even if he did, but it had been nice to watch him squirm. She had wanted to thank Nova, but the opportunity to speak alone never arose. It seemed like forever since they had woken up together this morning.

As she entered the lobby, she saw Jeremy carrying a cup of coffee away from the café. "Hello again. Long night?"

"James pulled me in. Two of his clients are wrapping up dinner now but want to go clubbing afterward. Are you going home, I hope?"

"Yes. I was just waiting for Nova." She managed to say it without blushing.

"There she is."

Nova was hurrying across the lobby toward them, and the sight of her sent a current buzzing beneath Vesper's skin. She was wearing the same board shorts and sandals that she'd had on all day, but sometime in the past few hours, she had acquired a Royal Flush hoodie.

"Hi," she said as she approached. Her gaze slid down and up Vesper's body, and when their eyes met, Nova's were dark with desire.

"Hi," Vesper echoed, marveling at the way her body lit up in Nova's presence. Their chemistry only seemed to be growing stronger with time, not waning. "How did everything go?"

"I inked a three-year contract." The note of disbelief in Nova's voice was endearing. "My first appearance is in LA in a week."

One week. It was a reminder that days were all they had left before reality separated them. Vesper was careful to let none of the disappointment color her voice. She had been the one to set the terms of their relationship, after all. "That's fantastic."

"Pretty crazy." Nova seemed more shell-shocked than anything else. She shook her head slightly. "Anyway. Shall we?"

"Let me give you a ride." Jeremy cut in. "I have the time, and the champion shouldn't be taking the city bus."

Vesper smiled at him gratefully. When they slid into the back seat of the limo, she reached for the champagne in the mini-fridge. Nova seemed oddly subdued when she should be celebrating. "Will you share this with me?" she asked, pressing her thigh against Nova's.

That earned her a smile. "I sure will."

They only had time for one glass before Jeremy stopped in front of Vesper's building, but Vesper took the bottle as she stepped out onto the sidewalk. As the car slid off into the night, she joined their hands together.

"How do you feel?"

Nova waited until they were inside to answer. "It's so strange," she said quietly as they climbed the stairs. "I'm happy—I really am. Obviously. But at the same time, I can't...I just can't escape this numbness. It's like all of this is happening to someone else, not to me. I can't really *feel* it."

The vulnerability in Nova's voice tempered Vesper's rising desire with a surge of tenderness. She unlocked the front door and tugged Nova inside, pausing only to set the bottle on the counter before guiding her to the sofa. Nova was complacent, hands hanging limply at her sides. As Vesper stared up into her eyes, she read in them a plea that roused empathy in her every cell, even as it frightened her in its intensity. Swallowing hard, she looked down and reached for the hem of Nova's sweatshirt. There were things she wasn't capable of giving, but this much, she could do.

"Raise your arms," she whispered, and together they worked to strip Nova's torso bare. She grasped Nova's right hand, then, and carefully undid the clasp on the wide, sparkling bracelet that marked her as a WSOP champion. Its fourteen-karat gold band gave way to four rectangles denoting each suit of cards, two outlined in rubies and two outlined in black diamonds.

"It's heavier than I expected," she said, cradling it in one palm.

A smile flickered across Nova's face. "I don't think I'll ever wear it again. But I didn't mind tonight."

Carefully, Vesper deposited it on the end table. When she returned, she cupped Nova's waist with both hands, thumbs tracing the ridges of her abdominal muscles. "I'm so proud of you. I hope that doesn't sound patronizing."

Nova shook her head, then gasped as Vesper ran her hands up over her ribs to cup her breasts. Vesper smiled at the reaction and gently brushed both nipples with her thumbs. When Nova caught her lower lip between her teeth, she did it again. God, she loved this—the soft weight filling her palms, the tender power she wielded in these moments. Need sliced through her like a knife—the need to test the limits of Nova's responsiveness and then push her over the edge into ecstasy. Hurriedly, she unlaced the front of her shorts and pulled them down her narrow hips.

"You, too," Nova said hoarsely, reaching out toward the collar of Vesper's suit jacket. Vesper let her push it down her arms, and when she shrugged it off, Nova went to work on the buttons of her shirt. Within moments, she was nude as well.

"Sit." As Nova fell back onto the sofa, Vesper knelt between her knees. Planting both palms on Nova's inner thighs, she pushed her legs as far apart as they could go. For once, the words came easily. "Watch me taste you."

Nova moaned, repeating the sound more loudly when Vesper gently opened the folds of her sex with both thumbs. She was wet, and the sight and scent of her arousal sent Vesper's desire into overdrive. Dipping her head, she flicked her tongue lightly over Nova's most sensitive skin, teasing her for as long as she could stand it before finally leaning in to kiss her deeply. When Nova's hips bucked, she held her down firmly, alternating soft strokes of her tongue with the pressure of her lips.

At first, Nova chanted her name in breathless syllables, but soon her fluency dissolved until all she could do was whimper. Hips juddering, she slid one hand through Vesper's hair to cup the back of her head, trying to pull her closer. When Vesper retaliated by going perfectly still, Nova groaned.

Glorying in Nova's need, Vesper raised her head and licked her lips. "Hands on the couch. You'll come when I want you to."

In an instant, Nova had curled her fingers into the fabric on either side of her hips. Vesper smiled at her obedience, admiring the flush that spread across her breasts and the need that was plain in her wide, dark eyes. "Please," Nova whispered. "Just…please."

Caught up in her power trip, Vesper held two fingers to Nova's mouth. "Suck," she whispered, and Nova did, closing her lips around them and swirling her tongue. The sensation echoed between Vesper's legs, and she moaned unexpectedly. Nova's eyes flashed open, dark and hungry.

"Enough." Vesper pulled her fingers away, holding Nova's gaze as she reached down to press against her opening. A new flood of moisture greeted her touch, and with a smile of triumph, she pushed inside. Nova's mouth opened soundlessly, her head falling back against the couch as her spine arched.

Thrusting lightly, Vesper returned her mouth to Nova's clit. Immersing herself in the heat of her sex, she curled her tongue around the knot of nerves even as she curled her fingers up inside. When Nova's muscles quivered, she knew the time for teasing had passed. Pushing further, she hummed in pleasure as the contractions began, accompanied by Nova's soft, broken cries.

For a long time, she remained on her knees, coaxing every last shudder from Nova's body and refusing to think about how short was the time remaining to them. When Nova's body had quieted, she eased back and looked up, finally meeting her wide, dark eyes. With one trembling hand, Nova stroked her cheek.

"Vesper," she whispered. "I love you."

The words felt like a slap. Vesper pulled away, shaking her head. Dread sluiced into her chest, filling it with ice.

"Yes," Nova insisted. "I do."

"No." Vesper stood. "You don't. It's just…this." She gestured between them. "The sex."

A spasm of anger contorted Nova's features. "The hell it is! It's not the sex. It's you. Us. I've fallen in love with you. It's been happening for weeks."

Vesper stood, putting herself beyond the reach of Nova's touch. She felt so cold. "That can't be true."

"It can be. It is. You're the most remarkable person I've ever met. This…this chemistry between us is insane. But there's more to it than lust. Much more. I feel it." Nova took a deep breath. "And I think you feel it, too."

Vesper froze as Nova's words struck a note in her, pure and perfect like a tuning fork. But even if it were true—even if a part of her did feel the same—what good would that do? Falling in love with Nova was a risk she refused to take.

"We would never work," she heard herself say. Gathering momentum, she crossed her arms beneath her breasts. "You say you love me, but I don't think you have any idea what that means. Have you ever even *been* in love? Or have you always been content to screw your roommates?"

"What?" Nova rose, every muscle taut. "How can you say that? Are you still holding Emily against me? Don't you know that this…this thing between us is entirely different from that?"

"How could I possibly know that? And how can you say you love me? We've known each other for a matter of weeks." Nova was shaking her head, and in an effort to make her absorb the lesson, Vesper went for her trump card. "You don't even know my real name!"

Nova froze. "Your real name?"

"You want me." Vindication made Vesper's voice strong. "You don't know enough to love me."

"I do want you." Nova took one step forward. "But I also want to know you. I want to know everything, if you'll let me."

But Vesper had momentum now, and she refused to be derailed. "Even if I did let you, my career is here, in Las Vegas. You *hate* it here. Tell me you don't."

Nova didn't bother to deny it. "I won a million dollars today. And I signed a contract for the next three years. You don't need to stay here either. Come back to San Francisco with me."

A haze of red streaked across Vesper's vision as anger outstripped her fear. She couldn't believe what she was hearing. "Are you serious? I'm not going to be a...a kept woman!"

Even in the dim moonlight, Nova visibly paled. "That's not what I—"

"No. Shut up. You listen." Her fury was heat, banishing the chill, thawing her reason. "When I left home, I had nothing. *Nothing.* You'll never understand how that felt. It took a decade, but I managed to make something out of that nothing. Something good. Something *great*. And you want me to give that up?" She shook her head again. "If you really had fallen in love with me, you would have known better than to make that offer."

"I'm sorry." Nova sounded heartsick, but fueled by the righteousness of her emotion, Vesper couldn't care. "I didn't mean it like that. You work so hard. Harder than anyone I've known." She was babbling now. "You've never had a break. That's what I want to give you. A chance to rest."

Vesper didn't want to hear anymore. She stooped to pick up her clothes. "I'm going to bed. Alone. We can talk again in the morning."

Without a backward glance, she stalked into her bedroom and closed the door. The anger simmered as she hung up her suit and turned down the sheets, but when she eased between them, it began to fade. She didn't want to miss Nova's light snoring, or how she always took up more of the bed than she had a right to, but if that was the price she had to pay to respect herself, then so be it. She didn't want to wonder whether she had done the right thing, because of course she had. Hadn't she? The way Nova had behaved was ridiculous. Borderline misogynistic, even. Vesper certainly wasn't about to sacrifice everything she'd built for a romance that was less than a month old.

Turning onto her side, she curled her knees into her chest and closed her eyes, trying not to listen for Nova's movements and praying that exhaustion would drag her under quickly.

❖

Naked and alone, Nova watched the moon's slow descent toward the mountains. She hadn't moved once since Vesper had stormed off— just over an hour ago, according to the clock. A thousand thoughts had flown through her head between now and then, but they were slippery and she couldn't latch on to any but one: that she had messed up. Badly.

She had replayed their conversation a dozen times in her head, but it never ended well no matter what she tried to change. The beginning had been the greatest mistake of all. She should never have told Vesper the truth. *I love you.* Perhaps in some parallel universe, her gambit ended well, but in this reality, it had utterly failed. Vesper had made it clear from the beginning that she had no room in her life for anything other than a casual relationship, and she'd stuck to her guns. Nova could only blame her own wishful thinking. She should have bluffed for all she was worth.

Slowly, the ache in her chest expanded until her breaths grew shallow. When she finally moved, it was to stumble into the kitchen for a drink of water, but she found the champagne bottle instead. She carried it back to the window and sipped at it slowly, irony tickling her throat with every carbonated swallow. She had won her bracelet and her sponsorship but lost something infinitely more valuable.

No. That was a kind of wishful thinking, too. Vesper had never been hers to lose.

By the time the bottle was empty, she knew what she had to do. She retrieved her phone from her shorts pocket and fired off a text to Jeremy. *Still up? If so, I need a favor.*

While waiting for his reply, she slowly put her clothes back on, unable to stop herself from flashing back to how eagerly Vesper had removed them. With a shiver, she pulled her brand-new hoodie back over her head and tucked her bracelet into a side pocket of her shorts. Royal Flush had treated her like royalty today, but the victory felt hollow with Vesper on the other side of a locked door.

At casino. Just dropped clients. Wut do u need?

Nova typed back quickly. *Can u pick me up from V's? Going to airport.* A long pause ensued. She could practically feel his confusion from halfway across the city, but she wasn't going to say anything more until she could look him in the eye.

Omw, he finally replied.

Her bag was mostly packed, and after a quick stop in the bathroom, she had everything she needed. One hand was on the doorknob before she reconsidered, dropped her duffel, and hurried back to the refrigerator. Vesper kept a magnetized notepad there, and she tore off one sheet before replacing it. Its empty lines stared up at her, mocking her efforts to make verbal sense of the maelstrom in her brain. Should she apologize? Beg? Berate?

No. She couldn't go back; she could only move forward. The thought galvanized her into action. There was only one thing left to say.

I meant it, she scrawled in an unsteady hand. Beneath the words, she signed her initials—*AJN*. Much as she might dislike them, they were what she had to give. With one of Vesper's spare magnets, she tacked up the note near the refrigerator handle, where she was sure to see it. And then, forcing herself not to look back, she stepped out into the hallway.

Nova emerged from the building as Jeremy's car pulled up at the curb. When he stepped out to help her with the trunk, she waved him off. She slid into the passenger seat, but when he made to put the car in drive, she stopped him with a hand on his shoulder.

"There's something I need to ask you."

"Okay." He sounded uncertain, and why wouldn't he? Vesper was the one to whom he owed his loyalty, not her.

"I have to go back to San Francisco right away and won't be able to play in the main event. I'm hoping you'll take my spot."

"Me?" He blinked at her, clearly shocked.

"Why not? You know how to play poker, don't you?"

"Sure, but—"

"So, play. If you make it to the fourth day, you'll be in the money. Fifteen thousand dollars, and it only gets better from there."

Jeremy drummed his fingers against the steering wheel. "Why me?"

"You work hard, and you're damn good at what you do. Vesper's not the only person who can see that. Why not find out if you can catch a break? Plenty of amateurs have made the final table in years past.

If you do, the sponsors will flock to you. If you don't, well, nothing risked, nothing lost."

Nova watched as he thought it over. She may have made a ruin out of her relationship—or lack thereof—with Vesper, but at least she could try to leave on some kind of high note. Generosity was never a mistake.

The brief drive to the airport passed in silence until Jeremy pulled off the highway. Finally, the weight of things unsaid compelled her to speak. Vesper wasn't the only person she would miss. "When you next see TJ and his family, would you mind telling them that I'm sorry I didn't get to say good-bye in person?"

"No problem."

"Thanks." They passed by first one sign announcing the airport, and then another. Each time, Nova's chest constricted painfully. However much she disliked Vegas, she had never planned on leaving it like this.

Jeremy pulled up to the curb and popped the trunk but made no move to get out of the car. Instead, his eyes locked onto hers. "Any message for Vesper?"

Tell her I love her, Nova wanted to say. Tell her I'm sorry. Tell her I meant it.

Instead, she shook her head and opened the door. "Take care, okay? Thanks for everything. And good luck."

CHAPTER NINETEEN

Vesper intercepted TJ as he made his way toward the exit. When he saw her, he smiled tiredly. "Really thought I had him," he said.

"That river card was unlucky. I'm sorry." Vesper patted him on the shoulder, glad he wasn't more upset. "You came close to lasting through the day. That's something to be proud of."

"Is Jeremy still in the mix?"

"Yes." The monosyllable came out more sharply than she had intended. She didn't want to think of anything that would remind her of Nova, and his success throughout the main event so far did exactly that. Swiftly, she changed the topic. "Can I help you with any plans for the evening, now that you're free?"

"We're just going to relax in the suite, I think. Amelia wants to do a horror film marathon. But thanks." He cocked his head. "Want to join us?"

A night sacked out in front of the television was exactly what she needed, but not as a third wheel. "I have another obligation," she said, which was the truth, anyway. "But that sounds fun."

"Theo!" Amelia burst onto the scene, hurrying toward them with a distraught expression. "I'm so sorry I missed it." When she slid one arm around his waist, Vesper felt her eyebrows twitch. Clearly, something definitive had happened over the past few days. And since when had she started calling him *Theo*?

"Well, I'm not," he was saying. His hand stroked in gentle circles between her shoulder blades. "It was embarrassing. V can fill you in if you want all the gory details."

"Vesper! Hi. I didn't see you." Amelia blushed. "I mean…"

Seeing them so *together*, and so obviously happy, made Vesper feel hollow. She smiled in what she hoped was an encouraging fashion. "You're fine. Enjoy the scary movies. Let me know if there's anything you need."

As she turned away, she glanced at her watch. It was nearly time to meet Priscilla for an early meal before her flight left later in the evening. She had busted out yesterday and decided not to stay for the remainder of the event, citing a measure of homesickness: "You can take the girl out of Texas, but you can't take Texas out of the girl."

Vesper didn't agree on that particular point, but she wasn't about to argue. Priscilla had lost almost ten million dollars over the course of her first solo stay in Vegas, and Vesper wanted to keep her as happy as possible. When she arrived at Barri, Priscilla was already seated in a private corner booth, sipping an appletini and looking out over the Strip. The orange rays of the setting sun filtered through the window to set her diamond earrings ablaze with color.

"There you are. What's the news from downstairs?"

"Kris Winston has the lead. TJ was just eliminated, but Jeremy is still in the running." As she slid into the opposite booth, a waiter materialized at her elbow.

"Something to drink, Ms. Blake?"

Vesper was about to ask for seltzer water when Priscilla barged in. "She'll have what I'm having."

"Thank you," Vesper said, trying out a laugh.

"Don't thank me. You're buying."

That was true enough, though Priscilla's losses more than compensated for the casino's expense where she was concerned. "Are you all set for your flight this evening? Your driver will meet you in the lobby at seven."

Priscilla waved one spangled hand in the air. "Yes, yes, I'm fine. I'm a big girl. And getting bigger after weeks of this food."

Their waiter returned to drop off Vesper's drink and take their orders, but as soon as he was gone, Priscilla leaned forward conspiratorially. "Tell me something, Vesper. What's your greatest goal?"

The question might have been abrupt, but the answer jumped readily to her lips. "To be the best host in Las Vegas." She only wondered whether she would have the opportunity. Once the Hamiltons left, Steve would shut Valhalla's door in her face. Whether she would find another home elsewhere on the Strip was anyone's guess.

"And then?"

She could have made something up, but Priscilla would recognize bullshit when she heard it. "I hadn't thought that far in advance."

"Always think ahead. That's my unsolicited advice." She clinked her glass with Vesper's. "What do you love so much about being a host?"

Vesper had never needed to put it in words before. She felt like she was at an interview that she hadn't prepared for. "I like having so many tools at my disposal to bring in new clients," she said. "And I enjoy straddling the line between company and client. It's a tightrope sometimes, but one I like to walk."

"You crave the thrill," Priscilla confirmed.

Vesper was taken aback. She wasn't the adrenaline junkie. That was Nova. Her heart thumped painfully.

"But in the end," Priscilla continued, "what do you have to show for all your hard work? Your clients come and go. Their money disappears into the bottomless pit of the casino, and your relationships with them fall apart like a house of cards if that money dries up. What have you built?" She shrugged. "Nothing."

Vesper couldn't believe what she was hearing. The skin on her neck prickled in anger and she felt her cheeks grow hot. How dare Priscilla judge her life's work so harshly, after Vesper had spent the past few weeks making her every wish come true? Heat pounded through her head and she clamped her lips together, forcing herself not to speak.

"I see I've made you angry. Good." Priscilla looked bemused, which made her headache even worse. "You're much more interesting when you're emotional. The life's gone right out of you since Nova left. You're a walking shell of a human being."

Adrenaline poured into her blood, making her tremble, making her feel alive. How *dare* Priscilla bring Nova into this! "Excuse me?" she said icily, glad her voice remained steady.

"You heard exactly what I said, and I'm glad to hear I've hit a nerve. I was starting to think you're a robot under those perfect suits and elegant dresses." Priscilla took another sip of her drink as Vesper continued to fume. "Now keep listening, because I'm about to offer you a job."

"You're…pardon?" Vesper had never been more confused in her life.

"A real job, in which you go out and *build* something instead of spending your time pandering to people." Priscilla cocked her head. "Are you going to hear me out, or throw that drink in my face?"

"I'm listening." Vesper kept her voice cool, though some of her anger had already given way to curiosity.

Priscilla drained her martini, signaled the waiter for another, and leaned back in her chair. "I would think you'd be more grateful, seeing as you'll be unemployed as soon as I walk out the door."

Vesper clenched her jaw to keep it from dropping. How had Priscilla learned about her dismissal? Should she deny or admit it?

"Oh, don't look so shocked. That sleazeball James came sniffing around yesterday and he happened to *accidentally* mention that you were being forced out. He even told me why." She chuckled. "That sure did backfire on him, the fool." She pinned Vesper with a sharp gaze. "I respect you for standing up for yourself. And I told him I'd rather spend my money elsewhere than let him near one red cent."

Vesper's brain was doing somersaults, but she managed to focus on the mental image of James's face long enough for a strangled laugh. "What exactly are you saying?"

"What I'm saying is that I respect you and don't respect him." Priscilla leaned forward. "Vesper, my husband had a diverse range of interests. With the money he got from oil, he bought whatever he wanted—car dealerships, golf courses, restaurants, a luxury hotel chain. My son is going to take charge of most of it; the rest he wants to sell.

"Now, I don't know a damn thing about golf or cars, but I know plenty about luxury, and our hotels aren't getting it right. They're languishing. The old boys my husband put in charge don't have the right priorities. The chain needs a fresh hand at the wheel, or it'll go belly-up."

"You'll be taking the helm, then?" Vesper asked, dizzied by the turn in the conversation.

"Oh, no." Priscilla laughed. "I'm much too old to play entrepreneur. I was thinking of someone younger. Someone innovative and ambitious, who understands hospitality on both sides of the coin. Are you catching my drift?"

Vesper was, but she couldn't believe it. "You want me to…to take charge? Of a hotel chain?"

Priscilla laughed again, but not unkindly. "Not all at once. You'll need to prove yourself first. You can start by taking on one of the crown jewels and turning it around—making it more relevant to today's younger, affluent customers. It can be a prototype. Beyond that, we'll see."

A low buzz filled Vesper's ears. This was beyond belief. "Crown jewels?" she asked weakly.

"There are five: Tokyo, London, New York, Los Angeles, and Paris. You can have your pick." Priscilla was smiling above the rim of her glass. "London might be a good place to start. Ever been?"

"I've never even seen the ocean," Vesper said weakly. She drank deeply from her martini. "I'm honored that you're asking, Priscilla. I really am. But why me?"

"Because you can see the big picture without getting bogged down in the details. Because you're willing to sacrifice the traditional approach to get results. You were savvy enough to hunt me down, weren't you? When everyone else was trying to get their claws into my son."

Even as Vesper listened to Priscilla's praise, the part of her that would always be a poor kid from Houston remained skeptical. She didn't belong at this table, in this conversation. She didn't belong anywhere near it. "I don't have a background in hotel management. I don't even have an MBA."

"You think I give a rat's ass about credentials?" Priscilla let out an unladylike snort. "There are hundreds of bright, entitled kids graduating every year from hotel management school. What I need is someone with taste. With vision. Someone with the right soul to breathe life back into what used to be a grand old brand name."

She leaned forward, eyes bright as the gems in her ears. "I think you're that person, Vesper Blake. What do you think?"

❖

Nova sipped at her thirty-year-old scotch and tried to seem interested in the conversation around her. It had begun as a discussion about federal gambling laws, and whether there might be a glimmer of light at the end of the tunnel for online poker players. One of the politicians in the room had mentioned that both Nevada and New Jersey were making bids to legalize online gambling, but that tantalizing piece of information had been eclipsed by a bitchfest about taxes. Unlike most of the people in this room, Nova was a staunch Democrat and couldn't sympathize. At all. Struggling to maintain a poker face, she slipped her free hand into her pocket and closed her fingers around her conch shell. Yesterday, in a dark moment, she had almost thrown it back into the sea.

The only other woman in their group—a brunette in a dress darker than her hair, with a plunging neckline—had been flirting with the men around her all night, but now she turned to smile at Nova. She worked for the hedge fund that had cosponsored this event, and as she congratulated Nova on being the first woman to win the Championship, she made sure their elbows brushed. Nova chatted politely with her for a few minutes but was careful to keep her distance. Once, she would have been interested in what the woman was offering, but not now. Not since Vesper.

After twenty-four hours had passed with no word from her, Nova had reached out by text. A day later, she had called. The sound of Vesper's voice in her automated greeting had made her heart twist like a fish on a hook. Now, almost a week after she had left an apologetic message, she still hadn't heard anything back. Frustration was slowly giving way to despair, though she was trying to fight it. Was it so easy for Vesper to turn her back on what they had shared? Had it truly not meant anything to her?

Despite her silence, Nova couldn't believe that. Two things she knew for sure: that she had hurt Vesper badly, and that Vesper was very good at protecting herself. She had to be—that was how she had survived all these years. Nova wanted to believe that once Vesper's anger cooled and she gained some perspective, she would reach out. But if she was being honest with herself, the other possibility was just as likely. Love was risk. Even if Vesper did feel the same, her self-protective instincts might overrule her emotions.

Nova excused herself and meandered back toward the hors d'oeuvres table. She waved at a few people she knew but didn't stop to chat. This was her second appearance for Royal Flush since the World Series, and while the food was always good, the company left much to be desired. These "charity" tournaments were really just an excuse for corporate bigwigs to get together and schmooze. Sure, some NPO always made out like a bandit with the proceeds, but the whole thing felt hollow to her. Rich white men, checking a box.

Nova wanted to go home, only she wasn't sure where that was anymore. She had lost the easy synchrony she'd once shared with her roommates, especially since she insisted on sleeping alone ever since her return. Her parents were nice enough, and even proud of her in their fashion, but she wasn't about to move back in with them. Increasingly, other people were making her claustrophobic. She needed her own space.

One of the few women in the group approached her then, Royal Flush cap in hand, to ask for an autograph on behalf of her teenage daughter. That cheered her up a little. As she handed the hat back with a smile, though, she could have sworn she caught a glimpse of Vesper across the room. Her heart thundered and her palms broke out into a sweat, but when she looked again, "Vesper" was gone. Probably because she had never been there to begin with. Rolling her eyes at her own imagination, Nova downed what was left of her scotch. She needed to clear her head and get some fresh air.

At the far end of the room was an observation deck looking out over a stretch of pristine white sand that gave way to the Pacific. Nova walked down to the far corner of the deck and rested her forearms on the railing. Turning her face into the sea breeze, she closed her eyes and let its wild fingers comb through her hair.

"You were right about the ocean," said a familiar voice behind her. "It's incredible."

Nova spun so quickly she made herself dizzy. Vesper stood five feet away, wearing a dress the color of her eyes. Her freckles stood out vividly against the pale skin of her shoulders, and all Nova wanted in that moment was to kiss each spot in turn. Waves of emotion roared in her head: love, need, fear, desire. She swallowed and fought for breath to speak.

"Hi."

Vesper's lips quirked. "Hi."

"You...you're here."

"That's true." Vesper seemed to be enjoying her incoherence. "I am."

Nova couldn't seem to care that she wasn't making sense. Vesper was here. Vesper had sought her out. That had to mean something, didn't it? "How...what..." She shook her head. "It's good to see you. Great, even. You look amazing."

"And you look exhausted." Vesper took a step forward, then paused.

Nova had nothing left to lose. The realization was freedom. "It's hard to fall asleep without you next to me. I miss you." Vesper opened her mouth, but Nova soldiered on. "I'm so sorry. What I said, that night...I didn't mean it that way. I swear."

One of Vesper's eyebrows quirked. "Good. Because if you think I'm going to give up my career—"

"I don't." Nova leapt frantically into the breach. "I'd never want you to do that. I'll commute between Vegas and Frisco. I will." She knew she was sounding increasingly desperate, but she didn't care. "Really."

"I don't think that's a good idea," Vesper said into the silence.

Nova's heart froze. "Y—you don't?"

"I don't live in Las Vegas anymore. I live here, in Los Angeles." When she smiled, Nova realized her shock must be apparent. "Priscilla asked me to take over one of her investments."

Nova shook her head slowly. "I'm going to need you to spell this out."

Vesper closed the gap between them and raised her hands to cup Nova's face. At that first intimate touch, Nova shivered. "She inherited a chain of luxury hotels from her husband. I've taken charge of the one here in LA. I'm supposed to revitalize it—to transform it into a prototype for the entire international chain."

Nova couldn't believe what she was hearing. "But what about Vegas? You've worked so hard to build a life there."

"Priscilla helped me realize I've done everything I can as a host. Anything else would be variations on a theme. That's not what I want."

"It isn't?" Nova felt completely adrift.

"No. I want to build something that's lasting. With the hotel and with us."

"Us?" Nova thought she understood what Vesper was driving at, but she didn't want to make unwarranted assumptions.

"You know, Priscilla offered me a choice of hotels. Tokyo. London. New York. A few others. I chose this one because it was closest to you."

"You did?" Nova stepped back in surprise, severing their connection.

At the loss of contact, Vesper noticeably paled. "I just realized how presumptuous that sounds. If you don't—"

Nova couldn't suppress an incredulous smile. "You did all of this so we could be together."

"Yes. Together." Vesper's eyes were bright and intense. "Ocean and desert. A compromise. I'm going all in, here. I'll even tell you my name."

Nova's chest swelled with emotion. Vesper wanted her. Not just for the moment, but for the future. Sliding her arms around Vesper's waist, Nova pulled their bodies flush. "I love you," she murmured. "And your name is Vesper."

Vesper braced her hands on Nova's shoulders and searched her face through blurry eyes. "I love you," she said, her voice quivering. "You're mine."

Nova kissed her forehead; her cheeks; the dimple in her chin. She had never felt so certain, so content. "I'll call that bet."

About the Author

Nell Stark is the Chair of English, Philosophy, and Religious Studies at a college in the SUNY system. She and her wife live with their son and dog just a stone's throw from the historic Stonewall Inn in New York City. For more information, visit www.nellstark.com.

Books Available From Bold Strokes Books

Desire at Dawn by Fiona Zedde. For Kylie, love had always come armed with sharp teeth and claws. But with the human, Olivia, she bares her vampire heart for the very first time, sharing passion, lust, and a tenderness she'd never dared dreamed of before. (978-1-62639-064-5)

Visions by Larkin Rose. Sometimes the mysteries of love reveal themselves when you least expect it. Other times they hide behind a black satin mask. Can Paige unveil her masked stranger this time? (978-1-62639-065-2)

All In by Nell Stark. Internet poker champion Annie Navarro loses everything when the Feds shut down online gambling, and she turns to experienced casino host Vesper Blake for advice—but can Nova convince Vesper to take a gamble on romance? (978-1-62639-066-9)

Vermillion Justice by Sheri Lewis Wohl. What's a vampire to do when Dracula is no longer just a character in a novel? (978-1-62639-067-6)

Switchblade by Carsen Taite. Lines were meant to be crossed. Third in the Luca Bennett Bounty Hunter Series. (978-1-62639-058-4)

Nightingale by Andrea Bramhall. Culture, faith, and duty conspire to tear two young lovers apart, yet fate seems to have different plans for them both. (978-1-62639-059-1)

No Boundaries by Donna K. Ford. A chance meeting and a nightmare from the past threaten more than Andi Massey's solitude as she and Gwen Palmer struggle to understand the complexity of love without boundaries. (978-1-62639-060-7)

Timeless by Rachel Spangler. When Stevie Geller returns to her hometown, will she do things differently the second time around or will she be in such a hurry to leave her past that she misses out on a better future? (978-1-62639-050-8)